Changeling
Dawn

Changeling Dawn

DANI HARPER

BRAVA

KENSINGTON PUBLISHING CORP.

www.kensingtonbooks.com

BRAVA BOOKS are published by

Kensington Publishing Corp.
119 West 40th Street
New York, NY 10018

ISBN-13: 978-0-7582-6518-0
ISBN-10: 0-7582-6518-2

First Kensington Trade Paperback Printing: January 2012

10   9   8   7   6   5   4   3   2   1

Printed in the United States of America

A good beta reader is a gift from the writing gods,
someone who isn't afraid to tell you
that your literary slip is showing
or you have metaphorical broccoli between your teeth.
I'm extremely grateful to my daughter, Sam,
and my husband, Ron,
who have waded through countless rough drafts of this story
with great patience and eagle eyes.

There is no instinct like that of the heart.
—LORD BYRON

Chapter One

R*un.*
      Shadow and moonlight merged beneath her bare feet, the dappled forest floor blurring as the little girl ran fast, then faster. Her long plaid skirts were hiked around her waist, and bushes and twigs reached for the woolen fabric like bony hands.

They were close behind her now. The nervous whining of dogs, the hiss and flicker of torches, the stench of tobacco and ale and human sweat. The excited voices, rough with anger and a little fear.

Run.

Her heart threatened to explode from her chest, her lungs were in flames, but she had to run. She had to get away.

Run.

She stumbled yet kept her balance. She ran, knowing now that she couldn't outdistance the hunters. She was very young—still, there was one thing left, one thing that could help her.

It spoke to her now, whispered from deep inside her. *Call me*, it said. *Call me* now.

She did.

Within her, something stirred to life and the hair on her

scalp prickled, her skin felt hot and tight. A small stream was in her path and she leapt into the air with the last of her strength—

And landed as a young wolf. Faster now, streamlined, she was nature's perfect running machine, and it was only a matter of minutes before the hunters were left hopelessly behind. Her four paws took her off the narrow game trails and into the deep brush where even the dogs couldn't follow her—if they dared.

Run, run, run. She raced easily, faster and faster. Her fear became exhilaration and she ran with an unbridled joy . . . until the ground disappeared beneath her feet and she tumbled headfirst into darkness.

Kenzie Macleod awoke with the scream stuck in her throat. She swallowed it back as awareness dawned, and released the fear on a long shaky exhale.

What the hell was that?

Heart racing and skin slick with sweat, she freed her naked body from the tangled sheets and padded to the kitchen. She pulled a water bottle from the fridge and drank it down with hardly a pause, wiping her mouth on her arm. *Better.* Her heart rate had returned to normal by the time she stepped into the shower. Her thoughts slowed down as she ran her fingers through her dark hair and reached for a towel.

Fully awake now, stray riverlets of water licking over her skin, she stepped out on the porch of the guest cabin. Still clad in only the towel, she wasn't a bit cold, despite the breeze—Changeling body temperature ran much higher than human. Kenzie breathed in the scents, took in the sounds and sights of her brothers' farm. The sky was lightening, silver gray above the tall poplars. Roosters crowed, livestock stirred. Birds sang to the dawn and a flurry of ducks took off from the pond. She liked it here. She had always liked it here. The abundance of life that seemed to be in the very air made her feel alive, and she let it soothe her.

By the time she yanked on her old jeans and a worn plaid flannel shirt, she felt almost normal. Calm, as she plugged in the coffee pot. But the nightmare was still very much on her mind, because it wasn't a dream. . . .

It was a memory.

For the first half of her Changeling life, she'd had horrendous flashbacks to long-ago Scotland where she'd been born *Mackenzie Adair Macleod*, youngest child of six, to Ronan and Gwynn. The entire Macleod clan had lived on the Isle of Skye for centuries, but the wolfen sept of the family had gradually moved to the thick Caledonian forests on the mainland. Kenzie's parents had built a homestead in the ancient pine woods. The family grazed a pair of cows in forest glens and gathered medicinal herbs and plants for the market. In their lupine form, they chased big red deer and small swift roe.

The rugged terrain and poor soil precluded serious farming in the area, and therefore human settlement as well. What few humans lived in the forest and along its borders were safe from their neighbors' wolfen natures— Pack law forbade them to be harmed. Kenzie had spent the first six years of her life with playmates from both worlds, not knowing how quickly things could change.

Things *always* changed—she knew that now. Kenzie sank into an armchair and drank her coffee from a battered blue enamel cup, remembering. Allowing the memories to play out.

Legend had it that the last wolf had been exterminated in Scotland in 1743. History didn't mention that the report was premature by over a century in the remote highland wilderness. It also didn't mention that it was actually a war on Changelings that precipitated the wholesale slaughter of all wolves across the British Isles. The flashpoint had been a series of attacks on humans by rogues, *warwoolfes* or *wulvers*, and the result was that no wolf of any kind was ever safe again. The war on wolves had been slow to reach Kenzie's family, and at first the thick pine forests provided refuge for many displaced Changelings.

When she was seven, hunters began to enter the thick woods, keen to collect the rich bounty offered by the crown. The last time Kenzie accompanied her father to the marketplace in Torridon, she had seen tall stacks of wolf pelts. The death of so many creatures was heart-wrenching, but the true horror was revealed by scent—many skins had come not from wolves, but from Changelings in their lupine form. Ronan Macleod had never taken his family to the market again. In fact, they had stayed away from all of the villages after that. But the madness had already infected the forest. Heavy iron traps lay in wait, log falls and pits, ropes and nets. Although few dogs would chase a Changeling— and fewer still would do it more than once—there were some that could scent their nearly imperceptible trail and direct humans to them.

The dream had ended with her fall into darkness, but Kenzie remembered all too clearly everything that happened after that. The breath was knocked out of her as she landed on hard-packed earth. Her lupine body struggled awkwardly against something squeezing her tightly around the middle. As her eyes adjusted, she realized she had fallen into a deep pit filled with long sharpened stakes. Her small body had slid between the posts rather than been impaled upon them. The thick peeled wood would not yield to her young sharp teeth or her struggles, holding her in place as easily as iron bars. On the other side of the pit, a big black wolf had not been so lucky and the stench of blood was thick in her nostrils. Terrified, she had nonetheless obeyed the first rule of the hunted—silence. She neither howled nor cried, fearing the human hunters or their dogs would hear her. She screamed in her mind, however, until she was insensible. It had been the next day—an eternity—before her family came and freed her.

She wasn't entirely free, however. She'd remained a wolf for days, too traumatized to remember how to shift back. And when she finally did, she didn't speak for months, as if her mind was somehow stuck in instinctive silence because of the constant, overwhelming fear that gripped her. Gradually she recovered, but she'd never been free of the fear. Even when her parents moved the family to the raw wilderness of northern Canada, she hadn't been free. She had nightmare flashbacks of the chase, the pit. Of the dying wolf. And when those faded, she still felt distrust.

Her brothers and sisters had been able to build a life that accepted humans. Even Culley, whose leg still bore the scars of an iron trap, had managed to overcome that trauma and move on. For her family's sake, Kenzie pretended that she had too. Like her family, she lived among humans, grew up alongside them, talked and laughed with them. She even liked them—a great deal, if the truth be known. Deep inside, however, there was a part of her that didn't trust them. That couldn't.

Perhaps that's why she ended up studying them.

Kenzie Macleod had twin doctorates in anthropology and archaeology. She turned down many opportunities to teach in favor of digging, and the more isolated the site, the better she liked it. Most people forgave her reclusiveness, chalking it up as natural for an "egghead"—even an attractive one. Professionally, her papers were well-received, her research was respected, her opinion was sought, and her rare lectures never had an empty seat. Her last book wasn't on anyone's bestseller list—*Beyond Clovis: Oregon's Ancient People*—but it had sold a respectable number of copies so far and two colleges were negotiating to include it in their curriculum. Only last week, National Geographic had asked her to participate in a television program they were filming about Ice Age man.

She drained the cup and savored the nutty coffee grounds at the bottom, crunching them between her teeth. Wondered, as she had many times: *What would they think if they knew that the so-called expert on humans wasn't one herself? What if they suspect what I'm really searching for?*

Even her family didn't know what she sought. No one did, not even her closest, dearest friend, Birkie Peterson, even though Birkie could be trusted to keep a confidence forever. Until Kenzie had found what she was certain existed, discovered irrefutable proof in the form of tangible evidence, she couldn't bring herself to say it out loud. Couldn't bear to hear how crazy it would sound, even to herself.

Certainly her hard-earned credibility would vanish overnight if a single word got out about her true goal. Not only media but social networking sites would spread it far and wide like feathers in a hurricane. She'd be labeled a kook, automatic fodder for late night television jokes, and utterly dismissed in scientific circles. Finding her holy grail after that would be worse than useless—no one would listen to her when she explained its true significance.

Kenzie rinsed out the coffee cup and headed outside, down the wide wooden steps to the narrow path that wound through poplar and spruce trees toward the corrals.

She took her time, enjoying the scents and sounds, grateful as always just to be at the farm for a little while. Her oldest brothers, James and Connor, and their families co-owned the sprawling farm. In fact, they owned most of the forested land around it, all the way to the Peace River. Connor had purchased the huge parcel originally, but as a busy veterinarian and owner of the chronically under-staffed North Star Animal Hospital, he didn't do much farming aside from keeping an ever-growing assortment of rescued animals. Sure, he'd added a few purebred Highland cattle, but even he admitted they were more for nostalgia than any hope of profit. The big shaggy beasts were basically pets. And despite the fact that he was a gifted healer, he was a certifiable *black thumb* when it came to plants, so the fields lay fallow. The wild-grown pasture suited the cattle, being of an independent breed that could forage for themselves. It suited the herds of local mule deer too and even a few elk began to frequent the edges of the farm. Poplar trees encroached on the fields, as if nature was determined to reclaim the land.

All of that changed when James came on the scene. Connor's animals remained, of course, but they were joined by top-producing livestock. The unsown land and neglected pastures gave way to certified organic crops. The farm not only prospered but over the years, it had gradually grown until it became the gold standard for sustainable agriculture in this part of the country.

Despite their different talents, James and Connor shared one thing—a deep respect for the earth. While most farmers would cut the timber to add to their cash flow, the mature spruce and poplar forests that flanked the Macleod fields remained standing. Not only were they useful to Changelings as a place to run as wolves, safe from human eyes, but the woods provided refuge for many other creatures as well. And in recent years, James's wife, Jillian, had built a wildlife sanctuary in the northeast woods where she rehabbed injured creatures from owls and ravens to puma and moose.

Kenzie admired her siblings' talents with living things, with plants and animals and earth. Strange how her own aptitudes seemed to lie with things long dead. . . .

"You're up early." The voice in her ear made her jump before her mind registered that it was James. His stalking abilities were legendary, moving as a ghost, whether on two legs or four.

She punched him in the shoulder as hard as she could. "It's rude to sneak up on people."

"It's careless to let me," he countered, and ducked before her fist connected a second time. "I was thinking you might need a ride to town to pick up your truck."

"Thanks, but Zoey's taking me when she goes to the office."

"Not today she's not." A rare grin spread across his face. "Doc Miller arrived just after midnight. Birkie too."

"The baby? Omigod, Zoey's having the baby? When—"

Without warning, the Red Hot Chili Peppers belted out an old classic, *Can't Stop*. Kenzie dove into her pocket for her cell phone.

Connor was on the line. "Congratulations, you're an auntie."

She squealed, a sound that would have shocked her peers and had James covering his ears in mock pain. "What is it, what is it, what is it?"

"A girl. She has Zoey's hair, and we're still arguing over her name."

Girl, she mouthed to James, who pumped the air and

high-fived her. They had both bet against brothers Culley and Devlin, who had put their money on a boy.

"That's fantastic. Congrats to all three of you." She hurried up the trail and through the crowded farmyard until she could glimpse Connor and Zoey's house. Sure enough, Birkie's bright red truck was parked in front of the steps next to the Millers' old tan Lincoln. "I'm so happy for you. Is Zoey okay?"

"Never better. She says hi by the way, and so do Birkie and Lowen. Zoey's going to have a nap—"

It wasn't hard to hear Zoey protesting in the background.

"Oh, all right," sighed Connor. "She wants Aunt Kenzie to come over and introduce herself to the new arrival. And then *I'm* having a nap, even if no one else is."

"On my way. James is with me, too."

"No, he's not," said James. "He's *way* ahead of you."

He punched her in the arm and sprinted for the house with Kenzie hard on his heels.

Zoey finally did head off for a nap and Kenzie got temporary custody of her red-haired niece. She inhaled her soft baby scent and nuzzled her little wrinkly forehead, kissed her tiny fists.

"Looks good on you." Connor leaned over and gave her a gentle squeeze, mindful of his tiny new daughter in her arms. It seemed a little strange to Kenzie—normally he'd indulge in a full-out bear hug, which often would devolve into a wrestling match. Changeling families tended to be very physical, and the Macleods were no exception. "You know, sis, you love kids so much, why aren't you settling down with a family of your own? You oughta trade in those dusty old bones of yours for a mate."

She rolled her eyes. She didn't need her anthropology degree to know that it was the nature of both humans and Changelings who had found happiness themselves to automatically want everyone around them to experience it too. *Whether they wanted to or not.* It had been the same when James married Jillian, when their twins had been born, when Connor married Zoey, and now this. She also knew that it was well-intentioned—her brother adored his "little" sister—so she aimed for humor. "Just haven't found a man that my big brother would approve of, that's all. And my inner wolf is very picky."

"I'm not telling you what to do . . . Well, hell, I guess I am. I just hate to think of you being alone so much. I'll bet there's not another soul within twenty miles of you and your new dig site."

Twenty-seven and a half miles actually, but she didn't say so. "I'll tell you what, if a man drops out of the sky there, I'll be sure to date him."

"I'll hold you to that," he laughed, and headed upstairs to nap with Zoey.

Kenzie enjoyed walking around the house with her niece on her shoulder, yet she couldn't stop thinking about Connor's brotherly advice. As if he should talk—he'd been alone as long as she had until Zoey Tyler had arrived in their little northern town to take over the reins of Dunvegan's weekly newspaper. Connor had known at once that she was his mate. *Known.* What would that be like? Kenzie had heard since she was very small that Changelings—or more correctly, their inner wolves—always recognized their *true* mates when they saw them. It had even happened to her oldest brother, James, and that was a flat-out miracle.

It had definitely *not* happened to her other brothers, twins Culley and Devlin. Not yet, at least. Although she

couldn't imagine Culley ever being serious enough to settle down, or picture Devlin looking up from his physics
experiments long enough to notice a woman. Her only sister, Carly, was a different story. Years ago, she had been the
first in the family to take a mate, marrying a Changeling
named Jake after a courtship of barely a month. She con-
fided later that she had wanted Jake and her inner wolf had
simply accepted her choice. Knowing her sister's head-
strong and stubborn nature, Kenzie couldn't imagine
Carly's inner wolf bothering to argue with her about anything.

As for herself, Kenzie was married to her work. Not because she'd planned it that way—well, not exactly—but
hey, how many eligible Changelings did you run across in
the middle of the Egyptian desert or the Chilean jungle? It
was a good enough excuse to pull out and dust off at family gatherings anyway. She couldn't expect her family to
understand that there was something she had to do, something she felt she had to achieve before she could turn her
attention to a mate. Her discoveries would have to be her
children, because what she was looking for now just might
ensure the future of all Changelings.

Which sounded rather grandiose, even if it *was* true. She
nuzzled the baby as she wondered where her siblings found
their courage. How did they manage to build families and
bring children—*Changeling* children—into a human world
that would not welcome them? Especially after what had
happened to James—he'd lost his first wife and unborn
baby to a murderer, a human who thought it was his calling to exterminate *werewolves*. In his grief, her oldest
brother had run as a white wolf for three decades, determined never to walk on two legs again. . . .

And then Jillian had come along.

Birkie often said that love changed everything. Kenzie didn't agree—love changed the people involved. It didn't change the world. The baby squirmed on her shoulder and Kenzie sighed. Changing the world was what she had to do. *Had to.*

She pulled the blanket up and lightly covered the baby's head, then wandered out to the front porch. The sky was bright now, robin's egg blue with creamy streamers of clouds. There was dew on the purple irises and the orange and yellow daylilies that flanked the steps. Baskets of flowers hung from the porch eaves, cascading blossoms of mauve and blue. The railings groaned under an assortment of window boxes and brackets filled with pots of all sizes, nearly hidden by the flowers they contained. All James's handiwork of course.

Kenzie shook her head in wonder. She knew all the forest's plants by scent when she ran as a wolf. But in the wild, the plants looked after themselves—they needed nothing from her and she could just enjoy them. In human form, she couldn't even keep a cactus alive. She whispered to the baby, "You're *so* lucky I'm not your mom."

"I see Connor's being Mr. Sensitivity again." Birkie waved a hand at her from the depths of a comfortable old recliner tucked amid some tall potted plants. Kenzie grinned, partly because she was glad to see her friend and partly because Birkie never failed to look impeccable. Even though she'd been up all night assisting with the delivery of a brand new Macleod, her tangerine pantsuit was crisp, her white hair tidily swept into a chignon, her makeup flawless. Perhaps it was a glamor—after all, Birkie was rumored to have not just Fae blood but *royal* Fae blood—or perhaps her fashion acumen was a natural gift. Whatever it was, Kenzie knew she didn't possess it, and ran a quick hand through her wavy hair in spite of herself. She hadn't touched it since her shower and heaven only knew what it was doing.

"Connor just wants me to be as happy as he is, that's all. And in his book, that means having what he has."

Birkie reached up to play with the baby's tiny fingers. "Well, he does have something pretty fabulous here." She looked up at Kenzie's face, suddenly intent. "You'll have something fabulous too, dear. Something you truly want, very soon."

The hair stood up on the back of Kenzie's neck and her scalp prickled. Birkie often saw things, knew things before they happened. *Something I want . . .* "Maybe I'll find something exciting at my new dig?"

Birkie shook her head slowly. "What you need won't be in the ground. But you'll have to put away your fears to make room for it." She rose from the chair and smoothed the bright fabric of her clothing. Her long-fingered hands, festooned with many silver rings and bracelets, appeared to brush away the remnants of her psychic vision as well. "Always easier said than done of course. People often hug their fears to them like teddy bears, even though they're made of barbed wire instead of fluff. Human nature. Changeling nature too. Letting go of fear can be scarier than what you're afraid of."

"Fear serves a purpose. It can keep you safe." Kenzie didn't like the direction this conversation had taken.

"Not always." Birkie put her hands on her hips and laughed at herself then. "And my *goodness*, I'm not sounding much better than Connor! What a serious topic we've gotten onto when we ought to be celebrating this amazing little addition to the family." She bent and kissed the baby's fingers. "Let's have breakfast, shall we? It's nearly noon and

I'm famished. I made Zoey eat to keep up her strength—shoulda taken my own advice."

Greatly relieved, Kenzie followed her friend inside. "Do you want to hold the baby while I make breakfast? You've probably been up all night."

"Thanks honey, but I'm not tired enough to eat toaster waffles."

"Hey, I can cook!"

Birkie just looked at her until Kenzie rolled her eyes. "Okay, okay. I admit it, my culinary skills are limited to whatever can be made with boiling water, a toaster, or a microwave. But frozen waffles aren't that bad."

"Well, I guess they'll keep you alive," chuckled Birkie and patted her arm. "Oh, don't feel bad, dear, you simply have other skills, that's all. Being a top-drawer archaeologist takes up a lot of your time and attention—you were gone almost three years this last trip. Don't think I saw you more than once every six months or so. And now that this gorgeous baby is finally here, I imagine you'll be heading out all too soon to your next dig."

"In a few days. I was just waiting for the big event before I left." Kenzie paused and nuzzled the baby. Normally she would have started her new dig much earlier in the season, May at least. But she'd wanted to see her new niece or nephew. And the project she'd been on had encountered difficulties, taking longer than planned. "I'm glad I finished up at Monte Verde when I did. I was so afraid I'd miss this."

"I imagine working in Chile is a lot different from working up north."

"Won't miss the snakes and the spiders, that's for sure. But I'm afraid I won't find any plant species this time that you don't already have." By day, Birkie was the preternaturally efficient receptionist at Connor's clinic. In her off hours, however, she was a master of herbs and medicinal plants. Most of her home and its expansive grounds were lovingly devoted to their cultivation. Kenzie had delighted in keeping her friend well supplied with unique seeds and tubers over the years.

"That lemon verbena you brought me is growing like a weed in my greenhouse. The orchids, now, they'll take a while. Might have blooms next year. Do you know that over a hundred plants are routinely used in the Chilean health-care system? I'm thinking about making a little educational trip one of these days."

"How soon? Can it wait till I get back from this dig? I'll only be gone a few months this time."

"Well, I'm hardly going to go off and leave Connor just yet. We'll see how things are when you're finished with your project. Sounds like fun though, just like when we went to Scotland together a couple years ago."

Kenzie hadn't expected that trip to be so much fun. She'd never intended to return to her home country, even for a visit. But then her parents had moved to Skye, and Birkie had been a willing travel companion, so how could she say no? As it turned out, they'd had a blast. And thankfully no one commented on the fact that Kenzie hadn't gone near the Caledonian forest where their family home had once stood.

Birkie pulled out a skillet. "Omelet or scrambled?"

"Are you talking one of your Kitchen Sink Omelets?" Birkie's creation was so named because everything was in it *but* the proverbial fixture. "Because the answer is absolutely yes—if it's not too much trouble."

"No trouble at all, honey. I was planning to make one for myself. Saw a little ham in the fridge earlier. Just pass me that bell pepper on the windowsill there."

Kenzie grabbed the bright red fruit, then took a breath. "Birkie? You know what you said about *fear* a little while ago?"

"I didn't mean to upset you, dear. You know how these things just come over me."

"No, no, I was wondering . . . well, I had the dream last night."

Birkie didn't take her eyes off the onion she was chopping, but Kenzie saw her brows go up. "Now there's an interesting thing. It's been a mighty long time, hasn't it?"

"The dream's popped up once in a while when I've been really stressed, but I haven't had it in years and years. Think it means something?"

"Honey, everything means *something.*"

Anya's running shoes made little sound on the soft forest floor as she raced along a game trail, trying desperately to elude her pursuers. Her pink shorts and T-shirt were torn by the branches, there were scratches on her legs and arms from the wild roses and devil's club bushes. Still she ran on, ran as her mother had told her to do.

They know. They know. The men were closer now, although the dogs whined and strained at their leashes and refused to go with them. Some broke away and fled, their high-pitched yelps becoming fainter. Suddenly the roar of engines erupted from the bottom of the hill, filled the silent woods with noise. ATVs rammed into the brush, shoved their way along the trails.

She couldn't run much longer. The tears had dried in pale streaks on her small face, her grief and fear over her mother displaced by exhaustion and panic. What could she do? Where could she hide? Her mother had told her to run and now she couldn't.

The terrain was rougher here, boulders appeared as if they had erupted from the forest floor, and tree roots encased the rocks like octopus tentacles clutching hapless crabs. Anya dodged and darted among the trees, between the rocks, as the game trail led steeply upward.

It slowed her down. It slowed her pursuers too, but not enough. A quick glance behind her showed a flash of white—an ATV was looking for a path up the ridge. Finally she clambered to the crest, where a row of spruce trees marched like giant soldiers. The other side of the hill fell steeply away and its foot was cleft by a deep ravine. Anya could hear the rushing, tumbling water at its rocky bottom despite the noise of her pursuers. Without a second thought, she was racing, falling, scrambling down the hill. She gained a clear stretch of ground and put the last of her strength into running full tilt for the edge of the ravine. Trusting her instinct, she leapt—

And came down on four feet on the other side. The young wolf paused for only a moment, eyeing her pursuers gathered at the top of the ridge, committing their faces and their scents to memory.

Then she raced away into the welcoming forest.

Chapter Two

Kenzie took a plane to Seattle from Edmonton, where it had taken nearly two hours to get all her supplies and equipment through U.S. Customs. It was worth the wait to her. She preferred to bring as many of her own things as possible, the tools she was familiar with and the supplies that had been proven useful in many previous camps. The customs officer eyed her as he picked up each of her worn tools, the grips that had gradually assumed the shape of her own hand over time and been polished by her sweat. He no doubt thought she was eccentric for bringing what surely must look like junk to him. Was she even old enough to be eccentric? *Probably.*

The thick gray clouds gradually cleared away as her second flight headed up the coastline to Alaska. Blue sky greeted her as the plane touched down at the Ted Stevens International Airport in Anchorage. Kenzie had been in many airports all over the world, but she'd never seen one decorated with stuffed wildlife before. A glass case housed a taxidermic polar bear that towered over the bustling passengers, raising its paws toward the enormous *Welcome to Alaska* sign. She counted a half dozen bears of various types, a deer, a beaver, and several geese, and marveled at a huge salmon and a 400-pound halibut. Exquisite native art was everywhere and one piece in particular caught her eye. It was a reproduction of a historic piece, a carved wooden wolf mask, painted with the traditional coastal colors of turquoise, red, and black. The pelt of a large white wolf was attached to it and Kenzie found herself wondering if a shaman had once donned one like it. Had he been enacting a ritual, trying to ensure a successful hunt? Had he worn it in hopes of transforming himself? Or had he hoped to gain the skill that some members of the Tahltan tribe were rumored to have—the ability to detect a shapeshifter in human form?

As an anthropologist and archaeologist, she was fascinated. As a Changeling, however, she was repelled—James was a white wolf in his lupine form, and she had a momentary flashback to her childhood. To the marketplace at Torridon and its stacks of pelts, both wolf and Changeling . . .

She walked quickly away but came upon a glass case with taxidermic wolves. They were positioned stiffly with artificial snarls and plastic fangs. *Jeez, it's definitely past time to leave this airport.*

At the rental counter she flashed a worn membership card, signed forms and picked up her keys. The company had provided her with exactly what she'd ordered—a full-size pickup truck with four-wheel drive and a canopy to protect her gear. They didn't usually keep such vehicles at their airport lot, but had brought it over from another site. She hadn't specified color but noted with approval that it was a nondescript taupe. Or was it tan? Whatever it was, it wouldn't show all of the dirt and dust it was about to collect.

Kenzie slid behind the wheel and closed the door, relishing the sudden quiet and relieved to be alone at last. She was itching to get on the road but it was far too late in the day for that. By the time she arrived in the area, she'd end up looking for her site in the dark, so she conceded to spend the night at a motel.

Luckily, the sun rose early this far north, and she was up and on the road by five with a steaming mocha in the cup holder. The first leg took her northeast along the Glenn Highway. It was July and summer ruled—the breeze was warm, the sky was hazy blue, the forests boasted a hundred different greens. And the mountains . . . Kenzie found herself driving slower and slower, all but mesmerized by the stunning scenery. The gently rolling land of northern Alberta, especially the Peace River country where the town of Dunvegan had grown up, was beautiful, all the more so because it was dear to her heart. Yet it didn't compare to Alaska's raw wilderness and pointed peaks. Everything here was bigger, taller, grander somehow. Two of the massive snow-topped mountains on the horizon were actually active volcanoes but there was nothing except her guidebook to identify them as such—they were as high and jagged as the rest of the Wrangell range that marched along the horizon. She drank in the beauty but thought it was almost too much for one person. This caliber of scenery should be shared. . . .

Wildlife crossed the road frequently, moose and deer and even grizzly, all unconcerned by the few vehicles and in no particular hurry. One giant silver-tipped bear sat down on the yellow line as if to rest, or maybe he just liked the heat of the pavement. Kenzie slowed to a stop long before she reached him and waited until he decided to amble off. He must have weighed a thousand pounds, but she wasn't worried in the least, knowing that even grizzlies wouldn't attack a Changeling.

Only humans did that.

The highway was punctuated by a series of small communities and she found herself unexpectedly missing the little town of Dunvegan. It was the only place she felt a sense of sanctuary. Maybe because her family had lived there on and off since they'd left Scotland. Maybe because the Pack was there, a kind of extended family, and there was relative safety in numbers. Birkie was there, her dearest friend. And as Birkie had often said, home was wherever the people you cared about were. *I should have stayed longer, I really should have.* Kenzie rubbed at her eye with the heel of her hand—

—and had to swerve as a man leapt out from behind a truck at the side of the road, waving his arms. *Holy Jeez!* Quickly, she pulled over just ahead and jumped out, determined to give the stranger a piece of her mind. Her businesslike gait slowed a little as she got a better look at the white truck. There was a small flasher mounted on the roof—had she almost run over a state trooper? Her initial fury fizzled out like a wet firecracker. *Crap, crap, crap.* As she got closer, the insignia on the door gave her a little relief: *Alaska Department of Fish and Game.* It was somewhat better on the scale of offenses to nearly hit an ADFG officer than a trooper, wasn't it?

She fervently hoped so.

The man in question rolled a tire from behind the truck, straightened up and wiped his hands on his jeans. "Thanks for stopping. Didn't think you were going to."

For a long moment, Kenzie couldn't say a word. He was easily as tall as any of her brothers, lean like Culley and Devlin, yet his build was deceptive. He had power. It radiated from him effortlessly, naturally, as if he drew it from deep in the earth beneath his feet. Sure of himself, yet she detected no arrogance in the obsidian eyes that were studying her intently. Long strands of rich brown hair had worked themselves loose from where they'd been tied at the base of his neck. Kenzie had a sudden crazy urge to brush them back—and to let her hand linger.

"I—you scared the hell out of me!" she blurted.

The intensity of his gaze gave way as he laughed. "Sorry about that. I was trying to get this tire off and nearly missed you. Hasn't been a vehicle by here in a while and the cell phone doesn't work in this particular spot. Dead zone."

"Don't you have a radio?"

"Sure. I can radio my office in Glennallen loud and clear, no problem. But since I'm here, there's no one to answer it. And the local garage only takes phone calls." He balanced the tire against his leg and stuck out a large hand. "Josh Talarkoteen. Sorry about the dirt. I had to use the spare this morning already so I'm reduced to begging for a ride to town."

"Kenzie Macleod." Her hand was engulfed by his, but the sensation was more than pleasant. "Two flats in one day? That's just cruel."

"No, that's just backcountry Alaska."

She grinned then. Flat tires were also the stuff of backcountry Chile, backcountry Egypt and backcountry Oregon. "Sure, come on." She led the way to her truck.

He rolled the tire behind her. "You're not worried that I'm a serial killer? I can ride in the back, no problem."

She turned and looked at him with amusement. He was much too tall for one thing. He'd practically have to fold himself in half to fit beneath the truck canopy. For another, humans were usually only dangerous in a group. A single human—even one with an official sidearm—wasn't a match for a Changeling, even if she didn't take on her wolfen form. She couldn't say *that*, of course. "I have four older brothers who'll hunt you down like a dog if you try anything."

"Duly noted. I'll be sure to control my tendencies, homicidal and otherwise."

She flipped opened the canopy and yanked down the tailgate, began shoving gear to one side. He heaved the tire in and quickly brushed away the smudge of dirt it left on her sleeping bag.

"Going camping?"

"I work outdoors."

"Me too, most of the time. I was just checking out a report of someone taking deer out of season. What is it you do?"

"Dig in the dirt. Archaeology, ancient history."

"I've heard the National Park Service is doing some excavations in the Wrangell–St. Elias National Park. That you?"

"Nope, completely different project. And I work solo."

He didn't say anything to that, but looked like he was considering it as he got into the truck. She paused with her hand on the gearshift. "So what town are you going to?"

"Copper Center. We're about 50 miles from Glennallen, so no point going back there since we're more than halfway to Copper. How 'bout you?"

Copper Center? That didn't sound one bit familiar. Kenzie fumbled for her map, ran her finger over her planned route. It was true—she'd turned the wrong way at the intersection. "Dammit," she said aloud. She'd been too busy thinking about other things, something which seemed to be happening with alarming frequency lately.

Josh ducked as she threw the map behind the seat without folding it. "I take it you hadn't planned to visit the fair village of Copper?" he ventured.

"No. No, dammit, I turned right instead of left at the tee. I'm heading up near Chistochina."

"Well, the tourism committee at Copper Center will be deeply disappointed. Myself, I'd be more than pleased to go back to the turnoff. I can call Frank's Garage in Glennallen to come get me from there."

"You're sure?"

He nodded. "Frank's a buddy of mine."

She put the truck into drive, then swung a U-turn that a stuntman would be proud of. For a moment, he was glad he'd put on the seat belt. They settled into an easy pace, however, not *too* far above the speed limit, and he relaxed.

"So, you must be looking for old Ahtna stuff," he ventured.

She looked over at him, and there was a quick punch to his senses as her eyes, silver gray with long thick lashes, met his. Her fair skin was tanned and her dark hair was naturally tousled into pleasant waves. Like she'd just gotten out of bed . . .

"I'm looking for an Athabaskan fish camp north of Chistochina. The Ahtna tribe gave me permission to dig up along the river."

"That's pretty impressive. They don't give permission to just anyone to dig on their ancestral lands."

"I think a lot depends on how much respect you have for their culture. Plus they're very concerned about preserving that culture."

"True, especially after they've just signed a new oil exploration agreement. They don't want any ancient history trampled. So why do you work alone?"

"Lots of people like to work alone."

He should have paid attention to the defensive note in

her voice. "Well, if you ever get tired of being alone and want to experience the nightlife at Glennallen, I'd—"

"Why is everyone and their dog so concerned about me being alone? First Connor gives me grief, then James, then my mother phones me—I'm doing just fine by myself, dammit, and I don't need people worrying about my love life." She put her hand to her head then, as if she had a headache. "I'm really sorry, it's not your fault. I don't know why I'm yelling at *you*."

He wisely kept quiet for a whole minute before responding. "Family riding you pretty hard?"

"They mean well."

"That makes it tougher sometimes. You should hear my aunts and my sisters start in on me. They think I should have a dozen kids by now."

"They do?"

"Hell, yeah. It's like some kind of crime against nature to be single at my age."

"How old are you?"

"Thirty-two. And I know better than to ask yours."

She glanced at him quickly as if startled. "Why is that?"

"Well, because you don't go around asking women their age if you want to be popular," he laughed.

"Oh. Oh, right." She looked oddly relieved.

"So tell me about your dig. Why Chistochina?"

"I believe signs point to there having been a major settlement there."

"Well, there's still a settlement if you want to get technical. Most of the hundred or so folks who live in Chistochina and the surrounding area are Ahtna."

"I mean an *ancient* settlement. Just after the last Ice Age, in fact, ten or twelve thousand years ago."

He whistled in appreciation. "Okay, that's *old*. Even Mamie Dalkins wouldn't remember back that far."

"Who's Mamie Dalkins?"

"A sweet little old lady in Gakona who keeps trying to ply me with food. I met her after she shot a bear on her back porch.

Kenzie's eyebrows went up. "She shot it herself?"

"*Hell* yeah. She can't weigh more than 90 pounds soaking wet, but the bear made the mistake of keeping her up all night, trying to get into the house. I think it could smell the salmon she'd been canning in the kitchen, but whatever it was, when she got up the next morning, she shot him."

"Is that how you got involved?"

"She called me to report a dead bear, so yeah, I had to check on it. Christ, the thing was sprawled across her steps and it had to be nine feet tall. I don't know how much it weighed but it was one of the biggest grizzlies I ever saw. Mamie felled it with one shot too, although she shot it a second time to make sure. It's a wonder the gun didn't knock her down with the recoil."

"What on earth do you do with a dead bear on your porch?"

"Well, the rules say if you shoot a bear in self defense, you have to report it, which she did. They also say you have to skin it out and turn the hide over to Fish and Game. I couldn't ask a little old lady to skin a thousand pound bear—although I'll bet she'd manage it somehow—so I did it for her. Been friends ever since. Of course she keeps trying to give me jars of canned bear meat, but other than that, we get along great."

"She canned the meat?"

"No kidding, every last bit of it smoked, canned, or frozen. She even made some kind of bear sausage. I'm sure it'll last her the rest of her natural life—or maybe mine. I wouldn't put it past her to will it to me." He gave a mock shudder and Kenzie couldn't help laughing.

"I take it you don't like bear meat?"

"Had some when I was five. It was greasy and stank like bear, and it didn't agree with me. Put me off of it ever since. Funny how the little things that happen to you as a kid are so intense."

"Yeah." Her smile faded, and he wondered what she was remembering.

"Anyway, I don't know what kind of information you already have, but Mamie would know who to talk to if you need to do any research on local legends. She knows everything that goes on in the Copper River basin, past and present—and what she doesn't know just hasn't happened yet."

"Sounds like Lucinda Perkins and Mabel Rainier back home. Between the two of them, they know everything there is to know." She made a face then. "And they give free advice."

"Let me guess, they're concerned about your love life too?"

"*Immensely* concerned. So much so that they had to discuss it in the middle of the damn grocery store. That got Mavis Williams to leave the produce department and join in. Then Enid Malkinson got involved and if that old Siamese cat of hers hadn't suddenly jumped out of her bag and run through the store, I'd probably still be there."

"Four to one. That's tough odds. You usually only get that at family gatherings."

"Dunvegan's a small town and my family's lived in the area for decades. Even though I'm not there much, everyone feels entitled to an opinion."

"Dunvegan," he repeated. "Isn't that in Canada?"

"Northern Alberta."

He grinned then. "Nice to meet a fellow countryman." He pointed at the road ahead. "There's the turnoff. You can just drop me off up there."

"Wait a minute, you're Canadian?"

"It's a long story. I'll tell you about it when we go out for dinner. Would you prefer bowling or dancing afterward?" It was satisfying to see her control wobble as she steered the truck to the shoulder.

"Jeez, do you feel sorry for me or something? I'm not going out with you, no matter what country you're from."

"Naw-aw, I made the offer *before* I heard how concerned your family was, so it's hardly a pity date. How about giving me your phone number?"

"No," she said, and brought the truck to a jerky stop.

He shrugged, and produced a dog-eared business card with the Fish and Game logo from his shirt pocket. "I'll give you mine then. If you have any trouble with bears, give me a call. There's a lot of big griz up there, all gathered to catch salmon at this time of year, and they can be a problem when you're camping." He waited a second, then added. "It's my job."

He didn't think she'd take it, but at last she plucked the card from his fingers and stuffed it in her own shirt pocket—which he couldn't help but notice was tantalizingly rounded, and the button had to be directly over her . . .

"Thanks, I'll keep that in mind," she said without conviction. Damned if her bottom lip didn't look just a little bit sulky. He was torn between wanting to kiss it and wanting to laugh. Since either choice would likely be harmful to his health, however, he opted to get out of the truck. "Wait." He leaned back in the window. "Be sure to leave the Richardson Highway or you'll end up in Fairbanks. Take the Tok Cutoff and you'll come right to Chistochina."

She saluted him and Josh walked back to get his tire. He thumped on the canopy after he put the tailgate back up and watched the pickup drive away until he couldn't see it anymore. It was the Fourth of July, and he could swear that there were fireworks going off in his bloodstream, thanks to Kenzie Macleod. And her initial outburst had been downright endearing rather than irritating. Why would that be? And why would the woman who'd just turned him down be miles more attractive to him than that cute redheaded waitress at The Caribou? Could it be those big gray eyes that arrested him? Or maybe it was her long, long legs.

Or maybe it was the bright blue aura that surrounded her. She probably didn't know she even had it, never mind that he could see it. And Josh would bet money that she had no idea what it had revealed to him.

Last summer, Kenzie had ordered a high-resolution satellite image of the Copper River basin directly north of Chistochina. The results had helped her choose the site for the dig, but that was only the beginning. Now that she was here, she needed to perform a surface survey, walking miles upon miles in careful patterns. Most archaeologists assembled teams in order to cover more ground. Not Kenzie. She worked alone and efficiently, simply using her lupine form to pace out the vast area on four tireless feet. The advantage was that she had a feel for the terrain that went far beyond the visual. Archaeology was both a science and an art, and her instincts—as vital as her education—were telling her she'd found the right spot on a forested shelf of land above the river flats.

The Chistochina River wound a bright blue serpentine path between spruce-covered bluffs and hills on its way to the much larger Copper River. This high spot would be where the ancient Ahtna had set up camp, where they could see for miles, where it was safe from flooding, and where they had ready access to the salmon that came up-river to spawn each year. Moose and caribou were plentiful most years but the salmon were far more dependable, leaving the ocean to travel countless miles up the Copper and its tributaries.

Field conditions were excellent. At this time of year, the earth was dry, but not too dry. Kenzie dug a test pit about a meter deep and examined the colors and textures of the soil strata, confirming that the site did indeed have the potential she had hoped for. The scent of the earth was primal and exhilarating, and she found herself wondering if her brother James felt this way when he was planting fields. Perhaps they were a little bit alike after all.

Finally she selected her *datum* or mapping point at the southwest corner of her planned dig site and laid out excavation units with strings and metal stakes. Each unit was about two-by-two meters, and she marked off about twenty of them, although it was unlikely she would uncover them all. One of the rules of modern archaeology was never to dig up the entire site, saving some areas untouched for what future technology might be able to reveal. It was a principle that science had learned the hard way, after many early archaeologists threw away countless shards of broken pottery, bits of burnt wood, animal bones and shells, stone and obsidian fragments, mistakenly judging them to be worthless. Only the intact artifacts were kept and studied and all that the so-called *garbage* might have told future generations of archaeologists was lost forever.

It was late in the afternoon when Kenzie surveyed her initial work with satisfaction. Time to set up her campsite. Usually it would be within a stone's throw of the dig but she found herself strangely restless. Deciding to take a break and stretch her legs, Kenzie left the camping gear in the truck and went looking for possible cell phone reception. Her work took her to isolated places where her cell was usually little more than a paperweight, so it was a pleasant surprise to discover a reliable four-bar signal on top of a knoll. Even more pleasant was the stunning view of the Chistochina River. She decided then and there that she'd found her home base for the next four months. The site was high above the river and was a hike of nearly a mile to her dig. The distance was nothing to her, of course, an easy stroll. And if the dig site was *ten* miles away, it would still be worth it to have cell reception. She parked the truck on the flats below, next to the rough and overgrown miner's trail that had begun its life long ago during the gold rush days, and hauled her supplies up to the top of the hill.

Once the tent was pitched and her gear unpacked, she sank into a camp chair overlooking the river. The shadows were getting long, although the sun wouldn't actually set until 11:30—and then for only about five hours. She loved that about the north—lots of time to work. And the nights were never totally dark, the skies remaining more of a deep twilight. Further north in Alaska, the sun didn't dip below the horizon at all at this time of year, but Kenzie preferred a short night rather than none at all. As a Changeling, she instinctively appreciated those magical hours ruled by the moon, even if she didn't have to obey the moon herself.

Without warning she found herself wondering what Josh was doing, as she had many times throughout the day. She still couldn't remember his last name but she sure couldn't forget anything else about him. Those eyes had been the color of obsidian when they flashed in the sun, but it was the intelligence and humor behind them that intrigued her. Okay, well, he was also unquestionably *hot* and she figured he'd be a treat for any woman to look at.

But she had been the one to look, to notice, to appraise. . . . What was wrong with her? Why would she find a *human* so intensely attractive? If her inner wolf had been able to purr, she was sure it would have each and every time an image of Josh popped into her head. The strange feelings were no doubt left over from all the family stuff she'd left behind in Dunvegan. Her siblings, the new baby, the Pack, the sense of home, of belonging. Not to mention both the subtle and not-so-subtle pressure to find a mate. She was still mortified about blurting *that* out to a complete stranger. But it was just further proof of the stress she was feeling. And she was never going to see Josh again, so it hardly mattered, did it?

Her inner wolf whined a little at that thought. . . .

Kenzie rolled her eyes. Obviously she needed a distraction, preferably one with some sense and especially one that wouldn't lecture her. *Probably* wouldn't lecture her. Pulling out her cell phone, she speed-dialed Birkie and was relieved when her friend answered.

"Hey there, sugar. Good to hear your voice. You all set up?"

"Pretty much. Got a nice spot above the river valley—you should see it, Birkie. So has my niece got a name yet?"

"Well, they went through the whole family tree, figuring maybe they'd name her after somebody, but they couldn't agree. In the end it was Culley that accidently named her."

"*Culley?*" Kenzie was horrified. Her brother was a prankster extraordinaire, without a serious bone in his body. Heaven only knew what he'd come up with.

"Teagan. From a Welsh word for *pretty.*"

"Teagan." Kenzie tried it out. "Connor, Zoey, and *Teagan.* It's great. But—"

"It's a little unexpected from Culley, I know. The boy's a clown on the outside, but he's got a sensitive heart. Sometimes I think that's why he jokes so much—to keep anyone from getting too close to it."

The observation made perfect sense to Kenzie, although she'd never thought of it herself. And wasn't it strange that she hadn't? Maybe she'd been a little too preoccupied with her own issues over the years. She pushed that guilty thought away and chatted with Birkie for a while, describing her trip, the grizzly on the road, the volcanoes on the skyline—and the man she'd picked up and promptly dumped on.

"Was he cute?"

"Birkie!"

"Well, if you're going to accost people, they might as well be good-looking."

"I didn't accost him. Well, maybe I did, a little."

"Well, it's no surprise you had to blow off a little steam. You've gotten a lot of pressure from your family lately, and all the excitement over the baby hasn't helped."

"Everyone worries about me being alone. But I *like* working alone."

"Nothing wrong with working by yourself. Lots of people are more productive without distractions. Take James for instance. Some folks would find it unbearable to drive that tractor around all those acres for a whole day at a time. But it suits him. He's right in tune with what he's doing, thinking and planning as he goes."

"Exactly." Kenzie blew out a breath. Birkie understood. She always understood.

"The only difference between what James does and what you do is that at the end of the day, he has a home to go to and people to talk to. He works alone but he doesn't *live* alone. Your family knows your work is important to you. They just want to see you have a more balanced life, that's all."

"I know they mean well but—"

"But your brothers have conveniently forgotten that they didn't go out looking for their true mates—their mates came into their lives when the boys were ready."

"Even James?" Kenzie still marveled at the change in him.

"*Especially* James. Trust me, if he hadn't been ready to be healed and move on, he wouldn't have met Jillian. That's just the way it works."

"Not according to Carly. She thinks I need to get busy and find myself a man."

"That's Carly for you." Birkie was no doubt rolling her eyes. "If Jake hadn't fallen for her after she set her sights on him, I expect she'd have nabbed him with a bear trap. She's direct that way. But it doesn't matter what Carly or anyone else thinks. All that matters is what *you* think, honey."

"I think my work comes first."

"Perhaps that's true. It is for some. Just don't close the door on possibilities. The most important thing is to be openhearted. To be receptive to whatever relationship comes along that feels right for you. Could be a dog or a child, or maybe a whole group of people working to save the long-toed salamander."

"Maybe I'll be one of those old ladies with twenty cats."

"Cats are not to be underrated as a source of happiness, but it *is* possible that a man might come along too, you know. Take that fellow you gave a ride to—what if he asked you out?"

"He doesn't count, Birkie. He's not a Changeling." And she was *so* not mentioning that Josh *had* asked her out.

The older woman sighed into the phone. "Honey, it's the heart that counts. Being a Changeling doesn't necessarily make a man good relationship material. And being human isn't a reason to write somebody off. There are good and bad individuals in both species. We were all reminded of that after Bernie."

Kenzie shivered. Bernard Gervais had been old even for a Changeling, and nasty by any standards. She and Birkie had been away in Scotland when the miserable old loner broke the most cardinal rule of her kind by killing at least two humans, and possibly more. His bloodthirsty rampage had set human and shapeshifter relations back several centuries. Years later, the small rural community of Dunvegan remained suspicious of all wolves and often shot them on sight, and even Kenzie found it tough to blame them.

Good and bad in both species. "I'll try to remember that." She honestly wished she felt as Birkie did—her life would be so much easier. They'd discussed this concept since just about forever, but while Kenzie accepted it logically, she couldn't seem to do so emotionally. Humans, while likeable and even fun, were just not trustworthy. Their first reaction to the strange and unusual was fear, their second to destroy the source of that fear. Which made it all the more important that she focus on her work.

Ever sensitive, Birkie changed the subject. "Say, I nearly forgot to tell you. Bucky Simons drove his mother's car right through the window of Mavis William's sandwich shop. It happened at lunchtime yesterday. . . ."

Kenzie smelled him long before she saw him. Nate Richardson hadn't been a Changeling long, only about thirty years or so, but even a cub would know better than to approach her from upwind. Nate being Nate, however, he was all too happy to broadcast his highly masculine presence to her. Still, it was a hell of a surprise—she hadn't seen him in what, two years?

Kenzie got to her feet and pulled the bandana from her head, wiped her face with it and quickly ran her hands through her hair. She surveyed the careful grid of strings and stakes she'd created, the first square of earth she'd uncovered, and waited. Sure enough, Nate swaggered into view. He was tall, blond, blue-eyed, and as tanned as a surfer. Built like one too.

"Hey baby, why are you always working?" He smiled broadly and gave her an enthusiastic hug that almost pulled her off her feet—not an easy task when she was nearly as tall as he.

"Why are you always *not* working? And what the hell are you doing in Alaska?"

"I came, I lectured, I conquered—got a couple of corporate sponsors out of Anchorage for a dig near Petersburg."

"In the Tongass forest? Congrats. I saw the basalt tools they found there a few years back. Pretty unique with the carved finger grips and all, but not all that old."

He rolled his eyes. "You're such a snob, you know that? At about 1,500 years old, they're way older than even *you*." Moving in close to her, he ran a finger softly along the sensitive edge of her ear. "Good thing I like older women. A lot. Wanna see how much?"

She shook off his hand and stood back, giving him a friendly shove as she did so. "No thanks. I have work to do."

"I'll say. It's July and you've barely started here. Usually you'd have half the hillside excavated by this time of year."

"What can I say? Things dragged out at Monte Verde, then I went home for a couple weeks to see my brand new niece."

"Which brings me to my next question. Why are you still working by yourself? You could have sent any number of students up here in May to do the initial fieldwork for you. Even volunteers will jump at the chance to help with a dig for God's sake, and you wouldn't even have to be here."

"You know I prefer to be hands-on." It was an old argument, and not one they'd ever resolved. They'd gone to the same university, become roommates and occasional lovers (*friends with benefits*, as Nate had called it). They'd been on digs together from South America to Egypt to Ireland as they finished their degrees, then their doctorates. Several years had passed, and Nate was now a professor with full tenure at New York University. She'd been offered the same—long before Nate, if the truth be told. And just like the many other professorships she'd been offered, she'd turned it down in favor of her fieldwork.

"You just like getting dirty. Speaking of which, I could use a little down and dirty." He waggled his brows. "How 'bout it, baby?"

"You haven't changed a bit," she said as she dodged his grab. He teased her like this every time he saw her—and she knew it wasn't all teasing. At her insistence, they'd re-

turned to *just friends* between the time she got her first
doctorate and her second, but he hadn't been happy about
it. He had wanted to take the relationship forward, wanted
a commitment.

Commitment was not something Kenzie wanted, at least
not with Nate. Sure, he was charming and handsome and a
lot of fun. And she didn't meet many Changelings outside
of her own Pack. But it had become evident early on that
he felt more like a younger brother to her than a serious
love interest. He was barely full-grown in the wolfen world
even as he appeared thirty-five in the human world. Although she looked to be the same age, Kenzie was actually
well over a century—still very young for a Changeling, but
impossibly ancient for a human.

Still, age could be dealt with in a relationship. Different
life goals? Not so much. They just didn't seem to want the
same things. He placed enormous value on social standing
and cultivating powerful friends. Appearance was everything to him, and by the time they'd graduated, she'd come
to realize that he'd chosen image over substance, even in
himself. What was it Birkie had said? *Being a Changeling
doesn't necessarily make a man good relationship material.*

Whatever the reasons, what she felt for Nate Richardson
was affection and no more. That long ago no-strings liaison
with him hadn't worked for her either. Maybe it was because most Changelings mated for life, or maybe she just
wasn't designed for a casual relationship. But it was clearly a
case of all or nothing when it came to men.

She'd chosen *nothing*. All of her passion in the years since
had been channeled into her research and fieldwork, something else which Nate didn't understand. He complained
bitterly about the competition for sponsors, about the endless fund-raising that preempted his teaching time, but in

truth, he loved every public minute of it. He'd obviously found his niche. Kenzie suspected he'd forgotten what fieldwork was like even as she knew he wouldn't miss it. He'd never loved the hands-on work as she did, nor did he share her cause. Not that she'd ever told him about it. . . .

"How the hell did you get here, anyway?" she asked. "I didn't hear a plane."

"Are you kidding? You know how much I like to drive, and then I even got in a little four-by-fouring to get to your camp. I had some general GPS coordinates to go by but if I hadn't spotted your truck, I'd still be searching for you. By the way, why is your dig so damn far from your camp? I practically had to track you to find you."

"Family stuff, remember? I wanted a cell phone signal for a change."

"That's a first. You're usually incommunicado for months at a time. Hell, if I'd known there was a chance you'd answer your damn phone, I would have called you to join me in Anchorage."

"Why?"

"Why not? You need a good meal and a chance to shop. Maybe trade in your truck for something classier. Good God, couldn't you at least get a Volvo?"

"I like my truck. I don't like the city and I hate shopping." And she wasn't dumb. Nate would love to have her along on his fund-raising mission—while she wasn't exactly famous, her name meant something both in and beyond archaeological circles. "Besides, I'm busy."

"You're always busy. Take a break, for God's sake. Kick back a little. You've got nothing to prove and surely this site will keep. No one's ever found anything around here except for one little microblade—if it *is* one—and it was probably dropped by a passing hunter."

He'd done his homework, she'd give him that. A tiny chip of dark glass-like obsidian found by a hiker years ago had led to some initial exploration of this area, but there had been no further evidence uncovered to suggest there was an ancient encampment here. Kenzie, however, had found clues at sites in northern British Columbia and the Yukon that she believed pointed to this place. None of which she was about to share with Nate of course. She shrugged. "It interests me, that's all. Besides, I like the scenery."

"The scenery is a helluva lot better in Petersburg. Why don't you break ground there for me? I've already got the media prepped to do a story there, and the site's getting a mention in an upcoming special for the History Channel."

She shook her head and his face darkened. "I forgot, you don't give a damn about the media, do you?" he blurted. "You've never needed to compete for funding."

Here we go again . . . Kenzie sighed inwardly. No matter how he'd tried to hide it, Nate had always resented her financial independence. Like many Changeling families, hers was old enough to have accumulated a great deal of hidden wealth. Her personal net worth could fund many archaeological digs indefinitely, and while Nate had no idea just how *much* she was worth, he openly envied the independence she enjoyed. She could pick her own site and work there as long as she liked. Kenzie worked alone by choice, but that didn't mean she didn't work efficiently. She made good use of the latest remote sensing methods—proton magnetometer, electrical resistivity, ground penetrating radar—all without the need to beg for sponsors, making her a rarity in her field.

He scrubbed his hands over his face as if to change his expression. "That was a jerkwad thing to say. I'm sorry, I guess I'm grouchy from traveling. Took two Alaska Air connections to get to Petersburg yesterday and then I had to charter a bush plane to go back up to Juneau in time for a flight to Anchorage. God, I don't know how the locals manage to get anywhere in their own state." Sudden devilment appeared in his eyes and his grin was bright in the July sun. "You know, I could really use a run. How 'bout it?"

Kenzie felt the prickle of static electricity on her skin, the buildup of energy that heralded a Change. A moment later a large tawny wolf stood in Nate's place. He bowed on his front legs, his tail wagging as if he was a big dog inviting her to play. *Oh, what the hell. . . .*

She jumped to her feet and ran in the opposite direction, making the Change on the fly. Raced toward the river on four paws, her steely gray fur still throwing off a few blue sparks of static. Nate couldn't catch her, of course. Even her brothers couldn't when she ran as a wolf. She was fast and sleek, a streak of thundercloud as she loped along the bank. Without warning, she pivoted and ran full-tilt into the much larger wolf, knocking him ass-over-teakettle. She clamped her jaws over the back of his neck with mock growls, and he rolled over to pin her. They wrestled and played for an hour, only breaking apart to chase each other. Finally, they made their way to her camp and flopped on the sun-warmed earth, panting hard with tongues lolling.

Kenzie returned to human form first. She was fully dressed, right down to the cell phone and crumpled paper in her pocket, as was Nate when he shifted back a few minutes later. A Changeling's apparel (and anything else that was within their aura at the moment) passed into another dimension while they were in wolfen form. At least, that was the only explanation anyone had. Which dimension it was or where the hell it might be, Kenzie had no idea. Her brother, Devlin, was working on something called String Theory that might help solve the mystery, but physics didn't interest her. Neither did fashion, come to think of it. Nate's pants and shirt were pressed and clean, and obviously top of the line. Her no-frills jeans and plaid workshirt were still rumpled and dirty. Didn't he notice how different they were? Surely his attraction to her was just old habit, no doubt coupled with what he thought she might be able to do for him and his goals. *Especially* what he thought she could do for him.

She got her answer when they walked up the knoll to camp.

"God, I've missed running with you. We're good together, we've always been good together."

"Our *wolves* are good together. On two legs, the relationship isn't so smooth."

"It could be if you weren't so damn stubborn."

"Or if you weren't so damn pig-headed."

They both forced a laugh. "So why are you here, Nate?" she asked. "How the hell did you even know where I was?"

"No big mystery. I'm in Alaska for the summer and heard through the grapevine that you were somewhere on the Copper River. You had to get permission to dig here, so it was just a matter of asking the right officials before I was pointed in your direction. So here I am to say hello to a dear old friend and colleague. In fact, I'll probably drop in a few more times if I get the chance. Is that a problem?"

"Shouldn't be." She waited, sensing there was more.

"I miss you, Kenzie. I wish you'd come and work in my department. It needs you. I need you too, but you keep saying no to giving us a second chance."

She stifled a groan. "I've already said many times that I don't want a position at NYU. I like to work on my own." Besides, NYU didn't need her, it needed her *name*. "And as for you and me—are you crazy? We've talked and talked about this over the years. You know how I feel. No matter how you slice it, we're not true mates."

"Bullshit. You're using that old fairy tale as an excuse," he scoffed.

Actually she was using it to buy time while she tried to figure out what on earth to say. "Like hell I am. Two of my brothers discovered their real mates. They both said that their inner wolf knew."

"Yeah, well, *my* inner wolf thinks you fit in my bed pretty well. All that soul mate stuff is a human idea. Who wants to spend centuries alone hoping to run across one person who may or may not exist?"

"I've heard that the person is drawn to you when you're both ready." Birkie might be right about that. Kenzie's sisters-in-law, Zoey and Jillian, were from large cities on opposite sides of the country, and had both been inexplicably drawn to the little northern town of Dunvegan where Connor and James were.

"Well *I'm* ready—ready and waiting for you to wake up. Why would you choose to spend the rest of your life alone when I'm right here? It's not safe for Changelings to be alone, don't you get that? Or am I just not good enough? I wasn't born a werewolf, so maybe I'm socially beneath you?"

"Nate! For pity's sake, you know better than that. We've been through all this before, again and again. We're friends and that's all there is."

"Well it's not enough for me. Maybe I don't want to be friends either."

She goggled at him. "Are you blowing me off? That's so high school!"

"Isn't that just what you're doing with me?" He walked a few steps away and pinched the bridge of his nose as if he had a headache. When he turned toward her, his expression was grim. "I want it all, baby. I don't need a goddamn friendship—I got plenty of pals to hang out with. I want you to be with me all the way."

"Nate, I—"

He held up a hand. "Think it over. Just think it over. I'll be back this way in a few days and maybe you'll have come to your senses by then." He headed down to the twin ruts that passed for a road, rammed a flashy yellow Humvee into gear and drove off in a cloud of dust.

Crap, crap, crap. She kicked over her camp chair, then worked on sending each and every piece of her firewood pile flying. It didn't help much—she wanted to punch something. Hell, she wanted to *bite* something. Nate's arrival had been surprise enough, but his demands for a relationship had blindsided her completely. Where the hell had that come from?

She racked her brain, trying to think of what had been said, done, implied, or even hinted at during their last conversation. But that was two years ago. Two years! She'd congratulated Nate when he took over the archaeology department at NYU. They'd danced together, but only twice—she'd had a date with him, for heaven's sake. And in the past two years she hadn't even sent Nate a damn e-mail. Thought about it once or twice, but hadn't gotten around to it. Kenzie threw up her hands. How could anything she had done or said have led him to persist in hoping for a relationship with her?

And that other thing he'd said—it wasn't safe for Changelings to be alone. What the hell did he mean by that? If he was so worried about her, why wait two years to come and talk to her about it?

Men! She filled a water bottle, swore as it overflowed, and stomped back to her dig. It had never been safe for Changelings, alone or with a mate. But she hoped with all her might that what she was doing would change that.

Chapter Three

S *tupid rabbit.*

Anya sat down hard, her sides heaving and pink tongue lolling full length to help cool her furred body. She was fast in wolfen form, not as fast as she would be when she grew up, but a lot faster than she was on two feet. Not quick enough to catch the big snowshoe hare, however. She had been lucky to spot it despite its earth-brown summer coat, but it had dodged her first lunge easily, and continued to keep distance between them no matter how hard she tried. Finally it disappeared into the underbrush with a flick of its tail.

You probably taste stupid too.

Two days ago she'd caught a mouse, but that had been luck. She'd blundered on it by accident and had a paw on it almost before she'd realized what it was. If she had been on two legs, the thought of mousemeat would have been *icky*. As a wolf, however, the musty-smelling little ball of fur had tasted just fine. It had eased the hunger a little but not for long. Her mother could hunt—she'd often brought home a deer, and deer were *sooooo* yummy—but Anya hadn't learned how yet; she wasn't big enough. She wished and wished her mother was here with her. The men had hurt her, taken her somewhere . . . but where? She'd told Anya to run; she hadn't told her what to do next.

Anya wished she could Change back, but she didn't dare. She missed her bed with its pink fuzzy pillows. She could spread the blankets on it (almost straight) so she wouldn't be cold, and she knew how to make cereal with milk so she wouldn't be hungry. But she couldn't go home and besides, she didn't know where home was anymore. She didn't know where *here* was either. The forest had always been so beautiful with its sounds and smells, but now there was way too much of it.

Hungry, tired, and more lonely than she had ever been, even lonelier than when her best friend Sasha had moved away, she flopped down and rested her chin on her paws. She was almost asleep when her sensitive nostrils caught a faint scent from somewhere downwind. It wasn't wolf . . . and it wasn't human. It was like *her*. Hope dragged her to her feet and she trotted south on a narrow game trail that flanked the wide river.

Kenzie studied the satellite map, then eyed her grid lines. She'd had to set them up all over again after a young grizzly blundered through them in the night. He probably hadn't even noticed he was dragging several hundred feet of string festooned with fluorescent tape and dozens of wire stakes. She'd followed the broad trail for nearly a mile until she found the huge tangle wrapped around some wild rosebushes.

The string hadn't been salvageable, but she'd cut the stakes from the snarled mess before tossing it in her campfire pit. Luckily she had another roll. It had been one of the first things she'd learned about fieldwork, that somebody or something was likely to take out at least some of the gridlines on every dig. Her very first site had been trampled—and crapped on—by a trio of camels. At least the grizzly hadn't left anything nasty behind.

A flicker of movement at the far edge of the clearing caught her eye. Every sense alert, she waited. Tried to catch a scent but whatever had moved was downwind of her. She sighed and hoped it wasn't that damn bear again. If it was, she might have to Change and chase it off.

Nothing showed itself, but throughout the day Kenzie's eyes strayed often to the thick forest growth beyond the dig site. Intuition told her she was being watched. The movement in the brush told her that, whatever it was, it sure wasn't big enough to be the bear. And when daylight finally faded, making it too dark to work efficiently—long after 10 P.M. this far north—she sensed she was being followed all the way back to her camp. Still, her wolfen instincts didn't raise any alarm. Some creature was probably just curious. A mountain lion had tracked her once, puzzled by her Changeling scent, yet Kenzie hadn't been afraid. No animal in its right mind would attack her, not even the grizzly. The only creatures she had to be wary of were human beings.

Strings of tiny solar lights were glowing prettily around the perimeter of her camp when she arrived. She got her Coleman stove going, boiled water, and added it to a pouch of instant stew. It smelled, well, *reasonable*. The quality of camp food had certainly improved over the years but it was never going to smell *good* to her. Wasn't going to taste good either, but that was the price of convenience. The foil bag was too darn hot to hold in her hands, however, so she poured it into a bowl. Just as she turned to find a spoon, she spotted movement at the far edge of her camp.

The solar lights were strictly for ambience, not illumination, but it didn't matter. As a Changeling, Kenzie's night vision was acute. She watched as a small black nose eased out from under a bush. The nose was followed by a dark blunt muzzle, a pair of eyes, and two pointed ears that looked a little too big.

I'll be damned. It's a wolf cub. "Hey," she said aloud. "Have you been following me?" The creature's face disappeared among the leaves, but not for long. It reemerged a few minutes later, watching her intently. Eventually the face was followed by a thin body. The cub was somewhere between the fuzzy baby stage and the gangly teen phase. Its fur was dark brown tipped with black, but one front foot was oddly white almost to the elbow. Kenzie lifted a spoon to her mouth and the cub's eyes seemed to follow the movement. She frowned. "Are you hungry? Where's your mother?"

It didn't respond of course. Nor did it come any closer. Why was this cub alone? Wolves took very good care of their young, and if something happened to the alpha pair, the rest of the Pack often stepped in to care for the cubs. She ate her dinner slowly, trying not to feel guilty for eating in front of the little creature and reminding herself that people food would only upset its system anyway.

Eventually, Kenzie reached out her fingers and made a soft call, but the cub didn't move. She persisted only to see the cub retreat into the bushes. She wasn't as gifted with animals as her brother Connor, but most creatures came to her. She waited until the moon was high yet the young wolf didn't reappear. Hoping that the cub's family had collected it, Kenzie finally turned in. Dawn came early here and she wanted to be at the site when daylight arrived.

She slept fitfully. The nightmare recurred, but this time, it was Nate who chased her.

★   ★   ★

The orange-striped canopy looked like it belonged on a beach, not in a forest clearing. Kenzie had been forced to replace her old canopy before the trip, and was dismayed not only by the color of this one, but its *newness*. It seemed almost vulgar, clashing with the familiar items it shaded; her battered screening box on an old blue tarp, her trowels and brushes, her camp shovel and other nicked and worn tools. Even the electronic equipment—her handheld GPS was a prime example—looked like tired and dusty flea market finds.

"Tools are meant to be used," she told herself, a saying she had picked up from her father, Ronan. Come to think of it, her oldest brother, James, said the same thing. It was tempting to throw a little dirt on the brilliant canopy just so it would fit in with the rest of her gear. Maybe she'd be lucky and the garish thing would fade in the sun.

She picked up a trowel and headed for the grid. Today she would break ground in square three and the anticipation made her tingle. Not too many people got goosebumps from digging in the dirt, but Kenzie lived for this. She loved the entire process, from the moment of beginning, of possibility, to the patient brushing away of layers, the chipping of stone, the bagging of samples, to the rare and beautiful discovery of pure history. Before the trowel touched the ground, however, a movement from the forest edge caught her attention.

The wolf cub was back.

The great hooked beak snapped shut an inch from his face, and Josh Talarkoteen's gloved hand snaked out to grab it. Throwing his other arm around the large feathered body, he pinned the bird's powerful wings to its sides, praying he wasn't causing it more pain. "There we are, shhh, easy. Easy. I'm trying to help you."

It was a golden eagle, larger than a bald eagle, and a female. Goldens were superb hunters and seldom scavenged carcasses as their cousins did. This one was young, however, and had been attracted to a dead deer along the side of the road where she'd been clipped by a passing car. Another motorist spotted her hopping along the ditch and called Josh's office. Despite the bird's broken wing, it had still taken him the better part of an hour to get close enough to her to grab her.

"It's going to be okay, honey. We're going to get you fixed up and back in the sky in no time. But you're going to have to go for a little trip first." It was a struggle to get the big raptor into the large traveling kennel, but a short one—Josh was both strong and experienced. He'd rescued plenty of bald eagles but he'd never gotten this close to a golden, even though he'd seen them all his life in the Stikine River valley. He'd been surprised to see them soaring high above the hills in Afghanistan too. Their presence had helped center him, helped keep himself together amid the blood and violence. Once in a while a pair of golden eagles had flanked him as he flew his chopper over mountain and desert. Sometimes he pictured himself as an eagle too. Perhaps it was his Tahltan background—after all, eagles played a powerful role in clan culture, second only to wolves. Or perhaps he just plain liked to fly. Whichever it was, he felt a kinship with the extraordinary birds.

Fierce yellow eyes studied him through the bars, eyes that could see several times better than he could. He wondered what they saw. Josh instinctively wanted to stroke the eagle's bronze head but knew that wild creatures seldom appreciated the human gesture. To them, he was an enemy and not to be trusted. Sometimes the very young ones, cubs and fawns, were all too happy to be held and petted, but it wasn't good for them. They needed to retain a natural suspicion of humans—that's what would keep them alive. He patted the top of the kennel instead and strapped it down before closing the tailgate.

He shook back his long dark hair as he swung into the truck cab. Usually it was tied back, but he'd lost the damn leather thong again. Maybe he'd cut his hair. His head had been shaved when he'd joined the service after 9/11, and in the breathless heat of Afghanistan he'd been glad of it. Five years. He'd spent five years there. Some nights he was still there. . . .

Suddenly his cell phone belted out Nickelback's *If Today Was Your Last Day.* Josh had chosen the song with a nod to two of his buddies who hadn't made it back.

"Tark here." He used his nickname from his service days without thinking.

"Who? I'm looking for Josh Talarkoteen."

"You've got the right—Kenzie, is that you?"

"You remembered my name?"

Hell *yeah.* He'd only been thinking about her a hundred times a day, trying to come up with an excuse to see her again that wouldn't make him seem like a stalker. "Of course I did. What can I do for you?"

"I've got an orphaned wolf here that I need some help with."

His pleasure at having Kenzie on the other end of the phone was suddenly tempered with apprehension. Every year the Division of Wildlife Conservation was flooded with calls about abandoned animals, and most of the time, the creatures weren't in need of help at all. It was typical of most mothers to leave their young for periods of time. A mother bear would actually run her young cubs up a tree so she could go fishing. Deer left their fawns in order to feed. As a result, Fish and Game usually ended up with far too many moose calves, fox and raccoon kits, even grizzly cubs that had been "rescued" by well-intentioned people who had no idea they were actually kidnapping the young animals.

A wolf cub, however, was unusual. There hadn't been a report on one of those for over three years, and the last one turned out to be a lost malamute pup. Kenzie Macleod proved to be unusual as well, giving Josh a concise assessment of the animal and its condition. He found himself nodding into the phone. "Sounds like you've pegged it right. The cub wouldn't be alone this long, and it's definitely too young to fend for itself. What's your location?"

And please, honey, read me the phonebook while you're at it. Dr. Mackenzie Macleod's voice was low and sultry despite her all-business attitude. He caught himself wondering how it sounded in the dark and yanked himself back to reality as she gave him a GPS reading. He spread out a dog-eared map and whistled as he pinpointed the locale. "I thought you said you were going to Chistochina."

"I said *near* Chistochina."

It was near the village like he was near the frickin' beach. At least he knew the area. "Let's see—I've got a few errands to finish up. I can probably make it there in three, maybe four hours or so."

Three or four hours *if* he didn't spend too much time at the animal clinic and *if* he took the chopper. The highway in the Copper River basin was decent but any road that left it was almost guaranteed to be a rodeo for the toughest four-wheel-drive trucks, and an axle-breaker for anything less. Flying was the most practical way to get around if you were in any kind of a hurry. Most small towns, including little Chistochina, had a grass airstrip, but Dr. Macleod wasn't anywhere near it. Studying a satellite map, Josh chose a wide spot on the nearby riverbank where he could set down—he didn't need much. His government-issued copter was an R44 Raven. It was like flying a dragonfly compared to the big Blackhawks and Apaches he'd flown out of Baghram. A gifted pilot, Josh could land the military birds in extremely tight spaces. By comparison, the little Raven was pure play. Plus, other than a poacher once, most people didn't shoot at him these days, and that made flying a damn sight simpler.

It was a twenty-minute drive to the town of Glennallen to deliver the eagle to the local animal clinic. He half hoped that the veterinarian, Bygood Stanton, was out on a call but immediately felt guilty—after all, Stanton had been his friend for years. A veteran of earlier wars, he'd helped Josh a lot during his first year back from Afghanistan. And Doc Stanton was nothing short of brilliant when it came to treating injured wildlife. *If only the guy didn't have such an obsession about conspiracies . . .* Once the man got started on his favorite topic, any conversation tended to be both long and lopsided. Interesting, but escape was difficult if you had other places you had to be.

Josh grabbed the kennel with both hands and tried to keep it level as he backed through the front door of the clinic. He was glad to see there were no clients in the waiting room, then remembered it was lunch hour and the clinic was technically closed. There was no one at the front counter but Stanton's voice came booming through his office doorway.

"Hey Tark, that better not be another damn bear cub."

"Nope. Rattlesnake."

Stanton snorted loudly. "Do you know how hard it is to find a place that wants grizzlies?"

"It's not a bear. Not a deer either." He set the cage on the counter.

"Well, what the hell is it?"

"Get your ass out here and look—I promise it's worth the trip."

"Damn well better be." Stanton appeared in the doorway. He was short and slight, with an unruly head of gray hair and immense salt and pepper eyebrows that failed to overshadow his sharp gaze. Josh knew those eyes didn't miss much—the man had been an accomplished sniper in two wars. And Stanton could never remain grouchy for long. His gruff features relaxed into a grin, and he punched the younger man's shoulder hard before he peered into the kennel.

The big eagle promptly fluffed itself up to appear even larger and hissed at the old vet. His shaggy eyebrows rose. "That's one damn big eagle. Is that what I think it is?"

"Yup." Josh was smug. It wasn't often anyone could impress Stanton. "An honest-to-god golden, a female. Told you it was worth getting off your butt to look."

"I'll be damned. Never had one in here before. What's her story?"

"Broken wing, but I think it's a clean break."

Stanton nodded. "Well then, she'll be back in the sky before you know it. I'll probably send her down to Sitka while she's healing, though."

"Good deal." The island community was the site of the Alaska Raptor Center. The place specialized in rehabbing predatory birds and Josh had sent them several over the past few years. He'd toured the facilities once and been impressed. There were large indoor flights where recuperating birds could strengthen their wings. Every effort was made to ensure that the wild birds remained wild, and he'd been lucky enough to witness the release of a fully recovered bald eagle. Josh hadn't expected it to affect him so deeply as the bird soared up and over the forest clearing until it was only a speck in the sky. He had spent several years in Fish and Game, both before and after his service in Afghanistan, but sometimes he thought he'd like to change career paths, start rehabbing wildlife. The golden eagle had brought that feeling back to him. Maybe it was a sign. . . .

"You going to stay and help me work on this bird?" asked Stanton.

"Wish I could, but no time today. I've got appointments in Tanacross and Slana, and then a wolf cub to pick up north of Chistochina." Josh told him about Dr. Macleod's call, expecting the vet to be interested in the wolf cub—after all, he probably hadn't had one of those in the clinic before either. To his surprise, Stanton went to a yellowed map on the wall and followed one of the Copper River's many tributaries, the Chistochina River, with his finger.

"That woman digging around here?"

Josh squinted at the spot where the vet's finger had come to a stop. "Maybe about three, four miles from there. Why?"

"Some mysterious environmental group's built a fancy facility right in the middle of nowhere. No one knows who the hell they are or what kind of research is being done there."

Josh suppressed a groan. Any other day he would have humored his friend and listened patiently to his latest theories on government cover-ups and conspiracies, but *shit*, not today. "I didn't hear about that one, but I got no time right now, bud. Why don't you tell me about it over a beer at The Caribou? I'll be back this way in a couple days."

"Fine," said Stanton. "Go pick up your wolf and we'll talk later. But Tark?"

"Yeah?

"You're buying."

Josh made it back to base in fifteen minutes flat, and even managed to make a few phone calls. Radioed his plans to HQ as he loaded some boxes and another kennel into the chopper. Once again, he was grateful he'd persuaded HQ to take the rear passenger seats out—in this job, he needed every square inch of cargo space he could get.

Fully loaded and fully fueled, he could count on three hours in the air, long enough to stop by Dr. Mackenzie Macleod's camp before traveling further up the Copper River. The truth was, ADFG policy leaned toward letting nature take its course if possible when it came to orphaned animals. Knowing they were unlikely to rubber-stamp a special flight just to pick up a wolf cub, Josh simply planned it so that the Macleod camp would be on the way to an approved destination. He was concerned about the cub—and he definitely wanted to know more about the woman who'd reported it. Lucky for both him and the wolf, the tiny schools in Tanacross and Slana welcomed his impromptu lessons on wildlife. And he had a brand new presentation on brown bears to try out on them.

Chapter Four

K enzie sat back on her heels and studied the layers she'd uncovered. With trowel, scoop, and brush, she'd managed to dig down a good eighteen inches in her latest square. Not bad for a morning's work. Of course, being a Changeling helped—her physical strength allowed her to work at a pace that humans couldn't match. *Another excellent reason to work alone.* She'd bagged and labeled soil and rock samples as she went along, depositing them in a tidy row along the edge of the dig. Her netbook was there too, and she was thankful to the gods of technology for inventing a nine-hour battery that she could recharge in her truck. Still, the little computer was shut down and bagged as well—she usually didn't bring it at all because of the dust and dirt—in favor of her old paper notebook.

A speck of black in the earth caught her eye and she worked the spot carefully with a brush. Could be carbon, perhaps evidence of a fire—

The sudden throb of an engine erupted from the river valley and a bright blue and white helicopter hove into view. It swept low over her, the wind it created kicking up dust devils in the middle of her dig and sending string and stakes flying. *Stop! Dammit, not again!* The bright orange canopy that sheltered her screening area tumbled end over end and wedged itself in a tangle of legs and nylon in the bushes. Her notebook spiraled into the air and vanished from sight.

As she heard the copter settle to earth somewhere by the river, Kenzie scrambled on her hands and knees to gather her scattered sample bags, her tools, and whatever else she could find. Even her netbook was lying on its back in its plastic bag like a packaged turtle. Fuming, she swore to file a complaint against the idiot pilot right after she kicked his ass from here to next week.

Suddenly a large hand bearing her flyaway notebook appeared in front of her. She snatched the wrinkled pad and bounced to her feet, opened her mouth to unleash a tirade—and closed it again.

"I'm really sorry about your site," said Josh Talarkoteen. "I hope I didn't damage anything."

"You? *You* did this?" Her brain switched back on. "Dammit, I've got an archaeological dig here." She waved at the scene behind her. "My grid is ruined and my equipment is scattered. What the hell were you doing?"

"I saw your camp up there on the knoll but I didn't see you down here. I was looking for wolves, hoping to find the pack that the cub might belong to. Look, let me help you put things back together and you can tell me about your wolf."

Kenzie's first impulse was to tell him not to bother, that she'd pick up her own damn stuff without any help from him. But he was already gathering string and tools so she simply joined him.

Last of all, they wrestled the canopy out of the bushes. The orange canvas didn't look so obscenely new anymore, but the legs were bent and battered. Josh frowned at it, then set to work. She shrugged and went back to camp to get more string, hoping she had enough for another round. Maybe this site just wasn't meant to be gridded. . . .

She returned to find the canopy set up almost exactly where it had been before. The legs were fairly straight, although she didn't miss that one was splinted with a tree branch and duct tape. The overall effect was strangely pleasing—the silly thing finally fit in with the rest of her stuff. "Thanks. I'm, uh, sorry I yelled at you."

"Sorry I buzzed your site. Truce?"

"Truce," she said and offered her hand. "I'm afraid it's dirty."

He grinned as his own engulfed it. "It's a working hand. My Gramma Kishegwet says that makes it beautiful."

She couldn't help grinning back. "Yeah? Then I think I like your gramma."

"And me?"

"The jury's still out, buddy." She showed Josh where she'd last seen the cub, although she doubted it would reappear anytime soon after the noisy arrival of the chopper. He walked the area and quickly found a few incomplete tracks. Kenzie was impressed—for a human, he was unusually adept at reading the forest floor.

"I think you're right," he said, crouching over the prints. "This cub is maybe five or six months old—much too young to survive on its own. I didn't see any wolves from the air, so its pack may have moved on. Strange that they didn't track him down."

"*Her.* I'm pretty sure it's a female, although I haven't gotten very close to her."

"Her, then." He straightened, but continued to study the ground. "You know, this cub's size is unusual for this time of year."

"Why?"

"Do the math. This far north, most wolves don't mate until April. After that it takes 60-plus days until the pups are born. Then they spend the first two months of their life in the den."

"It's July."

"Exactly. So the pup is small, but not small enough. It shouldn't be this old yet."

"Maybe its mother mated out of season? I heard it was a mild winter."

"They're not usually affected by the weather. Now if food was unusually abundant, *that* might have had an effect." Abruptly he pointed to a faint line of bent grass stems running parallel to the path she'd made between her camp and her dig site. "The cub may have headed in that direction. Mind if I take a look?"

"No, go ahead. If you don't need me, I've got a dig to straighten out."

"Sure. I work better alone when I'm tracking, anyway." He headed into the trees, and she stared after him for a long moment, before sighing and unrolling the string.

Josh Talarkoteen had a very fine ass.

From beneath the broad umbrella-like leaves of a devil's club bush, Anya eyed the man as he picked his way slowly through the camp. She'd been so scared when the helicopter came, scared that it was those men again, the mean ones who had taken her mother away. This man was different. He wasn't like her, and not like the woman who worked in the dirt, but he wasn't like most humans either. He smelled good, smelled like the forest. He seemed . . . *safe*.

But he couldn't be, could he? She'd heard them talking about her, and knew he was looking for her. Bad things happened to Changelings when humans found out what they were. Her father had been a Changeling just like her, and when she was very little, he had been killed. *By humans.* That's why she needed to be a wolf, stay a wolf. As a little girl, she wasn't very fast or very strong. As a wolf, she was both. Her mother had told her that if she ever got lost, she should let the wolf inside her take care of her until her mom found her again.

She wished her mom would find her soon.

Kenzie painstakingly scraped away another layer of dirt. The string that marked the grids was back in place, although it had obvious knots and splices in it. The metal stakes weren't very straight either, but as long as nothing heavier than a mosquito tripped over them, they would hold. She hoped. She needed them in order to document the site properly, but hell, she'd use spruce root and twigs if she had to. The site was already proving interesting.

So was Josh Talarkoteen, if she was honest about it. Two days ago he'd had to leave without finding the cub, but he'd returned each morning since. Kenzie hadn't seen the little wolf at all, but Josh had managed a fleeting glimpse. Most people would have gone charging after the animal, but he had simply sat down where he was and pretended he *didn't* see it. Kenzie was impressed with the man's intuition, his desire to approach the cub on its terms.

Too bad he's human . . . She brushed away the thought and tried to work, but her focus evaporated when Josh came over.

"I couldn't get my hands on a live trap," he began. "We don't have a lot of them and they're in big demand at this time of year. There isn't one in any of the local offices that isn't being used. They can fly one up from Southeast at the end of next week, but that's too long. So I'm going to have to use a dart." He opened his hands to reveal a large black handgun with a wood grip.

Kenzie felt her breath catch in her throat and immediately tried to tamp down her reaction. He was too perceptive not to notice, however.

"It's air-powered so it's bulky," he explained. "Looks a lot worse than it is. I got enough of a look at the cub to get a good weight estimate, so she should be fine."

"I don't like it. I don't like it at all. Can't we wait for the trap?" Her voice caught on the word *trap* and she swore inwardly. Her past was poking at her with a sharpened stick.

"Dr. Macleod—*Kenzie*." He knelt at the edge of the dig next to her. "The cub's too skinny. It can't wait until next week. It's weak and it may hole up somewhere and die before we can find it."

"We could feed it, put out food for it. Keep it going until we get the live trap."

"It's in danger from more than starvation. Think about it—it's amazing that a predator hasn't snatched it by now. If we're going to save it, we need to do it now."

She took a deep breath, then another. Put a hand to her head. "You're right. I know you're right. I just, well, I've had some bad experiences and now I have a thing about guns and traps and such." And *that* was a whole lot more than she'd intended to tell him or anybody else, but it was all too easy to talk to Josh Talarkoteen. She'd have to be more careful around him.

"I'm going to see if I can come up with a rabbit. The cub needs to eat and we need bait. Is that going to be a problem for you?"

"No. Not at all." Her feelings had nothing to do with squeamishness. In fact, she should have thought to Change to her lupine form and hunt something for the little cub herself. But that would have made it dependent, and it wasn't fair to turn a wild animal into a pet. "In fact, I've seen some snowshoe hares over by that tall stand of spruce."

Jeez, the man was efficient. She didn't hear a thing, but it wasn't long before she scented the gamey tang of rabbit. She looked up in time to see him carrying a big brown hare by its enormous hind feet, and laying it near the bushes at the far end of clearing, about 50 yards from her dig. It was downwind of her, and her inner wolf reacted with interest. She wondered what Josh would say if she told him she caught rabbits—not to mention much larger game—on a regular basis. She'd bet *that* would raise his eyebrows a little, then wondered why the idea of rattling his calm demeanor was so appealing.

Out of the corner of her eye, she saw Josh plant himself in a stand of alder across the clearing, no doubt deliberately ensuring she was out of the line of fire. This was a man who would be careful of such things, a man who protected those around him. She wasn't sure how she knew that, but she did. Kenzie lay on her stomach on the ground, reaching down into her first square and working a tiny spot with the point of a trowel. She didn't want to think about Josh right now and she especially didn't want to watch what was going on. Besides, if she acted naturally and did what she normally would do, the cub wouldn't be suspicious, would it? That was all she could do to help. She just hoped the young wolf wouldn't pick up on how much she was having to quell a rising sense of panic. It wasn't a cage, it wasn't a pit, but the little creature was walking into a trap just the same.

The breeze picked up. Even leaning down into the earth, the gently moving air brought her the essence of the freshly killed rabbit. She scented the hungry cub approaching it. Knowledge suddenly shot through her like lightning, certain knowledge that the scent was all wrong. . . .

"Stop!" she yelled, springing to her feet even as the echo of the gun lingered in the air. She ran, covering the ground at inhuman speed, her inner wolf a hairsbreadth from breaking free. Josh hadn't moved and she shoved him roughly aside, looking frantically around for the cub.

"Where is she? *Where is she?* Did you shoot her?"

"No."

The sheer relief brought her mind a moment's clarity. Her inner wolf was frantic, in full protective mode, and if she didn't get a grip, she was going to Change right in front of this human. She whirled on Josh, fully intending to release some steam by reaming him out—

Her voice dried in her throat as she realized he was furious. No, far beyond furious—the fire-bright anger radiated from him. Barely held in check, its sheer energy overwhelmed and extinguished her own as a backfire quenches a forest blaze.

"You didn't tell me it was a child," he said tightly.

"I didn't know, I didn't—" Stunned by his perception, she faltered, unsure of what to say and realizing she'd already said far too much. "How?" she demanded at last.

"My people are Tahltan. I knew you were a shapeshifter as soon as I met you. I can see it in your aura, sense it. I never got close enough to the cub to tell until it was almost too damn late. I had my finger on the goddamn trigger, for Christ's sake. Do you think I would have darted the poor thing if I'd known it was a *kid*?"

Tahltan . . . Kenzie had heard legends about the Stikine River tribe, but she'd never met a member of it. It was true then, that they recognized Changelings! She hoped like hell it was also true that they were ancestral allies to her kind. Because Tahltan or not, this man was 100 percent human and he not only knew what she was, but what the cub was. "I'm so sorry. I didn't know either. The cub—the *child*—always stayed downwind of me. I wouldn't have called you, wouldn't have bothered you at all if I'd suspected what she was." Her keen eyes spotted a slender muzzle amid a distant stand of huckleberry bushes. "You're certain she's all right?"

"Better than I am, that's for sure." He took a deep breath, rubbed the back of his neck which made his hair fall loose around his shoulders. Most of his anger seemed to dissipate. "Do you have any idea who she is?"

She shook her head. "I'm new to the area. I had no idea there were any other Changelings here." Suddenly the cub dashed from its hiding place. Kenzie was about to follow, but Josh seized her arm. As strong as he was, he wouldn't have been able to hold her if she hadn't felt what he was feeling—that there was no point in terrifying the cub further by chasing it. Instead, she watched the little wolf disappear into the forest beyond.

"Now what?" she wondered aloud. "I can't leave her out there by herself."

Josh's hand released her arm and rested on her shoulder instead. "We. *We* can't leave her."

She turned to look at him. "This isn't your responsibility. I'm sorry to have wasted your time."

"I'll let you know when I think my time's been wasted. And that's a kid out there, so it damn well *is* my responsibility. I'm not leaving." Anger flashed briefly in his black gaze, and she was reminded of sheet lightning on a moonless night. It didn't frighten her. He was pissed because he cared. But there was something behind the anger that puzzled her—pain.

"Okay, so what do *we* do? We just scared that little girl six ways to Sunday. She's not likely to come near either one of us again."

"Not in this form. But I'm betting she'll come to you if you're a wolf."

"But—I—but . . ." Josh was right. She hadn't taken on her lupine form before to help the cub because she didn't want to interfere with a wild creature. The situation had changed dramatically. She had to interfere. *Right now.*

Kenzie ran across the clearing, feeling the static electricity in the earth following her the way it followed thunderclouds. Feeling Josh's gaze too. Although he already knew what she was, *no way* would she shift in front of him or any human. Not until the dense brush of the forest closed behind her did she call the energy to her and let the Change take her as she ran.

Immediately the world was different. With every breath came a thousand scents, each as vivid as a photograph, but only one scent was important and she honed in on it. With a flick of her storm-dark tail, she slowed to a trot and followed the trail of the frightened cub.

Chapter Five

Josh's eyes were open but he didn't see Kenzie disappear into the trees. The clearing had dissolved to become a dusty school playground. Pools of blood soaked into the sand, bits of clothing and shoes littered the ground. A white concrete wall was pitted by shrapnel, sprayed with blood. Over by the fence was a row of six small bodies, each hastily shrouded with brightly colored fabrics. It was eerily silent, and Josh knew that was wrong. *Where is everyone?*

Suddenly she was there, standing by the wall. The little girl with the big brown eyes. She couldn't have been more than seven, but she looked older in her red and green tunic, with the matching shawl pulled around her head. She smiled at him—

And sounds abruptly poured into his head: shouting, screaming, sirens, crying. He was shoulder to shoulder with frantic people, coalition medics and civilians, all trying to tend to terrified and injured children. He recognized it all now. Two Taliban rockets had slammed into Salabagh Primary School, and he was airlifting some of the wounded to Baghram for surgery and acute care.

He was in his Blackhawk now, heading for base. The throb of the blades above him couldn't drown out the sounds from the bay behind him. He'd transported plenty of wounded men, but this was different, this was worse. Medics talking loudly, parents crying. There were few sounds from the children—they were too badly hurt. Among them, the little girl with the red and green tunic—

Without any warning, Josh came back to himself. Took a deep breath, then another, and sat down hard next to the dig in the forest clearing. Among Kenzie's tools was a water bottle, and he poured half of the water over his upturned face, then guzzled the rest. Part of him wished the liquid was something a helluva lot stronger.

Jesus H. Christ. That had been one mean-ass flashback. He'd had plenty of them the first year he'd been stateside, all gut-kickers and every one related to the attack on the school. It had been one of the last missions he'd flown for Task Force Falcon, Tenth Combat Aviation Brigade. He'd served with distinction for five years, flown countless missions, come under fire and returned it, transported countless soldiers and lost two of his best buddies. And yet it was the transporting of the children that continued to haunt him.

It was flat-out weird to him that he remembered the school so well—he hadn't even been there. The children had been brought to the airfield in Asadabad, already waiting for him when he'd set down his Blackhawk. But back at Baghram, he'd been helping to unload the stretchers when a little girl had suddenly seized his thumb. She'd wrapped her small fingers around it tightly, looked up at him and smiled. There was blood drying on her face and he'd brushed her hair away from the stickiness. Smiled back, told her she'd be all right. Then the medics had taken her away.

She hadn't been all right. She hadn't even made it out of surgery.

He rubbed his face with the back of his sleeve. No surprise he'd had the flashback of course. He'd already been squeezing the trigger when he spotted the tell-tale blue aura around the little cub. Thank God, he'd been able to skew his aim at the last millisecond—because she wasn't a wolf, wasn't an animal, but a shapeshifter who just happened to be a *little girl*.

What was it that Kenzie called herself? A *Changeling*. Well, Changeling or shapeshifter, something bad had happened to separate this kid from her parents. He needed to check that out, call a few sources, including friends who were State Troopers. Surely somebody had reported a child missing. Or maybe wolf-people didn't do that, maybe they handled these things themselves? He knew exactly who to ask about that too. Maybe he could get a cell signal up where Kenzie had her camp.

Josh stumbled as he tried to get back on his feet. Why the hell was there string around his ankles? Realization dawned as he glanced over at the dig—he'd been wandering during the goddamn flashback and taken out Kenzie's grid. Again.

He hoped like hell he could reassemble it before she got back.

Kenzie trailed the cub—*the child*, she kept reminding herself—to a rocky outcropping a couple miles beyond her camp. There, she scented the cub inside a small cave. She could smell its fear too, and cursed herself again for not realizing the cub's true nature sooner.

How the hell did she start over with this child? *Number one, don't scare her any further.* Then what? Finally, she lay on the mossy ground with her head on her paws. Perhaps the cub would come to her. . . .

She reached out with her mind to talk to it. As wolves, all Changelings could use mindspeech to communicate—surely this little one was no different. *I'm really sorry you almost got poked with a dart. And Josh is sorry too. You did such a good job of being a wolf that we both thought you were a real, wild wolf. Josh works for Fish and Game, and he protects animals. We were trying to help you. We didn't know you were a little girl, or I would have just asked you to come with us.*

There was no response. Kenzie focused hard, listening with both ears and mind, but heard nothing. She kept trying, talking about anything and everything, from what she was doing at the dig to all about her family back in northern Canada. She mentioned her niece and nephew, Hailey and Hunter, a lot, hoping that the little girl would relate to them, or at least see that Kenzie really did like children and didn't go around darting them for fun.

Two hours later, the cub still hadn't emerged. It had poked out its head once during the first hour to peer at her but didn't reappear. Kenzie had been so sure that Josh was right, that her wolfen form would be less threatening, but she hadn't counted on a communication problem. Could the child hear her at all? She'd never heard of a Changeling who wasn't telepathic, but she supposed it was possible. The other possibility was that the little girl was deliberately not talking to her. Why?

In the end, Kenzie hunted down a fat rabbit and left it in front of the cave. *No tricks,* she said to the cub. *I just don't want you to be hungry. It's hard to keep warm at night if you don't have a full tummy.*

A Changeling had extraordinary hearing—she caught a faint rustle from inside the cave, the first sound she'd heard for some time. *I'm going back to my camp now to see what Josh is doing—you can come visit me anytime, okay? Even in the mid-*

dle of the night. She forced herself to walk away then. She had to keep her word, had to do exactly what she said she'd do or the child would never trust her.

Leaving a child alone in the woods, however, was one of the hardest things she'd ever done. Still, she couldn't help smiling a little when her ears picked up tiny growls accompanied by the sounds of voracious eating.

The fire had died down to coals, perfect for cooking, and Josh added the floured pieces of rabbit to the cast-iron fry pan. They sizzled in the bacon fat, a satisfying sound.

A movement at the far end of the camp caught his eye—Kenzie was back. He didn't miss that the fire's glow flattered her as she approached, lent highlights to her dark hair and golden shadows to her skin. He did forget all the things he'd planned to say to her.

"Omigod, you're cooking!" she said.

"And you're alone."

She dropped into a camp chair near him. "Yeah. It didn't go so well. At least I got her to eat something, but she wouldn't come to me. Wouldn't even talk to me."

"Probably made you feel like shit." He patted her arm, then got up to turn the rabbit over with a fork. Sucked on a finger when a splatter of grease hit it.

"I could have forced her to come back with me, but that just felt wrong. I hate the thought of her out there by herself, though."

"You're trying to win her trust. Once you have that, you'll have her cooperation." He salted the sizzling meat. "You know that something happened to her to make her so afraid. It wasn't just us, it wasn't just the dart gun."

"Yeah, I know. And something is making her stay in wolf form too."

"Maybe she's not old enough to shift by herself?"

Kenzie shook her head. "No, Changelings can do that pretty early. It's instinctive, not something that has to be learned. They—"

He saw her stop herself. She probably figured it was dangerous enough that he knew what she was, without telling him all the details of her species.

"They just know," she finished.

"So how old is this kid? As a wolf, she looks to be maybe five months old. Please tell me that's not her human age."

"No, not at all."

She was quiet for a long moment, and he hoped like hell this wasn't going to be like pulling teeth. Finally he pointed the fork at her. "Hey, how am I going to help find where this kid belongs if I can't even narrow down how old she is? Do you have any idea how many missing person files there are in this state?"

She held up her hands in mock surrender but she didn't look happy about it. "Okay, okay. How much do you know about Changelings?"

"In my Gramma Kishegwet's stories, you live forever."

She gave him a faint smile. "Not quite that long. As children, we grow at the same rate as humans. It's not until we reach adulthood, somewhere in our late twenties, that the aging process slows down."

"So that's how it goes when you're walking on two legs. But what about your wolf side? Real wolves mature somewhere between two and three years old. So how the heck does that correspond with your human self if you can shapeshift as a child?"

"The wolfen body grows very slowly, so that it doesn't reach mature size until the human body does."

He nodded as he poked at the meat, noted that it was almost done. "Okay, that makes sense. So back to my original question—how old is this little girl?"

"Somewhere between six and ten, as near as I can tell."

Christ, what were the chances? Had he sensed how old she was, known somehow that she was about the same age as the little girl from Afghanistan that he still saw in flashbacks and dreams? He ordered himself to breathe, to focus. Turned all the pieces of rabbit again although they didn't need it. "All right then. So now I can ask around—discreetly—to see if there's a little girl in that age bracket gone missing." Too bad the poor kid didn't seem to want to shift to human form. He could really use a physical description but all he had was her fur color. Did that correspond to hair color at all? At least her age gave him a starting point. "Thanks."

Kenzie shrugged and apparently decided it was time for a change of subject. "That smells pretty good—is that the same rabbit you caught earlier?"

"You bet it is. My gramma would take this fry pan to anyone who wasted good meat. It's disrespectful to the animal. Without respect, a hunter won't find any more game and then everyone goes hungry. The animals know."

"I guess they might. So you must be one of those wilderness types that can make a full-course meal out of weeds, roots, and berries," she teased.

"I don't eat too many weeds and roots as a rule, but my mother drafted me to help pick berries as soon as I could walk. I can make a half-decent salmonberry pie."

"Salmon and berries?"

"No, *salmonberries*. They're like raspberries, only twice the size. There's blueberries around here too—you could have them every day for breakfast if you didn't mind competing with the bears to get them."

"Thanks, but I'll stick to digging. So where'd you find the bacon? I've never seen any pigs around here."

"I had it in the chopper. Old Mamie Dalkins gave me a couple pounds of her home-cured pork, a bag of flour, and a box of groceries before I left Gakona School yesterday. Said that no self-respecting bush pilot would leave home without grub in case they crash-landed in the middle of nowhere."

"Makes sense to a point. But bacon—wouldn't that just attract bears to the site?"

"That's what *I* said. But Mamie said that's a good thing, that then I could just shoot the bear and have groceries clear until the following spring."

Kenzie laughed. "Spoken like a true Alaskan. And all this time you've never told her that you hate bear meat?"

"You have to know her. She wouldn't understand. Although I'd sure as hell rather eat bear than that freeze-dried camp food crap you're stocked with."

Shamelessly, she borrowed a line from Birkie. "Hey, it'll keep you alive."

"Yeah, but why?" He handed her a plate of fried rabbit, then dropped a pair of foil-wrapped baked potatoes on it. It was rewarding to see her jaw drop.

"I'm not even going to ask where you got these gorgeous things."

"Not from your pantry, that's for sure. You didn't even have an onion. How can you cook without onions?"

She shrugged. "I don't cook. I'm busy."

"I'm busy too, but I like real food. I did my time in the military, figure I earned the right to eat non-instant chow."

She bit into the rabbit and closed her eyes in mock ecstasy. "This is good, *really* good. So were you a cook?"

"Hell, no—there are no cooks in the military, just burger

flippers and spoons. Me, I learned to fly before I learned to drive. Signed up the day after 9/11, spent five years as a pilot in Afghanistan."

She didn't reply to that and they ate in silence for several minutes. Josh was certain he must have said something stupid, although he couldn't guess what. Maybe she was against the war or something. Finally Kenzie tossed the rabbit bones from her plate into the fire and licked her fingers. "So tell me, why would a military type be tolerant of werewolves?"

"What the hell kind of question is that?"

"A damn good one from my perspective. Guys in uniforms tend to like their world orderly and secure. The very existence of a Changeling threatens that. Yet you're sitting here having dinner with me, knowing I'm not human, and you're trying to help a child who currently has four feet. Why?" Her gray eyes flashed in the firelight.

"Are you always this suspicious?"

"Let's just say I've had plenty of reason to be. You've stumbled on my secret identity, so to speak, and that makes me extremely nervous."

He thought about that as he finished eating. *Hi, I'm Josh, and I know you're a shapeshifter. . . .* Yeah, he could see that would be downright terrifying for someone like her. "Okay, I'll do my best to answer your question. But on one condition—"

"What? Why do you get to put a condition on it?"

"—I'll tell you anything you want to know, but then you tell have to tell me something about you."

"You know too damn much about me already."

"I promise I won't ask any questions about being a shapeshifter. Just about ordinary stuff, like what kind of music you like and your hometown and nonthreatening stuff like that. Deal?"

She eyed him warily. "Maybe."

"I slaved over a hot campfire and all I get is a maybe?"

"A *strong* maybe."

"Fine. I'll take it." He put more wood on the fire, then flipped open a little cooler and passed her a bottle of beer. "This is to wash down dinner. You'll have to make it last, though, there's only one each."

"It'll be a treat, thanks. Don't think it'll loosen my tongue, though."

He snorted and sat down, took a long swig as the fire crackled and grew. "I told you I was Tahltan. I was born in Telegraph Creek on the Stikine River, which meets the ocean just across from Wrangell, Alaska," Josh explained. "But thanks to the bureaucrats who penciled in the border so it runs right across the river, most of the Stikine is in British Columbia, and that's where I was born. My folks moved to Wrangell when I was eleven, so I actually have dual citizenship."

"Handy."

"Very. Gramma Kishegwet was head of the Tuckclar-waydee clan for many years—it's a matriarchal system—and she has some pretty incredible abilities. I just happened to inherit a few."

"Like seeing shapeshifters. You've seen others, then?"

He nodded. "A few. Anyway, Tuckclarwaydee is the Tahltan word for the wolf clan, the oldest Tahltan clan there is. My dad's name, Talarkoteen, comes from another wolf clan, one that migrated in from the Peace River region."

"*Two* wolf clans? So are you telling me you've got Changelings in your family?"

"Nope. Not a one. But we owe our survival to your people." God, her eyes were pretty when they got wide like that. . . . He had to shake himself mentally to be able to continue. "This is the story that my gramma told me many times. There was an old man named Xe'nda who led the Tahltan hunters. There had been very little game that winter and the people were starving. Xe'nda found the trail of a small caribou herd, and he and his hunters tried to follow it, but although they had snowshoes, the snow was much too deep and they moved too slowly. They couldn't get close enough to kill any caribou, and the people would die if they didn't bring back meat.

"Suddenly they came to a spot where there were strange snowshoe tracks on top of the snow, trailing the caribou herd. The other hunters made camp and rested, but Xe'nda followed the tracks and found a number of strange people standing beside several dead caribou. He couldn't see any weapons and asked them who had killed all the caribou, and they said that they had. Xe'nda was very weak and fell down. The strangers kindly built a fire near him and cooked some caribou for him to eat.

"As he ate, the strangers told him that his snowshoes were much too narrow but he would be able to run fast on top of the snow if he made snowshoes like theirs. They showed him very carefully just how to make them. Then they told him that he could have all the caribou they had killed so the Tahltan people would live.

"Xe'nda fell asleep and when he awoke, all the strangers were gone. There was no sign of any fire, but the dead caribou were still there. To his surprise, all of the caribou had been killed by wolves. He looked for snowshoe tracks but found only wolf tracks. Then he understood that he had been helped by the Wolf People.

"Xe'nda went back and told the hunters to fetch all the meat. The Tahltan people were saved, and from that time on, they all made their snowshoes the way that Xe'nda taught them, just as the wolves had showed him."

He looked at Kenzie for her reaction and found her frozen in place, staring at something. His eyes followed her gaze to the other side of the fire. Something small and furry was curled up under the camp table—

The wolf cub was sound asleep.

Chapter Six

"I'll be damned," said Josh, lowering his voice. "How long has she been there?"

"Quite a while. I think she was close to the camp already, and then she moved in when you starting telling the story." Kenzie whispered, afraid to break whatever spell had brought the little cub close to them. "I guess she likes you."

"Naw. Every kid loves a bedtime story, that's all. She wouldn't have come if you hadn't gotten through to her."

Was it true? Had the child heard her words after all? "Now what do we do?"

"Not a damn thing. We continue our conversation like nothing happened."

"She might leave again."

"Then she leaves. We're looking for trust here, remember? So if she wants to go, we let her."

Kenzie nodded. It was damn hard, though, when what she really wanted to do was scoop up the little cub and keep her safe. "Okay. So, you were saying about the Wolf People . . ."

"The Tahltan have been friends to the Wolf People ever since."

She'd heard that, but had never heard the story behind it. "You think the legend is true?"

"Come on, you're an archaeologist, aren't you? You ought to know there's some truth behind every myth and legend. This one is no different." From his chair, he stirred the fire with a stick, pushed wood into it with his toe. Settled back. "Yeah, I believe something like that happened, that your people helped ours when we needed it. I hope you believe it too."

"Why?"

"Because you look like you need to believe in something."

Her inner wolf should have been on high alert with this human, yet it was completely at ease. Either it was as charmed by the story as the cub—very unlikely—or this man just might be trustworthy. Could that be possible? "I do believe in some things." *Like a future for Changelings.*

He nodded but left it alone. "So, my turn now. You live in Dunvegan?"

Kenzie didn't usually talk much about herself, but supposed she could share a little bit. It wasn't as if Josh couldn't find out the basics on his own if he really wanted to. "That depends. I travel a lot, but I guess Dunvegan's still my home base. It's where my family lives, up in the Peace River region of Alberta. I think you said your dad's clan is from around there, but I haven't met them."

"That's because the Peace is a big river. My father's clan originally lived up by the headwaters, where it begins in the mountains of British Columbia, west of Alberta. So your home would be hundreds of miles downstream and it's no surprise you haven't run across many Tahltans. Although one of my sisters lives in your province now, over on the Saskatchewan border near Two Hills."

"Hey, I've been there," she said. "I conducted a dig there

a few years back. Didn't find what I was looking for, but I came up with three sizeable chunks of a meteorite."

He whistled low and the cub stirred in its sleep. Kenzie held her breath until it settled again.

"Sorry," he continued softly. "It's just that I've always wanted to find a space rock. I'm really jealous of you right now."

She laughed. He sounded a lot like her brother Devlin, who would have sold his eyeteeth for a *space rock* as a kid— and might still. "So how many siblings do you have?"

"One sister in Telegraph Creek. A sister in Alberta, like I said, and another sister lives in Wrangell. All three younger than me."

"Now *I'm* jealous—you have no idea what it's like to be the baby of the family. I've got four older brothers and an older sister, all with good intentions I have to endure."

"Lots of unsolicited advice, right?"

"Tons. From everyone and their dog, except Birkie."

"Who's Birkie?"

"My friend, but that doesn't begin to describe her. Kind of like a mom and a favorite aunt and a BFF all rolled into one. She's been around since forever, and she runs Connor's clinic for him. Wonderful gardener; you've never seen a green thumb like hers. Even my brother James can't top her."

"So she's a shapeshifter too?"

"No, she's—well, I'm not sure. Not Changeling and that's all anybody knows. Even my parents don't know and she's been close to them for years."

"Must be really hard to keep your secret from her." He made it sound matter of fact, laying his trap carefully.

"I—we *don't*. Birkie knows what we are, she's always

known. She can see it." Kenzie frowned. "Like you can, I guess."

"But she's totally reliable, definitely not evil, and even your BFF?"

"Of course she is—"

"*Aha*. So you have to concede that it's possible for a non-shapeshifter to be trustworthy?"

"I didn't say that!"

"You should." He looked at her steadily. "Because it's true."

She was saved from answering by her cell phone beeping. Kenzie looked at the text message and made a face.

"Everything okay?"

"My brother is just being *brotherly* again. Connor can't stand that I'm alone out here. I finally had to promise him that if a man dropped out of the sky, I'd date him."

"Really? Bet you didn't count on meeting someone with a helicopter."

She opened her mouth and closed it again, momentarily stunned.

"I'm thinking dinner at The Caribou in Glennallen, followed by dancing at the Tapout Lounge," he continued. "What day works for you?"

"I'm—we're—I'm not going out with you!"

"Sure you are, or I'll have to tell your brother."

"I wasn't serious when I made that promise."

"Maybe, but I'm serious about helping you keep it. Consider it an educational experience—did you know that The Caribou has a ceiling made of copper? They used to mine the stuff in this region back at the turn of the last century."

She folded her arms. "Big deal. The Ahtna discovered

copper *thousands* of years ago in this region. Your restaurant isn't exactly a historic site."

"Taste their poached salmon or their *Halibut Olympia*, and you'll change your tune. Saturday is good for me by the way."

Exasperated, she got up. "Thanks for dinner, Josh. I'm going to bed now."

"Now? It's still early." He sat back in his chair and looked at the twilight sky. "Okay, it's not early but hey, it's not dark yet."

"I like to be at my site when the sun comes up." She glanced around. "Just where were you planning on staying tonight?"

"In the chopper. Unless I'm invited somewhere else of course."

"Nice try. Good night."

"Night." He gave her a mock salute. "Make sure you dream about me."

Anya opened her eyes ever so slightly. The fire had died down but was still giving off plenty of heat. She wasn't being watched—Kenzie had gone into her tent and Josh had dozed off in the camp chair—and she rolled on her back in pure bliss. For the first time in days she'd gotten enough to eat, she was warm and safe, and she wasn't quite so lonely.

Josh told good stories. And just like Anya and her mother, Kenzie was a Changeling. Her wolf was pretty, blueish gray like rainclouds. Anya's mom was pretty too when she was a wolf, and her fur was soft. If only she were here. She'd like Kenzie and Josh, Anya was sure of it. And maybe her mother wouldn't be so lonely anymore either.

She sighed and rolled over to rest her head on her paws.

Her mother had told her not to talk to strangers. Ever. But was a person still a stranger if you knew their name?

It was hard work to keep a grown-up Changeling from seeing what was inside your head, but Anya was very good at it. It was even harder, though, not to answer questions, not to say a single word in her mind, and especially not to ask for help. Anya wanted so badly to tell Kenzie what had happened—she might help her find her mother. That would be all right, wouldn't it?

Anya closed her eyes. Maybe she'd talk to Kenzie tomorrow.

Nate paced his hotel room, occasionally glancing at downtown Anchorage through the wide fourteenth floor window. The Chugach mountains lined the horizon, capped with snow even in July. His inner wolf was restless, wanting Nate to Change and head for those mountains, wanting to run free, to hunt and howl.

Later, he murmured. He had to think, had to figure this out. The IBC wanted his *expertise* again, but what did he have left to offer them? It wasn't his fucking fault that things had gone south in the last operation. He'd earned his pay, delivered exactly what they asked for.

But now they wanted more.

He flopped on the king-sized bed, gazed at the expensive teak furnishings. The money he'd earned from the IBC allowed him to stay in places like this, the kind of places he belonged. Travel often kept him away from home, but he finally *had* a place worth coming home to—a luxury loft in Manhattan, not far from NYU. There was a sleek Audi in his private parking space these days. His tenure at the university was assured for life with the kind of funding he'd been able to bring in lately—after all, being able to wine and dine the big dogs meant big donations. Gone were the days of a crummy apartment in a crummy neighborhood, with a long and crummy commute. And everything was paid for in full, thanks to IBC.

He didn't owe them a thing of course. He'd fulfilled their orders, provided them with what they needed, and they'd paid him on the spot each time. There was no contract, no obligation to do more. Only his own desire to *have* more. And he could have as much as he wanted if only he had more items to deliver.

Too bad there were only so many of those. . . .

There was the one delivery that had gone missing—he could definitely go looking for that. Those idiots employed by IBC couldn't find their asses with both hands, but he had no doubt of his ability to find the lost item himself. The reward would be substantial too, more than enough to pick up that second home in Mendocino. It'd be a luxurious retreat, and the redwood forest there would be a great place to turn his lupine side loose. After all, his inner wolf didn't really care for the whole Manhattan scene. . . . In fact, that little romp with Kenzie had been the most fun he'd had, well, since the *last* time their wolves had run together. God, how many years ago had that been?

Only this time, there'd been no sex at the end of it. Make that *stupendous* sex. He'd been with plenty of women, including two last night in this very bed. None of them compared to Kenzie Macleod. And then she'd gone and decided to live like a nun. *Sorry Nate, we're just friends now.* . . .

What the hell was her problem anyway? Sure, she was older than he, but damn she was hot. And thanks to her lupine genes, she was likely to stay that way. They looked good together, a matched set, light and dark. Nate groaned with pleasure as he imagined walking into a room of potential donors with Dr. Mackenzie Macleod on his arm. Whatever wallets couldn't be loosened by his charm and their looks would be opened by her reputation. Their social success as a couple would be nothing short of stellar. He headed the archaeology department now, but who knew how much further he could go?

It was perfect. Meant to be, even. So why did Kenzie refuse to see it?

Well, maybe it was about time he *made* her see it. And if she still insisted on brushing him off, maybe she could be useful in another way. She just might be able to help him solve his little supply problem with IBC.

Kenzie felt like cheering when she emerged from her tent and found the cub curled close to the fire pit. Its head was resting on its front paws, one white, one black, and she couldn't help thinking of her brother Culley. In wolfen form, he was pure black, but an odd white snippet on his nose gave him a comical look. His tail was tipped with white and there was a white star on his chest. Trickster that he was, he delighted in utilizing those unwolf-like colors to the max by pretending to be a monstrous dog among unsuspecting humans. He'd even learned to make his pointed ears flop like a collie's—although *how*, she couldn't imagine.

"Good morning," she whispered. The young wolf pricked its ears and opened its eyes. Yawned and stretched. And looked at her expectantly.

"Breakfast time, right?" She considered the problem. A Changeling in wolfen form usually couldn't eat people food—not without causing an upset stomach. Culley insisted on eating pizza whether human or wolf, but he had a cast-iron digestive system so he didn't count. As for herself, Kenzie had never had much luck with it. "You know, if you were a little girl, I could make breakfast for you." She rifled through her freeze-dried packets for something that looked like morning fare. "Scrambled eggs?"

"Hold it right there! Back away from that instant crap!" Josh walked up the knoll to the campsite, whipping the packet out of Kenzie's hand, flinging it into the bushes.

"Hey—" She clapped her hands over her mouth when she saw the big rabbit hanging from his belt. Josh had been up early this morning.

He knelt in front of the cub. "Okay, kiddo—this is what wolves eat. This is all for you." He laid the rabbit at its feet. "But whenever you feel like being human again, I can make pancakes for you. Real ones with syrup. Kenzie can't cook—"

"I can too!"

"—but I can, so I'll make pancakes for you anytime you're ready." He dropped his voice to a stage whisper. "Even for *supper.*"

"Josh!"

"Bet I'm in trouble now, eh?" He winked at the cub and turned to Kenzie.

She played along and put her hands on her hips in a classic exasperated mother position but spoiled the effect by laughing at him. "You're a completely bad influence, you know that?"

"I know. And now this *bad influence* is going to fly back to base and see what I can find out, okay? I got things to do so I'll be two or three days. Anything I can bring you on the flip trip?"

"I'm fine, thanks."

He leaned in a little then. "You're very fine," he whispered. He cupped the back of her neck and placed a gentle lingering kiss on her forehead. . . . The next moment he was heading back down the trail.

Kenzie stood where she was for a long time. She barely heard the throb of rotors from down by the river, hardly noticed the shift in sound as the helicopter lifted off and headed away over the valley. All she could think about was the pleasant thrum in her blood and the realization that she wanted Josh to kiss her again, this time on her lips. *And everywhere else. . . .*

"Stop that right now," she ordered herself through gritted teeth. Exasperated, she shook off the spell and sternly told her inner wolf to settle down as well. The last thing on the planet she needed was to get involved with a human. It was just hormones—had to be. After all, it had been a helluva long time since she'd had sex, so *of course* Josh looked good to her. Almost any guy would, right? Case closed.

Before she could banish it from her mind, however, a little rebellious thought pointed out that neither her hormones nor her inner wolf had responded in the slightest to her former Changeling lover, Nate Richardson.

Chapter Seven

When Josh arrived in Glennallen, he discovered that his best hope for information was out of town for two days. While he waited, he pulled in favors right and left with friends in the state troopers but came up empty. There were no recent reports of a missing girl of the right age in the region. He even phoned Mamie Dalkins, praised her home-cured bacon to the skies and sat through two and a half hours of the latest gossip from several communities. He came away with no useful information (other than some things he'd rather not know) and the promise of a jar of smoked bear meat the next time he was in Gakona. *Ugh.*

He put the waiting time to good use, catching up on all the paperwork in his cramped office and answering phone messages—and damn, somebody was keeping a very young moose as a frickin' pet in their backyard. He dealt with that, and referred a call about hunting deer out of season to the troopers in that area. Finally, thankfully, his best contact returned to town. Surely Josh would get some answers now.

After all, Bygood Stanton was a Changeling.

It wasn't hard to find the old vet at The Caribou. He was the one with his table covered with papers and file folders.

"Christ, did you chair a meeting in here?" Josh counted

five coffee cups lurking under the documents, and those were just the ones he could see. He checked his watch but he wasn't late.

"Hey, Tark. Sit yourself down, boy, and have a look-see."

"What the hell's all this?"

"Just a little information I've been gathering about the International Biodiversity Conservancy—the IBC—who built that little facility I told you about, the one near your lady friend's camp."

Josh flagged down a passing waitress for a menu. "Okay, but I've got a couple important questions for you first. Like, did you order already?"

"Nope, but I'm going with the halibut burger."

"You always have the halibut burger."

"I stick with what works. By the way, I had Mimi stash half a rhubarb pie in the kitchen for us, before it was all gone."

"I love you, man." He ducked the file folder that swatted at him. The waitress took their orders to the kitchen and Josh glanced around to make sure he couldn't be overheard. The last of the lunch crowd was shuffling out the door. A gaggle of teens was slumped in the far corner booth but they were giggling over their iPhones. It was more than enough noise to cover anything he might say. "Stanton, I've got a lost shapeshifter. A kid."

The vet nearly dropped the papers in his hands. "You're shitting me, Tark. Where on God's green earth did you find an unattended werewolf *child*?"

He told his friend all he knew, and for once, Stanton didn't interrupt him. The food arrived and the older man remained quiet, frowning as he ate. Josh made it halfway through his triple Pioneer burger before the vet finally spoke.

"Finding this kid's folks is going to be tough. You have to understand, there's no organized Pack around here. Werewolves in this region tend to be loners like myself or isolated families."

Josh noted that Stanton had never used the term *Changeling*. As blunt as the old guy was, he probably felt that *werewolf* was plain and to the point. Or maybe it conjured up a more dangerous image, one that the veteran of two wars and God knew what else could relate to. "So I take it you haven't heard any rumors or anything."

"How the hell would I hear something? I'm trying to tell you there's no natural network. If you want to talk to a werewolf in this part of the country, Tark, you have to damn well go out there and find them or wait until they come to town, because most of the ones I know don't even have a bloody phone."

"See, that's why I need your help, because I'm not a shapeshifter. It'd take me forever to find them, and they're not likely to talk to me if I did. But someone's got to get a message out somehow, or we're never going to find who this kid belongs to. Or what happened to her."

"Something happened to her?" For a split second, Josh saw the wolf behind Stanton's eyes plainly.

"The little girl's still on four feet. She won't shift back to her human form, so something has to have scared the hell out of her. Put that together with missing parents and it doesn't look good."

"Bloody hell, okay, okay. I could go out tonight, hunt down a couple wolves I know. They could relay the message further on and so forth. They'll do it for a kid, believe me. But it's damn well going to cost you."

Josh rolled his eyes and held up his hands in mock surrender. "All right, what do you want?"

"Not much, just a ride in your bird." Stanton tugged a map out from under a folder. "I want a look at this IBC place I've been telling you about."

"What, you can't use Google Earth?"

"Doesn't show up. The entire area is blurred out. You'd think it was a military site or something. So are you going to fly me over it or not?"

"Sure, no problem. But it's a department chopper so any passenger has to be on official business. You'll have to check on some animal's condition or something. I'll have to get creative and find just the right case, something where your services are genuinely useful, so you'll have to give me a little time."

"Good deal. Now let me show you what I've got." Stanton spread out some papers in front of Josh, who stoically assumed an interested expression while preparing himself to be bored to tears.

"Here's a copy of the permit issued to IBC, allowing them to build this facility. Notice that it doesn't say specifically what it's for."

Josh pointed to a square on the form. "It says *environmental research* right there."

"And just what the hell does that mean? If I take my fish finder out in the middle of the bloody lake, I can say I'm doing *environmental research* too. Now look here." He spread out another paper. "They're not one of those non-profit organizations either, they're a business of some sort. It took me quite a while but I finally found the IBC's website. And that's weird right off the bat—the point of having a website is to have what they call *an internet presence*. Any business wants their site to be easy to find, right? Not these guys. Know what I found on their site?"

"No, but I'm sure you're going to tell me."

"Sweet nothing." Stanton slapped the paper with his hand. "Zip. Zero. Nada."

"I don't get it."

"Most businesses list their hierarchy—you know, their CEO, board members, stuff like that. This has no names on it whatsoever. And you know what? That stuff isn't listed in their LLC application either—that's *limited liability company* by the way."

"Yeah, but come on, there're signatures on all these papers. Somebody's in charge."

"Somebody, yes, but not one of these names. As far as I can determine, these people don't exist."

Stanton took his conspiracy theories seriously enough that he had computer programs that could locate almost anyone on the planet, plus where they lived, how many people were in their family, where they shopped, banked, and worked. Josh wouldn't have been surprised if Stanton knew what they ate for breakfast. "Phony names?"

"And phony addresses. Cell phone numbers that are no longer in service. This is a ghost company, Tark."

"But you're saying there's a very real building—"

"The permit says a building. *I* think it's more likely an entirely self-contained complex. It would have to be, just look at where the hell it is."

"Okay, so there's this *complex*, just a few miles from where Kenzie's digging."

"Yup. And we don't know a thing about it."

Josh waited a beat. Then two. "Aren't you going to tell me it's a secret government project?"

"Even when it's being secretive, the government tends to be predictable—after all, why change tactics that work? I don't see their fat fingerprints on this one, Tark."

★   ★   ★

Kenzie liked children—she adored her nieces and nephew—but on the rare occasions that she babysat James's twins, Birkie usually came along to tag team. Nothing surprised Birkie (not even a crayon wedged up Hailey's nose or Hunter painting the cat green), but then she was a mother herself. Maybe both competence and confidence came over time to a parent, but as an aunt, Kenzie mostly played with the kids and then gave them back to their parents. She felt responsible for this little Changeling child, but couldn't think of what else to do for her other than make sure she was fed.

The cub seemed perfectly happy with that. And appeared content to follow Kenzie around too. They were settling into a routine of sorts: They both went to the dig every morning, where Kenzie talked aloud about what she was doing and why, hoping that the cub would get used to her, and maybe eventually trust her. So far, the cub always stayed a few feet away, close enough to see what Kenzie was doing yet still far enough to flee.

The whole day would go like that, until Kenzie decided enough work had been done. Then, for the cub's sake, Kenzie shifted to lupine form and declared a play time. The gray wolf chased the little Changeling, then turned and allowed it to chase her. They played tug of war with sticks, then hide and seek. Kenzie wished that wolves were physically capable of laughter—there were times she was sure that she would explode with built-up mirth, especially after the cub came pouncing out of the ferns and attacked her with mock growls and tiny teeth. They wrestled until it was obvious that her little charge was tired. While the cub rested, Kenzie would hunt down something for it to eat, then the two of them would head back to camp.

The wolf cub continued to make its bed under the camp

table, close enough to be warmed by the fire yet far from Kenzie's human reach. *At least she's safe here.* No predator would come near her camp. Adult Changelings were generally accorded a healthy respect by the animal population.

"So what do I call you? I have to call you *something*," she said on the second night, as the cub stalked a cricket in the grass. "I know you're a little girl, but I don't know what your name is. If you don't tell me, I might have to make up a name for you."

The cub looked up in surprise.

"How about Gertrude," tested Kenzie. "Or Penelope? Ernestine or Beulah might be nice." She tried out every unfashionable name she could think of, knowing how her niece, Hailey, would respond to such dreadful suggestions. "There's Minerva. Maybe Prudence or Ursella."

The cub stopped playing and stared at her with wide eyes.

"I know," Kenzie clapped her hands in mock glee. "I could call you Frederika! Then I could call you *Fred* for short! You know, I'll just bet that's your real name, isn't it?"

The cub took a step back and sneezed. Twice.

Anya! The voice was loud, clear, and indignant in Kenzie's head. *My name is* Anya*, not Fred. Fred's a stupid name! And my mom told me not to talk to strangers!*

Anya whirled and stomped off—actually *stomped*, although it should have been physically impossible for a wolf—then curled up under the camp table with her back to Kenzie.

Kenzie sat stunned, a slow grin spreading over her face. Then she rubbed it off with both hands—she had an apology to make, and for that, a sober expression would work a lot better.

★   ★   ★

Josh's chance to make good on his promise to Stanton came up almost immediately. A Mentasta Lake resident had a pet fox tied up that had bitten two people plus its owner. Josh had rolled his eyes when he got the call. People never seemed to learn that they couldn't take the *wild* out of a wild animal. Sure, the fox was undoubtedly cute and friendly as a pup, but as it grew, it would become what Nature intended—a predator—and its personality would change. In this case, rabies was a possibility too and a vet's expertise could be helpful. Usually Josh would submit a proposal and request to HQ, and then there'd be paperwork prior to approval, liability forms out the wazoo . . . and the damn fox could have bitten six more people before he got up there. *Easier to get forgiveness than permission.*

"Make sure your receptionist doesn't bill the department for this," he cautioned Stanton as he belted himself into the passenger seat. "I'm bringing you along as a *volunteer consultant*. That way, you're allowed to ride in the department's bird and you'll be covered by their insurance. As soon as I do the damn paperwork. If you need reimbursement, I'll pay for it myself."

The vet snorted. "You just fly over IBC on the way back and we're good. And Tark?"

"What?"

"Don't crash."

It wasn't long after they arrived that Stanton diagnosed distemper in the fox and also in the neighbor's two young Labradors. The fox was too far gone to be helped and was euthanized. To be safe, Stanton was taking the body back with him for rabies testing. He ordered both Labs to be kenneled immediately. Distemper was highly contagious and usually fatal. There was no cure for the disease but it hadn't advanced very far in the dogs. Supportive treatment,

such as IVs for hydration, might save them. With all the ef-
ficiency of his military background, Stanton drafted a local
retired nurse to help manage the Labradors' care, then made
arrangements with the community leaders for an emergency canine vaccination clinic to be held on Saturday.

"Are you sending somebody up here or coming back
yourself?" Josh asked when they returned to the chopper.
He didn't get a chance to see his friend in action very often
and had almost forgotten what a force of nature the man
could be.

"There's no one to send—not many veterinarians in the
region. Doc Baker over in Wasilla might travel up with me,
though. An outbreak of canine distemper could take out
most, if not all, the dogs in the village—and from what I
see, there's more damn dogs than people. We'll vaccinate
for rabies and parvo at the same time."

"Good deal. Now how about giving me the coordinates
for your mysterious building."

"I told you it's gotta be more than just a building." Stanton produced a crumpled piece of paper from his jacket
pocket and read off the location. "Gotta be."

There was forest and more forest below, broken only by
ribbons of water and the occasional overgrown logging
road. Josh wondered why on earth anyone would base their
operations in such a remote place—and exactly what operations were suited to this degree of isolation? Of course,
there *was* that research station, HAARP, which studied the
aurora. To do so effectively, it required a clear view of the
northern lights, unobstructed by the artificial lights of a
town or city, and so the installation had been built in the
middle of the forest north of Gakona. It made sense—
weren't most observatories located far from human habita-

tion? Stanton, of course, had other theories about what was really being studied at HAARP and expounded on them frequently. Josh usually stopped listening somewhere between *military conspiracy* and *blowing up the ionosphere*.

A break in the trees appeared ahead.

"There it is—that's it, that's *it*." Stanton sounded excited. "Get us closer, Tark."

It seemed to be a natural clearing, a rocky outcropping flanked by a river. There was nothing natural about the tall chain-link fencing that surrounded it, or the razor wire along the top that gleamed in the sun. Inside, near the west side of the compound, was a very large metal-clad building with only a few small windows. A number of smaller service buildings stood in a tidy row along the forested north side, while a long row of what looked like bunkhouses lined the east boundary, overlooking a river that ran just outside the fence. Power was obviously supplied by an enormous wind turbine looming on the north side like a futuristic tree. The method of communication was also obvious—a sizeable signal dish was perched on the roof of the main building. And in the exact center of everything was a target-like helicopter pad, occupied by something very familiar to Josh. "That's an old Sikorsky Jayhawk."

Stanton squinted at it. "I thought only the Coast Guard had those."

Josh shrugged. "They upgrade their equipment like everyone else. Maybe they sold off some of their older choppers." Made by the same company, the Jayhawk boasted a similar basic design to the Blackhawk he'd flown in Afghanistan. Of course, the Coast Guard version didn't require the machine guns, rockets, and missiles that the Blackhawk had. And this one's color didn't resemble either one—its shiny new paint job was the same sterile white as the buildings. But the outline, the shape, was true to his warbird. A strange mixture of sentiment and apprehension settled into his gut.

"Didn't I tell you they'd have a whole compound? Self-contained, just like I said. Damn, it's nearly big enough for *two* football fields. And the main building could be used as a hangar."

"Okay, okay, you told me. But what the hell's it for?" Josh could see no specialized equipment, just three white pickup trucks and six white ATVs parked neatly in an open garage. Who the hell would paint an ATV *white*? All-terrain vehicles were built for one thing in Josh's book: getting as dirty as possible.

Suddenly three men came out a side door, each leading an enormous dog. They crossed the compound, heading toward an outbuilding. Both animals and humans glanced up at the government chopper but didn't seem concerned.

Stanton grabbed the binoculars first. "Don't recognize those guys. Wonder what they use the big-ass dogs for."

"Maybe to chase off bears."

The old vet snorted. "Tell you what, it looks like a damn POW camp to me."

Josh didn't recognize the men either, at least not from what he could see of their features. If he'd had his M22 binocs from his service days, he could have counted their nose hairs. He gave the glasses back to his friend and circled the perimeter one last time. Rubbed the back of his neck where a headache was taking root. "Are we done here?"

"Yeah." Stanton sounded reluctant. "Yeah, I guess. Not much to see, really. Not a goddamn hint of what all this is for. It has to have been a big investment to put up this place—it's a helluva long way to haul building supplies and construction equipment, not to mention bringing in workers."

"Yes and no. That old Sikorsky can carry a lot, believe me. You know, maybe you could find somebody who helped build the place, talk to them. They had to have hired some locals for a project like this."

"When I come back for the vaccination clinic, you bet I'll be asking questions."

Josh was just a little bit glad he wasn't going to be part of that expedition. Maybe it was part of his Changeling nature, but the old vet could be a lot like a damn pit bull when he wanted information.

"I didn't see a sign or a logo or even a name, did you? Seems like they're trying to be anonymous. Maybe we should go around again. I want to look at—"

Josh didn't hear the end of Stanton's sentence. He was staring at the Jayhawk on the tarmac pad, its white surface gleaming in the sun—and the tiny figure beside it. She looked up at him and waved, her red and green tunic and shawl fluttering in the breeze.

Chapter Eight

Something rocked Josh, battered at his awareness. The figure vanished and he realized that Stanton's fist was bashing the hell out of his shoulder.

"Tark! Put down now!"

"Yeah. Yeah, sure." Instinct guided him, and he landed the Raven on the wide grassy clearing away from the buildings with barely a bump. Powered down the rotors. Their throbbing slowed and subsided, unlike the pounding in his head.

Stanton was out of his seat at once, checking Josh over like a boxing coach and shining a penlight in each eye. "What the bloody hell was that? Where were you? You seemed to go completely blank, like there was nobody home, and you were still flying the damn helicopter like some kind of human autopilot. Stick out your tongue."

"What? Hey, I'm not having a stroke. It was just a flashback." Josh tried to brush off his friend's ministrations. "Quit playing medic. I'm okay, it's over."

"Well, I'm not okay; you scared the shit out of me! We're going to get out and walk around, get some air. And you're going to tell me when you started having these damn episodes again."

The sun was bright and hot in a cloudless sky, a rarity in

Alaska. Stanton pulled a cola out of the cooler and insisted that Josh drink it. All he could think of as he tipped it back was how good it would have gone down in Afghanistan. The hot dusty wind over there made this summer day seem downright frosty. Until you got into higher elevations of course, or when winter set in with a vengeance. . . .

The vet waited until he'd finished. "Okay, let's hear about your episode—what happened?"

"Beats the hell out of me. You know I had a lot of flash-backs the first year I was stateside. Nightmares too, normal stuff—everyone comes home with at least a little of that shit, right? I finally talked to someone, a guy who'd been in another unit, and he sent me to a good counselor. I went to a few sessions and got some relief. Hell, I talked to you a few times too."

"I remember. But I thought it helped, the counseling and all."

"It *did* help. There's been nothing since my second year back—not a single damn incident—until I was at Kenzie's camp the other day." He shook his head. "Fucking flash-back came out of nowhere, sucker punched me. And it was every bit as bad as the first one."

"Same event as you used to see? The school, the little girl?"

Josh nodded. "When it happened at Kenzie's camp, I fig-ured, okay, it's because the wolf cub turned out to be a kid, a little girl who needed help. Kind of a natural trigger, right?"

"And this here?"

"I just saw the little girl, the one from the school. Noth-ing else. She was standing beside the Jayhawk."

Stanton looked thoughtful. "Maybe because it looks a lot like your old Blackhawk?"

"I don't know, maybe. Hell, it could be the hot weather we're having, for all I know. You gotta admit it's not a typical summer for Alaska."

"But you're okay now? Because the welcoming committee is on its way over."

Two men, a short one in a lab coat and a tall one in coveralls, were hurrying across the compound. "You can't land here—" began Coveralls, but Lab Coat interrupted.

"I'm Jurgen Shumacher, IBC Project Manager." He extended his hand and greeted first Stanton, then Josh. His English had a trace of some European accent, but it wasn't German. "This is my coworker, Carl Meikle. We're a little surprised to see you here—are you having problems?"

"Nothing major, thanks. The pilot here has low blood sugar and we just had to stop and get him leveled out," said the vet. Josh obligingly held up the empty cola can and waggled it.

"I hope you are feeling better now, Mr.—"

"Talarkoteen. I'm with Fish and Wildlife." Josh could swear that the man flinched, although he covered it quickly. "This is Doctor Stanton, and we've just been on a case in Mentasta Lake. Took longer than expected and I missed lunch. My own damn fault." He smiled and Schumacher's answering smile contained relief.

"So this is quite the place you got here," said Stanton. "Beautiful facility, must have cost a mint. You know, as a veterinarian, I'm always interested in science. Any chance you could show us around while we're here, tell us what you're working on?"

Meikle jumped in at once. "We don't do tours; they're not allowed."

"What Carl means is that IBC has a strict no-visitor policy," explained Schumacher. "Information is a commodity these days and corporations have to be concerned about security."

"Yeah, of course, but I'm really interested in the environment—"

"I'm sorry, I can't answer any questions. It's a condition of employment that we sign nondisclosure agreements, so I couldn't even tell you what color the cafeteria walls are painted." He shrugged. "It's the world we live in. I'm sure you understand."

Josh could see that Stanton was warming up to argue. "We don't want to intrude," he said, catching the vet's elbow. "I'm feeling a lot better now, so we'll be taking off in a few minutes. Thanks for the landing spot."

"I'm glad we could help. Have a nice afternoon." The men walked away and Stanton fumed in silence until he got inside the chopper.

"What'd you do that for? I could have found out something."

Josh fastened his four-point shoulder harness. "Not from that guy. If he was an Afghan local, I'd bet my boots that he's working for the Taliban. Jumpy and a terrible poker face."

"Yeah, I picked up bogus vibes too." Having Josh agree with his assessment of the man seemed to mollify Stanton somewhat.

"I picked up a helluva lot more than vibes. There was somebody with a flak jacket and a sidearm holster watching from an upstairs window."

"You're shitting me."

"Believe me, I would never do anything to make you more paranoid than you already are, Stanton." He powered up the bird and prepared for takeoff. "The guy was talking into a radio. Hired gun by the looks of it, not a rent-a-cop."

"Added to that fence, it seems like an awful lot of security for an isolated scientific facility." Stanton glanced over at Josh. "So Tark, are you sure you're good for flying? I got a little air time in a chopper, I could get us home if you need it."

"My *blood sugar* seems to be back to normal now. Good story by the way."

"Hey, I figured they didn't need to know why we were here. But you're certain you're okay?"

"Good to go, bud." At least he sure as hell hoped so. He'd never had a flashback in the air before and didn't ever want to experience another one. Fortunately he'd never had back-to-back flashbacks so he was reasonably certain he was okay for a while. "Sorry if I spooked you."

"My heart needed the workout. You know, maybe we should make a little side trip."

"Where?"

"I think I should meet this gal of yours and the little werewolf kid. They're on the way, right?"

"She's not my gal."

Stanton snorted. "Only because you haven't had time to work your mojo on her."

"Maybe I'm not interested."

"Don't try to shit me, boy. Besides, I'm thinking somebody oughta make sure she's not mixed up in this IBC stuff—what if she picked this site for a reason? Maybe they hired her to look for something."

"I'm not taking you to meet her if you're going to interrogate her."

Stanton rolled his eyes. "I won't scare her off, if that's what you're worried about."

For a moment Josh considered it, he really did. After all,

Stanton was right, Kenzie's camp was on the way. Seeing her would be like a breath of cool, fresh air, balm for the headache that was throbbing in time to the rotors, and a great antidote for the flashback he'd just had. *But what if the presence of the little wolf brought on another episode?* His sensible side kicked in then—he had a passenger to worry about and the risk was too great. And as much as he hated the idea, he knew he needed to ground himself for a while until he was damn certain he was fine.

"I'll drive you there. Hell, I'll take you as soon as you finish your clinic in Mentasta Lake if you want. But right now, I'm taking this bird back to base." *And leaving it there.*

Kenzie had four squares excavated to about eighteen inches, and the one she was presently working on was a foot deep. She could see the striations in the soil, dark and light, layers that showed sections of time like pages in a book. By her estimates, she'd turned back those pages about 900 years. Far too early for what she was searching for.

She glanced over to see Anya still asleep under the salmonberry bushes. And still a wolf. The child refused to use mindspeech, other than that initial outburst to declare her name. She seemed to have accepted Kenzie's apology for teasing out that information, however, and followed her everywhere as if nothing had happened. But only when Kenzie was a wolf would the little girl come anywhere close to her. Anya's mom had done a terrific job of cautioning the child against strangers—but just how long was it going to take before Anya stopped seeing Kenzie as a stranger? Hopefully Josh was having better luck uncovering some clue that would help them locate her parents. . . . He hadn't been by her camp for an entire week and she had to admit that she missed him. Even though she most certainly didn't *want* to miss him.

Jeez, it's hot. Kenzie pulled back from the hole, wiped her hands on her jeans, and drained her water bottle. Tucked some stray wisps of hair back under the bandana on her head. The temperature seldom rose above 75 in the Copper River region, even on a July afternoon, but it felt a great deal warmer than that—well above 90. As a Changeling, her body temperature was higher than that of a human and truly hot weather could be tough to deal with, uncomfortable at best, dangerous at worst. Luckily, it wasn't that bad yet, and she was more acclimated than most Changelings. She'd been through far worse in Chile and Egypt. She knew the trick was to keep herself hydrated, and she'd have to make sure Anya did too.

It was early in the afternoon and the still air gave way to a faint whisper of breeze. The scent of a grizzly came with it, but it was well over a mile away so she didn't pay much attention. After all, this was bear country and the big creatures were plentiful. With spawning salmon coming up the Copper River and its many tributaries, there were countless grizzlies along the banks and in the water, each trying to gobble as many fish as possible to store fat for the coming winter. There might even be a few black bears here and there—as long as their much larger cousins didn't spot them.

Suddenly her sharp hearing caught the sound of a truck. Somebody was braving the rutted goat path from Chistochina but it didn't sound like Nate's Humvee. She held her breath and concentrated on listening—the vehicle didn't stop below her camp but continued in her direction. It had to be Josh. She could hardly wait to tell him Anya's name and hear what he'd found out. Mostly, she'd be glad just to see him.

Whoa, hold it right there. Kenzie squelched her impulse to head down to the road to meet him. She liked Josh but she wasn't going to let herself get carried away. She'd made that mistake with Nate and she wasn't going to do it again. Josh was a friend. Maybe he'd become a really good friend, but damned if she'd give him—or herself—the teeniest, tiniest reason to think they might ever be anything more.

To her surprise, her inner wolf whined softly. *Shut up,* she told it firmly. *I'm not asking for your opinion.*

Anya heard the truck too, but remained motionless except to wag her fuzzy tail. It was too hot to move from her cool and shady spot. The ground beneath Kenzie wasn't nearly so pleasant—the shade had vanished hours ago. Still, she remained on her stomach, working deep inside a square with the point of a trowel. She kept her head down, determined to concentrate, even when she caught Josh's scent and her wolfen self decided to do handsprings. What the hell was *that* about?

Suddenly there was a second scent, sharp and distinct, just as Anya yipped and Josh yelled, "Heads up!"

Kenzie sat up just in time to catch a cold bottle of iced tea. "Hey! Are you trying to brain me?" She blinked at the slight man with thick gray hair who had followed Josh. Piercing eyes looked out from under the wildest eyebrows she'd ever seen. But it was his scent that held her attention in an iron grip. She knew what he was.

And he would know what she was too.

She started to rise to her feet but the man shook his head. "Don't get up on my account, honey. It's too damn hot." His voice was thick and gravelly.

"This is my friend, Bygood Stanton," began Josh. "He's a veterinarian and a—"

"Werewolf," finished Stanton, plunking down beside her and shaking her hand.

Josh rolled his eyes. "Well, I was going to say *shitty poker player*, but yeah, he's a shapeshifter. He wanted to meet you. Hope that was okay."

"I'm glad to meet another Changeling," said Kenzie. And now that she could feel his energy, it was true. Her inner wolf was interested but not alarmed by this stranger. "And you're my very first Alaskan *werewolf*, Dr. Stanton, so it's even more of a treat." The smile on her face was genuine. But when she got Josh Talarkoteen by himself, he was *so* going to get an earful about revealing what she was, even to another Changeling. *Hey Stanton, I know another shapeshifter you just gotta meet . . .* Just because she'd been unable to hide what she was from his obsidian eyes didn't make it his damn secret to tell. Did anyone else know?

"And you're glad to see me too, of course." Josh plopped down cross-legged on her other side, took her bottle, twisted off the lid, and handed it back. "Especially since I'm trying to save you from dehydration. This weather is setting records across the state. I was afraid I'd find nothing but your bleached bones out here."

"Thanks," she managed, then turned her attention to the vet. "So tell me your first name again, Dr. Stanton?"

"No, no, Stanton's good. Nobody ever called me by my first name except my Edie when she was alive, and then only if I was in deep shit for something."

"Gotcha. So where's home for you?"

Their conversation didn't touch on anything lupine, yet it felt good to talk to one of her own kind. She was used to being a lone wolf among humans, but that didn't mean she didn't get lonely. A thought occurred to her—if Nate hadn't been a Changeling, would she ever have been attracted to him at all?

Stanton shared a number of funny stories from his work as a veterinarian that made Kenzie think of her brother, Connor. It was easy to lose track of time—until Josh poked her in the arm. She let him poke her a second time before she paid attention.

There was consternation in his dark eyes, concern for her that made it tough to hang onto her anger. She managed, though.

"You've got a lot of hours in on your dig, I'll bet, and you probably haven't eaten. I've got a cooler full of sandwich fixings and some more drinks."

"Let me guess, Mamie Dalkins gave you another care package?"

"Nope, threw stuff together myself. *Good* stuff, not that sawdust-in-a-bag that you pack. Wanna eat here or at camp?"

"Camp, definitely. I need to wash up." There was more shade there too, and the thought of taking her bandana off was appealing. Her hair was no doubt sticking up every which way, but sometimes if she brushed it, it behaved. Sometimes. Josh offered his hand to help her up but Kenzie ignored it. She sure didn't need her anthropology degree to tell her that he was trying to reassert himself and draw her attention away from the other male. Stanton might be older, but he was still competition. Men, both human and Changeling, could be pretty predictable, their behaviors ancient and instinctive, and often unconscious. "Just let me get Anya."

"*Anya?*"

"It's her name." She'd been looking forward to sharing

with him how she'd found out, but was too angry right now to tell him anything. Kenzie called the cub, who emerged reluctantly from the coolness of the salmonberry thicket. "It's time to go back to camp, honey."

"This is the little lost one?" asked Stanton. "She has a very distinctive coat."

"Do you recognize her?"

He shook his head. Her discouragement must have shown because he patted her arm. "We'll figure out where she belongs. We'll all work together and we'll figure it out."

Meanwhile, Josh knelt and addressed the cub directly. "Anya is a pretty name. Did you know that my cousin's name is Anya too?" He pulled something from his pocket and kept it hidden in his hands. "I brought you a surprise, one that both wolves *and* little girls can play with." A bright pink tennis ball appeared in his palm, and the cub's eyes went wide. He tossed it and Anya pounced on the ball with glee. A moment later she'd flopped on her side in the grass, holding her new treasure with her paws and biting it happily.

Kenzie was still pissed at Josh—and even more perturbed that he had to do something so damn likeable when she was trying to ignore him—but she had to give credit where credit was due. "That was thoughtful," she conceded as they walked up the rise toward the camp and the cub pranced behind them with the ball in her mouth. "I didn't even know they made tennis balls in pink. Bet she likes the color."

"It was a no-brainer. I've got little sisters, remember?"

"Bullshit," said Stanton. "I'll bet he picked it because it's *his* favorite color."

"Just remember it's a long walk back to your clinic, bud."

Kenzie was dying to ask Josh if he'd found out anything about Anya, but he hadn't said a word on the subject. Little wolves had sharp hearing, however, and Changeling hearing was even better—perhaps he was just waiting until they were alone to tell her? Still, she knew it was far more likely that he hadn't turned up any new information at all.

"Bloody hell." Stanton stopped ahead of her on the trail and it was all she could do not to run into him.

"What is it—" Her voice trailed away as she stared at the remains of her camp. The tent was a shapeless heap of shredded nylon. Clothes and cooking utensils were strewn everywhere. Chunks of blue foam from her cot were mixed with long ribbons of blankets. Her camp table was flattened, the chairs missing completely. Empty foil packages were scattered as far as the eye could see. Goose down from her sleeping bag floated through the trees and drifted against the bushes like snow.

"It looks like a tornado touched down," declared the vet, hands on his hips.

"This tornado had four legs," said Josh. He put an arm around Kenzie's shoulders. She was too stunned to shrug it off. "Welcome to Alaska, honey. You've just had a close encounter of the bear kind."

Chapter Nine

She should have known. She *had* known, dammit. "I smelled a bear and I didn't think anything of it. Bears are everywhere at this time of year." Maybe it was the same dumb bear that had taken out her grid. She should have chased him into next week, but Kenzie had assumed he was just passing through. *Crap, crap, crap.* She started picking things up and examining them. Outside of the cast-iron skillet, there was very little that wasn't completely ruined.

"Here are your culprits." Josh knelt by the campfire and pointed at a mish-mashed collection of prints in the soil. "Grizzly cubs, about a year old. At least two, maybe even three, had a blast playing with all your stuff." He continued to search the ground. "Look at that, Mama Bear joined the party too."

"You'd think *she'd* have known better," sniffed Kenzie as she stuffed a pair of salvageable underwear into her jeans pocket and searched for the mate to the sock in her hand. "What bear is crazy enough to enter a Changeling's territory?"

"An Alaskan bear, honey," said Stanton, picking up a knapsack that now had no bottom and only one strap. "I imagine your Pack's lived in northern Canada for a very long time. The animals there would be familiar with shapeshifters, and they know enough to steer clear.

"But here, it's different. Few Changelings for one thing and countless bears—Alaska's a big place. Hell, there are plenty of bears who have never encountered human beings and don't know how dangerous *they* are either."

"I know it's not their fault. It's just that everything's trashed and those damn bears ate all my food for the whole month."

"Poor bears," murmured Josh as he examined the empty packaging of some freeze-dried tuna casserole.

She punched him in the arm. Harder than she needed to.

"Hey, can I help it if they saved you from being poisoned?"

"The food wasn't that bad. The meals were portable, they kept well, and they were quick."

"So are my shoes," he said and grabbed Kenzie's hand before she could sock him again. She yanked it away. Ignored the protest that her inner wolf made. Ignored the way Josh's eyebrows went up, too.

He glanced over where Stanton was searching the bushes for Kenzie's belongings, then lowered his voice. "Look, it's a bad break but just forget this stuff. There's not a damn thing here that's salvageable. We'll head over to Anchorage or wherever you want to go. I know some good wilderness outfitters and we'll get you some more supplies, okay? Even more of this instant cr—*food*.

"And I've got a credit card if you need it. I know you scientist types are pretty dependent on funding."

Jeez, did he have to be so damn nice? She was still mad at him, after all, and he wasn't making it easy. "Thanks for the offer, but I can afford to replace everything, no problem. I have my truck too so I'm just fine, Josh. You don't need to worry about me."

"I'm thinking I do. And right now, I'm thinking you have something on your mind and we need to take a walk." He called out to Anya to stay with "Uncle Stanton" and headed back down the trail in the direction of the dig.

Kenzie watched him for a long moment, then decided that clearing the air was a good idea. She paced herself so she didn't catch up with him too soon—she didn't want Anya or Stanton to hear them either.

Josh stopped where the trail dipped beneath a monstrous leaning spruce. Folded his arms and settled back against the mossy trunk as if he was perfectly relaxed. She felt anything but calm, and it was downright annoying that he seemed as centered as ever, as if he belonged in the forest as much as the tree he was resting against.

"So what did I do or not do that pissed you off?" he asked, catching her by surprise.

"I—how do you know it was you?"

"I have three sisters, I know how it works. If a woman is upset, it's something the guy did or didn't do. So which is it?"

"Just because you know what I am doesn't mean you get to tell other people. It's not your business, it's not your secret, it's not your damn *life*. It's not automatically safe to reveal identities to Changelings outside the Pack. You had no right—"

"You're mad because I brought Stanton here?" he interrupted. "Look, I didn't tell him what you were. I went to him for help about the cub because he knows the people in this area, both human and shapeshifter. He asked to come here to see the cub but he also wanted to meet *you*."

"Because I'm a Changeling."

"No, because I like you a lot. He's been my friend for years and he's as bad as my Aunt Theresa when it comes to meddling in my dating life."

"Are you honestly trying to tell me that you didn't mention what I am?"

"Not a word. Christ, should I have planned something? Is there some sort of protocol that shapeshifters have to observe? Don't you ever just meet like normal people, run into each other by chance?"

"Not very often," she murmured, then blew out a breath. Josh hadn't spilled her secret after all. Of course, now she felt like an idiot. "I'm sorry."

"Me too. Sorry that you have to live in constant fear of having your cover blown. And maybe I should have phoned you, warned you that I was bringing Stanton by."

"You didn't know, you couldn't have known. You were just acting—"

"Like a human being," he finished.

She didn't feel like arguing, but he was absolutely right about one thing—she did live in fear. As independent and accomplished as she was, everything she did boiled down to that one fact. It was the reason she was here, searching for a needle in an ancient haystack, one key piece of evidence that might alleviate an entire world of fear. For a split second she could hear Birkie's words: *Letting go of fear can be scarier than what you're afraid of.* She brushed the advice away. "I overreacted. I'm just not used to having a human know what I am."

"Me, you mean." He studied her for a long moment, then reached out and took her hand. Watched her face with something like amusement as he tugged her closer. "You study humans but you sure don't know them very well."

"That's not true. I have a doctorate in anthropology for pity's sake."

"It's not the same," he said. "Knowing about them and knowing them. Not at all. 'Cause when you studied them, you missed something along the line. It's probably not written in any of your textbooks."

"What isn't?"

"That some of us can actually be trusted. Your secret is safe with me, Kenzie Macleod."

"How do I know that for sure?" she blurted, then wished she hadn't. It was a little too much like calling the guy a liar.

He shook his head. "You need to have a little faith."

"What I need is a reason."

Something in his eyes flashed then. His big hands traveled slowly up her arms, rounded over her shoulders and slid up to cup her head. Her eyes were wide and her hands were fisted, but she didn't move, couldn't move, as he simply, gently, brushed his lips over hers. She exhaled a shaky breath as he traced the contours of her mouth with devastating slowness. By the time he deepened the kiss, her arms were around his neck. She had no idea how much time passed—could have been seconds or days—before he lifted his head. All she knew was that the kiss had ended much too soon.

He didn't let go of her, and she was glad for that. Glad that he felt so solid, because she felt anything but. It should have seemed silly—in human form, she was physically strong and in wolfen form, there was no creature in nature that she needed to fear. Yet this man had shaken her entire world right to its foundations and rendered her helpless with nothing more than a kiss.

They stood like that for a long time, her head resting on his shoulder.

"Was that a good enough reason?" he asked at last. With her face against him she could feel the vibration of his voice, and something within her quivered.

"For what?"

He laughed and pulled out of the embrace. "You said you needed a reason to trust me. I could have given you a list, but instead, I just showed you how I feel about you."

She didn't know what to say, so she just nodded. Hoped she didn't have too dumb an expression on her face. And was hugely relieved when he suggested they head back to camp.

Stanton had the site organized when they returned. At least, it was organized if it was a recycling center and not a camp. Kenzie surveyed the mound of foam, the heap of nylon and fabric, the stacks of broken kitchen hardware, and the pile of empty foil packets in amazement. "Holy cow! How'd you get all this done so fast?" He'd gotten a roll of heavy duty garbage bags—must have come from Josh's truck because she hadn't owned any—and was systematically bagging the debris. She rushed to hold open a bag for him.

"Easy enough. I had help."

As if on cue, the wolf cub trotted by and deposited a scrap of blue foam on the appropriate pile. "Anya, that's wonderful," Kenzie said. "Thank you." She lowered her voice and whispered to Stanton. "I see you're great with kids."

"Me and Edie raised six of our own. You pick up a few things after a while. She was always better at it than me, though."

"You must miss her."

"Every damn day."

Josh grabbed two of the filled bags and an armload of bent and broken aluminum legs which had once held up the chairs and the table. "I'll put these in the truck. Looks like our first assessment was right—I don't see anything worth saving."

"Actually, Anya and I found a few little things that survived." Stanton pointed over to some objects in the skillet by the fire pit. "Not much though. The bears were pretty damn thorough."

Kenzie counted two more pairs of underwear, three socks, a handful of eating utensils, and a filled notebook with half its pages missing. Good thing she transcribed her penciled notes into the netbook every night. Had the small computer been in her tent and fallen victim to the bearfest as well, she had everything backed up on a pair of flash drives that lived in her shirt pocket. To someone who wasn't an archaeologist, it might have seemed obsessive, but Kenzie had learned the hard way to maintain copies of her work in every form possible. On a dig in Arizona, a rock had fallen from a canyon wall and crushed her laptop. On an Egyptian expedition, her notebook had been eaten by a damn goat. The bears might have annihilated her camp but they hadn't destroyed her work.

"Sorry we didn't find more," said Stanton, holding up what was left of her Coleman stove. It was crushed flat like an empty pop can. "They even ate your soap. I think you're going to have to go to town and start fresh. I'd skip the local trading posts and go up to Anchorage if I were you. There'll be a better selection on some of the bigger stuff. Josh'll know right where to take you. And the two of you will have much more fun there. Movies, restaurants, malls, museums. Glennallen's a great place, but it's just a little junction in the road."

She rolled her eyes. Josh had been right about Stanton's interest in his love life. Before she could form a response, another thought struck her. "Omigod, I forgot about Anya. She can't stay here by herself." The little wolf was on the other side of the camp, playing with the down feathers from the gutted sleeping bag.

"No, she can't," Josh agreed from behind her. She didn't jump but she was surprised she hadn't heard him approach. "We're just going to have to talk her into coming with us. We can probably pass her off as a dog with that white leg."

Kenzie didn't miss the *us*. He was still determined to accompany her. "That won't work. She still won't come within arm's length of either of us, so there's no way she's going to get into a truck. I'll just have to stay here. Maybe you could pick up some things for me in town and bring them by when you get a chance."

"That doesn't help you right now. You don't have a damn thing to eat or sleep on or even sleep *in*."

She shrugged. "Yes, but I'm a Changeling. I'll just be a wolf tonight. Anya seems to like me better that way anyhow, and I'm perfectly capable of hunting us something for dinner."

Josh was about to protest when Stanton held up his hand.

"I'll stay," said the vet. "You kids go ahead and spend a couple days in town. Don't even think about coming back until Friday. Anya and I will be just fine."

"That's way too much to ask," began Kenzie.

"Believe me, I'd enjoy the chance to get in touch with my hairier side. Seems like I don't get around to it much anymore." Suddenly an icy breeze swirled up out of nowhere, both strange and welcome in the heat of the afternoon. Dried leaves and bits of grass rose and played around Stanton, wind pulled at his hair with invisible fingers. The smell of ozone hung in the hot still air, as if lightning was about to strike.

Instead, a large and lanky wolf yawned and stretched where the vet had been standing only a split second before, a few stray blue sparks of static still crackling in his silver fur.

"Wow," breathed Josh. "That's the coolest thing I've ever seen."

"You haven't seen him Change before?" asked Kenzie.

He shook his head. "Totally amazing and so damn *fast*. I guess I expected a more gradual process or something. Hell, I thought you at least had to get naked first. And look at you, Stanton, you're bigger than any wolf has a right to be. You're like an *uber wolf*."

Stanton chuffed at him as if laughing, then rolled on his back and began wriggling like a puppy. A moment later, Anya stopped playing with the feathers and crept over to see what was going on. The silver wolf made whining sounds in his throat and remained on his back. He glanced at the cub, then at Kenzie and winked. Anya hunched down in the grass, eyeing Stanton's long bushy tail. Slowly, the tip of it began to twitch. . . .

She pounced. Stanton flinched once and Kenzie had to cover her mouth to stifle a laugh—the cub's teeth might be small but Kenzie knew well how sharp they were. To his credit, the old wolf managed to hold his position, but it wasn't long before Anya attacked a hind foot and all-out wrestling commenced. Stanton lifted his head once and yipped at the couple watching them, before he was forced to defend an ear.

"I guess that's our cue to get lost," said Josh.

"I don't know whether to worry about Anya or worry about Stanton. Are you sure this is a good idea?"

"You heard him. Stanton and his wife raised six kids. All of them Changelings by the way. He'll survive." Josh led the way to the trucks. "I'm thinking this might even be good for him. He doesn't shapeshift very often, not since Edie passed on."

"Wolves aren't designed to be alone. It must be hard for him."

"It must be hard for you too. I'll bet you're away from your family a lot in your line of work."

She was *so* not going there and changed the subject. "You're still determined to go shopping with me?"

"You bet. You're going to need some fresh clothes before we go out tomorrow night, and you'd probably like something a little dressy for dancing. Unless you'd rather go bowling, in which case jeans will work just fine."

She narrowed her eyes at him as he held the door of her truck open for her. "You can tag along shopping with me if you want but I'm not going on a date with you."

"Why not? We already kissed, which is what we would have done at the end of the evening. Why not enjoy everything that would have led up to that? By the way, I have to take my truck back to the office, so you can follow me there and then we'll drive your rig to the city."

"We shouldn't have done that. It was a mistake."

"Kissing? Why the hell would that be a mistake?"

"Because you're human. I can't have a relationship with a human, so there's no point in starting one."

"Can't or won't? Are Changelings physically incapable of pairing with humans or is this a form of prejudice?"

She opened her mouth and closed it again.

"I thought so. Now about our date, would you rather dance first or eat first?"

"I'm *not* going out with you. And if you don't drop it, I'm shopping alone too."

He just smiled. "I'll meet you at my office." He gave her directions, got into his truck, and left.

Her inner wolf was impatient but she waited until the dust died down completely and there was no reason to put off following the man any longer. She drove the entire way to Glennallen wishing there was another road to take. Any road except the one that led to Josh Talarkoteen.

Chapter Ten

Josh parked outside his little office in Glennallen, a stone's throw from the tee-intersection that connected the Old Richardson and the Glenn highways. It was late in the afternoon, still hot, and the sun would be up for a long time yet. He'd left all the windows open, but it hadn't helped much. He switched on the two fans—the last of the hardware store's stock of them—planted himself at his desk by the window, and waited for his quarry to appear. Like the Spartans at the passage of Thermopylae, Josh had an all-important advantage. There was no route Kenzie Macleod could take that wouldn't bring her right past him.

Unless, of course, she decided to stay in camp. Josh supposed she could rough it there for as long as she pleased, hunting for deer and sleeping under the sky. Would probably enjoy it for a while too—hell, he sure would. Sooner or later, though, she'd resent how much time it took away from her dig. And she would want to continue to coax Anya to shift to human form—tough to be persuasive on that point if she wasn't on two legs herself.

He snorted at Kenzie's anti-human bias. Most people were unaware they had any prejudices and he was certain she didn't think of her feelings that way. He knew that most prejudice sprang from fear of the unfamiliar, yet Kenzie lived her life among humans, even studied them, and spent at least half of her life in human form. He experienced discrimination rarely as a Tahltan in Alaska, perhaps because anyone who lived in this last frontier knew he might have to someday depend on his neighbor and be depended upon in return. The fury of nature was a great leveler. War was too—in Afghanistan, nobody gave a damn what color you were as long as you had their back.

If Kenzie rejected him because of his *ethnicity*—that was the ten-dollar word for it these days—he'd be disappointed in her but he could deal. Never in his wildest dreams did he expect he'd be written off because of his *species*. Under normal circumstances, he'd find it hilarious, except that he was already in over his head with this woman.

What made Kenzie so determined not to build relationships with humans? He supposed there was the age thing. He had no idea how old she really was. He did know that Doc Stanton was older than dirt, yet the vet didn't exhibit any animosity toward humans—unless of course they didn't treat their animals well. That brought up the point that not all humans were sterling examples of their species. As a shapeshifter, maybe Kenzie'd been on the receiving end of some poor treatment, perhaps even prejudice, herself.

That thought made him crazy. Every protective instinct he had rushed to the forefront, willing to take on all comers to defend a woman he'd known for less than a month. He laughed at himself and the aggression eased off, like a lion settling reluctantly for its handler yet remaining watchful.

Kenzie's pickup appeared and pulled in beside his. She didn't get out right away, and when she did, he could easily see the reluctance and the conflict in her body language.

She was fighting with herself again. Part of her was interested in Josh and the other part was . . . he wasn't sure but he'd put his money on *afraid*. And that was a paradox in itself because she didn't strike him as a woman who feared much of anything. There'd be no talking her out of her fear either, as he would a newbie in a firefight. In fact, getting Kenzie Macleod to accept him wasn't so different from coaxing an injured wild animal to allow him to help it. In the short term, he'd probably be bitten for his efforts, and likely more than once. The long term, he sensed, just might be worth it.

He decided to remain at his desk and allow her to come to him. He smiled as the door opened.

"Josh?"

"Right here, buried in paperwork."

She eyed the enormous moose head that dominated the cramped entry and came in. There was a grizzly pelt on the wall and several mounted raptors—eagles, hawks, and an owl—hung in various stages of flight from the ceiling. Visitors often instinctively ducked as they came in. The mounts were as much standard decor for a government wildlife office as the faded orange chairs from the seventies and the chipped countertop.

"Somebody does a lot of hunting," Kenzie said as she leaned on the counter.

"The animals weren't killed for display. Most of them ended up dead by accident—that moose was hit by a truck on a city street in Anchorage outside a Starbucks. Or else they were poached and then confiscated, like that bear."

"You look busy. I don't want to take you away from your work."

"No busier than usual, and I have a large number of days

off owed to me. You're doing me a favor by taking me away from all this." He slid papers into a file folder and stood up. "Ready?"

"I guess so."

"I love your enthusiasm." He held the office door open for her and nearly laughed at the glare she gave him. Then something occurred to him. "Hell, I don't know what I was thinking. I'll bet you'd like a chance to freshen up, maybe shower or something before we go to the city."

She looked down at herself—surveyed her dusty jeans, the smears on her shirt and the half-torn pocket over her breast—and he knew she hadn't given a single thought to what she looked like until now. It was easy enough to understand. She lived in a camp in the middle of nowhere and dug in the dirt for a living. Nobody to see, nobody to please . . . He almost laughed at that. Kenzie Macleod wasn't the type to be concerned about *pleasing* anyone. Surprisingly, it only made her sexier.

"Crap." She swiped a hand through her hair and only succeeded in making it stand on end. "I can't show up at a shopping mall like this. People will stare."

"Well, I'd still be proud to hold your hand, but if you'd like to tidy up, my house is yours." The wary look she gave him made him add something else. "And if you'd be more comfortable, I could just come back and finish up my paperwork while you're there." It sure as hell wasn't *his* first choice, but it did have a couple of advantages. One, she might feel comfortable enough to actually accept the offer if he wasn't going to hang around, and two, the thought of her in his shower was enough to make him need a shower himself—a cold one.

"You wouldn't mind? I'll be quick. And you certainly don't have to leave your own house."

"All right then." She'd probably deck him if she knew how happy that made him. He wondered if his sister, Sam, had left any clothes in the spare room the last time she'd visited. Probably not, but it was worth a look. Maybe they could find something at Whitford's Trading Post before they left town. Nothing classy there of course—the Post's selection consisted of souvenir T-shirts and Carhartt work clothes—but anything clean and functional would work until Kenzie could buy something more stylish in the city. That is, if she even possessed a fashionable side. Was she all practicality, he wondered, or was there a softer side to her?

For the first time in his life, he was excited about shopping.

It wasn't a surprise that Josh owned a house, but Kenzie was expecting a small bungalow in town. Instead, he drove back along the highway and entered a laneway that wound through thick trees. A sprawling log home, rustic yet modern, gracing a clearing and the vivid view of Mount Drum, snow-capped despite the summer season, made her heart ache. She got out of the truck slowly, drinking in the sights and smells.

"This is just like a *postcard*. And the house blends right in like it grew here. It's really yours?"

"Bought it as a fixer-upper the year before I signed up. The owners had started building years ago but never finished it, so it was just a shell. There wasn't a thing on the inside but some wires and a couple of lightbulbs. I figured the place would be a good investment and a good hobby, something to do in my spare time. When I first came home from Afghanistan, though, it was therapy. Worked for Fish and Game in the daytime, then came home and worked on the house half the night. Sometimes, if I couldn't sleep, I'd get up and work on something. That's how most of the drywalling got done."

She followed him inside to a massive great room with a vaulted ceiling. Wide windows faced the stunning mountain view. Armchairs and couches sprawled around a large woodstove. The walls sported an eclectic collection of artwork and artifacts—everything from deer antlers and snowshoes to sepia photos and paintings of wildlife. The effect was a "lodge" look that was comfortable and welcoming. Kenzie thought it would be even more inviting in the wintertime.

"Shower's this way." Josh led her to a guest bedroom that was dominated by a rustic four-poster bed and a colorful red and blue quilt. He crossed the room and checked the drawers of a wide pine dresser. "My sisters stay here when they visit. *Aha!*" He held aloft a pair of T-shirts, one pink with *Alaska Girls Kick Ass* emblazoned in rhinestones across the front, and a scoop-necked charcoal one with a black gothic pattern. He laid them on the bed and proceeded to check the closet, but it held only a couple of jackets and a bridesmaid's dress in a clear plastic sheath. "I'm sorry, I guess all we have are the shirts. Look, give me your jeans and I'll put them through the dryer while you shower."

"What? They're not wet."

"I probably shouldn't reveal this to you, but it's an old bachelor's secret. Put the jeans into the dryer with a damp washcloth and a couple of fabric softener sheets and *voilà*— they're fit for human company again."

"An *old* bachelor's secret, eh? Sounds like something guys learn in high school."

"Hey, you can't acquire life skills too early. Just leave the jeans outside the bedroom door and I'll take care of it.

Meanwhile, there're towels in the bathroom, and shampoo and all that stuff." He waved and left the room, closing the door behind him.

Kenzie stood for a few minutes gazing at the back of the door. She'd never met anyone like him. A little voice in her head warned her that the more time she spent with Josh Talarkoteen, the harder it would be to avoid becoming involved. And no good could come of having a relationship with a human. Sure, Connor and James would probably laugh at her if she said that out loud. Both of her brothers' mates had been human to start with, and everything had worked out great.

So why was she still averse to the idea? And if she was truly averse to the idea, why was she so attracted to him? Because there was no denying the pull she felt. Worse, her wolf seemed to feel it even more than she did, and she did *not* want to think what that might mean.

Still, what was it Birkie had said? *Don't close the door on possibilities.* That and something about being *openhearted* and receptive to the universe or some such thing. Kenzie sighed. What could happen if she just relaxed and tried to enjoy Josh's company? She'd been able to do that with Nate once upon a time. Just have fun and not worry about anything more. Her work and her cause meant a lot to her, but when was the last time she'd taken a break? A real one? Maybe it would be a good idea to relax and clear her head for a couple of days, and then she could go back to her project refreshed and renewed. She might even be more effective, more intuitive on the dig.

Right now there was a hot shower calling her name and a good-looking, intelligent guy who wanted to help her have a good time.

Kenzie decided she wasn't going to resist either one.

★   ★   ★

Kenzie thought that a man who caught his own rabbits and cooked them over a fire he'd made himself shouldn't appear so damn comfortable in an urban setting. But then, that was part of the unusual energy Josh Talarkoteen possessed. He was centered, as grounded as the ancient spruce that grew around her camp, as if his very soul had roots that went deep into the earth. At the same time he was fluid, in touch with everything around him, be it in the forest or on the main street—and apparently perfectly at home in either.

The drive between Glennallen and Anchorage was only a couple of hours, but they'd decided to stay in the city for the sake of time. He'd picked an upscale hotel and she was surprised that it was in the heart of the downtown. It was just down the street from what he called the *best Italian restaurant in Alaska,* and their rooms—two adjacent— boasted stunning views of the city and the mountains beyond. She teased him mercilessly about the décor, however. It was as rustic and lodge-like as his living room, replete with lamps made of antlers and paintings of moose and caribou.

The next morning they hit the ground running as soon as the malls opened. For someone who claimed to dislike shopping, Josh was unexpectedly good at it. He not only accepted it as necessary, he approached it like a mission. He had her make a careful list of every last item she needed, and added a few things he felt she should have. He knew exactly what stores to go to and which to avoid. In fact, Josh often knew more than the salespeople about wilderness gear and made some great recommendations. She might have expected that since it was something he was keenly interested in, but she was surprised when he made suggestions on clothing too, and said so.

"Hey, I had sisters. When I was growing up, somebody had to follow them around and keep them out of trouble."

"I thought you didn't like shopping."

"I don't. I just believe in being as efficient at it as possible. Then it's over sooner."

"What if I wanted to browse? Maybe look at jewelry or purses or something?"

He shrugged good-naturedly. "Then we'd be browsing. I'd hide the excruciating pain it would cause me because this expedition is for you and I want you to have fun. But it doesn't seem to be your thing."

"No, it's really not. My sister-in-law, Zoey, says I'm *shopping challenged*. I'm really more of a museum kind of person when I go to town."

"Yeah? I could get into that—we've got a pretty good museum here that I'll bet you've never seen." He held up the list. "As soon as we cross off *underwear*, we can go."

"I have no intention of shopping for lingerie with you."

"Well, I'm not keen on being seen in that department either. Unless of course, I get to pick out stuff that would look good on you—"

"No!"

"Then I'll wait in the food court with the rest of the banished males."

She ended up lingering over the lingerie. She'd picked up some packages of sturdy briefs that would be practical but couldn't pass by a bin of colorful little thongs and sleek high-cut bikinis. They were fragile and wouldn't last long in her camp environment—and they sure wouldn't be comfortable to work in—but they looked so vibrant and fun that she couldn't resist. Same with the bras. She already had what she needed in her basket but a couple of the brightly colored bras (and a satiny merlot one that called her name) made it to the sales counter as well. She refused to think about when she might wear them or why.

Josh saw her long before she spotted him, and for a few moments he enjoyed simply watching her. He liked the way she moved, her stride purposeful yet graceful. Those worn blue jeans sheathed long, long legs, and damned if he didn't wonder what they'd feel like wrapped around him. That old charcoal T-shirt definitely looked good on Kenzie—or perhaps she made it look good. For one thing, the color of it seemed to set off her big gray eyes. For another, it hugged her shape, something that was usually hidden away under a plaid work shirt, and it was a shape worth showing off. The palm of his hand ached to cup one of those nicely rounded breasts—

Quit drooling, Tark. He managed to put a semi-intelligent look back on his face just as she saw him and came over.

"Hey." She walked all the way around him, table, chairs, and all. "You got quite a haircut. Nice."

"I caught sight of myself in a mirror while you were looking at jeans. Felt like Shaggy on *Scooby Doo*." He'd had the hairdresser take it all off, right up to the ears. She'd styled it well too but he hadn't realized just how heavy his long hair had been. "Of course now it feels like my head's going to float away."

Kenzie laughed. "We'll tie a string to it. So, I've been good and finished all my shopping. Do I get to go to the museum now?"

The museum, the moon, anywhere you want to go. "I don't

know—I think I should inspect what you bought and make sure it's suitable."

She clutched the lingerie bag to her in mock horror. Maybe not so mock . . . He grinned. "Okay, we'll head out to the museum. And afterward we're going to dinner. I'm starving."

"You're in a food court—how is that possible?"

"I'm a fan of real food, remember? Besides, I made reservations for us at a great place."

"*Reservations* is such a strong word. Sounds an awful lot like a date. Which you will remember, I said I'm not doing with you."

"You did say that. But that was before we bonded over shopping."

"This was not true shopping. You consulted while I purchased necessary supplies. I'm not dating you."

"Is that your final answer? Because you're forcing me to pull out the big guns."

"What big guns?"

"I have a new phone number on speed dial that you might find interesting." He rattled it off and her mouth dropped open.

"Where the hell did you get that?"

"It's not hard. You said your brother's a veterinarian just like Stanton—and there aren't many animal doctors in your little hometown. Two, to be exact, and they both work at the same clinic. I'll just bet Dr. Connor Macleod would love to hear how you turned down a date with a good-looking veteran who has a respectable government job and owns his own house. You know how family works—you'll never hear the end of it from your big brother. Maybe you'll get lucky and he'll tell your other three big brothers and they'll all gang up on you. Not to mention your big sister."

She folded her arms then and her chin came up. "I don't care. Go ahead and call him. I'm not going out with you."

"And then of course, there's Mom and Dad, the sisters-in-law, great aunt, family friends . . . all of them wanting their little Mackenzie to be happy."

"I *am* happy, dammit." She looked like she was starting to sweat.

In slow motion, he pulled out his cell phone and poised his finger over a button. . . .

"Okay, okay, you win. One—just *one*—date. But that's all." She didn't look at Josh, just stalked off toward the nearest exit. "Do you get all your dates by blackmail?"

"Nope," he said cheerily as he easily kept pace with her. "Only the ones that matter."

Chapter Eleven

Nate left the curator's office, dodged a crowd of boy scouts trooping past a woolly mammoth skeleton, and headed for the escalator. The meeting had gone well, well enough to garner him an invitation to the museum patron's ball plus an idea of who else would be attending. He'd be able to work the room there, no problem, drum up enthusiasm for a cooperative effort between his department at NYU and the University of Alaska. The caves on Prince of Wales Island had yielded the oldest human remains in the Great State, but what was really going to bring in the donor dollars was—

His Changeling hearing suddenly picked out one very familiar voice amid the many. Startled, he followed the sound to a display wing to find Kenzie Macleod explaining the history behind an ancient copper knife to a tall native man. As Nate rounded a pillar, the man—a human—put a hand on her shoulder and she turned toward him slightly as she continued. The hairs on the back of Nate's neck bristled and the wolf within him snarled. *Who the hell is that?*

He dodged back behind the pillar and took several deep breaths. If he wasn't careful, he would Change right then and there. Kenzie was easily twenty yards away but he didn't need to be any closer to catch every word. His wolfen senses weren't as powerful when he was in two-legged form but his hearing still exceeded that of ordinary humans. He sniffed the air and wished he hadn't—renovations of one of the galleries had sent paint fumes throughout the building. He could pick out Kenzie's scent only with difficulty and that reassured him. The ventilation system was sending the air currents his way, making it highly unlikely that she would smell him.

"The Ahtna tribe have occupied the territory where I'm digging since before the pyramids were built," Kenzie said. "That makes it exactly right for what I'm looking for."

Nate peered around. Kenzie was flushed with excitement and he caught the faintest scent of it even through the paint fumes. She was a beautiful woman, something that work clothes and dirt could never hide. When she spoke about her work, however, it was as if something inside her lit up. She was vibrant, animated, *alive*. Dammit, if he could just get her to light up like that in front of an audience of potential sponsors . . . but right now, she shone for the tall human male she was with and Nate would've liked nothing better than to tear the guy's throat out. He counted slowly to ten, then thirty, then a hundred, holding on to control with his fingernails.

"Among the Ahtna, as with many peoples who live close to nature, all animals were revered and had to be properly thanked for providing food and clothing to the hunter."

"Good Karma. It's the same in our clans. Respect for the animal that gives its life so that yours can continue, gratitude for what is provided."

"Yeah, but the wolf was honored even more and for a specific reason. Ahtna legends are very clear about a time when there was no separation between human and animal."

The man whistled low, a sound which grated on Nate's already-stretched nerves. "So men and beasts were of equal importance."

"Absolutely. Among the Ahtna, it was forbidden to kill a wolf. It was one of the worst crimes you could possibly commit and there had to be an atonement made to prevent the rest of the wolves from exacting justice. The wolf's body had to be dressed in clothing and placed in a house. The shaman then had to prepare not just food but an entire banquet for the dead wolf. Do you know why?"

She was pacing now, using her hands as she talked, and Nate breathed a little easier that the guy was no longer touching her. He thanked all of his lucky stars that it was nearly closing time and there was no one else left in this display wing, no one to see him leaning his back against the pillar, shaking and sweating. No one to ask him if he was all right and dial up 911. No one to interrupt him as he fought to keep control of his inner beast.

"I'm guessing it got special treatment just in case it wasn't really a wolf. In case it was a Changeling."

Nate was shocked, the surprise helping to clear his head. This guy knew that Changelings existed! But did he also know that Kenzie was one? Nate couldn't imagine her ever revealing such a dangerous secret to a human. She liked humans, but she had never trusted them a bit. Remembering that, his inner wolf finally settled down. It simply wasn't possible for her to be in a close relationship with this guy, not possible for her to be more than good buddies with him. Nate snorted. Yeah, she kept that goddamn *just friends* sign firmly between her and everybody it seemed. It was long past time he tore it down . . .

Kenzie was still talking. "The Ahtna were isolated until the 1880s. I'm—Nate!"

He walked smoothly up to her, yanked her close and kissed her, hard. He might have expected the fist to his chin, but he was surprised that she put so much into it. Almost as if she meant it. *Almost*, because although a human would have been out cold, the blow wasn't enough to faze a Changeling.

"Quit that, you idiot!"

It was exactly how he imagined she'd speak to one of her brothers, and that bothered him more than the punch. He gave her a quick squeeze, kissing her hand before he released her, then turned his gaze on the stranger she was with. He allowed his inner wolf—firmly leashed at last but still furious—to glare through his eyes. Made certain, however, that all Kenzie saw was a big smile. She might be able to sense his real mood, but maybe he could keep her off-base with his trademark charm. "Great to see you, babe. Who's your pal?"

The *pal*, he noted, was one cool customer. Most humans would have at least backed up a step but if this guy was bothered in the slightest by Nate's possessive display, he declined to show it. Playing poker with him would be a serious mistake, Nate decided. Kenzie, however, smoothly glided away from Nate and took the man's arm.

"Josh, this is my *friend*, Nate Richardson. He's an archaeologist too. We went to school together and shared a lot of digs," she said. "Nate, Josh Talarkoteen. Fish and Game officer."

They shook hands, and Nate couldn't resist exerting a slightly more than human grip. Josh didn't flinch or blink, however. Nate resorted to a different tactic to try to get a rise out of him. "Talarkoteen, eh? I don't think we have any

Tahltan artifacts here—a *Canadian* tribe, aren't you?" He purposely allowed the tiniest hint of disdain into his words but it backfired when Kenzie was the one to take offense.

"Something wrong with Canadians, Nate?"

He could have kicked himself—he was off his game, that was certain. Why couldn't he have remembered that her family lived in some boring little town in northern Alberta? He'd never met them, of course. He'd always refused to go home with her on the few breaks she'd taken when they were in school together, preferring to stay in the Big Apple or head off to Vegas. Maybe that had been a mistake. Maybe if he'd made nice with her family, charmed them over to his side, then Kenzie would now be on *his* arm, where she belonged. Well, he'd just have to fix that . . . Meanwhile, he had to rescue the present situation.

"Not a gosh darn thing. They've given the world hockey, great beer, and *you*, babe."

She rolled her eyes and he relaxed.

"So, do you work here in Alaska?" asked Josh.

"New York, actually. I'm the head of the ancient studies department at NYU." Nate always enjoyed the way it rolled off his tongue. Someday—soon he hoped—being able to say he was the college president would sound even better. "Just setting up digs for my students and begging for donations. It costs a lot to run a world-class program like ours."

"You must know Professor Higby at the university here."

Too well. Higby hated him. They'd almost come to blows a week ago, when Higby accused him of stealing a major donor away from his project. Nate had done exactly that, of course, but he figured all was fair in love and corporate funding. "I'm sure I've met the man, of course. But

I can't recall his face at the moment." *Time to change strategy.* "Well, I've been in meetings all day and worked up an appetite. Why don't we go to dinner together—my treat. Josh and I can get to know each other and Kenzie can finish what she was saying about the Ahtna tribe. It sounded fascinating."

"You were eavesdropping?" A faint frown appeared between her brows and he waved a hand as if trying to sweep away her concern.

"I heard your gorgeous voice in here, babe. I just naturally caught some of your sparkling dissertation as I approached." Nate said to Josh, "Kenzie is the hands-down expert when it comes to truly ancient culture. I don't know how you talked her into mingling with modern civilization. She usually hates the city." And wouldn't accept his own invitation, he thought with no small amount of resentment, but that would change. That would definitely change.

"I had no choice," she said wryly. "A damn bear destroyed my camp and all my supplies."

His eyebrows shot up in genuine surprise. "Good God, Kenzie. I'm glad you're okay. How the hell did a bear manage to sneak up on *you?*"

"I've been a little preoccupied lately."

"I can see that," he said, nodding his head toward Talarkoteen.

"Josh has been helping me. I called him when I found an orphaned wolf cub at my dig. As it turns out, though, she's not a wolf."

For a moment he thought he'd gone stone deaf. Kenzie's lips were moving and he wasn't hearing anything. Only three words that repeated in his brain like a mantra—*not a wolf, not a wolf, not a wolf.*

"Nate, are you okay?"

He came to himself and blinked at her. "I'm sorry. I'm just, well, *shocked* I guess. I thought you said you found a Changeling—"

"Child. Yeah, it was a shock to me too. She just turned up at my camp."

Kenzie related the details and Nate had to work to keep an expression of concern on his face instead of the excitement he was feeling. It was too good to be true. Way too good. "So she claims her name is Anya," he said aloud. "That might be a made-up name, maybe a name from a storybook or something—kids do that, you know. My little cousin Morgan insisted her name was *Jasmine* for two years, from the character in her favorite Disney movie. And you still have no idea where this kid belongs?"

"Not until she tells us. She won't say anything else using mindspeech, and so far she refuses to resume her human form. So we're stuck looking for clues. You meet a lot of people all the time, Nate—have you ever run into any Changelings up here? Anyone you can ask?"

"Sure, I can put out some feelers," he began. "I think there's a pack over by—"

Josh interrupted then. "Make that *discreet* feelers. We don't know what kind of situation Anya came out of. And we're not letting anyone have her back without a helluva good reason as to why this little girl was left alone in the middle of nowhere."

"Naturally I'll be careful." Nate put on his most sincere face, the one that assured potential sponsors they were helping to uncover history and thereby becoming part of it. "But please tell me the poor kid's not alone in the middle of nowhere right now. I mean, you didn't bring her with you, did you?"

It was satisfying to see Talarkoteen's eyes flash but it was Kenzie who answered. "As if we'd abandon her, Nate! A friend of Josh's is staying at the site with Anya until we get back on Friday. She's being well looked after."

He put up his hands, palms out. "Of course—I was just concerned. The kid has to have been through a lot, she needs to be protected, that's all." Nate looked at his watch then. "Good God. I know I suggested dinner, but I have to meet with a sponsor. You know how it is with fund-raising—a schmoozer's work is never done. I'll call you later, babe." He reached for Kenzie, fully intending to give her an even better kiss than the last one just to piss off Talarkoteen. She wasn't caught off guard this time though and turned her head so he had to kiss her cheek. That was fine, though, she couldn't spoil his mood and besides, he was confident he'd collect a hell of a lot more than just a kiss later. Much later.

Right now he had a phone call to make.

Josh didn't see Nate leave. Didn't hear Kenzie apologize for his behavior or hear the voice over the sound system announce that the museum was closing in fifteen minutes. Was unaware of everything—except for the tiny figure next to a far white wall.

Suddenly the sounds of children playing, shouts and laughter, surrounded him. He glanced down past his dusty pilot's jumpsuit to his boots in the sand, felt the heat of the Afghan sun, inhaled the dry air and looked back at the little girl in the red and green tunic. Her shawl had fallen loose from her long dark hair and she was bright-eyed and laughing. Two other children ran past her and then it struck him—

This was *before*.

"Get down!" he shouted and leapt forward but he'd barely made it ten yards before the blast came. The concussion knocked him to the ground, where he clapped his hands over the terrible pain in his ears and fought to suck in a breath past the sand in his mouth. His insides felt like they'd been kicked repeatedly, his ribs had to be broken, had to be . . . then his brain switched back on and he struggled to raise his head.

Where was she? The clouds of dust obscured everything and he was half-buried in debris. It was eerily silent, or maybe he was deaf. He spat and sucked in a little more air, which cleared his head somewhat. The dust cleared too, and the courtyard came back into focus. The once-smooth white wall was dirty, the concrete pocked with holes and sprayed with lines of blood. Below it was a little red and green heap—

He jumped up and lunged forward, tripping and falling. Someone tried to grab his arm but he shook them off and kept going. He had to get to her, he had to help her, but the image faded as he got closer.

By the time he reached the wall, the damaged white concrete had become smooth wood panels. The shrapnel holes, the blood, all gone. *She* was gone.

Josh. Josh, it's all right. Come back now.

He heard the voice behind him, a voice that didn't belong in this time and place. His battered brain registered vaguely that he wasn't deaf after all. He also clued in that he wasn't in goddamn Afghanistan.

Oh, fuck.

He sank to the floor where the little girl had been standing—where he had *imagined* her standing—and leaned his head back against the wall. He saw Kenzie approach cautiously, concern on her face and that little frown between her brows that he'd love to rub his lips over. Not that she'd let him do that anytime soon. Not after this. *Shit*.

"Hey," she said.

"Hey," he replied. Damned if his throat didn't feel scratched and raw from sand and dust.

"Are you here now, Josh? Do you know where you are?"

"In a museum with a pretty woman who probably thinks I'm screwed in the head."

"Your head is just fine."

He eyed her, suddenly furious and ready to lash out at the slightest show of pity. That wasn't what he saw in her gaze and the anger stepped down a few notches.

"Wanna punch something?" she asked. "There's a stuffed polar bear by the front door. It's taller than you so it'd be fair."

He doubted that punching a *live* polar bear would drain the chaotic emotions that were swamping him. She offered him a hand but he brushed it aside and got up. Took a deep breath and wished for a goddamn beer.

"Everything okay with you folks?" A museum security guard appeared. "Mister, you don't look so good."

Josh waved a hand and borrowed a page from Stanton. "Just a little low blood sugar is all. Got a bit dizzy."

"The gift shop's got some candy bars if you need one. The museum's closing now but the shop stays open a little later for last minute customers. Right by the front door."

"Thanks," said Kenzie. She put her arm through Josh's as if he was escorting her, but in reality, she was both supporting him and leading him. On one level he was fascinated by her Changeling strength. On a more basic level, he hated that he needed it. Hated that they weren't going to have the evening he'd planned for them, hated that they were going straight to the damn hotel because he was in no shape to do anything else.

Hated most of all that she had seen him in full flashback mode. No way in hell she'd feel anything but sorry for him now.

Chapter Twelve

The rush hour had passed and traffic was light as Kenzie drove them to their hotel. Josh didn't feel much like talking but he was impressed that she remembered how to get there, even though he had been driving when they'd checked in to their rooms the night before. But then she was smart—not one but *two* doctorates. Way too smart to hang around with him and he should have damn well known better from the start. Resigned, he scooped up a double armful of her shopping bags—despite her protest—and followed her inside to her room, where he set them on her bed. To his surprise, she blocked him as he turned to leave.

"Sit. Relax a minute."

"I'm fine." He tried to brush past her but she put out a hand.

"I'm not. Please sit."

Reluctantly, Josh backed into the bed and sat down harder than he intended to. God, he was tired. The flash-backs (*hot memories* as his counselor had called them) often left him physically exhausted as well as emotionally wrung out. Kenzie produced a large bottle of water from the mini-fridge and he drained most of it. It hadn't been desert dust but the damn adrenaline that had left his mouth and throat dry as cardboard. Now they felt like *wet* cardboard, but still, it was a step up.

"Better?"

He nodded.

"Good. Now tell me what's wrong."

"What's *wrong*?" Without warning, he was angry again. He didn't want to be angry and that fact just pissed him off more, pushed him back to his feet. His voice rose. "You were in Anchorage and I was in Afghanistan. That's what's *wrong*."

She just shrugged, as if they'd been talking about the weather. As if he hadn't been all but shouting at her. "I figured that out when you yelled at someone I couldn't see to *get down*. I'm not asking about that. I'm talking about right now. I want to know why you've got this hang-dog attitude going on. We had a great day together and now you won't even look at me."

A dozen emotions rampaged through his brain, but it was the anger again that won out, snapping his head around so he was eye to eye with her. "You're too smart and too beautiful to be hanging around with somebody who's messed up. You don't need a head case, so get out of my way."

He got up and took a step toward the door but didn't get any further. Those gorgeous gray eyes leveled a look that could have pinned him to the nearest wall.

"First of all, I'll decide what I need and what I want, and I'm right where I want to be," she said. "Second of all, if you're feeling guilty or embarrassed or some crap like that, you can just drop it right now."

He stared at her. It wasn't the reaction he'd been expecting and he didn't have a clue how to respond.

"And third, everybody's messed up about something,"

she continued. "Trust me on that one, I'm an anthropologist. What counts is how you handle it and what you do with it. And right now, you don't have to do a single damn thing except relax."

His anger fizzled out like firecrackers in the rain. He unclenched his fists—he hadn't even known he'd closed them—and sat down on the bed again.

She waited until he'd taken a few breaths. "Is it okay if I sit with you? Touch you?"

"Sure." The raspiness of his voice had him drinking the rest of the water.

Again, she did the unexpected. No arm around the shoulder, no *there, there*. Instead, she settled in close to him and took his hand in both of hers, rested her cheek on his shoulder as if he was the one comforting her. It steadied him as nothing else had, brought him fully back to himself. He leaned his face so he could smell her hair and ended up nuzzling it.

"I have a brilliant idea," she said. "Why don't I dial up a pizza, and we'll just lie down and take a break until it gets here."

Could it really be that easy? "Guess you're relieved you don't have to go on a date with me, huh?"

She laughed. "Not as relieved as I might have been a day or two ago. I'll take a rain check on it, okay? Even though you blackmailed me into going out with you in the first place"—she punctuated that by poking him in the side—"I hereby solemnly swear to accompany you on another date."

"A dress-up date?" He eyed her speculatively, as he rubbed the spot between his ribs where she'd drilled him with her finger.

"Now you're pushing it. Jeans and a really nice shirt. Maybe earrings, but that's as far as I'll go."

He chuckled, then coughed because his throat was still rough. "Done."

"So, Mr. Food Snob, what about that pizza? Or there's room service—I think I saw a menu here somewhere. We've got cable and Pay-Per-View, so we can hole up for as long as we like if somebody delivers chow. Jeez, I haven't watched television in months. Is *Castle* still on?"

"I think so—there're summer reruns on Channel 4 for sure." A quiet night of TV sounded pretty damn good at the moment, although he'd usually be watching World Extreme Cagefighting. "But if we're going to order pizza, it has to be *good* pizza. Call up Esposito's on the corner."

"Hey, all pizza is good pizza." She laughed and crossed the room to the desk, leaned over and began thumbing through the phonebook. He allowed his gaze to slide over her shapely butt. A lot of people said that sex was like pizza, but he didn't quite agree. In his book there was junk food sex and there was gourmet sex (and would Kenzie tease him or be insulted if she knew he ranked sex like he rated food?). It was true, though. Junk food sex was what you had with partners you weren't particularly attached to. Quick, simple, even fun, but it didn't stay with you, nourish you, *change* you. Gourmet sex was something you had with somebody you loved. You savored it, reveled in it, wholeheartedly indulged in it, gave your all into creating it. It filled you up and fed you, heart and soul. You could build on it, and you couldn't help but grow. You wanted to.

At least he had it figured that way. And he knew that sex with Mackenzie Macleod would definitely never be the fries and burger kind. Not for him.

Of course, it was a helluva long way between shopping and sex, and he'd just had a major meltdown before they'd even gotten around to an official date. But she was still here and she didn't hate him and that was amazing.

He lay back on the bed and closed his eyes.

Anya liked the old wolf. He knew lots of games and was as much fun to play with as Kenzie, even if he insisted it was time for her to go to bed. She didn't understand why grownups made it bedtime when it wasn't even dark yet, but her mom had done that too. To her surprise, though, Stanton stretched out beside her. She snuggled up against the silvery fur and sighed, wondering if this was what it was like to have a dad. She didn't remember hers much— she'd been very little when he died. But he'd told her stories; she recalled that much even if she couldn't remember what they were about. Her mom read books to her sometimes and Anya had a whole shelf of storybooks in her room. She could read them herself now, but it was always more fun to hear them. Josh had been really good at stories but he'd gone with Kenzie to the city. She missed them both, missed her mom. Why did everyone have to go away?

Without thinking, she wished *really hard* that she could hear a bedtime story now.

Once upon a time there were three billy goats . . . Stanton's deep gravelly voice spoke in her mind.

She jumped up and looked at him. Had he heard her? She couldn't remember putting up the *gate* as her mother had called it. Anya thought of it more like a little door inside her head, a pink one. She slammed it tight now, and pictured locking it with all kinds of bolts and chains. As she scrutinized the old wolf with narrowed eyes, he gave her a long, slow wink.

The billy goats were brothers, and their name was Gruff.

She didn't know what to do. She wasn't supposed to talk to strangers, not even strange wolves, but what was she supposed to do if she *had*? What came next? Should she run? Hide? She was so tired of being afraid all the time, of never talking to anyone. Even if mindspeech was harder work than talking with your mouth, it would be awfully nice to talk to somebody. Just for a little while . . .

One day the three billy goats named Gruff discovered they'd eaten up all the grass in their meadow.

What were their names?

Stanton looked surprised for a moment, but quickly responded. *I told you. It's Gruff. They're the three billy goats Gruff.*

Yeah but that's their last name. What're their other names?

Well—the big one's name was Josh, and the medium-size one was Kenzie, and the littlest one was Anya.

She giggled. Only it didn't come out that way—it was hard to laugh when you were a wolf. It was more like a whuffing sound in her throat. He whuffed right back and Anya snuggled up again and rested her head on his front leg.

Josh and Kenzie and Anya Gruff decided they had to travel to the next hill where there was lots of grass to make them grow fat and strong. But to get there, they had to pass by the terrible troll who lived under the bridge. . . .

Chapter Thirteen

Josh had to admit that watching television had never been so much fun.

Propped up by all the pillows from his room as well as hers, they sat side by side on the bed with two boxes between them containing four different styles of pizza. Josh was surprised at how much he really *was* able to relax, and knew it was mostly because of Kenzie. Sure, he'd learned self-calming techniques years ago, but they were nothing compared with the easy acceptance she gave him and her refusal to let him indulge in feeling *less than*.

Saturday Night Live had just ended when the northern sun finally dipped below the horizon on the other side of the hotel. The entire sky in every direction was painted with brilliant sunset colors, which proved more interesting than late night talk shows. Kenzie grabbed the remote and flipped off the TV.

"The better to see the sunset with," she explained.

"I'll bet it's all part of your master plan to jump my bod."

"Sure. Step one was to stuff you full of pizza so you couldn't run away." She held her middle. "But I should never have let you order."

"It was part of my own master plan to turn *your* plan back on itself by making sure you couldn't move either."

"Interesting defense. We might be stuck here for days."

They watched a jet climb to clear the mountains, a silvery streak against the orange and pink sky. It seemed as good a time as any to ask the question that had bothered him all night.

"So the big shapeshifter we met at the museum—are you two an item?"

She stared at him for a moment, then put a hand to her head. "Damn, that's spooky. I forgot you'd be able to tell what he was." She blew out a breath. "As for Nate, no, we're not together. We tried that back in our college days and it didn't work. He's more like a little brother."

"He sure as hell didn't act like one." Josh was surprised by the hint of a growl that crept into his voice.

"I know. He'd definitely like more than a friendship. I've told him many times it's not going to happen. He sulks for a while, then comes back and asks me for favors like always."

Josh relaxed then. At least he wouldn't have to compete with one of her own kind. "So what are you digging for in Chistochina? Anything special?"

She sighed. "An end to prejudice."

"Against the Ahtna?"

"No."

He waited but she didn't say anything more. The darkening sky was reflected in her serious gray eyes as she stared out at the mountains, and he wondered what those eyes had seen, what was the source of the tightly-held pain in them. "I'll show you mine if you show me yours," he said suddenly.

"What?"

"You have a story behind this quest of yours. I'd like to hear it. I'll trade you, my story for yours."

"You don't need to do that. I don't have anything to share."

"You mean you don't *want* to share."

"Okay, I don't have anything that I *want* to share. Same difference."

"What if I wanted to share my story anyway? Would you listen?" He was really going out on a limb here.

Kenzie turned and studied his face. He had no idea what she saw there, but it must have satisfied her. "Well, of course I would listen. Do you really want to tell me, or are you just trying to barter with me?"

For a split second he was caught—and then awareness dawned. He did want to tell her. He wanted her to know everything. Well, what the hell . . . he'd already had a full meltdown right in front of her. What could it hurt to have her know the story behind it?

"It was one of my last missions. I'd been flying for Task Force Falcon for five years. . . ." The words emerged slowly at first, as if he had to pull them out one by one. Gradually, however, they gained momentum as Kenzie's genuine interest prodded him on, coupled with his own desire to have her know this part of him, to lay it bare and almost dare her to look at it. But then the story took on its own life, because it *was* alive and couldn't be killed, and he could no more stop telling it than he could stop a train with his bare hands.

When it was done, he was wrung out but at least he didn't have to brace for Kenzie's reaction. Somewhere during the telling, the pizza boxes had disappeared and she had curled up against him with her head on his shoulder, one arm thrown across him and a hand clasping his. She said nothing, simply allowed her closeness to speak for her. He closed his eyes and rested his cheek on her dark wayward hair, letting the scent of it wash away the last vestiges of the unwelcome memories. It was so blessedly ordinary, so welcome to be just a couple cuddling close as a few stars poked bright holes in the deep twilight. They lay together like that for a long time as a big round moon rose over the mountains, and Josh wondered if he had ever felt such a perfect peace. He pressed his lips to her forehead.

"I was seven when the hunters came to our forest."

He brushed his lips over her forehead again. "You don't have to tell me anything."

"What if I want to?"

"Then I promise to shut up and listen. You were seven?"

She nodded and told him what he realized she hadn't told anyone. He couldn't say how he knew, just that he'd heard plenty of vets relate their stories at group, and there was always a rawness to the first telling. Her family knew what had happened to her, of course, but that didn't necessarily make it easier for her. She'd been a child, she'd been scared out of her mind, and everyone would have been focused on soothing her—and that probably meant *never bringing up the subject again.* How could they know that some things needed to be opened not just once, but again and again like an infected wound until all the poison had drained away? A staff sergeant had made that analogy to him, and it had helped him to finally take the first and most difficult step—talking about it.

He sure as hell hadn't enjoyed it. He didn't like it the next time either, or any of the times he'd related the story, including tonight when he'd told Kenzie. But each and every time, it had eased something inside him and he gained a few more millimeters of breathing space.

What surprised him the most was that Kenzie's experience was not so very different from his. Did Changelings get PTSD too? Did they process trauma differently? If they aged more slowly than humans, maybe they recovered from some types of stress more slowly than humans. And she'd been a child at the time—wouldn't the whole experience be more intense if you were a just a kid? He didn't know how old Kenzie really was, but he had some notion of history and was pretty damn sure that the wholesale slaughter of wolves hadn't been popular in any country he knew of for quite a while.

"Why did it take so long for your family to find you? Don't shapeshifters have some kind of homing system? And why were you alone?"

"It wasn't planned that way. My parents hid Carly and me in the loft of the barn and told us to stay put. The boys were helping our uncle shear sheep, over on the western edge of the forest. So my folks went to get them and scout things out. But dogs came sniffing around and some hunters followed them. They set fire to our house . . . we didn't understand why, couldn't imagine why anyone would do that. But that's when Carly grabbed me and we ran away. We got separated pretty quickly, though. She was trying to lead the hunters away from me, because she was faster. But more hunters came.

"As for the rest, I asked Culley about it a few years later. Well—I didn't exactly ask. I was fifteen and we were arguing. I accused him of taking too long to rescue me because he was *just plain mean*. You know, typical brother and sister crap."

He nodded. "Believe me, I know."

"Anyway, Culley told me what had been going on. That there weren't just a few hunters, but a big party of them organized by some wealthy landowners to drive the wolves out of the forest once and for all. There were several packs of dogs, and a lot of them weren't afraid of Changelings like most dogs are. Some of the Changelings stayed in human form, thinking they'd be safe. And—they weren't."

She fell silent and Josh didn't expect her to say any more. He could guess what had happened next. History was replete with examples of people being killed on the slightest suspicion of being werewolves.

"There was such a lot of confusion, friends and family being chased down, others trying to help them. My uncle and aunt, and both my cousins—they were cornered by an enormous pack of dogs, almost a hundred. The four of them fought back but they were overwhelmed." She rubbed an eye with the heel of her hand. "Sadie was my age. We used to play together.

"Anyway, James and Culley figured out where I was, but they were busy keeping the hunters away from me—the boys were scared that I'd be shot or given to the dogs before they could get me out. My brothers did a good job too because no humans ever came near the pit, at least not until after I was freed."

"Jesus. That was a helluva lot for anyone to go through, never mind a child. And what about Anya?" Josh asked. "You must have seen yourself in her right from the get-go."

"Yeah. Yeah I did. And I'll bet you're having flashbacks because of her too, a child in distress, a little girl that needs your help."

He nodded.

"It's kind of strange, don't you think? That this little girl should be such a powerful catalyst, that her situation triggers the most difficult memories for both of us?"

"Maybe that's why we're meant to help her."

"You think so?"

"Hey, it's natural karma. Circle of life or some such

thing. If my Gramma Kishegwet was here, she'd say it was because it'll help us both if we help Anya."

Kenzie looked up at him and smiled. "I like that. I like that a lot."

He took a chance then. "So what are you looking for, really, in that dig of yours?" Intuition told him it was related to what had happened to her although he couldn't imagine how.

Her smile faded, and she was quiet for so long that he wasn't sure she was going to answer him. "Changelings can't remain hidden forever, Josh," she said at last. "Science is moving forward in leaps and bounds. DNA testing has become so sophisticated, and everyone and their dog has a cell phone camera. It's like a net drawing tighter and tighter." She shivered and he rubbed his hand up and down her arm. "I know that it's natural for humans to be repelled by things that are different, that they see as alien. *Other.*"

"Not everyone. Not all humans."

"It's an instinctive response, a survival mechanism. Human beings were suspicious of strangers in the Pleistocene and they're suspicious now."

"Maybe that's their first response. But we can choose our actions. We can decide to be tolerant, to accept the new."

"Exactly. It's a conscious decision. Some people can make that decision easily and some aren't interested in even trying."

"Okay, so you're worried because shapeshifters are going to have to come out of the closet one of these days. Or be outed by science."

"Yes. And that's why I have to find the evidence before that happens. I have to be able to show that we're not so different. That we're not alien and other, but that we were once the same."

"The Ahtna legends? You started to tell me about them at the museum, that men and beasts were equal or something. And they knew about Changelings."

"It's more than that. The Ahtna believed that every person was able to shapeshift. Everyone, not just their family and their tribe, but *every human being had the capacity to change into an animal form and back again.* Think about it—shapeshifting is present in the ancient lore of almost every culture in the world. Why is that?"

"You think it might be true?"

She nodded ever so slightly, her fingers pressed across her lips as if she was afraid of what she was revealing. "My instincts tell me it is. But I have to prove it. I have to find that point in time where a few humans discovered they could become wolves at will. Right now, the genes are still present in every human being, but inactive unless saliva from a Changeling bite awakens them. How did the first Changeling come about then? Was it a spontaneous shift? A mutation? An attribute like that would be sure to improve the odds of survival. So why doesn't everyone have the ability to change their form now?"

"I'd like to know the answer to that one. None of my people's stories tell about being able to shapeshift. We only get to be friends with those who do. I feel deprived."

"Hey, this is serious." She pulled back as if offended, but allowed him to gather her close to him again.

"I *know* it's serious. And I can see this means a lot to you. You want to establish a solid link to the human race before the scientific world learns that shapeshifters exist."

"I've got to. If science figures out Changelings are real, they'll also figure out how to identify us. There'll be no hiding, no choice about whether to reveal ourselves or not. It'll be so much better if we're able to point to common ancestors, common roots, before humans panic and assume that the Changelings living among them are alien monsters."

It dawned on him then, her real goal. "You're trying to stop history from repeating itself."

Her eyes were solemn. "I remember what it was like when humans were at war with *werewolves*. I have to prevent that from ever happening again."

"That's a tall order," he said, even though he also knew that if anyone could pull it off, it would be Kenzie Macleod. "And a helluva lot to take on all by yourself."

She didn't reply but suddenly he could see the toll that her quest had taken on her. Sure, she was brave and strong and smart. She was also a woman, and lonely.

He slid his hand up from the small of her back to the nape of her neck and applied the gentlest of pressure until her lips were barely brushing his.

"After all that emotional work, I think a little physical therapy is in order."

"It's not a good idea."

"Because you're shy?"

"Because you're human."

"You keep pointing that out. For someone who wants to do away with prejudice, you're pretty adamant about not getting too cozy with me because of my species. What are you afraid of?"

"I'm not afraid of *you*, that's for sure."

"Prove it," he murmured against her lips and kissed her.

It was dark when Anya woke up, and the moon floated just above the trees like a big golden balloon. She should have been cold but Stanton's tail was wrapped around her, a thick and furry blanket that kept away the chill. She automatically looked toward Kenzie's tent, but it was missing because of those stupid bears. Almost everything was gone now. Stanton had burned all the wrecked things that could be burned, and Josh and Kenzie had taken the rest with them. In the moonlight, Anya could make out the bright white feathers scattered like snow in the grass and in the bushes from Kenzie's ugly brown sleeping bag. Kenzie was going to buy another sleeping bag in the city. Anya hoped she'd choose a pink one.

She yawned and stretched and snuggled back against the old wolf. Kenzie had asked her to come to the city with her, but Anya would have had to change back into a girl. That's when she'd run away like a big silly and hidden under the devil's club bush. She wasn't supposed to change. Her mother had said that the wolf would keep her safe, safe until her mother came back. . . .

Kenzie had promised to bring her a present though. A surprise. That would be okay, wouldn't it? Anya wished she'd come back soon. And Josh. She missed him too.

At least Stanton was nice—and she'd decided he was more like a grampa than a dad. She didn't have one of those either but the old wolf just seemed like what she imagined a grampa would be like. He was just a little bit cranky when she jumped on his head while he was *resting his eyes*, but he was kind to her. He was a good hunter too—they'd eaten deer last night, Anya's favorite. And he'd told her three whole stories before she fell asleep.

She was just dozing off again when Stanton's head suddenly shot up, his ears swiveling to listen. A moment later she heard it too. Engines. Not from the road below but from the forest behind them. She jumped to her feet, quivering.

Let's move away from the campsite. Stanton led the way

quickly, soundlessly, into the deep brush. He picked a narrow game trail and followed it, down the hill toward Kenzie's dig. Strangely, he seemed to be heading straight for the sound of the engines. They were louder now, coming toward them, and she whimpered just a little.

Okay Anya, duck down here with me. He'd found a spot beneath a fallen tree. *They're going to go right by us. It'll be close, but they won't see us if we keep still.*

He squeezed into the hollow spot and she burrowed quickly between his front paws and hid there, afraid to look. The ATVs went hurtling by in an earsplitting blast of sound and vibration. In the midst of it, Stanton's voice in her head was surprised. *I'll be damned. They're white.*

What's white?

The ATVs.

She shivered and pressed closer. *They're the ones that took my mom.*

There was no resisting Josh's talented mouth. Kenzie sank into the kiss as smoothly as a swimmer slides below the surface of the water, and the wolf within her seemed to sigh. In fact, her alter ego was as fully present as her human self, as if it was watching everything through her eyes, feeling everything through her skin. She was two beings at once, something which had never happened before, and yet she had no time to wonder at the oddity of her dual awareness. Because she wanted Josh, and that knowledge was both thrilling and freeing. She *wanted* him, and everything about him—his touch, his scent, his arousal pressing against the denim of his jeans—said he wanted her too.

She released the breath she'd been holding as Birkie's words about being *open to possibilities* once again ran through her mind. Then and there Kenzie decided she would *have* what she wanted.

Josh's strong hands on her were tender. And cool. A Changeling's body temperature was much higher than a human's, and right now she was burning up, but not with fever. She found herself craving the gliss of his hands, soothed by their coolness as much as she was aroused by their caresses.

The darkened sky cradled a buttery moon, glimmering between the mountain peaks yet outshining the city lights. Moonlight pooled in the center of the wide bed and Josh knelt in it, drew her up to her knees as well—then turned her as smoothly as if they were dancing so her back was against him. One powerful arm cradled her close enough that she could feel his erection pulsing against her crease despite their clothing. His other hand stroked her from shoulder to thigh.

"I've been wanting to do this," he murmured, and slowly, thoroughly kissed the nape of her neck. Exquisite sensation rocketed through her and her breasts tightened almost to the point of pain. As if he knew, he cradled them in his hands and softly thumbed the nipples. Her clothing felt cumbersome, hot, heavy, and very much in the way. She wanted to pull off the restraining fabric, but he had caged her with his arms and simply continued to place slow, deliberate kisses on the back of her neck. Kenzie had never thought of that spot as particularly erotic, but her body quivered like a taut wire. The new thong she was wearing was already soaked through with sheer anticipation.

He worked his way over to the side of her neck, bringing a whole new array of sensations. Her earlobe was seized in gentle teeth and she could swear that an electrical current suddenly connected every part of her to her ultra-sensitive core. Another touch like *that* and she was sure to start vibrating like struck crystal. . . .

Time to turn things around. She'd accepted Josh's lead, luxuriated in his touch, but now she wanted to do a little *touching* of her own. Her wolf was on board with that notion and she used the tiniest bit of its strength to swivel within Josh's powerful arms so she faced him. There was fire in his obsidian eyes, as if a volcano had awakened in the heart of the earth—yet it was tempered with something both softer and stronger at the same time. He released her and waited. She shook off the "deer in the headlights" look she was certain was on her face, then lowered her eyes and focused on his broad chest as if there were nothing else in the whole world.

As if his feelings for her hadn't been plainly written in his gaze.

Kenzie unbuttoned Josh's shirt, slowly, deliberately, trying to follow the unhurried pace he'd set, and finding it increasingly tough to resist her rising desire to simply tear his clothes off with her teeth. She tried to study his body as she revealed it, when every instinct was urging her to shove him to the floor and ride him hard. *Then it'd be over too quick, you idiot.* That thought helped her rein herself in somewhat. At least part of her wanted this to last as long as possible. . . .

She pushed his shirt from his shoulders and he shrugged it the rest of the way off. Her hands trembled a little as they roamed freely over his bare chest, hard with muscle beneath the smooth skin. She traced over his biceps with her fingertips, surprised that he was as powerfully built as any Changeling. And what she couldn't see was strong too, a sense of power, an energy that seemed to radiate up through him from somewhere deep in the earth's very core. She'd never felt anything like it.

Never met anyone like Josh Talarkoteen.

She kissed her way along his solid jawline and down his throat, from his collarbone to his nipples, then applied her teeth lightly to them. Heard him hiss in a breath with pleasure and she sternly reminded herself again that she need not hurry. She flipped open his jeans casually, as if she had all the time in the world . . . except the rising want within her had reached nearly unbearable proportions, and her inner wolf was becoming frantic. Was she in danger of Changing? And why the hell was her lupine self hovering so close anyway? It had never done that before, certainly not when she was, well, *busy*.

Go away, she shouted at it in her head.

Later, it replied. *Need. Now.*

The fact that her wolfen persona had just *spoken* to her stunned Kenzie. It hadn't done so since she was a child, and she paused in confusion. Only when her T-shirt was suddenly pulled over her head did she shake free of the distraction.

The rush of cool air was welcome on her burning skin, and one of Josh's fingers traced the inner edges of her bra. The sleek fabric was the color of merlot and her sensitive hearing could pick up the faint rasp of his fingertips against it. She was *so* thankful she'd worn one of the new ones and left her old bra (the one with one strap held on only by a safety pin—why couldn't the damn bear have eaten *that* one?) in the dressing room trash. New or not, however, she was even more relieved when Josh unhooked it, drawing the satiny material down her arms and away.

Josh pulled her close, pressing her hardened nipples to his skin. Sighing, she circled her arms around his neck, rubbing her breasts over his chest, and was rewarded when he leaned down to nuzzle them. He rolled a nipple gently between his teeth and at the same time squeezed her ass with his strong hands, causing her fingers to clench his hair *hard*.

"Ow," he chuckled.

"Ow, nothing. If you don't help me get my jeans off *right now*, I'm going to have to hurt you," she said through her teeth.

Chapter Fourteen

Josh laughed and tossed her backward onto the pillows, then seized the legs of her jeans and tugged them off without even unzipping them first. Stood back a moment in sheer appreciation. His gaze traveled up her long, long legs to her elegant vee and curvy hips, trailed over her belly to full breasts pleasingly draped with the moon's creamy light. With her tousled hair, she seemed more like a painting he'd once seen of a Roman goddess, the huntress that ruled the moon and all wild creatures, than a flesh and blood woman.

His own flesh and blood was satisfied she was real, however, and shucking his jeans was an enormous relief. His body was strung tight with arousal, his cock hard and heavy, but he tried to ignore it. After all, a goddess should be worshipped.

Thoroughly.

Josh slid his hands under her hips, pressing her legs apart with his shoulders. Slowly he kissed Kenzie's soft inner thighs, giving them the same attention he'd given her graceful neck. Soft, openmouthed kisses from each knee all the way up to the glistening triangle of her sex. Heat radiated from her skin wherever he touched her, not the parching heat he'd known in the Afghan summers but the welcoming heat of a campfire. Soothing, even healing. He dipped his head and ran a tongue along the crease of her leg, feeling her jump in his palms. He squeezed her shapely ass and licked again, parting her this time, seeking her hidden pearl.

The urgent little moan she made had his balls high and tight, as he indulged in tasting her, the rocking of her hips rubbing her clit along his questing tongue. The scent of her called to him as the taste of her made him crave more.

Instead he gave more, slipping a finger inside her, then two, stroking her soft, wet heat as he worked her with his tongue. Held her tight with an arm around her hips as she bucked frantically, as she was caught between trying to escape the intensity and wanting even more. He drove her now, pushed her on, drank his fill as he urged her to the very brink—and over.

Josh sat back and stroked his cock with his fingertips, thinking Kenzie might want a moment to regroup. Instead she glided up beside him and replaced his hand with hers. She squeezed him slowly, one finger at a time, from base to tip—*omigod, yes*—as her lips met his, and her kisses were hungry and hot. Suddenly he was consumed with need, burning up with it. Damn, if he didn't take her hard and fast, he was going to spontaneously *combust*.

That was when she shoved him backward, still holding his cock like a throttle and milking it with her strong fingers. Josh caught a glimpse of her silvery gray eyes in the moonlight and saw something feral in them. He tried to suck in a breath but all the damn air in the room disappeared as she settled over him, as wet heat came in contact with—

She slid down him and he nearly came off the bed. Then she readjusted herself, squeezing his cock with her inner muscles, repeating the milking motions her fingers had been making. Slowly she began to ride him in long smooth strokes, until he could feel his eyes roll back in his head. The pleasure was drawn out to the point of insanity. And then he went a little insane, he must have. Kenzie was strong but he reared up and flipped her over, following her down and sinking his cock deep. Something fell from his lips, not even words but a wild and primal sound as he pounded into her heat and she urged him on.

Sound and sight disappeared as the orgasm took him over, as powerful waves of sensation passed through him like a tsunami passes through the deep ocean, and for a brief instant he could feel them ripple through Kenzie as well. As he sank bonelessly beside her, his last act before oblivion was to throw an arm and a leg over her and gather her tightly to his heart.

The white ATVs would have been easy to see even if there hadn't been a full moon. Out in the open like this, there was little true dark in an Alaskan summer night—the sky retained its deep twilight glow until dawn. The vehicles rolled with earsplitting precision past Kenzie's dig and on up the rise, finally coming to a halt in the middle of the destroyed camp. Stanton welcomed the sudden quiet as he counted six machines, ten riders, and one large empty kennel mounted on a trailer. The riders dismounted and began casting over the ground, dressed alike in camo coveralls and armed with bulky-looking rifles—tranq guns most likely. There was no mistaking the night vision goggles, which would amplify the moonlight into something approaching daytime sight for the humans.

None of that was cause for concern. Any Changeling worth his salt could elude human hunters. But the men hadn't come alone. Their ATVs were trailed by several massive dogs, of a type Stanton had seen only a few times in his veterinary practice and once in the IBC compound: Anatolian Shepherds. Big, powerful, and totally fearless, these animals were a favorite in many parts of the world among farmers with flocks to protect. Two or three Anatolians could do a lot of damage to a wolf pack—the dogs were bigger than many wolves and heavily muscled—and Stanton had a sinking feeling they might not run from a Changeling either.

He had to get Anya out of here *now*.

The little wolf shivered beneath his chin and he licked the top of her head to comfort her as he quickly considered which direction they should go. There was no room for mistakes. North, the direction the searchers had come from, was out of the question. And right now the searchers had split into three teams, beating the bushes west and south of Kenzie's camp. That left east—which meant he'd have to leave the bluff and lead Anya down to the river flats. There was thick cover along the water and, if they could just move quickly enough, maybe no one would see them or pick up their trail until they were too far away to follow.

Stay close behind me, Kiddo. He crept from their hiding spot, flattening his body as much as possible. Wished his coat was inky black again, as it had been in his youth. Tough to blend into the shadows when his damn fur was silver, and the bright moonlight would reflect off it like snow.

As he slipped through the thick brush, Stanton could feel the breath from Anya's tiny nose within an inch of his left hind foot. When he stopped at the edge of the embankment, she bumped into his leg and sat down hard. The river below looked oily in the moonlight as it wound its multi-fingered way through hazy clumps of willow and tall grass that grew on endless sandbars. Stanton eyed the steep embankment, noting that probably nothing larger than a mink had ever climbed it here. About thirty feet straight down. A few decades ago, he would simply have jumped. Now? Probably break a damn leg, and no way could little Anya make it.

But there wasn't time to look for an easier way, and it didn't seem that his wolfen form was going to be a lot of help. *Stand back a minute, honey.* His fur rippled as though stirred by a sudden breeze. A moment later, he crouched at the edge of the embankment as a human being. Thanked the powers that be that Changelings brought their clothes with them during transition and he was fully dressed. He tucked his worn T-shirt into his jeans and cinched up the belt as tight as he could, then grabbed the neckline and stretched it out wide with both hands. *Okay honey, you're going to squeeze in here and I'll carry you down.*

In there?

Sure. It's just like a— He almost said *baby carrier* but stopped himself in time. No self-respecting kid wanted to be thought of as a baby. *Like a secret compartment.*

What if I fall? Her voice in his head was small and tight with fear.

You can't fall unless I do, and I'll make sure I'm on the bottom. I'll be like a big fluffy pillow for you, okay?

Pillows are soft. You're too bony to be a pillow.

Better. She still had her sense of humor. *A lumpy pillow beats no pillow at all, Kiddo. Let's go.*

She wriggled in nose first and curled up over his belly, making herself as small as possible. He remembered carry-

ing his own kids like this from time to time, but they'd
been a little younger and more compact. Still, it would
work. Probably.

Stanton made his way over the edge and started down,
instinctively feeling for handholds and toeholds. He might
be an old fart, but his Changeling nature still gave him
more strength than a human to make the climb. The
toughest job was trying not to squish Anya between the
hillside and his body.

For her part, the cub was doing well. She remained still,
curled up tight and quiet. He wondered if she was holding
her breath. His T-shirt was holding up too. It was stretched
nine ways to Sunday, probably permanently, but functioned
well as a sling. Still, he was relieved to make it to the
ground. He extricated Anya and they crept along the wall
of the embankment as snatches of voices drifted down to
them. The dogs were still silent and Stanton hoped that was
a good thing. He remained in his human form for the time
being, heading south past Kenzie's camp high above them.

Suddenly, a deep continuous barking erupted from
somewhere overhead. It wasn't the excited baying of a
hound, but the business-like voice of a guardian, one that
had discovered a threat and was on its way to neutralize it.
The rest joined in. Had the dogs discovered their trail or
simply run across the bears that had wrecked the camp earlier? Stanton hoped it was the latter, but as he rounded a
bend, that slim hope was dashed.

A massive sow grizzly stood directly in their path. One
by one, three young bears as big as their mother emerged
from the brush.

The ripe moon was high above now and tugged Kenzie
awake. She wasn't subject to the lunar call, but she felt it

nonetheless, loved it as all Changelings loved it. Tonight, however, her inner wolf was already sated and it wasn't the moon that gave her such contentment and bliss.

She had a mate. *Holy Jeez*.

There was no doubt now about what her lupine self had been up to—witnessing and affirming a lifetime bond. The knowledge was exhilarating, outrageous and completely terrifying at the same time. Her inner wolf hadn't consulted her one bit, and she should have been more suspicious when it lingered so close to the surface. Maybe she had been, especially when it spoke to her as though it were a completely separate entity. But Josh had been there, and she had *wanted*. Wanted so damn bad that she could no more have walked away than flown.

Sex, as she had known it in the past, would never have satisfied such a soul-deep yearning. But sex with Josh had taken her to a whole different level, involved her entire being in a way she hadn't imagined possible. The thrill of discovery had vied with a fierce joy of something almost like *homecoming*. Josh was still a mystery yet he was familiar in some way she could neither describe nor deny. Was this how Connor had felt when he found Zoey? Or what James experienced when Jillian walked into his life? Kenzie had thought the feeling would be more subtle, perhaps easy to mistake for something else. She hadn't expected it to pulse in her with every breath like a second heart.

An odd thought ran through her head. *If you're close enough to hear the thunder, you're close enough to be struck by lightning.*

She nestled closer to Josh and his arm tightened around her, though he was sound asleep. One leg was thrown over hers. It all felt intimate and familiar and right, but how could it? Wolves didn't question their attraction to a possible mate. Changelings didn't question it much either. *It is or it isn't*, her mother had once said. Yet Kenzie didn't see how this relationship could possibly work, human and Changeling together, didn't even know how strong Josh's feelings for her were. And—

He has no way of knowing what just happened to us.

To me . . .

Omigod. What if it happened only to her and not to him? Her inner wolf was bonded to him now but what truly connected a human? Her anthropology studies were not much help in this area. In fact, Josh had been annoyingly right about one thing. She knew *about* humans but didn't really know them.

Still, she had seen something in his eyes, felt something in his touch that was far more than physical. Because of it, for the first time in her long life, she was daring to trust, daring to be vulnerable. It was flat-out terrifying, and she would have run as far and fast as she could, except for something else that she was experiencing for the first time.

Hope.

Chuffing, the grizzly sow flattened her ears and shook her head from side to side, popping her jaws at Stanton with gunshot-like noises. He knew it meant that she felt threatened, but it was nothing compared to what he was feeling at the moment. She might decide to charge, and there was no way of knowing if it would be a bluff charge and she would stop at the last minute, or an all-out attack. Never taking his eyes off the bear, he backed up one step at a time, using his leg to push along poor Anya, who was half-paralyzed with fright. If he could get a little room, he could call up his inner wolf and any threat by the grizzly could be dealt with. But Anya was too close. It took a lot of

energy to make the transition, and Changelings were efficient at drawing it from their surroundings—so much so
that the immense buildup of static became dangerous to
anyone standing too close. The little wolf would be injured
for sure. For now, all he could do was hope that backing off
would be enough to mollify the mother grizzly.

"Come on, old girl, you don't want to mess with us," he
said in the soothing tones he usually reserved for nervous
patients at his clinic. "We're not going to hurt you or those
fine big cubs of yours. Just move along and let us by, why
don't you?"

For a moment he thought she was going to do just that.
Then the dogs barking on the bluff above became louder
and more ferocious. Stanton realized they'd found the spot
where he and Anya had climbed down, and were racing
back and forth along the edge searching for a way to follow. Christ, it was only a matter of time before he and Anya
were trapped between the dogs and the bears. As it was, the
roar of the dogs was agitating the big female further. She
was slapping the ground now and her mouth was foaming
with saliva, sure signs of an impending charge.

"Anya," he said aloud, and pushed home the message
telepathically as well. Most Changelings had to be in
wolfen form to do that—but then, most weren't as old as
he was. "Listen to me. I need some room, I need you to run
back away from me about ten feet. Can you do that,
honey?"

The little wolf didn't move immediately, and he was
afraid she wasn't going to. Then, hunching low to the
ground, she slowly crept back along the way they'd come.
He never got a chance to make sure she was far enough
away. The bear launched herself with terrifying speed and
Stanton called the Change.

Anya hid under a stand of willow and watched in horror as the grizzly reached the old man within a heartbeat. But a flash of light and a rain of blue sparks erupted and the angry sow was tossed back abruptly onto her rump. The younger bears jumped backward, making whining sounds of distress despite their size as they found themselves suddenly facing a very large silver wolf, its broad head lowered and fangs bared. Anya was surprised too—her mother had told her *never* to Change too close to anyone. She'd never gotten to see what would happen before. The mother bear looked dazed, and it held a paw to its head as if it had a headache.

The big wolf held his ground as the grizzly recovered and flattened her ears at him. Two of her cubs were making short dashes forward. Suddenly Anya heard Stanton's gravelly voice in her head again.

Anya! Get out of here! Run as fast as you can! I'll catch up with you!

She dashed out from under the willows and sprinted away, ducking under bushes and leaping through reeds and standing water. She could hear an awful ruckus behind her, growls and grunts and breaking twigs. Her mother had told her that full-grown Changelings were too strong to be eaten by bears, but Anya wasn't so sure about *old* Changelings like Stanton. And he'd sent her away just like her mother had done. What if he disappeared too?

You'd better not go away!

She was so busy thinking about Stanton and the bears that she nearly ran full-tilt into something else.

Several *somethings* that towered over her and showed very big teeth.

The dogs had found her.

★   ★   ★

Stanton figured he might have fought one bear—*might*, since it had been quite a while since he'd flexed much wolfen muscle—but fighting four of the damn things was asking a little too much of an old fart. The young grizzlies were following their mother's lead now. He ducked one swipe only to be caught by another that tumbled him over and over as if he weighed nothing. Lucky for him that the cubs were inexperienced. With strength like that, if they pursued their advantage, he'd end up looking like Kenzie's tent in no time.

He rolled to his feet and crouched, waiting until they were about to rush him again, then spun and ran east across the river flats. The bears were agitated enough to pursue him, and although grizzlies were capable of outrunning a horse for short distances, he was still a little faster—for the moment at least. His plan was to lead them off, circle around, and get back to Anya.

He should have known. The Copper River and all its tributaries were filled with spawning salmon, and every bear in Alaska was on a riverbank right now. With four bears hard on his ass already, Stanton's nose told him his luck wasn't about to improve. He was coming up fast on yet another grizzly—a boar, and therefore likely to be twice as big as the sow he was trying to leave behind. *Goddammit.* With his pursuers so close behind him, veering off to one side or the other wasn't an option. It was straight ahead or nothing.

Stanton put everything he had into running flat out for the huge dark shape he could now see ahead. Fortunately the business end of the new grizzly was facing away from him. With an enormous leap, he landed on the bear's broad back and was up and over before the surprised creature had time to react. And when it did, it no doubt found four other bears frantically trying to put on the brakes before they ran into it.

A wolf's body was designed for running and built for speed. Until it got too damn old and the joints got a little arthritic. Stanton wanted nothing more than to flop down somewhere and pant openmouthed until his heart rate returned to normal. Instead, he kept going. He gritted his sharp teeth as adrenaline wore off and aches and pains dragged at him. And something else—a hot line of pain now ran from his shoulder to his hip, and he could smell his own blood. Dammit, one or more of those four-inch claws must have connected while they were cuffing him around. He could barely manage a soft lope, but still he pushed himself, determined to find Anya. He called for her in his mind but heard nothing.

Back at the base of the bluff, he nosed the ground, casting back and forth until he found her most recent trail—and where it ended. There, another scent filled his veins with ice water.

Uncle Stanton! Her voice was faint in his mind, but there. She was okay, at least for the moment. He reassured her as best as he could as he ran along the bluff, searching for a place to climb the bank. For the place where the damn dogs must have found their way down. . . .

Chapter Fifteen

Josh pulled his jeans on rather reluctantly. They had made love twice last night and again upon waking. They'd showered together, giggling as elbows were banged and the curtain fell down. He'd be willing to attempt another round of sex, maybe something slow and tender this time, except Kenzie wanted to get back to Anya.

Fair enough. He did too, if the truth be known. Sure, Stanton was an experienced parent but it had to take a lot of energy to keep tabs on a little girl. Even if she was a wolf. In addition to relieving his friend, however, Josh was anxious to continue building a relationship with Anya, hoping to establish trust. All of Stanton's contacts had come up empty. No one knew who she was or where she'd come from. And so all of the answers would have to come from Anya herself. He didn't know how long it would be before she felt comfortable enough to resume her human form, but for now, he'd be happy if she'd just be willing to communicate.

And he'd be *really* happy if the flashbacks quit. Somewhere around dawn he'd opened his eyes to see a little dark-haired girl in a green and red tunic standing by the window. She vanished as he came fully awake, but something about her—well, something besides the fact he was having yet another damn *hot memory*—was different. He lay awake puzzling over it until a naked Kenzie had rolled over and blinked up at him. . . .

Anyway, the dream/vision/hallucination still bothered him, a niggling sense that there was something he should know, something he should see. He chewed it over as he went to check out, only to find that Kenzie had been there ahead of him and paid the bill for both rooms. *Damned efficient woman.* He resolved to fuel up the truck and pay for breakfast as he returned to Kenzie's room.

"Can you talk to them anytime?" he asked her.

Kenzie was rubbing her hair with a towel and looked up, baffled. "What?"

"Can you talk to Anya and Stanton anytime?"

"Like now?"

"Yeah, like right now."

"No. It doesn't work like that. Most Changelings can communicate telepathically only as wolves, you know. Connor and I can both manage it in human form, but he's way better at it. I'd have to be a lot closer—at least within a few miles. Right now we're too far away from camp, even if I was on four feet."

"That's too bad. Cool that you have the ability, of course, but too bad we have to wait."

"Is something wrong?"

"No, just wondered how things were going, that's all." The way he figured it, the sooner he helped Anya get back where she belonged, the sooner he'd stop having the damn flashbacks. At least he hoped she was the trigger of all this—after all, he'd had the first major flashback at Kenzie's camp. But what about during the flyby of the IBC compound? Or the museum incident—God, that one had been a *bitch*. And now the dream. They just didn't fit a pattern. Not that he could see, at least. His Gramma Kishegwet said there were patterns to everything but this one made no sense to him.

He watched Kenzie run her fingers through her damp wavy hair and smiled at her. That was all the grooming she was likely to do, and she still looked hot enough to melt a glacier.

"Why didn't you run screaming down the street?" he asked.

"Somebody had hold of me in the shower."

He flashed a grin. He'd like to have hold of her again too. . . . "No, I mean yesterday. When I had the flashback. You didn't freak out."

Kenzie shrugged as she shoved things into a bag. "Maybe because I've seen it before. One of the best archaeologists I've ever worked with, Magdi Ahmed, was at the Temple of Queen Hatshepsut in Egypt's Valley of the Kings. In 1997."

Ninety-seven . . . "Luxor?" Josh guessed.

She nodded. "Six terrorists opened fire on unarmed tourists. They gutted some and beheaded others. Over sixty people were killed and I don't know how many were wounded. Magdi was struck by three bullets, but worse than that, she saw it all."

He understood perfectly. The inner wounds could be far worse.

"Magdi left Egypt after that. Never went back. I worked with her on a project in Monte Verde, Chile, for three years, and she still suffered from post-traumatic stress disorder after all this time. She'd have nightmares. Bad ones where she'd start screaming and it took forever to wake her up, bring her out of it. Twice while we were on a dig, she just zoned out on me. Couldn't see me, couldn't hear me. She was terrified. Started yelling things in Egyptian and ran away."

"Flashbacks. Like mine." And damn depressing to think the poor woman was still having them after so much time had passed.

"Magdi had warned me ahead of time that she sometimes got them so I was able to just wait it out and make sure she was safe. She'd get so depressed afterward though."

"Of course she did. You think you're done with that shit, and then *kabam*, it happens again. I hadn't had an incident in years until I met up with Anya."

"Magdi said they didn't happen to her very often anymore. Not unless there was a trigger, something that reminded her. Monte Verde isn't much to look at, just some sandy banks along a creek surrounded by hills and trees, but it's completely different from Luxor. It didn't look the same or even smell the same—I mean, the artifacts are in a peat bog, not a desert. We finally figured out what the trigger was. The sound that one of the workers was making with his hammer was just like the ping of bullets hitting stone at Luxor. We got the man to use a different tool, which changed the tone and that was it. The trigger was gone and Magdi didn't have another episode. So maybe your flashbacks will go away again once we figure out where Anya belongs."

"I sure as hell hope so. Hate to think you might have to chase me through museums on a regular basis."

"Hey." She wandered up to him with swaying hips and seized his shirt collar with both hands. Pulled his head down and kissed him long and slow. "Maybe I'd *like* to chase you on a regular basis."

"Only if I get to chase you sometimes too."

"Deal."

They stood for a few moments, just holding each other. Finally Josh said, "Okay, you have to choose, sex or breakfast."

"What do you mean?"

"Either we go for breakfast right now or we stop and have sex again. You feel just too damn good to me."

She backed out of his arms hastily. "Breakfast. Definitely breakfast because I'm starving." Kenzie made her way to the door and paused on the threshold. "But once I'm refueled, I'll just bet there's dozens of spots on the way back to camp where we could pull off and have a little fun." She waggled her brows.

He knew there was a goofy grin on his face but there was nothing he could do to wipe it off. Didn't even want to. "Well then, if it's refueling you need, I know where the biggest Alaskan breakfast in the state is served."

Josh hadn't been kidding about the breakfast. Their plates were laden with wild blueberries, reindeer sausage, and sourdough pancakes, and afterward, Kenzie was certain she wouldn't have to eat again for the rest of the summer. Certainly not during the drive back. But by the time they were coming up on Glennallen, she found she had an appetite for something else. She turned off the highway and followed the tree-lined lane to the log house.

It was only a matter of minutes before clothing was flying across the guest room.

Happily naked, Kenzie perched on the very edge of the bed. She could feel the energy of the vibrant colors of the quilt through her skin, but most of her attention was on

Josh. The window was behind him, the sun illuminating his powerful body. He had no uniform, no weapons—in fact, he was as naked as she was—yet there was no mistaking his warrior's build and ready stance. His energy was as calm as ever, grounded and centered, but she could sense clearly that this man would be tough to catch off guard.

And didn't that just sound like a challenge?

As he approached and leaned in to kiss her, she succeeded in surprising him by cupping his tightened balls, caressing their taut velvet with her fingertips. He froze in place as she ducked her head and flicked her tongue experimentally over the head of his cock, tasting, savoring. Lapped at its hypersensitive underside and saw his stomach muscles twitch. Satisfied, Kenzie smiled against the smooth broad tip before licking her lips and sliding them over it.

Her wolf was still hovering in the background but it had made no further move to be involved since the night before, and she ignored it now. *This* moment was all hers. It was Josh's fingers tangled in *her* hair now, his breath hissing between his teeth . . .

Until he seized her wrists and pulled away, drawing her to her feet. Anticipation throbbed through her. Already she was oh-so-wet, needing him, wanting him, now, now, *now*, but her hands were captive. Seeking relief, she parted her legs and rubbed her slick clit hard against his thigh.

A moan escaped them both and he seized her hips, positioning himself just so—and drove his cock upward. She gasped and gripped his shoulders for balance, reveling in the glorious sensation of it as he took her standing up, lifting her to her toes with each powerful thrust. *Yes, yes, omigod yes.* Relentlessly he pushed her pleasure higher and higher, faster and faster, until she peaked when he did.

They clung to each other like prizefighters at the end of a bout, their muscles gone lax and their bodies languid from pure pleasure. Staggering to the bed, they collapsed in a fit of laughter and didn't move for half an hour.

Whereupon she surprised him all over again. . . .

They'd barely gotten dressed and into the truck before Josh's cell phone rang. He answered it and winced. "Where? Is everyone okay?" He gave Kenzie an apologetic look as he listened to the caller. "On my way. I'm just in Glennallen so it'll only be a few minutes."

"Duty calls?" asked Kenzie.

Why the hell did I answer the phone? "I know I'm supposed to be off but a mother moose has treed some sport fishermen from California across from Tazlina. That's about five miles south of the turnoff."

"Tazlina? How do tourists hear about a place like that? I'm sure that's not even on my map."

"Are you kidding? I had a buddy who was addicted to fly-fishing. He'd go anywhere to fish, even brought his damn rod and reel all the way to Afghanistan *just in case.* Tazlina's well known in fishing circles for its red salmon run. Or *sockeye*, if you're a cheechako. That's a—"

"*Greenhorn*, I know, and I'm not one. Anyway, sounds like you're busy so I think I should drop you at your office so you can get your truck. I'd like to get to camp and start getting set up."

"That'll work fine. I'll follow as quick as I—oh, no. No, no, *no.*" Josh groaned as the Fish and Game office came into sight. His truck sat out front listing drunkenly to starboard with two flats on the righthand side. The two that *hadn't* gone flat on him the day he first met Kenzie.

"Wow. Do you always get two flats in one day?" she asked. "Guess we better take the tires to the garage or something."

"No, drop *me* at the garage and I'll get Frank to send somebody over with some tires. I'll get a loaner from him and go save the tourists. You go ahead and I'll follow along shortly."

Kenzie looked hesitant, but then nodded. "Okay, but only because it's getting late in the day and I'd like to get set up before dark."

"I'll be there soon to pick up Stanton. Hey, uh—"

"What?"

"Don't give the kid all her presents till I get there, okay?" He didn't want to miss seeing how Anya reacted to the gifts they'd gotten for her.

"I'll save some, don't worry. We went a little overboard so there's plenty. Geez, we're probably going to spoil her."

"Naw, she'll be fine. The kid could use a little spoiling."

Kenzie grinned at him and the short goodbye kiss he'd intended stretched out to something more epic, like they were being separated for years rather than an hour or so. He even entertained the notion of taking the big bear pelt off the office wall and laying her naked on it. . . . Instead, he sighed and waved as she drove away.

Later. They'd definitely try out that bearskin later.

Chapter Sixteen

The late afternoon sky had gathered a number of clouds, and a warm breeze stirred the alder leaves as Kenzie parked her truck. Thinking she'd like to be closer to her dig site, she'd spent the last hour planning out where to set up camp this time. And anticipating Anya's delight when the child saw the toys and the pink sleeping bag that had been picked out for her. Kenzie tried to tell herself not to get too excited—after all, Anya would probably remain in her wolfen form. But then again, what if she didn't?

With that happy picture in mind, Kenzie decided to leave most of the stuff in the truck for the moment and give Anya a couple of small presents first. She selected two brightly colored bags and wondered how the hell there had gotten to be so many. *It looks like Christmas.* It's Josh's fault, she decided with a chuckle, knowing full well that she'd bought just as much, or more, than he had. She tucked a couple of folding camp chairs under her arm and headed for her site.

The grid around her dig was missing again.

Instantly she froze, her inner wolf on high alert. She could see that the entire area was disturbed, the grasses trampled down and limbs broken on the devil's club and salmonberry bushes that surrounded the area. Had the bears returned?

"Anya? Where are you?" There was no answer. "Stanton!" The only sound was the throaty rattles and clicks of a raven high in a spruce tree. She called out to them in her mind but there was no response. Maybe Anya wouldn't reply, but why didn't Stanton? Kenzie tried to shake off her apprehension. After all, the little girl and her guardian could be doing any one of a dozen different things right now: hunting, swimming, fishing, or just plain napping in a cool spot. Still, she set the packages and the chairs down and paced carefully across the clearing, examining the ground as she went.

Her head spun when she found the first tire track. She quickly found another and another, crisscrossing each other and mixed with prints, both human and canine. *Large* canine. Even in her human form, she could easily tell the scent was dog, not wolf, and her heart skipped a beat.

Stop it, she told herself sternly. It was just some local hunters with their ATVs looking for deer or moose. Or maybe a few fishermen, heading out to catch those famous red salmon that Josh was talking about. Lots of people depended on fishing and hunting in this area, right? Stanton had probably taken Anya somewhere safer until the party moved on.

But her inner wolf growled long and low, and every instinct screamed at her that these were not ordinary hunters. She closed her eyes and focused again on *scent*. Suddenly, amid the odor of gasoline exhaust and human sweat, her senses caught a faint whiff of blood. *Changeling* blood.

"No, no, *no!*" Her hands fisted as she fell to her knees and an anguished howl was torn from her throat, a cry of pain and loss and rage. Memories slashed at her viciously as the ancient past erupted into horrifying life. Humans. Humans had attacked Changelings. And this time it was *her fault*, all her fault. . . .

Guilt and blame pounded her like merciless fists. She should have stayed at camp, should have watched over the little wolf herself. What did she think she was doing anyway, playing around with a human? Taking a human's word for it that Anya would be safe with a Changeling she didn't even know? And just where the hell *was* Stanton? Was Josh involved in some way? Had the getaway to the city all been a plan to lure her away from camp, away from Anya? Sure, Josh was a great guy but *he wasn't like her.* Maybe he hadn't done it intentionally, maybe he'd just been careless in trusting the old Changeling? *She'd* been careless to trust either of them.

And where was the little girl now?

Her inner wolf raged, clawed to be released. Kenzie held it off, her hands shaking as she pulled out her cell and pressed Josh's number, but it went straight to voicemail. She left him a message and vented her anger and frustration, then flung the phone aside as she Changed.

As a wolf, she cast back and forth over the ground, seeking information in the thick tangle of prints and tracks. Her senses were far sharper, keener, in her lupine form and it wasn't long before she zeroed in on the blood she had scented. Small droplets punctuated the clearing here and there, and all of them belonged to Stanton. What had happened here? And why wasn't there any sign of Anya?

An hour later, Kenzie didn't know anything more. She sat on her haunches and howled out her frustration. Her tracking skills had never been her strong point but she could follow a trail easily. *This*, however, was a goddamn mess. There were countless scents leading in and out of the forest, woven together in a knot so nasty that even her brother, James, the most skilled tracker she knew, would have problems with it.

She wished he was here. Hell, she wished *anybody* was here, but most of all she wished Josh was here. And raged at her mutinous heart for wanting a human. Disgusted with herself, she bent her nose to the ground and tried again. She had to find Anya. She had to.

The moose finally took her twin calves and left, grumbling as she went, and Josh breathed a sigh of relief. He hated to have to shoot animals because of human foolishness—in this case, they had offered the animals doughnuts. Tourists seldom took moose seriously, maybe because they looked ungainly and cartoonish, but the enormous creatures attacked people far more often than bears, and they could be every bit as deadly. Josh couldn't help wishing he had a camera, though, as the fishermen made their way clumsily down the tree—they'd climbed it wearing hip-waders, a testament to just how terrifying a 900-pound moose could be.

Only one of the men complained as Josh took their names and issued fines for feeding moose—$110 in the State of Alaska. Josh didn't miss a beat, simply cupped his hands around his mouth and produced a long, drawn out tone followed by several explosive grunts.

"What—what're you doing?" asked the man, his eyes wide.

"Calling the moose back," Josh said.

"That's okay, it's okay, I was only kidding," he stammered. "I'll take the ticket, no problem." The man fell silent as Josh resumed writing and handed him his copy of the page. Luckily, the men were from California and didn't know that it wasn't breeding season and the cow moose was unlikely to respond to Josh's call.

As the would-be fishermen drove away, the muffled beep of Josh's cell reminded him that he'd thrown the phone on the seat of the loaner truck before mounting the rescue. It took a minute to locate the damn thing in the clutter—Frank really had to clean off his front seat one of these days—but when Josh pressed the voicemail button, he was almost sorry he'd found it. A furious Kenzie delivered a message that would have melted the ears off a lesser man. Somewhere between telling him she never wanted to set eyes on him again and that her trust in a *human* had been seriously misplaced, he heard the raw pain in her voice and gleaned what was really wrong.

Normally it took an hour to get to Chistochina but he covered the distance in record time, cursing the fact that Kenzie wasn't answering her phone. He left message after message, asking, telling, ordering, and finally begging her to *wait for him*. Something wasn't right, his gut said so. And his time in Afghanistan had taught him to pay attention to it.

As the truck bumped along the old logging road leading to Kenzie's camp, Josh wondered about her words. She'd said *hunters* had taken Anya. But there shouldn't be any hunters in the woods until August unless they were poaching. *Or unless they were deliberately targeting wolves.* Many Alaskans depended on game for subsistence—and wolves were often seen as competition. Some hunters wouldn't even flinch at shooting a wolf cub—or setting their dogs on it.

He rammed the truck into park and ran for the camp. There wasn't much there except the interwoven tracks of several ATVs. Fresh human footprints and enormous canine paw prints formed part of the mix and Josh studied the ground as he headed for Kenzie's dig site. Dogs, he decided at last. The size said *wolf*, but the structure subtly leaned toward *dog*. And the canines were definitely mingling with the humans, sometimes walking at their side. This couldn't be a party of hunters, nobody hunted in such a large and noisy group. Could be kids, just having a little four-wheeling fun. Like he and his buddies had done growing up. No doubt got their hands on a little beer too—

He never saw it coming. One moment he was studying the ground, the next he was lying on it, looking into the long, sharp teeth of a seriously pissed-off wolf. Its storm gray pelt suited its snarling demeanor, but the size . . . Jesus Christ, he'd never seen a wolf this big in his whole life and never from this vantage point. The enormous front paws pressed down on his chest, making it difficult to draw air, and its breath was hot on his face. His fingers inched toward his service revolver, flipped open the holster—and stopped as he got a good look at the creature's unusual eyes.

"Kenzie?"

The teeth snapped together inches from his face with a sound that chilled his blood and the wolf sprang away. Turned and growled at him as he slowly got to his feet.

"What? What the hell's wrong with you? Quit that." He took a step toward the wolf but stopped as the growling got louder. Christ, it was like being in a horror movie—didn't she recognize him? He hoped like hell she was in control of her animal side. Suddenly an icy breeze sliced through the summer heat and his skin prickled. Kenzie stood where the wolf had been. Tiny blue sparks winked out on the ground around her and he caught a whiff of ozone, as if lightning had struck nearby.

One look at her eyes, the color of thunderclouds threatening to spawn a tornado, let him know that her wolf was still present. He elected to treat her as a wolf and stood dead still, his body slightly sideways to appear nonthreatening. "Kenzie," he said, more calmly than he felt. "Tell me what happened here."

"What happened? Anya's *gone* and I can't find any sign of her that isn't at least a day old." Her voice was raspy, and he wondered if she'd been crying, or if it was a side-effect of shapeshifting. "She must be so scared. And I don't think Stanton's with her."

His insides clenched at that. "I'm sure you've covered every inch of this place. What else did you find?"

"Too much." Her face was pale and she rubbed the back of her neck as if she had a headache. "And not enough. I don't know which way they went, I don't know if Anya's with them. I can't even track them out of the damn clearing."

"Let me help. I was reading a trail when I was six, maybe I can help sort it out."

He walked toward her now, wanting to comfort her, but as he reached out she stepped back and the anger flashed in her eyes again. "Don't. I don't want you to touch me."

Ouch. "Okay. Is it you or your wolf talking?"

"This all went too fast, just too fast—you're getting the wrong idea."

He didn't like where this was going. "Well, way too late for that. What the hell's up with you?"

"Look, it was a memorable night, we had a lot of fun, and that's all. That's it."

"That's it?" He stared at her, unable to believe what he was hearing. "What, you want us to just shake hands and walk away or something?"

"Yeah, we should be smart and do exactly that. No harm, no foul."

No harm? An invisible knife had just sliced through him, virtual guts were spilling out everywhere, and it was tough to draw a breath. "We're both worried about Anya but we should be pulling together, not pulling apart. What the bloody hell are you afraid of, Kenzie?"

"Nothing, I just think it best that we don't—"

"No, not *we*. You think it's best that *you* don't get involved with a human. That's what this is all about, isn't it? Last night was more than just simple fun, a helluva lot more, and you damn well know it. We made a connection and now you're scared spitless. All because of something that happened to you a fucking *century* ago. And yeah, it was bad and it's wrong that it happened to you, but you've judged most of the people on this planet by it ever since. Including me."

"Don't you say that to me. Not now, not with Anya missing."

"I don't think Anya has a thing to do with it. You're using her disappearance as a goddamn excuse to blow me off. Because you're scared."

"I'm *not* scared!"

He paced, needing to channel his frustration before he grabbed her and shook her. "Not of some things, that's for sure. You've got a lot of courage and a lot of strength. You have to, in order to spend years digging in the dust for any tiny clue that might protect your family and your people. For chrissakes, Kenzie, you're preparing to stand the entire world on its ear with your work. Why can't you find the courage to give us a chance?"

"Don't you understand? There's no *us*, there can't be."

He stopped in front of her and looked her in the eye. "Why the hell not? Give me one good reason."

Her lips pressed together until they were almost white. When she spoke again, her words were sharp and clipped. "I don't love you and I don't want you. I was curious and now I know. I need a mate of my own kind."

The invisible knife finished carving his heart from his chest, and he stepped back. "That's plain enough. But Anya's missing and she needs help. So we're going to work together until we find her. And then we'll talk." At least that's what he thought he said. Tough to be sure when it was hard to get the words out and when it cost him even more to make them calm and steady. He didn't believe what Kenzie had said, didn't believe for a moment that she didn't have feelings for him, yet he still felt like he'd been gutted. Funny how there was no blood on the ground— with this kind of pain, there sure as hell should be.

The grass of the big clearing had been flattened by all the traffic, and trails had been punched into the forest in every direction. Kenzie resumed her wolfen form right in front of him—and he was acutely aware of the symbolism of the act. She wasn't displaying her abilities because she trusted him but because *he no longer mattered*. She bared her teeth at him as if to underline that message, then made a point of searching the ground as far away from him as possible. He sighed and drew heavily on his experiences in Afghanistan—there, you had to focus on the mission, and you learned to block out everything else. *Everything*, like someone you knew getting shot out of the sky or an IED taking out the truck ahead of you on the street. You not only had to keep functioning, you had to stay sharp or you'd be the next casualty. So you dealt with pain, felt the pain, *after*.

Moments later, Josh found a few drops of blood on the ground—but whom it belonged to, he couldn't tell. It was on top of the tire tracks, however, and on top of the dog prints too. So whatever or whoever was wounded was following the hunters. It could be one of the dogs, trailing behind. What if it was Stanton? Josh hissed out a breath between his teeth as he realized how much sense it made. He couldn't imagine any human hunter getting the drop on the wily Stanton, yet the only way anyone could have gotten to Anya was if the old wolf was physically unable to prevent it.

One thing Josh wasn't seeing, however, was any print belonging to Anya. Either she'd been successful in getting away—unlikely, considering the dogs—or she'd been captured and carried. Damned if he knew where, though. Kenzie had been all too right about the condition of the ground. The humans had been searching for something, and it must have been small because they appeared to have looked under every goddamn leaf and blade of grass to find it. Had Anya been their target to begin with? If so, why the hell did they want her?

It seemed impossible to sort out the collage of footprints, tire tracks, and paw prints, and yet he *had* to figure out where the hunters had gone, where Anya had been taken. And right now he didn't have so much as a general direction. The only thing he'd been able to determine was that the party hadn't headed south to Chistochina. Nor did they come from there, which added to the mystery.

A movement drew his eyes to the trees and his mouth dried at the sight of a small familiar figure. The red of her scarf was like a gash against the bright green salmonberry bushes. She wasn't smiling this time and he realized that *that* was what was odd about the dream he'd had the night before. She had always smiled at him. Always. But the last couple of times he'd seen her, her dark eyes were big and solemn. She wasn't waving at him either, but pointing at a break in the thick brush. When he looked back, the child had vanished.

Josh jogged to the spot she'd pointed out and pressed through the broken branches and past the scraped trees. A hundred feet later, he wasn't sure why he'd been directed here. If anything, this was one of the few areas the hunters *hadn't* forced their way into. No tracks, no prints, not even a stalk of bent grass. Nothing but a narrow game trail through dense and prickly brush.

Kenzie wasn't there when he returned to the clearing. He knew damn well she'd set out to try to find Anya and even if he succeeded in tracking her, he didn't have a hope of catching up to her, not in her lupine form. He sat on a fallen log and breathed out a curse. *This is what I get for listening to spirits.* In fact, the little Afghan girl wasn't even a spirit, just a nasty trick that his own brain conjured up because Anya was in trouble. And now Kenzie could be in danger as well because he'd been stupid enough to take his eyes off her.

That's when a new thought pushed its way to the forefront of his mind. What if the visions he'd been having hadn't been flashbacks at all?

What if they'd been warnings?

Chapter Seventeen

Anya curled up in the farthest corner of the cage with her back to the door. She didn't care what the men said, she wasn't going to eat one bite of their dumb food. Or even look at any of them. She was tired and scared, and tired of being scared. Her shoulders hurt where one of the big stupid dogs had picked her up by the scruff of the neck like she was a *baby*, even though she was way too big for that. She'd tried to squirm and shake herself loose, but the dog had carried her straight to the hunters. She'd managed to bite one of the men before he tossed her in a kennel and locked the door. Inside her mind she'd hollered for Stanton, again and again. The old wolf hadn't answered. Not when the ATV bumped and bounced along forever. Not when it stopped inside a strange building. Not when a man reached in and stuck her with a needle, and not when she woke up in this cage. She was afraid of this place, but she was also afraid that maybe Stanton had been hurt by the big mean bears. And how would Kenzie and Josh know where she was?

Most of all, she missed her mom, and wished they were home together *right now*. Anya raised her head and howled her heart out.

Nobody came.

★ ★ ★

Warnings, not flashbacks . . .

To his surprise, the idea felt *right*. Josh's grandmother often had visions—hell, even Mamie Dalkins had them regularly—but he'd never experienced anything similar. Still, one thing he'd learned during his deployments was always to go with his gut. It had saved him more than once. Maybe it could save Anya too.

He returned to the trail the Afghan child had pointed to, covering the ground as fast as the uneven terrain would let him, until suddenly a familiar voice popped into his head. Josh stood listening intently, more than a little concerned he was losing his mind. "Stanton?"

Over here, boy. And be damn careful where you step.

Josh left the trail and pressed through the dense brush as he honed in on the voice in his head.

I said careful!

He came to a stop and crouched where the ground fell away into dark empty space. The scent of damp earth, mineral-laden water, fungus, and wet limestone rose up to meet him. "Christ, Stanton, you've got yourself a bunker now? I think you're taking this conspiracy theory shit way too far."

"Just see if I let you in here when the world's blowing itself up, smartass."

As his eyes adjusted to the darkness of the cave below, Josh could see the old man sitting against a rock wall opposite him. Blood ran down the side of his face from a cut on his head. "You all right?"

"Hell no. I've broken a wing down here and I'm still stupid from the fucking dart they shot me with."

The distance to the cave floor appeared to be about thirty feet, with piles of rocks waiting below. Josh leaned as far over the edge as he dared and felt around for any possible handholds. "Where's Anya?"

"IBC has her. They came looking for her, you know, specifically looking for a *female wolf cub*—and when they saw me, they decided they wanted me too."

"That's 'cause you're so cute and cuddly, bro." Damn it, he couldn't find a place to climb down. Stanton was lucky he'd broken only an arm. "How the hell did you get down there?"

"Jumped." Stanton held up a fluorescent orange dart. "Right after they shot me in the goddamn ass, but they weren't loaded for a full-grown wolf, and especially not for a werewolf. I barely had enough time to lose the dogs and drop in here before I passed out. Kenzie with you?"

"No. She went after Anya on her own."

"And you let her?"

"What can I say? She blew me off." Josh cursed as his boot slid off a rock.

"And I repeat, you *let her*?"

Jesus. Definitely time to change the subject. "So what's with the Vulcan Mind Meld? Since when are you Professor Xavier?"

"Ha," Stanton snorted. "Took long enough to get the message through your thick skull."

"Why am I getting a message at all? I thought shape-shifters—"

"Can only communicate with each other. Yeah, yeah, yeah. Well guess what, most werewolves aren't nearly as old as I am. You pick up a few tricks if you live long enough."

Josh crawled back onto the edge. "Hate to leave you, but I've got to go back for a rope, okay? Even if I get down there with you, I can't pack your ass back up." He wasn't sure he could get *himself* back up the slippery cave walls. "I'll bring the first-aid kit too."

"Hell with that. Bring me a beer."

The ground beneath Kenzie's paws was a blur. The average wolf could reach a speed of 35 miles an hour, but Changelings were faster. Especially *motivated* Changelings. Now that she finally had the trail, nothing, not even six humans and a dozen dogs, would prevent her from reaching Anya.

The further away from the trampled clearing she got, the easier the trail was to follow. Although grasses were gamely trying to stand up again and branches were springing back to their original places, there was no hiding the broken stems and scraped bark, the scents of disturbed earth and crushed leaves. The tracks showed that the ATVs had traveled in single file, heading dead north. Kenzie followed the tracks until the trail veered off and met up with a road of sorts—if you could call it that. More like twin ruts in hard-packed clay with tall grass growing between.

It looked like the ATVs had followed the road, but Kenzie slackened her speed just the same, alert for any sign that they had gone off into the bush again. Miles later, she stopped to drink at a cold stream and wondered where on earth the hunting party was headed. Her maps hadn't shown any villages in this direction. And it still made no sense that they had taken Anya. Why would anyone want a wolf cub?

Not for the pelt, that was for sure. Although many Alaskan furriers sold wolf skins to tourists, most hunters took them in the winter when the pelts were thick and lush—and at their most valuable. Plus, Anya was far too small anyway.

Sled dog? Kenzie had watched some of the winter races near Dunvegan, and a few of the dogs were wolf hybrids. Maybe the hunters thought Anya was a hybrid because of her unusual markings. Zoo specimen? Private pet? More people were keeping exotic animals as pets, despite whether it was legal or practical to do so. Kenzie's brother, Connor, had been called in to treat a full-grown tiger at a farm last summer.

She sighed—she wasn't asking the right question. Instead of why Anya had been taken, Kenzie knew she should be thinking about how she was going to free the little girl when she found her. With a twinge of guilt, she knew she'd picked a really stupid time to brush Josh off. If he were here, he could have thrown a little law enforcement weight around, quoted some Fish and Game regulations and probably walked away with Anya tucked under his arm, no problem. Instead, the logical and meticulously scientific Dr. Kenzie Macleod was charging into an unknown situation without a plan and without backup. She wondered if Birkie would be proud of her newfound spontaneity or horrified. . . .

Shadows were deep and the sky had slid into twilight, where it would remain until morning. Kenzie trotted along the road until her keen hearing picked up the sound of an engine. She dove into the brush, hunkering down on her belly to watch until the vehicle roared slowly into view, bouncing methodically over the potholes and ruts. *Omigod.* Only one person could be driving around central Alaska in a bright yellow Humvee. . . .

In an instant she resumed her human form and walked onto the road. The Humvee braked abruptly. There were some awkward noises from the transmission as the driver fumbled the vehicle into park and jumped out.

"Good God, Kenzie, is that you? What on earth are you doing out here?"

"I could ask you the same—" was all she got out before he grabbed her in a bone-crunching embrace. "Wow, that's pretty enthusiastic, Nate. Put me down, 'kay?"

He stood her on her feet and stepped back. "Just glad to see you. *Really* glad."

"Glad enough to give me a ride?"

"Absolutely. I'm just on my way to drop something off to the IBC execs and then heading back to Anchorage. Your camp's along on the way."

"Actually, I'm headed the same direction you are." Buckling into the Humvee's deluxe leather seat, she explained about Anya.

"No problem," said Nate. "IBC's an international research group. Probably thought they were collecting a regular wolf cub, but there's no need to worry about Anya. They won't hurt her. It's all part of a study."

"What, are they collaring wolves or something?"

"Something like that. Some Alaskans feel that wolves compete with them for deer and moose and—what's that other thing with the antlers?"

"Elk? Caribou?"

"Caribou, that's the one. So the government's had this aerial shooting program for the last few years to reduce the wolf population. But it's really unpopular with the general public as well as with wildlife groups. So IBC is collecting their own data to prove it's unnecessary."

"But why would they contribute to your archaeology department?"

"Good PR and a tax break, of course, just like the oil companies get for *their* hefty contributions. And IBC has more than one branch of interest worldwide. Besides, I suggested they make the case that indigenous peoples were able to subsist comfortably for centuries without killing off the wolves. And they liked the idea."

"So what about Anya?"

"We'll just go get her. She's got a white leg, right? So we'll tell them she's not pure wolf. She's a cross or a pet or something. I don't know—you think up the story and I'll ask for the cub back."

"They'd actually do that for you?"

"Hey, IBC is a major donor to my cause. *Major* donor. We're on really great terms. So no worries."

Kenzie settled into the leather seat, hardly able to believe her luck. "I don't know how to thank you, Nate. I've been beside myself since I found Anya gone, and I have to tell you I thought the worst."

"You'll be with her in no time." Nate reached over and put his hand over hers. "So now, how about being with me? Didn't throw me over for that tall native guy, did you?"

"Josh and I aren't together, Nate. You know I wouldn't go for a human." She injected a hint of distaste into *human*, to cover the fact that she'd really like to see that particular human. A lot. *Right now*, in fact.

"That's what I figured. But I gotta tell you, it was tough to put on a happy face when I saw you with him. You and me, we're a team, honey. Don't you think it's about time we made it permanent?"

Her mouth dried. Crap, crap, *crap*, he was going to press her for a relationship. Again. And if she didn't give him the right answer, would he still help with Anya? How on earth was she going to handle this without pissing him off? None of her anthropology studies covered this kind of thing.

"We've always been close, Nate. As for more than that, let's discuss it after I get Anya home safe and sound—my emotions are totally wrecked right now." She laughed a little. "I wonder if this is what it's like to be a parent?"

She was relieved when he started talking about other things, his plans for the department in the fall, the latest contributions he'd scored, the discovery of cave paintings in the Dominican Republic . . . Through it all, however, something was niggling at her, something that wasn't right. She reached for it with her mind—

And then the compound came into view. "Holy Jeez, Nate, is this Jurassic Park?"

"Some fence, eh? But it's to keep things *out*. This complex is in the middle of nowhere, so grizzlies used to just walk right in. One of the biologists got mauled last spring. So IBC installed the fence, electrified it, and *voilà*, no more bear problem."

"Obviously I should have had one around my campsite," said Kenzie, trying to make light of it. The fence creeped her out, and it didn't look any friendlier when they pulled up to the gate either. Hollywood could film a prison movie here. Her inner wolf growled softly.

Nate snapped open his cell phone. "Hey Jurgen, *open Sesame.*"

The gate slid apart a few moments later and Kenzie quelled the rising sense of alarm she felt as they drove into the compound. Every building was shiny-new and much too clean looking—why would someone pick *white* as a decorative color in the middle of the wilderness? Even hospitals weren't this sterile and had more windows. Oh God, she wasn't going to start hyperventilating, was she?

"So you're sure Anya's okay?" she asked as they parked the Humvee in front of the main building. "You know, I just don't understand why they picked her up in the first place. I've never heard of any study that didn't gather their information in the field." In a flash, the thing that had been bothering her came clear. "Nate, how did you know about Anya's white leg?"

"You told me, silly. Remember how we figured it was a mutation?"

No. No, they hadn't, because they'd never discussed it. Ever. She laughed a little, trying to play along even as her eyes darted back to the gate that was now slowly closing. "Oh right, I forgot. See, Nate, I *told* you I was an emotional wreck." She pivoted fast to launch herself into a run, fast enough that a human would be unable to react to it. To another Changeling, however, her move was obvious and Nate's reflexes were as sharp as hers. Knife-like pain jabbed her hard in the thigh and set fire to her entire leg. Momentum carried her only a few steps before she stumbled to her knees. Her eyes were already blurring as she saw a grinning Nate hold up a bright orange dart.

Chapter Eighteen

The concrete was cold against her cheek. Layers of scent, laced with the cloying reek of disinfectant, crowded her brain with information. There were Changelings in the room with her, several of them, and all in wolfen form, but they were strangers to her. Wolves, real ones, were somewhere close by. Humans had come and gone recently, people that she didn't know. But as for Anya, there was no sign the little wolf had ever been here. Wherever *here* was.

Do not *panic. Do* not *Change.* She talked sternly to her wolfen self, so close to the surface that any surge of fear from her would cause it to take over. It was a survival reflex that could backfire badly in the modern world. *Be calm, be calm.*

Kenzie opened her eyes then, taking in the galvanized steel mesh that formed the walls and ceiling of the enclosure. It was like a dog kennel on steroids, about 20 by 10 and everything heavy-duty enough to hold a rabid grizzly—or an angry Changeling. She was in the end unit of a long set of these big runs, inside a room that could double as a warehouse. She turned her head to see who her neighbors were.

A huge jet-black wolf was sprawled in the adjacent cell.

She'd never seen fur so dark on any animal. The creature's sheer size told her he was Changeling, and scent confirmed it. One green eye was open, regarding her with guarded interest.

"Hey there," she croaked, suddenly aware of how thirsty she was. Her mouth tasted like she'd been sucking on nickels. As she struggled to sit up, she didn't think the dark wolf was going to answer but finally a word crept into her mind, slowly as if unsure of its welcome. *Hey.*

She found a stainless steel bowl set into an iron bracket at the side of the cage with a continuous water feed. The water looked and smelled clean, and she scooped some into her mouth with her hand. The cool liquid soothed her throat and she cupped her hands and drank deeply.

You okay? It was the dark wolf. Other Changelings in the cells beyond were now sitting up and looking in her direction.

"I think so, thanks." Her thigh was sore as hell where Nate had jabbed it with the dart. She ran her hands over it, noting that it was swollen and bruised, but she could use her leg. "How long was I out?"

Maybe half an hour. Name's Roy.

"I'm Kenzie." Others chimed in then. *Dempsey, Keith, Dan, Guillermo . . .* Roy introduced one grizzled wolf as *Shaggy Sam.* With the longest fur she'd ever seen on a Changeling, he could have passed for a giant collie. Two of the other wolves, Beau and Rico, didn't speak or move, but remained huddled, unmoving, in their cages. Were they unfriendly or were they ill?

Drugged, explained Roy.

She realized suddenly that all of her fellow prisoners were male.

"What, am I the only girl here?" She'd intended it to be

humorous, but to her surprise, several of the wolves hung their heads. One whined softly. Another howled, a bone-chilling sound that reverberated off the concrete walls.

Roy was the one who answered. *There was another female, but she had a bad reaction to the tranquilizer dart. They brought her in and put her in your cage, but she didn't wake up. She seized and died within a few minutes.*

"That's horrible." Kenzie had to suppress her wolfen self again—it was going to be damn tough to stay in control in this dangerous situation. Instinct kept pressing her to assume lupine form. She took a deep breath and asked, "How long ago was that, Roy?"

When he told her, she gripped the chain link and sat slowly down on the concrete. "Anybody know her name?" No one did. Maybe it was some other female . . . it could have been some other Changeling woman, couldn't it? But one of the other wolves, Guillermo, piped up.

I heard the scientists talking about her cub. I guess it got away, because they were pretty pissed about it. They really wanted the kid, more than all of us put together.

The sickening truth washed over Kenzie. The cub had escaped all right, but then she'd told Nate about Anya—and Nate had told IBC exactly where she was. He'd even had the damn GPS coordinates from that first visit to Kenzie's site. Anger and pain at his betrayal surged through her system, along with grief and guilt. She'd all but put Anya on a silver platter.

"They've got us both now," she whispered, unshed tears making it hard to speak. "The child was with me." Actually, the child had been with *Stanton* at the time. Where was he? She asked if anyone had seen an older silver Changeling, but no other wolves had been brought in. Did that mean he was all right or was he another casualty of IBC? Kenzie felt sick. She'd endangered Anya and Stanton both by trusting Nate. But never in a million years had she expected him to turn on his own kind. To turn on *her*.

So much for her work. She hadn't yet found enough evidence to prove that Changelings and humans had the same origins, and now it was everlastingly too late. The world was going to know all about the existence of shapeshifters, and the humans would start hunting the "monsters" among them. History was going to repeat itself and there wasn't a damn thing she could do about it.

I don't think so. Roy got up and paced his cage. Had she been broadcasting her thoughts? *Some of us have been here over a year now, and we've been able to piece some things together. The facility's funded by a group of foreign investors.*

Extremely well-funded, Dempsey added. *We're talking about people so rich they can buy whole countries.*

"Well, they're going to get a whole lot richer when they tell the world about us," sniffed Kenzie, unable to keep the bitterness out of her words.

Roy shook his head, a distinctly un-wolf-like mannerism. *That's just it. They're not interested in capitalizing on that. In fact, they don't want anybody ever to know about us. They're researching our longevity—and how to replicate it in humans.*

"What?" Kenzie goggled at him. "You gotta be kidding. You mean like a Fountain of Youth?"

From the other end of the cell block, Shaggy Sam finally spoke. *If you own half the world, you don't need more money. You need more time to enjoy it.*

Kenzie had tried and tried to make contact with Anya, but without success, in spite of pushing her mindspeech abilities to the max. Either the child was still too scared to talk to her or she wasn't awake. Were they keeping her drugged like Rico and Beau? Exhausted herself, Kenzie was half-dozing in a corner, despite the fact that the concrete was chilling her right through her jeans. Without the high body temperature that was typical of her kind, she would have been ill in no time. Suddenly the last person she ever expected to see again walked into the room and in a flash she was on her feet, gripping the front of the cage.

Nate Richardson's expression was smug. "Not so high and mighty now, are you, Dr. Macleod?"

"Nate, what the hell is wrong with you? Let me out of here! Let us all out!"

He surveyed the long row of caged runs. "Why would I do that when I worked so hard to put all of you in here? It's a pretty good collection, don't you think?"

"Collection for what?"

"For research of course. You'll be making a great contribution to science, just not the way you planned."

"Nate, please—you can't betray your own kind."

"*My own kind*," he mocked. "Like hell you are." His expression grew hard.

"I don't understand."

"No? Of course you don't. It's all so easy for you." He paced in front of her cage as if he were the captive. "You and your werewolf family and friends. You've all been around for a century or two or six and you've all made your fortunes long ago—you're fucking rich now without even trying. Well, some of us weren't born Changelings, remember? Thirty years ago, I was human—then one of you bit me. Three decades might be long enough to benefit from long-term investments, even though I didn't have much money to put into them back then. Then the market fell and took everything I had with it. Everything. Well, thanks to IBC, I don't have to sit around and wait a hundred years or so to be able to live the lifestyle I deserve."

It was all about money. *Of course* it was about money. She should have known, should have at least suspected. "How long have you been planning to sell me out?"

Nate shook his head. "I didn't. Not at first. I wanted you to be with *me*, remember? I wanted you by my side from the very beginning. Remember when we were students together? We were the perfect team. I had so many plans for us but then you went and changed your mind. I hoped maybe this summer we could get it back, that if I could just get you by yourself, then you'd see the incredible potential we had. We could have had it all, you and me. But you didn't even want to consider it. You didn't even want to talk about it. And suddenly, there you were at the side of the road, just begging me to bring you here . . . kind of a sign, don't you think?"

"So you're leaving me here?" she asked, incredulous.

"It's not hard to do the math. Since the beginning of the project, we've captured ten males and only one female, but she died."

"I heard. You killed that child's mother."

He shrugged. "Allergic to the tranq, who knew? The cub got away, but now we've got her back *plus* you. And as for me? I collect a hefty bonus—that's *hefty* as in my second home in Mendocino is paid in full as of right now. So, yeah, too bad for you but I'm leaving you right where you are, babe." He leaned in close to the mesh and lowered his voice. "Wouldn't want you to miss me though. I have a copy of the lab schedule and I know exactly when they'll tranq you for blood and tissue samples. I'll be sure and stop by for a visit. After all, you still have the best ass going—and this time you won't be able to say no to me."

She lunged at him, jamming her fingers through the mesh and raking one side of his face with her nails before he could jump back. Swearing, he pulled out a handkerchief and blotted the blood from the long furrows that marred his all-American face from cheekbone to chin. His eyes were cold, and there was neither wolf nor human in them. "You want to play rough, babe? Good. I'll make sure we do when I come back."

He stalked out and she slid down the unyielding mesh to the cold concrete floor, her hands fisted on her knees. Fury and revulsion vied for dominance until finally she let the Change take her.

When awareness returned, Kenzie's cheek was resting on the cold concrete again, only this time her skin was cushioned by storm-gray fur. She rolled to her belly and sucked in her breath as her paws protested sharply. The pads were raw and bleeding, every claw cracked or broken.

You okay? Roy asked. *You went a little crazy for a while there.*

Kenzie looked around. The concrete was spotted with garish rosettes of blood—her own paw prints. The chain mesh at the front of the cage was bowed outward in several spots. She vaguely remembered clawing at it and howling out her rage and frustration when it didn't give way. After that, she didn't remember anything.

At the moment, her inner wolf was quiet yet very far from subdued. It was waiting. Watchful. *Didn't you go a little crazy too when they locked you up?*

Didn't get the chance. I was drugged when they brought me in, and they kept me that way. At first, I wouldn't eat the food they brought me, thinking there might be something in it, but they would just come along with dart guns and shoot me through the cage mesh. Went like that for the first couple of months. Same with everyone else. If you make any noise, give the docs or the handlers any trouble, you get juiced. Beau and Rico, they've been shot up more than anybody because they won't play along. The handlers probably would have done that with you too, except the jerk that brought you in here wanted you awake.

He said he brought you all here. How?

Simple. He'd become a wolf and hang around the area for a few days on four legs, although I don't know how he figured out where anyone lived. Maybe he was just fishing to see if there were any Changelings around and sometimes he'd get lucky. Anyway, he'd strike up a friendship, propose a run or a hunt. Not hard, considering how rarely any of us see another shapeshifter here. There are few packs in this state, and most of those are just members of a small family.

No, not hard at all to get close to another Changeling, Kenzie thought. Nate could be charming and personable and oh-so-entertaining. It was what made him so successful as a fund-raiser. People enjoyed his company, wanted to be around him. Liked him.

Sooner, rather than later, he'd make the switch to two legs—and then punch us with a dart. Call in his IBC buddies with the chopper for pickup.

Where the hell did these people come up with a formula that would work on us? We're usually immune to pharmaceuticals.

Don't know. Somebody's been working overtime, that's for sure.

More than that, she thought. *Somebody's been* practicing *on Changelings for a very long time.* Thick fear rose like bile in her throat, threatening to cut off her air. Her worst nightmare had exploded into raw life and she was a child trapped in a pit again. Rising to stand on her lacerated feet, she willed the pain to clear her head, keep the terror from choking her. She had to remember that she was a full-grown Changeling, a grown woman, powerful and smart. She wasn't a little girl anymore, but there was one depending on her. She had to find Anya and get her out of here. Had to. Had to get all of the Changelings out.

We're going to have company soon. It's almost time for Nikki to make her rounds. Dr. Yeung is the veterinarian here.

Great.

She's pretty decent, actually. I've overheard her arguing with her bosses about our care. She fights a lot with Gessler, the guy in charge of the handlers. He's the muscle around here. He's some kind of expert on capturing and transporting wild animals—the big ones, like elephants and rhino. Used to work for zoos in Europe. Mostly he's an asshole.

Does he come here too?

Not often, thank God. Only if he's got a new prisoner. Nikki tore him a new one when the female died—she was trying to protect her cub and he darted her twice. She wasn't allergic to the drug, she was overdosed.

Kenzie felt sick. *Speaking of the cub, why isn't she here with us?*

Don't know. I heard she's upstairs somewhere.

She didn't even have to think about what her next move would be. She Changed and checked her hands—the shift healed most superficial wounds. Then ran her fingers through her hair and smoothed out her shirt.

What the hell are you doing?

"Getting ready to meet the veterinarian."

You're not going to get special treatment by cooperating, you know. Or by providing the scientists with more footage of the Change. Roy inclined his head and she followed his gaze to a camera high on the wall near the ceiling. She spotted three more. *None of us perform for this crowd.*

"Believe me, Roy, I'm not performing." She understood his surprise. All of the Changelings were in lupine form, a natural reaction to a dangerous situation. And instinct would press them to conceal their abilities, their identities. The way she saw it, however, her identity was already out of the bag. And all those anthropology classes just might come in handy after all. She adopted a casual pose, leaning against the wall of the cage just as a young woman in a white lab coat entered the room.

The woman didn't notice her at first, starting at the far end of the runs. Nikki looked over Shaggy Sam with a practiced gaze, but her voice was kind. "How are you today? You didn't eat all of your kibble again. I got the boss to send Carl out to get a couple of deer so there'll be fresh meat for you soon."

Nikki talked to each and every one of the Changelings. They didn't move, didn't trot over to see her or anything, but some of them wagged their tails ever so slightly, which pleased her. She came over to speak to Roy and stopped dead in confusion as she caught sight of the woman in the cell next to him.

"Hi," said Kenzie. "I understand you're the veterinarian here. My brother's a vet too. Nikki Yeung, isn't it?"

She nodded slightly, still bewildered.

"I'm Dr. Mackenzie Macleod. Could you please tell me where the cub is? I've been really worried about her. Is she okay?"

"Fine," said Nikki, who then abruptly left the room.

That went well. Roy chuffed as if laughing.

"Actually it went very well. You've never shown her your human side, have you? Any of you?"

Nope. Better for them not to know.

"I disagree. They see you as animals. Different from them, and *different* is easy to dismiss or ignore. If you're not people, then it's easy to do the things they do to you. The Nazis did the same to concentration camp inmates—dehumanized them so they were different, treated them worse than livestock so the guards couldn't relate to them. And the more they saw the prisoners as different, as somehow less than human, the easier it was to brutalize them."

Several of the Changelings were looking at her now. "I have nothing to hide—these people already know what I am. So I plan to use my human form as much as I can. I'm going to talk to my captors at every opportunity, whether or not they listen to me. I'm going to remind them in every way possible that *I am like them.* That woman just fled the room because she was unprepared for that reality. I'm not a wolf, I'm not a zoo animal, and I'm not a lab rat. I'm a person, and I'm being held prisoner. Somebody's bound to get uncomfortable with that."

She sat cross-legged, facing the front of the cage so she could watch the doorway on the other side of the room. Her body was still, but her mind was busy. Despite her words, she didn't have a lot of hope that she'd find an ally among the humans who worked here. If IBC paid Nate as much as he'd said for her and Anya, they weren't likely to let her go just because she was wearing blue jeans.

No, her best chance was to try to make contact with someone on the outside. More than anything, she wished she could talk to Josh. She owed him a huge apology for the hurtful things she'd said, made all the worse because they weren't true. He'd accused her of being scared, and he was right. Fear had made her push him away, deny her own heart. She was still afraid, of course, but Nate's casual betrayal had given her a whole new perspective on Birkie's words—"*Honey, it's the heart that counts. Being a Changeling doesn't necessarily make a man good relationship material. And being human isn't a reason to write somebody off. There are good and bad individuals in both species.*"

Good and bad. And Kenzie had ditched the good in a meltdown of misdirected fear. *Way to go.* She sighed and tried to focus on the task at hand. She couldn't broadcast a general message that all shapeshifters could hear or Nate would pick it up too. Instead, she had to tightly focus her mindspeech and direct it to a specific individual—and there was only one Changeling she knew of who might hear her. If he was in range. And if he was still alive.

Chapter Nineteen

"Jesus, Stanton, you're bleeding like a stuck pig." Josh blotted at the head wound, trying to clean it so he could get a better look, but the old vet's unruly hair kept getting in the way. Finally Josh gave up and simply applied a pressure bandage.

"Ow, dammit, be careful."

"I thought you said it's not as bad now."

"It's not. Changing form tends to improve things. But that doesn't mean it doesn't sting like a sonofabitch."

Improve, hell. How bad had the gash been before? And his arm was definitely broken. "Come on, we're going to the clinic."

"Fine. I can take care of my own wounds, you know."

Stanton obviously thought he was going to his veterinary office and slowly but willingly followed his friend back along the game trail to the clearing and then to the truck. Josh wisely didn't say anything different until he pulled up in front of the Glennallen Medical Clinic. There, they argued for ten full minutes before Stanton reluctantly agreed to be looked at. Once a doctor came on the scene and Josh was confident Stanton wouldn't sneak out, he left to gas up the truck and *think*. It had nearly ripped him in two to leave the trail behind with Kenzie and Anya both missing, and he was anxious to return, even though the sun had dipped below the horizon.

At least Josh now knew where Anya was because Stanton had overheard some of the hunters' conversation. That information plus the familiar white ATVs and unusual dogs cinched it: the little wolf had been taken to IBC. Kenzie was certain to have followed her to the facility and heaven only knew how that had turned out. The minute he was sure Stanton was going to be okay, Josh was going after her. Maybe Kenzie had simply walked up to the gate, talked nicely to the IBC staff, and walked away with Anya. Maybe Josh didn't have to worry about rescuing either one of them. But if everything was rainbows and unicorns, why had the little Afghan girl been appearing to him? Nope, he was going with his gut on this one and his gut said he needed to be prepared.

As he paid for the gas, a monstrous yellow Humvee pulled up to a pump. The big vehicle looked ridiculous in that color—it practically glowed in the goddamn dark. The thing sported a shiny chrome bumper too, unlike the practical dust-colored workhorses that Humvees were in Afghanistan. . . . With a start, Josh recognized Nate Richardson behind the wheel and instantly all of his senses shot to high alert. When he was a child learning how to track, his father had told him to *look for things that were out of place.* Richardson was definitely out of place in such a small town, even more so than his silly macho truck.

"Nate, isn't it? Didn't expect to see you outside of the big city."

Richardson looked up from the pump as Josh approached. There was a split second delay between recognizing Josh and putting on a smile. Josh could also see a faint ripple of unearthly green in the blue aura that surrounded the big Changeling, usually a sign of anger. So Richardson was pissed to see him? *Good.*

"Fund-raising takes me to all kinds of exotic locations. Just passing through. What about you?"

"Home base."

Nate glanced around. He made no comment but his expression made obvious what he thought of Glennallen. Josh ignored it and pressed on. "So, Nate, you're good friends with Kenzie. Didn't happen to visit her camp today, did you?"

There was a faint, barely perceptible change in the man's pupils, but he recovered quickly. "The last time I saw her, she was with you," Nate said lightly, as he clicked off the gas nozzle. "Lose her already, did you?" He smirked and swiped his credit card on the pump face.

It was obvious to Josh that the guy was hiding something. Civilian life was complicated, however. In Afghanistan, Josh could have pulled Richardson in for questioning, but here, he hadn't the slightest authority over this man unless he mowed down a moose with that big-ass vehicle. "Haven't been able to raise her on her cell phone, that's all. With all the bear problems she's had, I'm a little concerned."

"I'm sure she's happily digging in the dirt somewhere. Probably just forgot to turn her phone on. You don't know her like I do—we have a long and *intimate* history—or you'd know how forgetful she gets when she's working on a project."

On the outside, Josh didn't react to Richardson's baiting and maintained his casual facade. On the inside, he couldn't help wishing the jerk was human. . . .

"Tell you what," said Nate, wiping his hands. "If I see her, I'll let her know you're looking for her." He waved airily as he got in the Humvee. "See you around."

Bet on it. As the Humvee sped off toward Anchorage, there was no doubt in Josh's mind that the jerk knew exactly where Kenzie was. And if Josh hadn't *also* known where she was, he had no doubt he'd be cleaning Richardson's clock right now to get the information. The guy was a shapeshifter, sure, but his attention could probably be gotten with a two-by-four.

Josh turned to look at the tiny figure standing where the bright yellow Humvee had been parked. The air was still but her red and green clothes fluttered in some cosmic breeze and her big dark eyes regarded Josh solemnly. "I know," he said to her. "He's involved with this somehow but I'll deal with him later. I'm going to get Anya and Kenzie first, make sure they're safe." The apparition faded from his sight then, and he released a shaky breath, glancing around to see if anyone had observed him talking to himself.

Christ, he was never going to get used to this.

The harsh fluorescent lighting of the hospital lobby contrasted starkly with the moonlit night just outside the door. Josh blinked, willing his eyes to accept the unnatural brightness, and nearly ran into a young doctor in the hallway.

"You brought in Bygood Stanton, right? Your friend will have to give up rock climbing for a while." The guy referred to a clipboard in his hands. "Fracture of the radius and ulna—that's both bones of the right forearm. The usual treatment is surgical placement of a plate and screws, but Mr. Stanton has refused this. I've set and cast it as best as I can, but it's going to be incredibly fragile. Maybe you can talk some sense into him, because I just can't guarantee it'll heal properly."

A plate and screws . . . Josh imagined that wouldn't work so well on a shapeshifter. The thought of what would happen to them during the conversion from human to animal made him queasy. Small wonder Stanton had refused the surgery.

"The proximal humerus is also fractured—that's his shoulder—but the only way to manage that is to place his arm in a sling."

"He's okay otherwise?"

The doctor all but rolled his eyes. "Depends how you define *okay*. There's extensive bruising. Had to stitch a couple of the lacerations in his scalp. And he'll have a lot of pain in that arm and shoulder, of course. We'd like him to stay overnight for observation, but he's not receptive to that idea. If *you're* willing to watch him, I'll discharge him." He headed off down the hallway, no doubt to spread cheer to some other poor souls.

Josh entered the hospital room and was jolted by how pale Stanton seemed against the white sheets. His eyes were closed, and his eyebrows looked wilder than ever when unrestrained by his glasses, but he was perfectly alert. "There's a woman who won't stop talking in my head," he muttered.

"What?"

Stanton opened his eyes. "There's a woman who won't quit talking to me. Here I am, a shell of a man, and I can't get a lick of sleep until I pass on the message."

"Kenzie? Are you talking to Kenzie?"

"Barely. It's quite a distance. But her broadcast is coming in loud and clear. Adrenaline will do that to you."

"Why would she need—"

"Looks like she's been captured, bud, just like Anya. IBC's got her locked up tight and they know what she is."

It happened too fast. Josh wasn't prepared for the emotions that suddenly ripped through him, and he plowed his fist into the nearest wall. "*Shit.* Why'd she have to go off by herself? I shouldn't have left her alone, I should *never* have left her alone." *And I should have cleaned Richardson's clock when I had the chance.*

Stanton surveyed the large hole punched in the drywall with a barely raised eyebrow. "It's *my* fault that any of this happened. Kenzie wouldn't be a prisoner if I'd managed to protect Anya."

"Bullshit. You might be a shapeshifter but you're not a superhero. Who knew that you were going to have to deal with bears and dogs and hunters all at once? You wanna lay a guilt trip on somebody, then put it on Kenzie and me for leaving you alone." He blew out a breath. "Or we could all come to our senses and go after who's really responsible: IBC."

"You're mounting a rescue mission?"

"Damn right."

The vet nodded. "Count me in."

"You're supposed to stay here overnight for observation."

"So observe me. But I'm going."

You didn't go into a situation without intel, you didn't go in without a plan, and you sure as hell didn't go in alone.

Those were basic rules that kept soldiers alive in Afghanistan. It was tough to pay attention to rules, however, when every instinct Josh had was screaming at him to fly straight into the IBC compound and beat down their door with an M240 machine gun. The woman he loved was in a cage and a child was in danger. His heart wanted to charge in now, but his head knew better. This was a mission he couldn't risk failing.

Already there were complications. Kenzie and Anya were not kept in the same area. At least eight other shapeshifters were imprisoned as well. At least he had some maps of the compound, thanks to Stanton's conspiracy theorist hobbies. They'd gone to the vet's house and Stanton had dug out the maps before Josh insisted he get some sleep. There were even some general layouts of the main building from its construction permit application. Added to the little sightseeing tour Josh had taken with his friend, he had no trouble orienting himself. But that was only part of the equation. He knew nothing about the security once he got past—*if* he got past—the formidable front gates. Just how many people lived and worked at IBC? Plus, he had no idea who their friends were, or who they'd call on for help if they were threatened. State troopers? Military? On-site mercenary? How fast would they respond?

He was trying to plan an operation that wouldn't get anybody killed, and was rapidly realizing it might not be possible. His watch beeped—another hour had passed and Josh went into Stanton's room to check on him again. He was sleeping well, his breathing even and easy, and his color looked better. Technically, Josh was supposed to *wake* him every hour, but his friend had assured him that it wasn't necessary with werewolves. It was probably bullshit—Stanton likely just wanted to sleep.

Earlier, Stanton had gleaned everything that Kenzie could tell him, mind to mind, but she didn't know much of what went on beyond her cage. What she *did* know was scary. IBC obviously had a hell of a lot of money, enough that they could afford to kidnap a dozen people with incredible abilities unknown to science, imprison them, and keep the whole thing secret. Worse, those prisoners were far more valuable to IBC's purposes than the untold millions of dollars the company would make if they revealed them to the world.

With so much at stake, Josh knew that IBC was potentially more dangerous than a drug cartel. They'd have state-of-the-art electronic security in those shiny new buildings. The presence of dogs was already confirmed. And although IBC probably felt their isolated facility was safe, it stood to reason they'd have hired guns as well. He'd spotted one in a window when he and Stanton landed there. Now he was certain there'd be more. Not rent-a-cops, but people trained to protect IBC's investment. Josh surveyed the weapons he'd laid out on the table. He could be dangerous too.

So far, however, he had no idea who he was going to tap for backup on this, and going alone was stupid. At best, he'd get taken out and then there'd be no one to help the prisoners. At worst, Kenzie and Anya could be hurt or killed. Stanton healed fast as a shapeshifter, but his arm and shoulder were going to take a few days. Meanwhile, Josh couldn't involve law enforcement, not even his fellow wildlife officers, because he couldn't risk Kenzie's secret being revealed and the existence of shapeshifters making the national news. Too bad he didn't know any changelings besides Stanton who could help him—

Or did he?

Josh pulled his cell phone out and looked at it. He had a number and a name. To borrow a phrase from Mamie Dalkins, the Macleods didn't know him from a bar of soap. Plus, it was the wee hours of the morning. They'd probably think he was a lunatic and hang up. But Josh knew what it was like to be a big brother, and what he'd do if anyone ever threatened one of his sisters. Hell, he knew what he was prepared to do right now for the woman he loved. Shapeshifters or not, he had a feeling that the Macleod brothers would react along the same lines. Kenzie would likely kill him for involving them of course, if she ever spoke to him again. He figured he'd manage to live with that if she was safe and sound.

He punched the number.

Kenzie figured she must still be experiencing the effects of the drugs in the dart. How else could she have slept so soundly, and on a hard floor to boot? There was a rubber mat in each cage for sleeping, which provided some insulation from the cold floor. Nikki's doing, Roy had said. But the mat wasn't much more comfortable than the cement. She rose and stretched, wincing at her bruised thigh and wanting nothing more than to punch Nate in the face. Repeatedly.

To her surprise, three of her fellow prisoners were on two legs; Roy, Dempsey, and Shaggy Sam. Sam, as it turned out, was rather shaggy in human form as well. He sported waist-length hair in a long thick braid that hung down his back, and eyebrows that could rival Stanton's. "Morning, guys," she said. "You're looking unusually good today."

Roy grinned sheepishly. "Thought about what you said and figured it was worth a try. Who knows, maybe they'll finally give us some coffee."

The veterinarian came in at that moment, and paused to take in the changes in her charges. For a moment, Kenzie thought she might turn and run, but Nikki appeared to square her shoulders and approached the cages—slowly. She walked along each one, saying nothing, until she came to Kenzie's cage.

"You didn't really believe it, did you?" Kenzie asked softly.

Nikki shook her head.

"Can you tell me if the wolf cub is okay? She's just a little girl and I'm worried about her."

The woman's eyes widened. "F-fine. She's okay. We've got her upstairs where it's warmer."

"Thanks for that. Can you help us get out? We'd all like to go home."

A crash at the door interrupted them and five men came in wheeling a low stainless steel cart. Two of the men had dart guns at the ready, but Kenzie could see that all of them had sidearms—and the holsters were open. The leader strode over to Nikki without hesitation and stood looking at the Changelings with one hand on his holster.

"What the hell is this?" the man demanded.

"They're werewolves, Gessler, what did you expect?" said Nikki, as if finding human beings in the cages hadn't thrown her for a loop too. "They have a human shape."

"Well, whatever shape they are, the clipboard says Number Six is due at the lab." With one smooth movement, he moved forward, drew his dart gun and fired through the mesh. Dempsey's lupine instincts were fast enough to try to dive out of the way but the fluorescent dart caught him in the shoulder.

"No!" shouted Nikki. "We don't know how it will affect them in this form."

Kenzie was horrified at how quickly the drug took effect. Within a few seconds, Dempsey's eyes rolled back in his head and he slumped bonelessly to the cement floor. Despite Nikki's protests, Gessler nodded to his men. They wasted no time opening the cage door and loading Dempsey onto the cart like a sack of potatoes. Nikki knelt and checked his pulse, used the stethoscope that was around her neck and pushed back his eyelids to check his pupils. "I don't like the way he's breathing. You idiot, you could have killed him."

"My job is to dart subjects and transport them back and forth to the lab. I was just doing my job." He motioned at his men to wheel Dempsey away. "You don't want them darted, maybe we'll go back to tying them up. Remember how much fun that used to be? After all, we only had to shoot three of them to keep them from killing the staff. Besides"—he pointed at Kenzie—"it's that one's fault. Dr. Richardson warned us she was a troublemaker and to keep an eye on her."

"That's crazy," retorted Nikki.

"Is it? She's been here one day and already we have werewolves trying to look like people."

Kenzie narrowed her eyes at Gessler. "We *are* people."

"Only when it suits you. The rest of the time, you're killers."

"If you're so sure of that, why isn't Nate Richardson in a cage? He's a werewolf too."

Gessler laughed out loud. "Sure he is, and the pope wears a thong. Nice try, lady." He was still chuckling when he left the room.

"I need to look after Six," said Nikki, and she turned to leave.

"It's Dempsey," said Roy suddenly. "He has a fucking name. *Dempsey.*"

"Dempsey, got it." She hurried across the room and out the door.

Roy slid down the wall to sit on the floor. "Damn that Gessler. He's the one that should be in a cage. Tell me why we're in human form again?"

"Nikki might help us," piped up Sam from the end cage.

"Might," snorted Roy. "And then Gessler will just dart us or shoot us. I don't think he cares which."

"They don't know that Nate's a Changeling?" asked Kenzie. "They honestly don't know?"

"Richardson's got himself a sweet racket. Nobody at IBC can tell if a human is Changeling or not. So he's taken full advantage of that. Pretends he's a psychic and that's how he can find us and turn us in."

"I think we should turn the tables on *him*," Kenzie said, folding her arms. "I think we should expose him for what he is."

"How? You saw how Gessler took it when you tried to tell him."

"We could show them. There are enough full-grown Changelings in this room. If we all pushed at Nate at once with our mindspeech, we could order his wolfen side to come out and play."

Roy looked at her openmouthed. "Holy shit, lady," said Sam. "That'd be a neat trick if it works. Where the hell did you learn about that?"

"My family's part of a Pack. It's pretty basic stuff, although you use it only in an emergency."

"Well, I'd say this qualifies. But it's not as basic as you seem to think," said Roy, recovering somewhat. "What we know, we've had to learn on our own. There's not a lot of Changeling Packs in Alaska. In fact, I don't think any of us have ever been part of one in our lives. Land of the *rugged individualist* and all that."

Sam nodded. "Probably why it was so damn easy to grab us."

"Probably why we're still here, too," Roy said wryly. "Nobody's looking for us."

Kenzie sat in a corner, rested her elbows on her knees and closed her eyes. She was lucky to have more hope than her fellow prisoners. Stanton had told her that Josh was going to get her and Anya out, but it was hard to imagine how anyone could get past Gessler, his goons, and who knew what other security. Still, Josh had once told her she needed to *have a little faith*. She certainly hadn't shown any in their relationship. At the very first obstacle, she'd turned on him and pushed him away. Her inner wolf had permitted it only because it was fixated on finding Anya, and perhaps because it was inexperienced. After all, she'd never had a mate before.

Sadly, she didn't know if she had one now. Josh was the kind of guy who would rescue her and Anya whether he knew them or not, and whether he liked them or not, just because it was the right thing to do. So maybe he planned to free her and then walk away. She could hardly blame him—after all, her last words to him had been pretty ugly. All because of her own fears.

Kenzie sighed and ran her fingers over the steel mesh of her caged run. She'd told Birkie that *fear serves a purpose, it can keep you safe*. Ha. The joke was on her—all her fears hadn't kept her the least bit safe. In fact, every fear she'd ever had about humans had just come true.

And, thanks to Nate, should she now have fears about Changelings too? Good and bad in both species, just like Birkie had said.

She hoped she got a chance to tell her friend how right she'd been.

Chapter Twenty

"Helluva way to meet the in-laws," whispered Stanton, obviously enjoying Josh's discomfort as they waited at the side of the highway in Stanton's jeep. The old vet had managed to locate the hidden turnoff to the road—not much more than an overgrown goat path, really—that meandered to the compound.

"They're not my in-laws."

"Not yet. You have to impress them first."

"I'll settle for them not killing me. Tell me again how this isn't a bad idea—we're asking civilians to help break prisoners out of a high-security compound."

"They're werewolves. They'll take care of themselves, trust me."

"That's not comforting when all of the prisoners we're trying to rescue are *werewolves* too. And somehow they managed to get themselves captured."

"They were *alone* at the time they were picked up. You send werewolves in a pack, it'll take a tank battalion to stop them."

"How big's a pack?"

"Anything more than one," Stanton grinned.

A full-sized pickup truck was slowing as it approached. A few moments later Josh—who was accustomed to being taller than anyone he knew—found himself looking up at a blond Viking with murder written in his blue eyes. Two men flanked him, twins, their faces grim. Suddenly, a small white-haired woman stepped down from the driver's seat of the truck. She was dressed in camo coveralls and her eyes contained immense intelligence—and something like amusement—as she surveyed him. He didn't miss that she edged herself in front of the Viking. Her gaze lingered for a moment on Stanton before she extended a hand with many silver rings and bracelets to Josh. "I'm Birkie Peterson. We talked last night."

When he'd called Connor Macleod's office, he'd expected a recorded message to give him a home number for emergencies, as Stanton's clinic phone did. Instead, the machine forwarded to this woman. He'd had no intention of discussing the situation with anyone but a Macleod but Kenzie had spoken fondly of Birkie—and said that she knew all about Changelings.

"I had a feeling my girl was in trouble," she'd said, but otherwise had seemed unfazed by a complete stranger's calling in the pre-dawn hours. Josh ended up explaining the entire situation to her, but certainly hadn't expected her to show up in person. The three men were clearly shapeshifters, their strong auras glowing blue. But Birkie— he looked down at her slim hand clasped in his and saw a shine that had nothing to do with the jewelry she wore. Incredibly, her *aura* was as silver as her rings. What the hell was she?

As if she knew what he was thinking, she winked at him and retrieved her hand. "These are Kenzie's brothers. James"—she waved at the glowering blond giant—"and Culley and Devlin.

Although a smaller force was better suited to stealth op-

Dani Harper

eration, three men—even shape-shifters—did not seem like nearly enough. "I thought there were four of you. Where's Connor?"

"Kenzie said he's the one with the newborn, remember?" Stanton whispered from over Josh's shoulder. "Werewolf imperative. Can't leave if there's young to guard—not for a while at least. It's a biological thing."

"It's *Changeling*, if you don't mind," said Culley. "But you're right. He had to call another veterinarian to fill in for a while because Connor can't leave his mate's side. Actually, it's starting to drive Zoey crazy—" Elbowed by Devlin, Culley shrugged and fell silent.

"There're more than enough of us," said James.

Out of the corner of his eye, Josh saw Birkie reach behind her and place a restraining hand on James's much bigger one, the one that was balled into a formidable fist at present. Josh wasn't sure if James was pissed at him because he was casting doubt on their ability or questioning Connor's absence. Both, he decided.

"We're here to get our girl back," Birkie said to Josh. Her voice was as friendly as ever, but he could hear the resolve and the certainty in it. "And we will. Like James said, there are more than enough of us to do the job."

"Like Texas Rangers," added Stanton.

One riot, one Changeling. Josh fervently hoped his friend was right. "Let's get down to business then. We'll want to reach the facility before sundown."

"Wait a second. I want to know how my sister ended up a prisoner in the first place." It was James again, his voice still low and dangerous. He obviously thought Josh was to blame for the situation. Stanton narrowed his eyes, about to say something scathing no doubt, but Josh signaled him back.

Best to meet this one head on. He locked eyes with the bigger man. "Kenzie went after Anya alone while I was checking another trail because we'd had an argument."

"That so? And just what were you giving her a hard time about?"

"That *hard time* was pretty mutual as I recall, and the subject's none of your business—it's between me and Kenzie." Josh didn't miss that the twins almost took a physical step back, as if expecting an explosion. "You want to go a round with me, James, that's fine. Name the place and time. But it can damn well wait until Kenzie and the others are safe." Josh deliberately turned his back on the big man and spread out his maps and papers on the hood of his truck. "Culley, I hear you're the electronics expert. I've got a live fence around the compound and the power shed appears to be *here* on the north side . . ."

As Culley peered at the map, his face had lost its threatening demeanor. In fact, Josh could swear that he was trying not to laugh. The others circled around and a moment later, James silently joined in.

Four more Changelings now stood on human feet. Only three remained as wolves, and of those, Beau and Rico were still unconscious. Kenzie was worried about them both—whatever they were being drugged with was heavy-duty stuff. And, hours later, Dempsey still had not been returned to his cage.

A couple of handlers had brought in fresh deer quarters, using butchers' chainmail gloves as they shoved them through the narrow steel flaps in the cage doors over the brackets that held the food dishes. Kenzie decided she needed to keep up her strength. She couldn't stomach raw venison as a human any more than she could handle pizza

as a wolf. So she Changed as soon as the men left and gob-
bled down the fresh meat, even cracking the bigger bones
and licking out the marrow. The others followed suit.

Nikki came in as Kenzie finished eating and gingerly approached her cage. "Dempsey is in ICU. I think we've got
him stabilized now, but he's had a rough time of it. The
tranq obviously affects you differently when you're in
human form than it does when you're a wolf. I'm so sorry."

It wasn't going to hurt anything to shift her form in
front of the young vet; she already knew what Kenzie was.
And maybe it would be a gesture of trust between them.
Kenzie stood and resumed her human form.

The others followed her lead, and for a few moments,
blue sparks rained in the room and unseen vortexes of icy
air spun wildly about.

"Oh. My. God." Nikki's face was awestruck. Her sleek
black hair was mussed from all the static electricity. A pair
of blue sparks winked out on her lab coat. "I didn't think it
would be so fast. That was amazing."

Kenzie noted with satisfaction that, except for Beau and
Rico, every one of the Changelings had now put away
their wolfen forms. After all, brute force wasn't going to get
them out of their cages. But a little charm and some op-
posable thumbs just might. . . .

The crash of the door on the far side of the room dis-
pelled her optimism. Gessler strode in, obviously enjoying
his noisy entrance, and handed Nikki a thick sheaf of
paper. "New security rules, Dr. Yeung."

"What are you, a secretary now? I don't have time to go
over this bureaucratic—" she began but Gessler put up his
hand.

"It involves you and your staff," he said and pointed to a
paragraph highlighted in yellow. "For your own safety,

you'll be accompanied by one of my men each and every time you enter this room."

"Since when? What the hell is this about?"

"It's about our research subjects assuming human shape in order to elicit sympathy from the *real* humans. You could be seriously wounded or even killed in an unguarded moment, Dr. Yeung. This is for your own protection."

"That's a load of horseshit, buddy, and I'm going to the top about this right now." She stalked from the room.

Gessler turned a mocking smile on Kenzie. "Whatever you're planning isn't going to work," he whispered, and sauntered after Nikki.

"I hate that guy," said Roy.

Kenzie clenched her fists in frustration. "Not nearly as much as I do." Just then a voice popped into her head. It was Stanton, only it was *so* much easier to hear him than it had been before. She listened carefully, then beamed at Roy and the others.

"They're coming," she announced.

Roy looked toward the door. "Who is it now?"

"No, no, not from here. My friends on the outside. They're coming to get us."

Whispered cheers came from the other cages. Dan and Shaggy Sam high-fived each other through the mesh.

Kenzie paused as Stanton continued. "He did *what*? Omigod." *He couldn't have.*

"What's wrong?" asked Roy.

"Josh called in my brothers." And even Birkie had come along to help. The mix of emotions was overwhelming, almost dizzying, and Kenzie sat down to try to make sense of them. Elation and relief warred with stark fear for her loved ones. Kenzie didn't want her family anywhere near this terrible place. Astonishment that a human would take it upon himself to apprise her Changeling family of her situation blended with worry—what if they blamed Josh? After all, hadn't she reacted the same way when she'd discovered Anya missing? Of course, her brothers were more accepting of humans than she was, and with Birkie on hand, maybe they wouldn't do anything to him.

Maybe.

The road was little more than a bulldozed path through thick forest, most likely created when the facility was being built and left to its own devices after that. Josh felt a headache coming on, partly from the constant jarring of driving over deep ruts and potholes, and partly from his own frustration at not being able to travel faster. His hands were tense on the wheel, wanting nothing better than to break someone in half over Kenzie's imprisonment, even as he knew emotions clouded judgement in battle. Still, his feelings refused to be quelled. The lowhung sky matched his mood, the dark clouds roiling like his gut. Fury at her captors warred with hurt over her parting words. What if she'd been telling the truth and couldn't love a human partner? What if she really didn't want him?

Then she doesn't want me, he told himself sternly. *But I'm getting her out of there so she can tell me that herself.*

He envied James and Devlin, who had shifted to their lupine forms and run on ahead as scouts. They didn't have to follow the road and could make far better time. Stanton and Culley were in the second truck but Birkie had elected to travel with him.

Josh was apprehensive about her company at first, but she didn't interrogate him, simply talked about the rest of the Macleod family and their life in the small rural town of Dunvegan. He relaxed after a few minutes, and allowed her to distract him a little from the maelstrom of emotions that battered him.

"You're not a Changeling but you sure seem to know a lot about them," he said finally.

She nodded. "I've been acquainted with Changelings my entire life."

"So tell me, can a shapeshifter have a successful relationship with a human?"

If she was surprised by his question, she hid it well. "Can and do, all the time. James's wife was human when he met her. So was Connor's."

What? "There're humans in Kenzie's *family*?" He'd make a point of bringing that little gem up in their next argument. And by God, there was going to be one.

"Plenty of them. Even her father was human when Gwen met him. Most Changelings find their mates among humans. For one thing, there aren't that many shapeshifters around. And for another, Changelings *are* human, really. They just have a few extra talents. And a few special needs—they mate for life, you know."

"So do I."

Birkie nodded but there was a satisfied grin on her face as she gracefully changed the subject.

It was dusk when they ditched the trucks about a mile from the IBC compound, pulling them into the forest and covering them with branches. Stanton had brought a veritable arsenal—Josh figured it represented a sizeable chunk of his friend's personal collection—and distributed rifles, handguns, and tasers.

"Holy crap," said Culley. "The government let you register all this? Hell, they let you *buy* all this?"

Stanton chuckled. "It's Alaska, son. No gun control here on the frontier."

"That's it, I'm moving here," he sighed.

"Use nonlethal force *if* you can," instructed Josh, taking one of the tasers. "But since we're dealing with people who think kidnapping's A-OK, chances are they won't hesitate to shoot us. So do what you need to do. Anybody have a problem with that?"

No one did.

Culley had his own contribution, holding up a camouflage hood. "IBC has more money than God. So everybody keep your face hidden at all times. I've got enough hoods for everyone, but if you don't want to use one, wear face paint, sunglasses, *something* that will obscure your features. Because if they catch you on a security camera, there'll be more than legal ramifications to worry about. Number one, they'll suspect you of being a Changeling and hunt you down later, and trust me, they have the resources to find you anywhere on the planet. In other words, your life is ruined if they see you."

"Encouraging pre-game speech there, coach," remarked Devlin.

Birkie passed out tiny leather pouches on rawhide cords. "This should take care of that little problem. Made them myself."

All three Macleods looked relieved and immediately put them on. Stanton scrutinized his, even sniffed it, then shrugged and followed suit.

"A medicine bag?" asked Josh. The traditional protective talisman was common to many Native American cultures, including his own. The bags usually held sacred herbs, stones, feathers, and other found objects.

Birkie patted his arm. "Not exactly. I guarantee they're not just decorative, son."

"Hey, I'll take any help I can get," he said as he slipped

the cord over his head and tucked the pouch beneath his shirt and T-shirt, next to his skin. "Thanks."

"Once we're inside, don't talk above a whisper if you can avoid it," continued Culley. "We don't want to take a chance on anyone's voice patterns getting recorded. And glove up. No prints."

The six of them took to the forest, following a narrow game trail through the thick brush until they came within sight of the gate. Birkie and Stanton dug in on the southwest side, hiding themselves at the edge of the treeline where they could watch anyone entering or leaving. The rest slipped quietly around the western perimeter of the compound, using the forest as cover.

The compound was more oval than square, following the natural terrain. Cutting off the corners made the distance much shorter on paper, but it sure didn't feel like it, thought Josh. It had taken forever to hike around to the north side where the wind turbine loomed over the power shed. Culley surveyed the high metal fence critically, then walked back to the treeline without a word. When he reappeared, he was dragging a huge log. Josh and James helped him position it upright about four feet from the fence—then let it go. A shower of sparks crackled and sprayed in all directions like fireworks as the log toppled onto the mesh. Parts of the timber blackened and caught fire and Josh was grateful that nobody had touched the fence—this was no wildlife deterrent but a full-fledged anti-personnel device designed to disable intruders.

Devlin, who was watching the compound from beneath a thicket of huckleberry bushes about forty yards further down, had a clear view of the front of the main building and signaled that they were clear. The power shed, the size of a city bus and located about ten feet inside the fence, was shielding them nicely from any IBC eyes, and the deep twilight would make it difficult for any casual glances to see the smoke. Particularly when the main building had no windows on this side.

A few moments later, Culley poked at the fence with a stick, then slapped it with his hand. "It's shorted out. Let's chop through it." James set to work with bolt cutters and started taking out a large chunk of mesh about six feet tall and almost as wide.

"I don't know about you, bro, but the rest of us could fit through a *way* smaller hole," said Culley.

"We've got a dozen people to rescue plus ourselves," James whispered fiercely. "If something happens that we have to get out of here in a hurry, I'd rather not try to do it single file."

"Wait." Josh pulled out his field glasses. He had a clear view of the ATV shed on the northeast and the dog runs between it and the garage. No animals were visible. Maybe they were sleeping, but it seemed unlikely. He held a hand to his ear where his headset nestled under the gray and brown camo fabric and spoke to Devlin. "How many ATVs do you count over there?"

"Five."

"Dogs?"

"None."

"We've got issues then."

As if on cue, Stanton hailed him. "Heads up, Tark. Got a guy coming up the road with a herd of dogs the size of ponies following him. He'll be at the gate in about ten."

Shit. The handler would have to bring the dogs all the way across the compound to their pens—and the animals were bound to sense the presence of intruders. "We're going to have to pull back," said Josh.

"We can if you want us to, boss," Culley said, helping to pull the mesh out of the way as James continued to cut the fence as if nothing was wrong. "But Birkie can handle the dogs."

"*Birkie?*" What the hell was a little old lady going to do? But then Josh remembered that strange silvery aura . . . He belly-crawled over to Devlin, reaching his hidey-hole just as a pinging sound from across the compound signaled that the gate was opening. Both of them trained their glasses in time to see a man on an ATV come into sight on the road. There were at least six dogs trotting beside him, maybe seven—and the old vet had been right; they looked *huge*, even from Josh's vantage point.

Suddenly an enormous mule deer, a pale buck with antlers like tree branches, leapt directly into the path of the vehicle and sprang straight up and over the head of its driver, who barely had time to duck. The big animal hit the ground running and bounded back down the trail at top speed. Every dog wheeled and followed the creature, barking madly. Their handler jumped off the ATV, waving his arms and shouting, but the dogs didn't return. He stood there for a long moment, then drove the ATV into the compound, parking it beside the gate and walking into the main building.

Josh returned to Culley, not quite sure what he'd just witnessed. "She's not—you're not telling me that was Birkie, are you?"

"Hell no," he chuckled. "She's not a shapeshifter. But that lady has some pretty impressive talents. Don't know where she found the deer or how she persuaded it to pull that stunt, but it'll keep those dogs busy for hours. Who knows, the gate might be left open for them tonight and we won't even have to use this fine doorway we're making."

Josh fingered the little leather pouch around his neck that Birkie had given him. She'd said it *wasn't decorative*—did he really want to know what it could do? "Let's keep an eye on the ATV just the same. The guy might go back for it and put it away."

"That's got it," said James suddenly and helped Culley pull the rest of the cut mesh clear of the hole they'd made. Josh checked his watch. Twenty-two hundred. Two more hours to *maximum dark* and they could enact their plan. Fortunately, the thick cloud cover was helping to dull the perpetual twilight of the northern night and the moon would be well hidden, at least for a while.

Devlin remained on lookout while the rest of them retreated to the cover of the treeline for the hardest part of the operation.

Waiting.

Chapter Twenty-one

Nikki was back for her late evening rounds, accompanied by one of Gessler's men. Her face was dark with anger, and the security guard was armed to the teeth—no question about how the young vet's visit with her boss had gone.

Kenzie sighed inwardly. When were they going to catch a break? She couldn't just sit on her hands and wait to be rescued. And there was no guarantee that any rescue attempt would work. Not with someone like Gessler around.

"Hey, how's Dempsey?" Roy called out to the veterinarian.

"No talking," shouted the guard, brandishing a dart pistol. "Not a word out of any of you."

Nikki went from cage to cage with a small cart, carefully pulling out bones and used dishes and replacing them with clean bowls. She paused in front of Roy's cage, and a tear ran down her face. "Dempsey didn't make it," she whispered. "I'm so sorry—the doctor and I both worked on him, but they wouldn't let us fly him out. And then he was gone." Several more tears followed the first.

The guard took a step forward. "You can't talk to the

subjects, Dr. Yeung," he said, almost apologetically. "Orders."

"They deserve to know what happened to their friend, Carl," she retorted, sniffing as she moved to Kenzie's cage. She removed the old dish and picked up the last of the clean bowls in her hands. Before she set it in place, however, she rubbed its stainless steel side with her fingernail ever so lightly. The sound was faint for human ears, but Changeling senses picked it up easily. When Nikki and the guard had left, Kenzie resisted diving for the bowl, knowing that the cameras would pick up whatever she did.

Roy stood clutching the front of his cage, leaning his head against the mesh with his eyes closed.

"I'm so sorry about Dempsey," she whispered. "It's horrible, especially with help so close at hand."

He shoved himself upright and appeared to pull himself together. "Thanks, but Gessler is the one who's going to be sorry. I don't know how, but the bastard is going to pay for this. What did you get from Nikki?"

"I don't know yet. I have to figure out how to grab it without being filmed. I'll bet Gessler is actively monitoring every one of these damn cameras now."

"Maybe we should give him a show then."

"A diversion?"

He waggled his brows and whispered to his cell mate on the other side. The message got passed on down until it reached Shaggy Sam and Dan. A few minutes later, the pair of them began a wild air guitar rendition of a Metallica song—with full volume vocals.

"They've done this before," she chuckled.

Roy rolled his eyes. "Sadly, yes. But if Gessler has this room bugged, he'll never hear us now. And if anyone but him is watching the monitors, they're likely to watch the more interesting prisoners instead of us."

Suddenly howls and low drawn-out cries could be heard from somewhere beyond the massive room that housed the Changelings.

"Sounds like the wolves are singing along," said Roy.

"Maybe they're trying to help us. Or maybe they don't like the playlist. Why the hell does IBC have *real* wolves?"

"They've got a dozen of them somewhere in the east wing. We think they keep them for comparison to us, maybe going through our bodies with a fine-toothed comb, searching for differences of any kind, including a way to identify us by our genes."

Kenzie shivered. "Now I want to howl too."

She sat beside the broad metal dish hanging low to the floor in its bracket and faced the wall that separated her from Roy. "Sit down here like we're talking or something."

He knelt close to the mesh. "Can you reach under the dish?"

"In a minute. We need to look like we're having a conversation so they're not watching my hands."

"Ah. I'll be Italian then so they'll watch mine," Roy said and began making hand movements as if explaining something. Gradually Kenzie squeezed her fingers between the dish and the floor and felt around until she found a tiny paper bundle attached to the bottom with what was probably duct tape. Dan and Shaggy Sam had moved on to cover Ozzy Osbourne before she was able to peel the little prize free. Carefully she gripped a corner of it between her fingers and turned her hand palm down. A moment later, the hand was in her pocket, where the treasure was deposited.

"So far, so good," said Roy. "I don't see any goons busting down the door to search you."

"Now all I have to do is figure out where the blind spots of the camera are."

"Easy. We figured that one out months ago. Guillermo used to install those things for a living."

With his guidance, she moved to a spot near the opposite corner. "Here goes." She pulled out her contraband and peeled the duct tape away to reveal a tiny envelope, containing far more than she had dared hope for. In it was a pair of key cards, what looked like a car key, and a series of numbers on a sticky note—a combination?—with a memo that read "cub on 2nd floor, unit 9." "Nikki really outdid herself."

Something Josh had said ran through her mind—*We should be pulling together, not pulling apart.* Now Kenzie had the means to make a contribution to the rescue effort.

Josh studied the sky with satisfaction. It was nearly mission time and they'd have ample darkness to be able to use their NVGs—night vision goggles—inside the facility. Or rather, *he* would. Culley had explained to him that none of the Changelings would require the equipment, since they possessed natural night vision even in human form. He rolled his eyes, wondering if perhaps Kenzie saw humans as an inferior species. He'd bet that Nate Richardson did. The Macleod brothers seemed different, however. They'd accepted his plan and his leadership without a hitch, even James, even though none of them struck him as a natural follower. It had surprised him—after all, in human form the brothers were stronger than he and had enhanced senses. And in wolfen form, they were far more powerful than he could ever hope to be.

His love for Kenzie, however, was no less deep and strong for its newness. And his determination to free her was absolute.

"We've got a vehicle, Tark." Stanton's voice in his ear made him jump. "Yellow Humvee approaching the gate."

Christ. What the hell was Nate Richardson doing here at this time of night? And how was it going to affect the mission? Josh got part of his answer right away.

"Vehicle's inside the compound, and the driver's on his cell phone." Stanton hadn't finished the sentence before a loud pinging sound echoed across the compound. The gate was closing, no doubt at Richardson's insistence. So much for the quick exit they'd hoped might be available. Josh was glad now that James had made the hole in the fence extra-large. He looked at his watch.

"Let's give this jerk a little while to finish up his business and hope he'll leave," Josh said into the headset to Stanton and to the Macleods sitting with him.

"What if he doesn't?" asked James.

"We're going in anyway." *And I'm going to punch him out.*

An hour later, they rose from their hiding place. It was as dark as it was going to get, and the yellow Humvee was still parked at the front of the main building. There were a few lights still on in some of the windows, but Josh wasn't surprised by that. His own experience with scientist types had led him to expect that some would naturally press on with their work into the evening hours.

The four made their way to the back of the power shed, then slipped around the side. Culley reached around and tried the knob. "Locked," he said and handed a small bag of tools to Devlin. "Thirty seconds, bro."

"Twenty." He had it unlocked in fifteen, but closed the

door again. "I'm going to shut down their communications to start with," he said, pointing at the satellite dish on the roof of the main building. "And then I'm coming back here. Call me when it's time for lights out." Devlin ran across the grassy terrain to the steel ladder mounted on the north wall.

Josh and the others headed for a small service door not far from the ladder. They'd be well hidden while they worked on the lock, and the door itself opened beneath a stairwell. With a little luck, they wouldn't be seen when they entered the building.

It was one thing to have the key card and another to be able to reach the lock to swipe it. There was no chance of hiding what she was doing either. Dan and Shaggy Sam continued to rock on, adding some wild choreography to the act, hoping to keep all eyes on them. Meanwhile, Kenzie had tried for several minutes before she finally managed to squeeze her hand all the way through the slight gap between the door frame and the cage wall. It took even longer to try to slide the card through the slot, as her wrist protested not just the pressure of being wedged in a narrow space, but the unnatural angle of her hand. After the first two times Kenzie figured out she had the card backward. On the third try, the card slipped from her fingers and fluttered to the floor.

"Dammit." She could have cried in frustration.

"It's okay," said Roy. "We've got a second card."

Yeah, but I don't have another left wrist. She thanked whatever lucky stars helped her arm to go through the gap a little quicker this time. And then managed to swipe the card all the way through the slot.

She retrieved her hand as the door swung open.

"Keep singing, guys," she called as she quickly stepped out and swiped Roy's cage. She handed him a card and together they freed the rest of the prisoners. "We've got to move fast. Unless someone's asleep in front of that monitor, we'll be busted any second. My friends and family are on the north side of the compound—they've made a hole in the fence behind the power shed."

"Aren't you coming?" called Roy, as he and Guillermo dragged the unconscious Beau from his cage.

"I have to get Anya." She turned to leave and froze—

Nate Richardson had just stepped through the door. The sight of Kenzie outside of her cage enraged him and he leapt straight for her, knocking her to the cement, banging her head hard enough to stun her. Before she could recover, his hands were tight around her throat. She gouged at his face, his eyes, as her own vision darkened at the edges, but suddenly he jumped away from her.

She rolled to her knees, gulping air until her head cleared. At least she *thought* it had cleared—a strange pale shimmer of greenish gold washed over Nate's skin. Suddenly she realized that every Changeling in the room had silently focused his gaze on Nate, and she could sense the *push* of energy from their minds. Nate began clawing and slapping at himself as if a thousand flies were biting him at once. Kenzie sprang to her feet and backed away as Nate's face elongated and his body reframed in a forced Change. Just as he screamed, his golden skin erupted in the tawny fur of a giant wolf.

He jerked a couple of times as if electrified, then scrambled clumsily through the open door. Kenzie turned to the others. "*Go*," she yelled. "Get everyone out *now*." She could hear a commotion somewhere above them, the sound of running feet. *Hurry!* She put every bit of energy she had into broadcasting her message to the rescue team outside as she ran down the hall. *We're free but they're after us.*

Her senses told her she was heading north, and Stanton had said there was a stairwell at that end of the building. She had to get to Anya, but she could hear the pounding of boots beyond a double door ahead. Quickly, she ducked into a side room, a surgical-looking place of cold stainless steel and tile that reeked of formaldehyde and other pungent substances. Kenzie managed to hide behind a big wheeled garbage can just as the lights went out.

The boots, about three pairs of them, stopped dead amid curses. Someone yelled for the emergency lights, but Kenzie knew that her brothers would have been thorough. Suddenly there was a crash from further down the hall and an immense commotion. "Drop your weapons!" shouted a familiar voice—it was Culley. A shot was fired high along the ceiling and there was a few seconds' silence, followed by the clash and clatter of weapons hitting the tiled floor.

Hey Kenzie. The good guys are here. You okay?

Fine, Culley, thanks. Follow the hallway and help the others get outside, okay?

Gotcha.

Her eyes had easily adjusted to the darkness, but when she stood up, she wasn't ready for what she saw. She'd thought she was in a lab but the cloying stench of the chemicals had blocked her ability to scent what the room actually was—a *morgue*. The steel tables closest to her were empty, but farther down, two had bodies. One was in a black bag, probably the ill-fated Dempsey because it was human shaped. The other was different, and it lay beneath a heavy sheet—

She had to look. She didn't want to, but she had to know. Kenzie forced herself to walk over to the farthest table and pull back the sheet.

An adult wolf lay spread-eagled, belly up. Kenzie peeled the surgical fabric back further, exposing that the animal had been not just autopsied but carefully *dissected*, nose to tail, and preserved in that hideous condition. A rush of horror overwhelmed her as she realized several things at once. The wolf was actually a Changeling. A female.

And one of its front legs was pure white.

You bastard, she thought, wishing now she'd been able to claw Nate's eyes out. *You unholy bastard*. Grim and heartsick, she headed to the hallway, which was empty except for a brass shell casing from the shot Culley had fired. Quickly she jogged north, heading for the stairs. She was getting Anya out of here *now*.

Josh and James swept the first floor, room by room, as Culley and the other Changelings locked the three guards in one of the runs. Two more of the staff were put into an adjacent run after being found hiding under a desk in the dark.

Josh assigned Culley and Devlin to help the Changelings get outside while he covered them. James disappeared. A few moments later, an entire pack of wolves came racing around the corner, eerily erupting from the shadows in strange shades of blue and gray thanks to Josh's night vision goggles. He gripped his rifle reflexively but stood his ground as the animals swirled around him, and wondered where the hell James was—until an enormous white wolf bounded into sight. Damned if the thing didn't wink a bright eye at him. *Jesus, James.*

"I'm heading upstairs," growled Josh. The white wolf

chuffed and wheeled to follow him, with the pack obedi-ently in tow as if they were well-trained dogs. Josh had no time to consider how surreal the situation was as he bounded up the steps. He was too busy watching for any opposition from IBC, uneasy that things were going smoothly and knowing it was unlikely to last.

Just as the strange group cleared the landing, a pair of men wearing lab coats came stumbling out of a room into the dark hallway and froze. Josh doubted they could see much, but the growling of a dozen wolves couldn't be missed. One man screamed and ran, the other threw up his hands and backed against the wall, shaking uncontrollably. James bounded after the runner and knocked him down within a few feet, where he lay too frightened to move. Josh leveled his rifle at the other man, whose eyes were bulging behind his wire-rimmed glasses. It was Jurgen Schumacher, whom he'd met on the scouting trip with Stanton. Funny how the *project manager* seemed much less arrogant when terrified. "How many people are on this floor?"

"N-n-now?"

"Now. Here tonight."

The man continued to shake as if palsied. "F-f-four, m-m-m-maybe f-five."

"Go lie facedown next to your buddy." The man walked on jellied legs to comply, half-lying, half-collapsing on the floor. To Josh's amazement, two wolves promptly lay down on top of the men, effectively pinning them. He spared a brief hope that the guys wouldn't have heart attacks, and tackled the second-floor rooms one by one.

A dozen rooms and four more scientists later, he still hadn't seen Kenzie and no one seemed to know where she

was. Culley said she'd gone after Anya and they were upstairs somewhere, but Josh was rapidly running out of
rooms to check. And no sign either of that *son-of-a-bitch*,
Richardson. It was the middle of the frickin' night and
most people should be in their barracks asleep, not *working*
for chrissakes. Stanton and Birkie hadn't seen anyone leaving any buildings—

Sudden shots rang out from outside in the compound.
"We've got five guards, maybe six, making a stand in the
ATV shed," Stanton's voice crackled in Josh's ear. "There's
no getting to the hole in the fence right now, they've got it
too well covered."

"All of us are still in the main building, retreated to the
south end, and we've got one prisoner wounded," said
Culley. "I'm trying to get the damn front gate open but it's
encrypted and I haven't figured out the password yet."

"I'm sending James. Maybe he can give you guys a hand
down there," Josh said. "I'll finish clearing the top floor and
we'll figure out something." The white wolf made a series
of high-pitched yips and dashed away, followed by all but
the two wolves guarding the prisoners. Josh studied the
hallway before him. There were at least a dozen more
doors to go. He was about to kick in the door of the nearest one when a fluttering motion caught his eye. . . .

He shouldn't have been able to see color with the
NVGs, but the little girl's tunic and shawl were vivid green
and red as always. Her clothing was stirred by a phantom
breeze, and tendrils of her dark hair escaped her scarf. She
stood, solemn-eyed, in front of the farthest door, with one
small palm upon its glossy metal surface—and then faded
from his sight.

Under normal circumstances, Josh would have continued sweeping every room along the way. But nothing was normal here, and whether spirit or hallucination, the little Afghan girl had never steered him wrong. Quietly he made his way down the hall and kicked open the door she had pointed to. His hands were steady and his rifle was instantly trained on Nate Richardson's forehead.

The man stood with Anya clutched by the throat in one hand and a gun pointed at Josh in the other. The little wolf's eyes were wide with fear and she was trembling. "Welcome to the party, Talarkoteen," he said. "Put the weapon down and you can have Kenzie." He nodded at a small locked cage on the other side of the room in which she was crouched. "The cub and I have other places to go."

"You said you'd let her go, Nate," Kenzie fumed, rattling the door in frustration. "You *promised* you wouldn't hurt her."

Josh's rifle was unmoving. "Put the kid down. Now. You kill her and you won't take another breath."

"I'm no soft human. All I have to do is close my hand," said Richardson smugly. "Her neck will snap and I can shoot *you*, all at the same time. And then I'll shoot the bitch in the cage just for laughs." He squeezed Anya a little harder until she made little choking sounds. "So put the rifle down and get out of my way."

Josh was about to lower his rifle when a brilliant flash of light blinded him and made him tear off the NVGs. Nate was flung backward into a bookcase, hard enough to stun him. The little wolf was gone and a small blond-haired girl blinked unsteadily and sat down hard on the floor, as blue sparks rained like falling stars all around her.

Spots whirled in front of Josh's eyes but despite the dark he could just make out that Richardson's hand still gripped the gun. "Get over to Kenzie," he said to Anya. "Hurry!" The little girl scurried to comply.

He brought his rifle to bear and when his opponent started to recover, Josh deliberately fired into the wall next to him. "Drop it."

Nate blinked and tossed the gun aside. He grinned strangely, as if the whole thing was humorous—and faster than Josh could react, a tawny wolf was at his throat.

Chapter Twenty-two

Kenzie screamed a warning but the big tawny wolf had already come up under Josh's guard, making it impossible for him to bring the rifle to bear. Only his instincts prevented his belly from being torn out. He brought the butt of the rifle down on the wolf's broad skull with a loud crack and used the momentum to spring out of the way. It barely bought him a second's respite, however. The wolf was on top of him in a heartbeat, its fang-filled jaws held away from Josh's face by only the rifle gripped crosswise in his hands, as if he were bench pressing a weight from hell.

It was getting hard to breathe and his arm muscles felt like they were going to shred at any second. Human strength was no match for a shapeshifter. But if he didn't stop Richardson, not only would he be killed, but Kenzie would be dead and Anya would spend her life in a lab. Josh held on, his own teeth bared even as the savage jaws snarled just inches away from his face. Again and again, he brought his knee up hard into the wolf's ribs and gut. For the longest time it didn't seem to have the slightest effect on the creature. . . .

Then abruptly the giant wolf jumped off to one side and Josh sucked in a lungful of welcome air. There was no time to gather himself, however, no time to move or think before snake-quick jaws had clamped onto his thigh. Yelling, Josh threw rapid-fire punches into the beast's tender nose, desperate to make the creature let go before it applied all the pressure it was capable of and took his leg off.

Suddenly a dark blur sailed over him and latched onto his attacker, ripping and tearing with tooth and claw. The tawny wolf released Josh to fend off Kenzie and Josh rolled fast to get out of the way. *The gun, where's the damn gun?*

"Did you want this?" asked a soft voice to his left. He turned his head to see Anya holding out the handgun to him in small cupped hands. Josh grabbed the weapon and held it in front of him with both hands to steady it. All he needed was a clear target for one split second, but the shapeshifters were rolling and snarling and snapping. It was too dark and the Changelings were moving too fast for him to separate Kenzie from Richardson. Blood and saliva and fur flew. "Anya, tell Kenzie to duck. In her head, tell her *fast*."

Abruptly, the gray wolf dropped flat to the floor and the larger tawny creature lunged with open jaws for the vulnerable spine at the base of her skull. Josh didn't even hear the retort of the gun, only saw two holes open up between the tawny wolf's eyes. It slumped over its would-be victim, its long fangs still bared in a permanent snarl.

Wriggling out from under the massive head, the gray wolf shook itself and Changed. Kenzie was bleeding from countless scratches, and a couple of long gashes along her ribs and down her back, but she caught the little girl who flew into her arms. Josh lay propped up against a desk, grateful to see the two together and safe. He wanted nothing more than to gather them both into his arms, but felt strangely weak and dizzy—must be his body dumping all its adrenaline after the fight. Then he looked at his leg and spotted the dark red pool fanning out around it.

"*Shit*," he said aloud, frantically ripping off his camo shirt in a hail of buttons.

Startled, Kenzie followed his line of sight and blanched. She was beside him in a flash, tearing off strips of the cotton material, folding it into pads and packing it tight against the wounds. "Anya, press down here, like this. And here too, okay? Atta girl."

"How bad's it look?" asked Josh.

"It's deep, and I don't know if the artery's been nicked. It's bleeding like crazy." She stopped and took a deep breath as if she'd been holding it. "But I can't believe it's not worse."

"You kept that from happening by jumping in."

She grinned a little at that. "We saved each other. And Anya helped, didn't you?"

"I made the lock open. Kenzie told me how."

"Nikki gave me some numbers, and they turned out to be the combination to that cage." She tied the last of the fabric around Josh's leg. "Anya was very clever—I know a lot of grownups who'd have trouble with a lock like that."

"We couldn't have done it without you, honey," said Josh, wishing he hadn't had to shoot Richardson in front of her. "But we've got to get out of here now." He grabbed Richardson's handgun and stuck it in the back of his waistband, slung his rifle over his shoulder. Anya found his NVGs for him. They still worked but his radio had been broken in the fight. He jammed it in a pocket, not wanting to leave evidence. Amazingly, Birkie's leather pouch still hung around his neck. He snorted—the amazing thing was that he still *had* a neck.

As he struggled to his feet, Josh had to lean heavily on Kenzie, and was grateful for her Changeling strength.

"Are you sure you can do this?" she asked. "You're going to start bleeding again."

"Hey, I got Wonder Woman and Super Girl to help me out. I can do anything." He began moving forward, but had to grit his teeth to manage it. Anya pushed herself under his other hand and tried to help. He tousled her blond hair, hoping she'd stay human for a while. "Let's catch up with the others now."

From what she could glean from her brothers using mindspeech, nothing had changed downstairs. Kenzie hoped they could break the standoff before anyone else showed up at the complex, or someone managed to get a message out. Plus Josh's leg needed attention—she had no idea how he was walking on it—and both Birkie and Stanton were on the outside of the compound.

Two wolves still guarded the door to an office holding terrified IBC staff. The big animals surveyed the threesome solemnly as they passed by. "Can you talk to them?" managed Josh between his teeth. "We oughta say thanks."

"James and Connor are the experts in communicating with animals—" began Kenzie, but Anya interrupted.

"I can tell them. I know how." Before anyone could say a word, the child had skipped over to the nearest wolf and gripped the thick ruff on either side of his neck, bringing her small delicate face close to his broad muzzled one. It was scary as hell for a grownup to watch, knowing the ease with which the wolf could savage the life from Anya if it chose, but she was perfectly comfortable with the big predator and repeated the performance with the second one. Whatever she said was passed silently to each wolf, and both animals sat calmly, as if they talked with little girls every day. "Jesus," breathed Josh, his hand gripping Kenzie's arm.

"They're gonna wait here for somebody to come and take their place," Anya said, as she came back and took Kenzie's hand. "But then they want to go home."

"I don't blame them," Kenzie said, with a *can-you-believe-this* glance at Josh. "I want to go home too."

The journey down the stairs was slow and difficult. Josh gripped the railing with both hands and hopped on his good leg, as Kenzie walked close in front of him in case he fell. They were only a few steps from the bottom when an unwelcome voice called out from the shadows.

"Freeze right there or I shoot."

"Gessler," spat Kenzie and swept Anya behind her.

"Don't move," breathed Josh and she understood at once. The way that she was positioned, half in front of him, he might be able to get to his handgun before Gessler saw him. She hoped.

"Glad to see you too. Hands up where I can see them." The man emerged from the dark hallway, wearing NVGs and pointing a small black Glock at them. Her friend Magdi had had one like it that she kept with her at all times. She'd said that the gun had a *light trigger* and Kenzie instinctively knew that this man would enjoy letting his finger slip.

"I have to hang on to the railing," said Josh. "Or I'll fall." His blood-soaked pants and smeared T-shirt, plus the makeshift bandages, reinforced his story.

Gessler shrugged. "All I want is the kid. IBC will pay me a helluva reward if I can produce her, so let me have her and you go free. Everybody gets what they want."

"How do we know you won't kill us?" asked Kenzie.

Gessler raised the Glock. "I'm *certainly* going to kill you if you don't comply. So better for you to take a chance that I'm feeling generous and give me my little prize."

It was obvious that the guy was concerned about harming his "prize" or he would have shot both of them already. Kenzie could feel movement behind her left shoulder as Josh no doubt palmed his gun—

Suddenly a slender black shape separated itself from the darkness behind Gessler and stabbed him in the neck with a small fluorescent yellow dart. The man cursed but the sound trailed off and he collapsed to the floor in an untidy heap, his NVGs skittering across the floor and coming to rest against a wall.

The figure pulled back the hood of her black sweatshirt to reveal goggles and a grin. "*Nikki!*" Kenzie ran down the rest of the steps to hug the young veterinarian. "Thank you. You were wonderful." She glanced over at Gessler. "I shouldn't care but you didn't use—I mean, it's not—"

"No, this stuff goes by body weight and it's less than half a dose for an ordinary wolf. I didn't want to kill him. Well, not much anyway."

Anya bounced down the steps and Nikki's grin disappeared. "Omigod, you're the cub, aren't you? I—I'm sorry." She dropped to her knees and took Anya's hands. "We didn't believe . . . we didn't know that you were really *people.*" She looked up at Josh and Kenzie. "Most of us thought we'd discovered a new subspecies of wolf, perhaps even a remnant of the old *dire wolf* from the last Ice Age. I'm so sorry."

Anya shrugged, not sure what to do. "The man with the gun is bad," she said simply. "He's the one that took my mom away. He caught me too and I bit him, but he didn't let me go."

"Yes, he was bad," agreed Kenzie. "And somebody had to stop him, so Nikki did that for us." The child nodded, apparently satisfied. Kenzie wondered how Anya was ever going to be able to adjust to everything that had happened to her. "Come on, let's go find the others."

Nikki was appalled by the condition of Josh's leg and made him promise to let her look at it. She helped Kenzie support him as they headed through the doorway into the blackness of the corridor. They'd gone only a few yards when a shot deafened them in the confined space and something whistled past Kenzie's ear. In a flash, Josh took the women to the floor with him and shielded Anya with his body. His pistol was pointed at the stairwell they'd just left.

"You're not getting away that easy." It was Gessler. His words sounded slow, as if played on low-speed, but there was no doubt he was still dangerous.

"*Shit*," hissed Nikki. "I *knew* I should have given him the full dose."

"Either the kid starts walking toward me or I start shooting," he shouted.

A muzzle flash blossomed in the darkness as Gessler fired another shot. Josh's NVGs didn't seem to be affected by the sudden brief light, and Gessler couldn't have found his own goggles or that last shot wouldn't have been so high. Kenzie figured that until Josh got a decisive shot, he probably wouldn't fire so as not to give away their position.

Suddenly the hallway echoed with the loud snarling of a massive animal. Despite her sensitive hearing, Kenzie couldn't pinpoint the source of the sound—it seemed to be coming from everywhere. Gessler exposed a little more of himself as he looked frantically around for this new threat and Josh trained his revolver. Before he could fire, however, a shape that was blacker than black sailed out of the shadows and knocked Gessler down. The man screamed but the sound ended abruptly as a monstrous wolf closed its massive jaws around his throat and dragged him out of sight behind the stairs.

"What was that?" whispered Nikki, clutching Kenzie's arm as they sat up cautiously.

"It was Roy," she said quietly as she hugged Anya, who was staring wide-eyed at the spot where Gessler had been a moment ago. Was it worse for the child to see someone killed by tooth and claw than by a bullet? Did it make a difference if she was Changeling rather than human? "And I think that was for Dempsey."

They made their way to the south end of the building, where both rescuers and the rescued had holed up in the main office. Metal desks were upended in front of narrow windows, and everyone was crouched or sitting on the floor. Kenzie, Nikki, and Josh automatically dropped to the floor too, pulling Anya with them.

James was back in human form, holding a rifle and peering carefully through a corner of a window. Only James, thought Kenzie, could look completely normal surrounded by an entire pack of wolves. As soon as he saw her, though, he made his way over to give her a quick hug before resuming his post. All of her fellow prisoners were gathered in a far corner. Beau and Rico appeared to be unconscious still. Dan was clutching the makeshift bandages that covered his shoulder. Shaggy Sam spotted Kenzie and grinned, touching his wild brow in salute.

She had only to follow a string of curses to find Culley and Devlin. The twins were crammed into a closet on the far side of the room that housed a large electrical panel and a great deal of electronic equipment.

"Try this sequence," said Devlin, holding some tiny device in his hand.

Culley's fingers flew, then he banged his fist on the doorframe. "Man it was so close. I got five characters in before it shut down this time." He looked over at Josh and Kenzie in exasperation. "But it changes the goddamn password every time I fail. I can do this, but it's going to take time."

"If anyone can do it, you can," said Kenzie, and it was true. Devlin's field was physics, but Culley could work miracles with computers. *Usually*, she amended as he cursed again. Miracles took time and they didn't have much.

Josh donned the radio headset that Devlin tossed him. "You there, Stanton?"

"Hey, Tark. We're working on the problem."

He snorted. "Which one?"

"Can't fix the gate for you, but Birkie's been working on the guards in the ATV shed. She says another couple minutes and we should have some results."

"Good. Keep me posted." Josh couldn't imagine what was going to help the situation unless the woman came up with a machine gun–wielding moose, but decided it was better not to ask. Instead, he focused on other problems. "James, do you think that Humvee could take out the gate?"

"Hard to say. It's a civilian version and not nearly as tough as military issue." He continued to watch out the window.

"Tougher than a pickup truck?"

"Maybe. Heavier than those ones over by the ATVs at least. Might work if we got it going fast enough, took a run at it."

"Birkie's doing something about the guards," said Josh.

He noted that James merely nodded as if the older woman took out nests of guards with guns every day. "As soon as it's clear, send a couple of guys to rig the Humvee."

"Sounds like a plan. I'll keep my eyes open for something to jam the accelerator with." Suddenly a grin crossed the big Viking's face, changing his entire demeanor. "Will you look at *that*."

Josh crawled over and peered through the bottom of the window. Six men spilled out of the ATV shed, slapping and swatting furiously at themselves. Guns tumbled to the ground, the fight forgotten. Two men threw themselves down and rolled, batting at their faces and yelling. Josh shook his head in amazement. Obviously Birkie had found herself an army of very small allies. "I'm going to kiss that woman."

"Get in line," said James, rising and shouldering his rifle. The wolves sprang to their feet around him. "I'll go round up the idiots, including that roomful upstairs. Then I'm sending my buddies here through the hole in the fence so they can go home."

"Thank them for me, will you?"

James nodded, then called over to the newly rescued Changelings. "Hey guys, I need a couple of volunteers to help with prisoners and a couple more to crash the gate." Four men scrambled to follow him and Josh handed his rifle to them as they passed. The pack of wolves trotted after the group.

Another volley of curses flew from the closet. "Forget the password, guys," said Josh, leaning back against the wall. Christ, he was tired. "Now that the guards have been neutralized, we're going to take out the gate the old-fashioned way, using that piss-yellow Humvee out there."

Culley held out his hands as if weighing something. "Computer finesse or wanton destruction, hmmm. . . ."

"Wanton destruction gets my vote," said Devlin.

"Hell, yeah." Culley looked at Josh. "We'll get started on the cleanup then."

On the way out, the twins passed Kenzie, Nikki and Anya, who had their arms piled high with what looked like first-aid supplies. Josh kicked himself mentally—he hadn't even seen them leave. "Dammit, the situation wasn't secure yet, Kenzie. You shouldn't have been wandering around."

"Hey, not dumb here. We raided a couple of the labs on the east side of the building," explained Kenzie. "We stayed low and we had at least three concrete walls between us and the shooters outside, which, let me point out, is more than we have here."

"Just the same, I'd like to get used to you not being in danger for a while."

"Nikki said we needed to get you some more bandages," added Anya.

Josh looked down at his leg. He'd left a wide smear of blood as he'd made his way over to the window. "Guess she was right."

"You bet I am," said Nikki. "From the looks of it, what you need is a hospital, but you'll have to make do with me because you can't keep bleeding like this. I've got everything from scissors and sutures to butterfly bandages and pressure pads, so let's get at it."

Kenzie helped Josh prop his leg up on a chair so Nikki could access it. He hissed a breath through his teeth as she began unwrapping the wound, releasing the pressure that had held it intact and kept some of the pain at bay. Anya laid out a couple of towels on the floor under the leg, while Kenzie used the scissors to take the pant leg off.

Jesus H. Christ. Josh had seen battlefield injuries that looked better. The wolf's fangs and scissor-like teeth had punctured flesh and muscle on both sides of his thigh, then torn it at an angle. The bleeding was profuse, although the vet agreed with Kenzie that the femoral artery had been missed.

Thirty minutes later—a damn *long* half hour filled with peroxide and sutures—Josh was surveying his neatly bandaged thigh. His T-shirt was soaked in sweat, but he was grateful for the doctoring, even from a veterinarian. All he needed now was some calories and fluid to compensate for blood loss, and Anya had gone to raid a vending machine for him. Nikki was already working on her next patient, one of the Changelings who'd caught a bullet in the top of his shoulder.

Taking advantage of a moment alone, Kenzie leaned in and kissed Josh soundly. "Thanks," she murmured as she nuzzled his face and planted delicate kisses on his eyes and brow. "Thanks for coming back for me."

He cupped his hand behind her neck and directed her lips back to his. Feasted on her luscious mouth. There were a few whistles from the Changeling posse but he ignored them and took his time. "I would never have left you here. Never." *Not while I was breathing.* She was straddling his lap and it was a damn shame that his leg was in such tough shape. . . . As part of his anatomy began to rise to meet her just the same, he decided he needed to move that tempting ass of hers to a less distracting location. "Come sit beside me," he suggested.

"Sorry, too close to your leg, aren't I?" She snuggled in under his arm.

It's not the leg that's the problem. Josh pulled her tight against him and reveled in the feel of her. The unusual warmth of her body seeped into his. He wanted to kiss her again, long and slow, wanted to feel the weight of her full breasts in his hands . . . but he needed to let his body cool down. They were in the middle of a rescue operation after all. Not to mention how awkward it would be if her brothers walked in and found him with a hard-on . . . "You're sure you're okay?"

"I'm fine. You know, you called in my family," Kenzie said, pressing an accusing finger to his chest. "I'm not sure how I feel about that."

He grabbed the finger and kissed it. "I would have taken on IBC alone if I had to. But the chances of successfully getting you out of here were a helluva lot greater if I had some backup."

"I guess I can't argue with your reasoning. But you better stick up for me when they chew me out for getting myself captured."

"Hell with that, I'm on their side. You went off on your own because you were pissed at me."

She rested her head on his shoulder and sighed. "You're right and I'm sorry. I shouldn't have taken off and I *especially* shouldn't have been angry with you. It was a knee-jerk reaction and a crummy one. I'm pretty ashamed of myself for it."

"That's okay. You can make it up to me with sexual favors later. And believe me, I have a list." She laughed, no doubt knowing he was only half-joking.

"So what was the cleanup that Culley was talking about?"

"We came here to spring you, but while we were waiting for full dark, we decided that we needed to eliminate as much information on Changelings as possible. IBC has a ton of data we don't want them to have."

"How much of that information has already gone to their headquarters?"

The million dollar question. "No way of knowing. Maybe all, maybe some, maybe none. Culley talked about sending a computer virus to IBC, maybe even uploading one to the satellite, just to try to take out their existing data. Talented fellow, that brother of yours."

"You don't know the half of it," said Kenzie. "I have Culley to thank for all the IDs in my passport pouch." She explained how difficult it had become for Changelings to hide their longevity—and of course, telling her actual birth date to the government was out of the question. Culley manufactured identification for the entire family, and his formidable hacking skills allowed him to manipulate official records to reflect the facts he'd created. "So I guess now you know enough to put us all in jail."

"Are you kidding? I just got you out." Josh realized there was nothing criminal intended by Culley or the rest of the Macleods, only survival. Just like what they were doing right now in rescuing one of their own. But how much longer could they keep this up?

Sooner or later, the existence of Changelings would be revealed. And what would happen to them then?

Chapter Twenty-three

The massive gate gave way with a satisfying crash before the bull-like onslaught of the speeding Humvee. Surprisingly, the driverless vehicle *continued* to run, leaving a trail of parts and pieces, including the hood, the grill, the front bumper, and both front quarter panels. The heavily potholed road eventually slowed it down and changed its trajectory so it meandered into a steep ravine and turned turtle in a creek, its tires still spinning.

Stanton and Birkie had rushed into the main building as soon as the gate was down. The old vet had approved heartily of Nikki's treatment of Josh's leg and Dan's shoulder. Birkie had hugged Kenzie hard, then sat down and taught Anya how to make origami ducks using office paper. Meanwhile, the others had performed a building-by-building search and rounded up the rest of the IBC staff without any resistance. Culley and Devlin had gone along behind them through the bunkhouses and snatched up any computers, cell phones, flashdrives, and so forth. All of the staff, including those held in the cage runs, were transferred to the end bunkhouse and guarded there. The confiscated technology was piled in the main building's office.

"We've got hair and tissue samples, slides, photographs, security cameras, and all kinds of data in every lab in this

building," Devlin reported to Josh. "We've got seven bodies—"

"*Seven*?" exclaimed Kenzie, glancing quickly to make
sure that Anya was out of earshot. "Where the hell did we
get *seven*?"

"There were three more bagged in a freezer in a storage
room," he said grimly. "That's six Changelings altogether
and the remains of one of the human guards. What I'm
saying is that there's so much evidence here that I think the
only sure way to destroy it all is to torch this building."

Josh glanced around the room. "It's a steel-clad concrete
building—how the hell are we going to get it to burn?"

"Culley and I have put together some chemicals that'll
act as an accelerant. And Birkie says she can take care of the
rest. Don't ask me what that means, but if she says she can
do it, I believe her."

"Let me get out of the way then." Josh let Devlin and
Kenzie help him to his feet. It didn't hurt quite so much to
put weight on his leg now. He was weak from loss of
blood, but he wasn't about to complain. At least he still *had*
his leg, which was more than one of his buddies from his
unit had.

"Will you take Anya and Nikki outside?" Kenzie whispered in his ear. "We have some Changeling business to attend to in here before we bring the place down."

He nodded his understanding. "Sure," he said and kissed
her forehead.

It was a relief to get outside. Anya was restless and Nikki
volunteered to take her for a walk, along with Guillermo
and Shaggy Sam. Josh leaned against the building, not quite
ready to sit down, although his leg was throbbing. Daybreak was still a couple hours away, but the breeze was cool
and fresh. The heavy night clouds had cleared away, leaving

a few bright stars pinning the dark blue sky and the declining moon was still visible behind the far mountains. Suddenly Josh heard wolves off in the distance and realized it was the pack they'd freed. He noticed several of the Changelings paused to listen—and smile. He smiled too.

So did a tiny figure over by the helicopter. Josh sucked in a breath but let it out easy. He waved his hand at the little dark-haired girl, and whispered *thank you*. Vision or spirit or creation of his own mind, she'd helped him. She laughed, a sound like tinkling bells, waved her red scarf over her head and danced as she vanished into the night air.

A firm hand on his shoulder made him jump. "Who the hell are you waving at?" It was Stanton. "You're awake, aren't you, Tark? Because we need to talk." Birkie was with him, and she wasn't smiling.

"What's wrong? What's happened?"

"A Changeling bit your leg. Not just a scratch but bit it deep."

"Richardson gave me a souvenir. So?"

"You have a decision to make, Josh," said Birkie.

He sighed. "I know, I know, but I can't figure out how the hell to report that I shot him. He's still got a wolf body and—"

Birkie put her hand on his arm. Her voice was quiet and kind. "No, honey, you don't have to worry about that. But you do have to decide whether to stay completely human or become Changeling."

Josh stared at her, then looked at Stanton. The old vet's face was as solemn as a funeral and his eyes were troubled. "What, you mean like a goddamn werewolf movie? I get bit by a werewolf, so I turn into one?"

"Only if you want to," said Stanton, clearing his throat.

"If you want to be a Changeling, we don't have to do any-thing. The first Change will happen involuntarily at the next full moon, and then whenever *you* want it to after that."

Birkie nodded. "But if you wish to remain as you are, son, we have to treat you, and we have to do it soon."

He wasn't sure if his wounded leg gave out or his knees, but he sat down hard on the ground. "Jesus H. Christ."

Stanton crouched down beside him. "Silver nitrate has to be administered within twelve hours of the bite, or it won't work. So you have a little time to think about it, Tark, but not much."

"Does Kenzie know about this?"

"Every Changeling knows about this. Our most basic law is *never to harm a human.* And the second law is *never to turn a human without consent.* So yes, she's very aware of your situation."

My *situation.* Pretty mild terminology for having to choose what species you wanted to be. And what would Kenzie want? If he decided to be like her, then she'd have no reason not to accept him and all their problems would be solved, right?

"Fine then, I've made my decision." He told them. Birkie nodded as if he'd chosen exactly what she expected but Stanton's wild eyebrows went up.

"Tark, are you sure about this?" he asked Josh.

"Dead certain."

Kenzie stood with the others on the far side of the com-pound. Nikki was watching over Beau and Rico, who were slowly coming out of their drug-induced stupor. The young veterinarian had asked to go with the Macleods when they left, saying she wanted a new start. Kenzie knew that James's wife, Jillian, would love to have Nikki's help at her wildlife rehab center. She'd have to thumb-wrestle Connor for her, though. He wanted Dr. Yeung at his chronically understaffed animal clinic. The real winner might be Devlin, however. Kenzie had caught him looking in Nikki's direction several times. Wouldn't it be great if they hit it off?

Thinking about her brother's love life brought hers to the forefront. How could she be so glad to see Josh and feel so awkward around him at the same time? There was no question that she wanted him, wanted to leap into his arms and stay there. But now things were even more complicated. Before, it had given her pause that he was human. Now, he'd been bitten and he'd have to choose. Thankfully, Birkie and Stanton had said they'd handle it—Kenzie didn't want to be the one to tell Josh what was about to happen to him. She was afraid she'd consciously or unconsciously try to influence his decision. She already felt guilty for wanting him to be like her, but it would be the perfect answer to everything for them. And she wanted so much to share the world of the wolf, the exhilaration and the joy of it, with this man whom her own inner wolf had claimed as a mate.

It was obvious, too, that her brothers were going to accept him. Culley and Devlin were already treating him like one of the family. And she'd witnessed James clasping Josh's shoulder, quietly saying "Good job, bro," before heading off to some other task. Those few words represented immense approval coming from her taciturn brother.

She glanced around until she spotted Josh sitting with his back against a bunkhouse and grinning at her. He patted the grass beside him hopefully. *Oh good grief.* How could she resist an invitation like that? Just as she was about to sit down with him, however, a small hand slipped into hers.

"Kenzie?" Anya had Birkie in tow as well.

"Yes, honey?"

"Did anybody find my mom?"

Omigod. Kenzie exchanged a stricken look with her friend. Birkie gave her a slight nod, which confirmed what she already knew. It was time to tell Anya *now* and it was very clear that it was her job to do it. But what on earth was she going to say?

Josh moved first, gathering Anya in to his lap, and Kenzie sat beside him. Birkie stood a little ways off, and Kenzie was reminded of her own mother long ago, having to break the news to her that her uncle and aunt and cousins were gone. She took a deep breath, held Anya's hand and stroked her hair. And in simple and plain words, she told the child that her mom had died. That the bad men were to blame and *especially* that it wasn't the little girl's fault. She threw an arm around Anya and together she and Josh rocked her as she cried her heart out. There were tears in both of their eyes too.

Finally, the tears slowed a little, and Anya looked up at them. "Where is she?" she hiccupped. "I want to see her. I want to see my mom."

Oh honey, not that. Don't ask for that. Kenzie wracked her brain to think of something, anything, to tell the child. Because what was left of Anya's mother was in no condition for viewing.

"I can help," said Birkie. She knelt beside them. "Anya, sugar, I want you to lay your head on Josh and close your eyes."

"I'm not tired! I want to see my mom."

"I know, and I'm not asking you to go to sleep. I just

want you to think about your mom for a moment. Think about being at home with your mom, doing something nice together. Can you do that?"

"Like when she reads me a story?"

"Just like that."

" 'Kay," Anya sniffed loudly and scrunched up her eyes. "But just for a minute."

Birkie stroked Anya's silky blond hair and whispered something. It was so low and soft that even Kenzie had to strain to hear the words and even then they seemed to be in a language she didn't know. Anya's face slowly relaxed and the hiccups eased away. Soon she was breathing evenly and deeply.

"You made her go to sleep?" whispered Josh.

"Not exactly." Birkie spoke normally, as if Anya could no longer hear her. "I can't bring her mom back to life or prevent the pain and grief that Anya will have to go through, but I can give her a little closure so she can heal."

"How?" asked Josh, frowning. "You're not fiddling around with her memories, are you?"

Kenzie opened her mouth to protest, but Birkie patted her arm. "No, Josh, I'm not fiddling with a single thing in that child's wonderful mind. All I've done is open a door for her. And I promise you that whatever she finds there will be just as real as you and me."

"The little dragon ran and ran and ran, and as he ran, his wings opened up. Suddenly he was lifted right up into the air! The wind blew him all the way home to his cave in the mountains, where his mother was waiting for him with supper."

Anya had heard that story many times but this time something was different. She lifted her head from her pillow to look. "Mommy?"

"Right here, honey."

And she *was*—sitting on the bed beside her, with Anya's favorite pink blanket and a storybook just like always. Anya hurled herself at her mom and wound her arms around her neck, burying her face in her mother's long blond hair. "The bad men took you, they took you *away* and I couldn't find you and then they took me too, and Josh and Kenzie helped me but I still couldn't find you and I looked and looked." She burst into tears and her mother hugged her tight, rocking her back and forth until the sobs subsided.

"You were gone for so *long*." Anya sniffed and rubbed her face on the shoulder of her mom's sweater, taking in the welcome, familiar scent.

"I know I was. I'm sorry."

"I did what you said to do. I ran away and I stayed a wolf for a long, long time."

"Yes, you did. You did exactly what I told you, baby, and I'm so proud of you. I know it was hard."

Anya looked into her mother's face. "But the bad men got me anyway. I did what I was told—why didn't it work?"

"Sometimes, even if we're very, very good, bad things can still happen. That's just life sometimes. The important thing is that you know it wasn't your fault. It wasn't your fault at all, Anya. You did everything just right. And you're going to be just fine."

Something was different. Anya could feel it but she didn't understand what it was. She looked around. "When did we go home? I was with Kenzie and Josh. I helped them when one of the bad men was trying to hurt them and take me away."

Her mother nodded. "You were very clever and very brave, honey. And you have to be very brave now, too.

We're not home, sweetheart, not really. We're just visiting while you're asleep."

"I'm not asleep, I'm awake!"

"This is a dream, honey."

Suddenly Anya remembered everything Kenzie had said to her, and her lower lip began to quiver. "They said you were dead, but you're *not*. I can see you! You can't go away again—I don't want you to!"

"People who love you are never far away, baby." She held Anya tight and rocked her again. "Let's just cuddle for a while. You like Kenzie, don't you?"

"Yeah." Anya hiccupped as the tears spilled down her cheeks again. "But she's not *you*."

"No. But she loves you."

"But I love *you*. I missed you!" Anya sat up and knotted her hands in her mother's sweater. "I don't want Kenzie, I want you!"

Her mother smoothed Anya's hair away from her face, which was sticky with tears. "I love you too, honey, with all my heart. And I would stay right here with you if I could, but I can't. That's why I need you to be with Kenzie." She cupped Anya's face in her hands and touched her forehead to hers. "It's okay for you to be sad or mad or upset about it. But there'll be good things to look forward to. You'll be part of a pack—remember we used to talk about how nice that would be? Kenzie's pack has kids that are almost as old as you are. You could play together. I know you'll have sad days but you'll have happy times too. I promise you, honey, it'll get better."

"No, it won't. It'll never, *ever* be better if you go away," declared Anya.

"Kenzie rescued you, didn't she? She must love you very much to go to that scary building to get you back."

"Yeah, but she got caught and I had to help. I opened the lock all by myself."

"That's my clever girl. Maybe Kenzie needs you around to help her?"

Anya thought that was probably true but she wasn't going to say so. "You're still gonna leave me, aren't you?"

"Not forever. Sometimes we'll visit when you're dreaming, just like we are right now."

"Really? You'll come back?"

"Yes, I will. Not every day but *sometimes*. Just like this. And next time, you can read *me* a story, okay?"

" 'Kay. Can I pick?"

"You bet." Her mother gathered her close. "Just rest now, baby."

Anya laid her face on her mother's shoulder and let herself be rocked for a long, long time.

Chapter Twenty-four

Kenzie helped Birkie to her feet and hugged her. "Thank you for whatever you did for Anya."

"You did the tough part, sugar. I got the easy job."

Josh still sat with his back against the bunkhouse and his powerful arms curled protectively around the little girl. She was snoring ever so slightly and her tear-streaked face appeared peaceful at last. "I don't know what she's dreaming about but I can feel that it's good," said Josh. "Thanks. Anya's a really great kid, you know."

"She's that and more." Birkie surveyed Anya's serene features with satisfaction and murmured softly, "She's an amazing child. And she'll be an amazing woman. . . ." Her voice trailed away and she seemed lost in thought for a long moment.

"Are you all right?" Kenzie studied her face in consternation, but Birkie shook herself and waved her off.

"Never better, dear. I have some other things to attend to now. My goodness, this is the slowest escape I've ever seen."

As she left, Kenzie smiled down at Josh as Anya slumbered on. "Birkie has a point, you know. We're not exactly running for our lives."

He snorted. "We're just lucky we don't have to, not yet at

least. The IBC staff can't call for help from this remote location thanks to whatever Devlin did, so we've been able to take our time so far. Still, we want to be gone by daybreak. After the fireworks of course."

"Of course." A rumble of thunder made her jump. Culley, Devlin, and Birkie were grouped together near the helicopter pad. A large white chopper gleamed in the waning moonlight like a newly stranded whale still wet from the ocean, but the trio wasn't paying any attention to it. They were watching the main building, and as Kenzie turned to look too, she saw the stars over it disappearing one by one as if being switched off. A massive cloud, dark and ominous, appeared to boil up from behind the building, eerily rising higher and higher until the building was dwarfed. The moon illuminated the roiling cloud as it gathered strength, and the top of it flattened out into a looming anvil shape. Flickers of greenish light shone briefly here and there in the monstrous column. Kenzie rubbed her arms, aware of the buildup of static energy in the earth, the air. It was exactly what every Changeling drew on in order to shift their shape, but *this*—this was on a colossal scale.

Kenzie's Changeling hearing picked up Birkie's voice: "I think *now* would be a good time, don't you?"

"You bet," said Culley. A sudden explosion had Kenzie throwing herself over Anya. The glass blew out of the building, and flames and smoke erupted from the windows. There was nervous laughter from the crowd behind her and she knew she hadn't been the only one taken by surprise. Although they were all a safe distance away, it was unnerving just the same.

Unnerving didn't begin to cover what happened next. Kenzie knew her friend had a lot of powerful abilities, but had very seldom seen them demonstrated. Birkie took great pleasure in doing ordinary things. She went to work at Connor's clinic every day and ably dealt with paperwork that would choke an elephant and customers that would frighten a Marine. She grew and nurtured her plants from seed, shopped and cooked like everyone else, watched movies, and ordered pizza for fun.

Yet the immense storm that had gathered directly over the IBC main building was there at Birkie Peterson's bidding.

Kenzie flinched as the first lightning bolt struck the building, and thunder pealed almost simultaneously. She held her hands over her ears and felt the vibrations roll through the earth beneath her, through her. Lightning flashed again and again, and the thunder became continuous. She wasn't afraid of storms—in fact she'd always found them to be exhilarating—but this monster was overwhelming. She turned her face away from the blinding spectacle to check Anya again, certain that the little girl would be terrified. To her surprise, the child slept on. Her head was still on Josh's chest and he had a protective hand over her ear, but she appeared peaceful.

"She's okay," said Josh, shouting to be heard over the thunder. He held out his arm on the other side, and Kenzie didn't think twice about diving under his shoulder. The deafening thunder drove away any further thought.

Eventually the lightning slowed, then ceased, and the cloud itself began to slowly disperse. Whether the storm had lasted a few minutes or a few hours, Kenzie couldn't tell. All she knew was that her ears were ringing from the thunder and even her body felt jarred from its loud assault. Yet Anya slept on as if nothing had happened and Kenzie reached over to brush her hair away from her face. "How on earth did she manage to sleep through it?" she asked.

Josh shrugged. "I don't know what Birkie did, but I'm glad she did it. A storm that size would have been terrifying for a little kid."

"It was almost too much for *me*."

The storm had definitely been too much for the building. Kenzie realized with a start that part of the vibrations she'd felt hadn't been thunder at all but the collapsing of the walls and roof. Nothing was left standing but heaps of fine rubble, punctuated by strange blazes of blue-white flame crowned with daffodil yellow. The effect would've almost been pretty if it hadn't been so alien. "I thought fire was supposed to be orange."

"Depends on the temperature. Concrete doesn't burn but it'll crack if you get it hot enough."

"It's not cracked; it looks like the stuff you dump out of the bottom of a toaster."

"And if the heat was intense enough to do that, everything else is ash."

Kenzie closed her eyes for a moment. Josh and Nikki had taken Anya outside with the others, while the Macleods had lingered in the building to perform one last task. Five Changeling bodies were carefully laid out in one of the larger rooms. Culley and Devlin had surprised Kenzie by singing over them, and even James had joined in. Birkie had scattered fireweed flowers and birch leaves over each of them and said what sounded like a blessing. Kenzie hoped they were at peace now, especially Anya's mother.

As for Nate and Gessler, their bodies had been placed in a room as far from the others as possible. It wasn't right for their ashes to touch those of the Changelings who had died from their actions. Birkie hadn't visited that room, and no one sang for them. It was sad, thought Kenzie, but it was just.

Culley approached, with two laptops tucked under one arm. "I'm taking these with us." He patted the black one. "In this one, I've got a good overview of what the scientists here have been working on. This one"—he tapped the silver one—"is my ticket to linking up to IBC's satellite. Between the two of them, we've got a helluva lot of email addresses, so we know who's been getting all this information. We may need to know that in the future. And of course, I'll be sending them all a little *present* which I hope will wipe out whatever data about Changelings they've got stored on their own computers."

"That's damn good news," said Josh and touched his brow in salute. "Wish you could do the same with the staff's memories of us."

"Some of us don't have to worry about that." Culley pulled a little leather pouch from beneath his shirt. "Thanks to Birkie's mojo."

Josh looked at Kenzie, obviously hoping for a translation.

"Don't ask me how it works," she said. "I only know that if you're wearing one of these little bags, strangers can't remember your face. Our pack has used them before."

He looked at the smoldering rubble that had once been a very large building, then put his hand over the pouch that hung around his neck. "Birkie and my Gramma Kishegwet would have a lot to talk about," he said quietly.

Guillermo and Shaggy Sam walked by, supporting Beau between them. Rico hadn't yet Changed, and trailed the group on four feet—but at least he was walking. Everyone was on their feet now and organizing to leave.

"I guess it's time to move out." Kenzie leaned over to pick up the sleeping Anya, but Culley was quicker. He scooped the child up over his shoulder, winked, and walked away with her.

Josh put out a hand and let Kenzie help him to his feet. "It's been a great party but we want to be gone before the sun comes up and somebody reports a forest fire from all the smoke. And IBC might send someone from the outside once they figure out that communication's been disrupted."

"It's going to be awfully crowded in the trucks," said Kenzie. "Too bad we couldn't have kept the Humvee for a while longer."

"Stanton's going to take my truck back, and your brothers are taking their own of course. Can't leave the vehicles here after going to all the trouble of eliminating evidence. There'll be two IBC trucks and the ATVs for the staff to make their way elsewhere—they'll be free to go as soon as we leave.

"But there's a perfectly good chopper right over there just begging to be borrowed. In fact, I have a flight leaving right now for Telegraph Creek."

"You're leaving?"

"Just for a short while. I want to visit my gramma and my sister, all the rest of my relatives. You should come; you'd like them. And besides, wouldn't you rather fly than bounce over that damn goat path again?"

She sighed. "Sounds a *lot* more comfortable but I really have to get back to my camp, get back to work."

"It's not safe anymore, Kenzie. Why don't you have your brothers collect your stuff and take your truck back to the rental place. Your camp's too damn close to this compound and it's the first place IBC will look for you."

"Look for *me*? But . . ." Her voice died away as realization hit her hard. "IBC is never going to stop, are they? Not if Nate told them who I am."

"We can hope that he might not have had time or didn't want to. But for a while at least, you'll have to behave as though IBC knows your identity. They'll probably resist trying to kidnap you again since you're practically famous, but you're a known shapeshifter—they'll want to ask you questions, maybe even win your cooperation somehow."

A known shapeshifter. The other prisoners had said that Nate was IBC's only means of knowing who was a Changeling and who wasn't. That role was vacant now— what if IBC wanted *her* to fill it? The thought filled her with revulsion.

And then there was her family . . . "Omigod, they'll assume everybody I know is a Changeling too."

"They'll suspect it, yes. The other prisoners are in a better position, even Anya. They were taken while they were wolves, and none of them shifted during their incarceration until you did. So IBC has no names, and photos of their human faces are in the ashes of the security cameras. All the company has to go on are the different locations where each one was captured."

"I guess it's a good thing after all that none of them belonged to a pack." No one else would be in danger from IBC because of them. Not like her own pack, back in Dunvegan.

"Actually, they *do* have a pack now. Stanton says the guys have decided to pull up stakes and leave the state, but they're planning to stick together."

"That'll be good for them. But where do seven Changelings go to start over?"

He grinned then. "To the ancestral friends of the wolf, of course."

"You look like you swallowed a canary," she laughed. "That's the real reason you're going to Telegraph Creek, isn't it? You're taking them to your people." She turned and sure enough, there were several Changelings boarding the helicopter.

"Why don't you and Anya come along for the ride? There's lots of room."

Anya. Even if it was perfectly safe to go back to camp, Anya had no one but Kenzie now. She had to start thinking in terms of what the little girl needed. Did the child have family? Relatives? Godparents? Kenzie had a lot of searching to do. And maybe Josh needed some time to himself too. She was still afraid of influencing his decision; even if there hadn't been a cardinal rule about it, she wanted him to choose for himself to be a Changeling. Kenzie sighed and put a hand to her head. Obviously it was way past time for her to regroup.

"I should have thought, I need to take Anya to Dunvegan," she said. "She needs some stability and a safe place to grieve and heal. It'll be a good place for me too. I can hang out there for a little while and just *think*. I have to figure out what to do next if I can't go back to the dig. Maybe I can get someone else to work it for me or something, and—"

Josh tipped her chin up with his fingertips and kissed her, warm and soft and slow. She shivered as his strong arms slid around her, as his lips traveled along her jawline and nuzzled her ear. "Take your time," he whispered. "But make sure I'm at the top of the list of things you're thinking about, because when I'm done delivering these shapeshifters and getting them settled in, I'll be on my way to *you*."

His strong fingers made little circles at the back of her

neck and she ached for them to touch her everywhere. Her inner wolf definitely didn't want him to leave, and despite Josh's reassurance that he was coming back, her heart hurt and she felt like howling aloud. She rested her head on his shoulder and just breathed in his unique scent, allowing it to comfort her. *Once Josh accepted the Change . . .* He had to. Because once he was like her, then everything would be all right.

Everything.

Chapter Twenty-five

Fall was coming. September was fast approaching and the tall poplars' coin-like leaves were just beginning to turn yellow among the dark stands of spruce. It was still warm enough, however, to make it worth claiming a hammock in the late afternoon sun. It made Kenzie feel marginally better to be outside, but after nearly a month on the Macleod farm, both her human and her wolfen selves ached for Josh on every level. *No one talks about the downside of having a mate—that being apart sucks. Big time.* She wondered if Josh felt as desolate as she did. And would it be better or worse for him once he was Changeling?

James's children, Hailey and Hunter, had taken Anya along to feed some of the livestock. The little girl still had sad moments and sometimes tears, but with the resilience of a child, Anya had gradually been able to take an interest in her new surroundings. The process was no doubt helped along by Connor giving her a puppy of her very own, something she could hold and hug whenever she needed it, especially at night. With the dog to encourage her, the little girl was running and playing again. She would never forget her mother, but there was no doubt that Anya would heal.

Kenzie had managed to get some college students to

take over her dig north of Chistochina, and she'd also sent some students to three other sites in the Copper River region. Plus she'd laid plans to make two digs herself in Alberta. One would be very close to home, east of Dunvegan, where a member of the Pack had spotted what looked like a petroglyph on a rock face. The other dig would be further north in the Caribou Mountains that surrounded a strange inland plateau. Both digs would have to wait for another summer of course. Snow came early to the Peace River country.

Kenzie's winter project would be compiling her private research into a manuscript on the shared origins of humans and Changelings. The secret of shapeshifter existence might be spilled sooner than anyone wanted, but Kenzie would have a book ready for a publisher the minute it happened. Connor's wife, Zoey, had also talked her into being prepared to do TV talk shows and magazine interviews. Kenzie was far more comfortable with college lecture tours and scholarly papers, but Zoey made her see that the people she needed to reach were not scientists, but the average human on the street. She sighed and tried not to think about it. Right now, she just wanted to lie in the hammock and zone out—

A shadow fell across her and she looked up to see James blocking her sun. "Hey!"

He adjusted his stance so she was once again bathed in sunshine. "Got a minute?" he asked.

"Sure. Several, in fact. What's up?"

In answer, he reached out a hand and deftly dumped her out of the hammock.

"What the hell was *that* for?" She sat up and brushed bits of dried grass off herself, eyeing her brother as if he'd lost his mind. Culley would be the one to pull a stunt like that, not James.

"I figured it'd be kinder than the smack upside the head that I'd prefer to give you."

She stared.

"You've been moping around this farm for almost a month now. It's pretty damn obvious that you're pining for Josh. Why aren't you two together?"

"I am *not* pining." Come to think of it, maybe she was. "And Josh has been busy."

"I know he went to Telegraph Creek, but he didn't stay there."

"No, he had to wrap things up in Glennallen. He has some years in at Fish and Game and he can't just walk away without—"

"The full moon is tonight, sis."

There it was. For those who had been bitten, the first Change always occurred at the next full moon. It was a special and sacred occasion in her world, and Kenzie had hoped Josh would want to be with her when it happened. He hadn't said a word. In fact, it had been almost two weeks since she'd last heard from him when flowers arrived at the farm addressed to her. "I know. I guess he decided to make his first shift in Alaska, probably with Stanton."

James sat beside her on the ground. "Do you love him?"

"Hey, why all the questions all of a sudden?"

"I want to see you happy. I know the family gets on your case all the time about settling down, and I've tried to stay out of it. But I need to tell you something. All those years ago, when you were little, and Culley and I found you in that pit . . . we thought we'd rescued you, but I swear part of you never left that hole in the ground."

"What are you talking about?"

"I know a little bit about being alone. And I know a lot about closing yourself off—I ran as a wolf for three damn decades, remember? I didn't want any more pain, any emotional risk, but I had to learn that I wasn't alive without it.

"You've lived all this time in fear, done everything you can to keep humans at arm's length, even though you walk among them all the time. I'm concerned that you're letting fear dictate your love life too. Josh is a good man. *Better* than good. And I think maybe you need him."

She sighed. "Yeah, I think I do too. I'm just waiting for him to—"

"Decide to join your world? Sounds like you're putting conditions on your relationship. *I'll be with you as long as you agree to be like me.*"

"I am not." Was she?

"You already know how he feels about you, and what he risked to get you out of that facility. You know he could have been killed. Have you thought about what he's willing to sacrifice to be with you now?" James counted off his fingers. "His career, his house, his friends, his—"

"Not his career, not really. Jillian wants him to oversee the wildlife center, and—oh hell, it's *still* a big move. I've already been feeling guilty about all of it. Is that what you wanted?"

"No. I just want you to answer one question. You don't have to tell me, but for God's sake, answer it for yourself: *What are* you *willing to give up in order to be with him?*"

The Changelings were welcomed by the Tahltan, as Josh knew they would be. The ancient friendship had not been forgotten. Shaggy Sam and Dan turned out to be gifted mechanics, especially with ATVs and outboards—critical equipment in the remote area—and decided to stay in Telegraph Creek to ply their trade. Roy was better with horses than machines, and signed on with a Tahltan outfitter who guided hunts into Kawdy Mountain. The others melted away into the vast territory beyond the town. Josh didn't know where they would end up, only that IBC would never find them again. Their friends would, however—the seven intended to meet up to run as a pack under the full moon.

As for himself, Josh felt like a child again as he knocked on his Gramma Kishegwet's door. She was a tiny woman, and he'd been taller than she since he was ten, but she felt like a china doll in his arms as he hugged her. Her personality was anything but small, however.

"Where the heck have you been, boy? I haven't seen you since forever." A plate of cold sliced moose tongue and thick bread was set in front of him.

"Meduh," he said. *Thank you.* "Now, Gramma, I was here at Christmas to visit you."

She pointed the mayonnaise knife at him. "And what month is it now?"

"April, isn't it?" he teased.

"You always had a smart mouth." She chuckled and shook her head. "I missed it; it's good you came. You've got something different about you now though." Her bright eyes scrutinized him and he nearly squirmed. He knew that look, knew that she always saw far more than the physical. "A wolf spirit walks with you. Got bitten, did ya? One of these boys you brought here?"

"No, it was another shapeshifter, a bad one, and he's dead now."

"By your hand?"

He nodded and so did she, apparently satisfied with that answer.

"Now tell me about this *wolf woman* I been dreaming about."

Josh laughed out loud—there was no hiding anything from his gramma's inner sight. So he told her about Kenzie. Gramma Kishegwet was unusually quiet, sitting with her hands folded around her teacup as he talked, and when he finished, she got up and left the room.

Just as he was wondering if he had upset her somehow, the old woman returned with a carved wooden box the size of a paperback book. He'd seen it in a place of honor since he was very small. "This is for your wolf woman, boy," she said, and set the box in front of him. "It's waited a long time."

Josh hugged her and kissed her cheek. His throat was tight as he stammered out, "Meduh, Gramma."

The sun rose as he flew through the Stikine River valley, heading back to Alaska. Josh had decided to leave the helicopter at the Chistochina airstrip where IBC would be able to reclaim it—after he wiped all his prints off, of course. For now he just enjoyed the trip. It always felt good to be in the air again.

Warm light brushed the hilltops, glittered in the water. Suddenly Josh realized he wasn't alone. A pair of golden eagles flanked the chopper, their seven-foot wingspans gleaming in the morning sun.

Josh had to remind himself to focus on his flight panel. He settled for stealing regular glances at the great birds. Goldens were beautiful and rare, but they were also powerful spirit animals and often signified *new beginnings*. He fervently hoped so. He'd made his decision and was standing by it, and hoped with all his heart that Kenzie would understand.

Kenzie knew the very moment Josh arrived at the farm. Her inner wolf woke her from a restless sleep and she sat upright in the darkness, shivering with anticipation. Skipping the underwear, she quickly pulled on a pair of jeans and a hoodie, and ran outside in bare feet. The waning moon hid behind midnight clouds but her Changeling vision guided her along the path without hesitation, through the woods, alongside the corrals and the barns. Finally, she spotted the truck in the laneway.

Josh was standing in the middle of the open yard, studying Connor's house. There were no lights on at this time of night and he was no doubt wondering where to start looking for her. Silently she ran across the grass, coming up behind him undetected. He remained unaware of her until she quietly whispered "*Boo.*"

Instantly she was in his arms, his hands running over her body, his mouth on hers. A wildness rose in both of them, a frantic desperation as if they'd spent years apart instead of weeks. He came up for air long enough to ask "Where?" and she knew what he was asking. Knew, too, that they'd never make it all the way back to her cabin. Instead, she grabbed his hand and led him to the closest barn. It was a vintage building, used to store feed for the horses, and she ran lightly up the sloping ladder to the loft. The sweet smell of fresh alfalfa permeated the cool night air and slivers of moonlight sliced across the darkness through gaps in the planked walls. James had a favorite napping spot carved out in a corner where some broken bales beneath an old quilt made what he called *the best bed in the world.*

At the moment, neither Josh nor Kenzie could care if it was a bed of nails. In seconds, he had stripped the hoodie and the jeans from her and she helped him shuck his own clothes. That first breathless meeting of skin against skin, as her nipples pressed against his hard muscled chest and their thighs entwined, was both primal and profound. The wolf within her leapt for joy and she threw her head back in purest bliss as body and soul sang out that she was home at last.

Josh took advantage of her exposed throat with teeth and lips and tongue until shivers of pleasure radiated outward, tightening her breasts and electrifying her nipples. He seized her hands and placed them behind his neck before cupping her ass in his palms. She barely had time to wrap her legs around him before he hefted her high against the smooth wooden wall. She'd admired the corded muscles of his arms before, but still his strength surprised and thrilled her. Her heart beat faster as he both balanced her and pinned her in place, and she was wet for him long before his fingers slid into her.

He worked her mercilessly, thumbing her clit as he stroked the subtle secret spot just inside her folds. She gasped and writhed, caught between wanting to escape the unbearable intensity and wanting more of it. He fastened his mouth on her breast, sucking it hard in time with the plunge and stroke of his fingers in her heat. Her own fingers dug into his shoulders but not out of fear of falling. Instead, she was clutching for an anchor as his touch had her dizzily spiraling up and up to impossible heights of sensation. Up and up, higher and higher. She had a fleeting impression of a roller coaster car ratcheting its way slowly but unrelentingly to the edge of what surely must be a cliff. . . .

Without warning, Josh took them both down to the quilt. The momentary absence of his fingers created such a chasm of pure *need* in her that she twisted in his arms and desperately ground her bottom into his groin. She could feel his cock, hard and hot, pressed against her ass and she was nearly wild with want. Still he held her, running his hands down her arms, pressing her palms to the quilt as he shadowed her kneeling form with his own body. She shivered as he drew back, his fingers trailing over her arched back then kneading her taut cheeks. His knees nudged her legs further apart and he slipped a hand between them, delivering lush broad strokes from clit to tailbone. There was no slow ride to the brink this time, no easy climb, just a straight rush skyward to teeter helplessly on the very edge of the world.

Kenzie fell over the precipice the moment Josh's cock slid home and she screamed as she came. He drove her without mercy and she wanted none. She needed this, lived and breathed and ached a hundred thousand days for this mating, this man. As she came a second time, a century's worth of empty nights were finally put to rest. The third time, Josh exploded with her. And somewhere between the breathless rush and the blessed release, it seemed as if even their souls had joined.

They tumbled as one to the quilt, hearts hammering, and Josh's arm drew her in close to his side. He kissed the top of her head as she laid her face on him and sighed, content with the taste of him on her lips, the sound of his heart in her ears, the soothing coolness of his skin and the familiar scent of him—

The coolness. The scent.

Kenzie's eyes flew open and she rose on one elbow to look at Josh.

"What's wrong?" he asked.

"You're still—" She drew in a long deliberate breath and

ran a shaky hand over his skin to make certain. "You're still *human*."

He nodded. "One hundred percent. I had Stanton give me the shot of silver before I left—although he didn't tell me what a goddamn big needle it was going to be."

"Why?" Kenzie blurted before she could stop herself. "Why would you do that?"

"Because I love you."

"But that makes no sense at all." Horrified, she sat up and hugged herself. "You had a chance to fix *everything* and you didn't want it?"

"Listen to yourself. What the hell needs to be fixed? I'm here, you're here, I love you, you love me. The only thing in our way is your fear. You don't trust humans and that's why you think you need me to be a shapeshifter like you. So you can feel safe. So you can trust me."

"That's not true."

"I hope not because it won't work. If I become a wolf tomorrow, I'm still going to be Josh Talarkoteen. Having four legs won't make me one bit more trustworthy than I am today with two legs. For chrissakes, Richardson was a shapeshifter and look at what he did to you. And what about Nikki? She's human, but she helped you and all the others escape."

Kenzie took a deep breath and thought of her brother's words. *What are you willing to give up in order to be with him?* Birkie had once warned her that she would have to give up her fears to make room for what she really wanted. And she had no doubt that she wanted Josh.

"I'm learning," she said finally. "I understand—now— that there are good and bad people in both species. And you're right that I *thought* I needed you to be a shapeshifter, but now I—I just want to share it with you.

"You're right that I have a lot of fears, and I want to let go of them. It's a slow process because old mindsets are so automatic. So it's going to take me some time but there's one thing I do know right now. And that is, the only thing I really need is for you to be *you*. Because I *do* trust you."

He stroked the side of her face with gentle fingers. "Trust me now then. If I accept the gift of the wolf, then you don't have to deal with anything. That might be convenient for you but it's not healthy. So I'm staying human for now, and you'll have to accept me as I am."

"I can live with that."

"Are you sure? Because I'm definitely asking you to live with that. I'm asking you to live with *me*. Permanently."

"I can live with that too," she laughed and kissed him soundly. Hands and lips traveled over bare skin and passion flared anew.

"Wait," he laughed. "Hold that thought but give me a second. I want to do this right."

As she surveyed his naked body with an admiring smile and plotted new moves to try out, he went looking for his jacket and rummaged in its pockets until he produced a small wooden box. Pulled something from it but kept it palmed out of sight as he settled in beside her. "Okay." He took her hand and tenderly kissed the back of it, then set something cool and heavy on her wrist that gleamed in the moonlight. She looked at it, her Changeling eyesight making out the details of a wide gold bracelet. Her practiced eye told her that it was incredibly old, definitely a museum-worthy piece. Wolves and humans mingled together over its entire surface, carefully crafted by an ancient artisan.

"It was my gramma's," explained Josh. "Her mother gave it to her when she got married. And her mother received it from her mother and so forth. Nobody even knows how old it is."

"Omigod." She shook her head in disbelief. "Josh, this is priceless. I can't take this away from your family."

"Gramma Kishegwet says you're to have it, that it's meant for you. And you don't argue with her, believe me. See the story pictured on this bracelet? It shows that one day a wolf woman would join our clan and connect the two peoples forever. Clan jewelry is usually silver, but Gramma says this bracelet was made of gold so that it could rest against the skin of the shapeshifter that would come."

"You're making that up." She looked up at him in amazement but his obsidian eyes were steady.

"Nope. It's the real deal. And so is this—I love you, Kenzie Macleod, and I want us to be together always."

She slid her arms around his neck and snuggled in close. "I want that too." Their lips met and there were no more words. . . .

Epilogue

The young girl jogged along the riverbank, the loose shale beneath her soggy running shoes crunching like clay pots breaking. She'd laid a false trail, then ran in the shallow water for what felt like a mile, hoping to throw off her pursuer. If she could just reach—

A sound behind her sent a burst of adrenaline through her lithe body. Her own footsteps were loud, but she could still pick out the determined lope of four large paws on the telltale shale. She was close, *so* close, to safety, but only the fastest sprint would get her there in time. Lungs heaving, arms pumping, she threw everything she had into one desperate dash up the wide bank, heading for the base of the cliff that towered above the broad Peace River.

Hot breath on the back of her calves let her know she'd lost the race. An enormous shape the color of strong coffee came into her peripheral vision—

"You are *so* not going to pass me!" She squealed as the monstrous wolf nipped her sock, but it wasn't in fear. Seeking to put space between her and the creature, she leapt high, shifted in mid-air, and came down running on four legs.

In her lupine shape, she was much stronger and faster. She raced ahead of the brown wolf, then abruptly wheeled and leapt at her pursuer's ears. He danced out of reach but she managed to bite the bigger wolf's tail, and then he was shaking her by the scruff of the neck. They rolled and tumbled, until the mock battle took them crashing through the tall grass at the base of the cliff where a number of squares were marked off with string.

Suddenly Kenzie's voice rang out. "Hey, be careful, you two! If you mess up my grids, I'll have to kill you both." A moment later, her head appeared above a mound of sandy soil that had been dug away from the cliff face. "I think I've got something here."

The wolves resolved into human forms, breathless and grinning.

"I'm faster than you," declared Anya, with satisfaction.

Josh shook his head. "No way. I tagged you down by the river."

"You didn't tag me, you tripped. I saw you. *Twice*. And you fell off that log into the stream and then tried to tell me you were swimming."

"Hey, so I don't have a driver's license yet for my wolf body. Gimme a break, kid, I'm new at this. In fact, shouldn't I be allowed some sort of handicap since you were born a Changeling and I wasn't?"

"Uh-uh. It's like Darwin said, *survival of the fittest*," she laughed.

"I'll remember that when you ask for your allowance." He made his way carefully through the obstacle course of string and stakes to the enormous hole that Kenzie stood in. Anya followed. The three of them had been working on the project for a month, gradually exposing a 20-foot wide expanse of the rock face below the foot of the cliff. They'd found a number of petroglyphs, carvings in the rock that

dated back thousands of years. Most were classic shapes—
spirals and circles, some faces, even a fish.

"Look what I found," said Kenzie, and stepped away so
they could see.

Etched into the rock was the unmistakable image of a
wolf walking upright among several human figures.

"Is that what I think it is?" asked Josh, leaning down to
place a hand on his wife's shoulder.

Kenzie grinned up at him. "It's a beginning."

Have you tried the other books in Dani's fabulous series? It starts with CHANGELING MOON . . .

He roams the moonlit wilderness, his every sense and instinct on high alert. Changeling wolf Connor Macleod and his Pack have never feared anything—until the night human Zoey Tyler barely escapes a rogue werewolf's vicious attack.

As the full moon approaches, Zoey has no idea of the changes that are coming, and only Connor can show her what she is, and help her master the wildness inside. With her initiation into the Pack just days away and a terrifying predator on the loose, the tentative bonds of trust and tenderness are their only weapons against a force red in tooth, claw . . . and ultimate evil.

Freezing rain sliced out of the black sky, turning the wet pavement to glass. Zoey stared out at the freakish weather and groaned aloud. With less than two days left in the month of April, the skies had been clear and bright all afternoon. Trees were budding early and spring had seemed like a sure bet. Now *this*. Local residents said if you didn't like the weather this far north, just wait fifteen minutes. She gave it five, only to watch the rain turn to sleet.

Perhaps she should have asked more questions before taking the job as editor of the *Dunvegan Herald Weekly*. She was getting the peace and quiet she'd wanted, all right, but so far the weather simply sucked. Winter had been in full swing when she'd arrived at the end of October. Wasn't it ever going to end?

Sighing, she buttoned her thin jacket up to her chin and hoisted the camera bag over her shoulder in preparation for the long, cold walk to her truck. All she wanted before bed was a hot shower, her soft flannel pajamas with the little cartoon sheep on them, the TV tuned to *Late Night*, and a cheese and mushroom omelet. Hell, maybe just the omelet. She hadn't eaten since noon, unless the three faded M&Ms she'd found at the bottom of her bag counted as food.

As usual, the council meeting for the Village of Dunvegan had gone on much too long. Who'd have thought that such a small community could have so much business to discuss? It was well past ten when the mayor, the councilors, and the remnants of a long-winded delegation filed out. Zoey had lingered only a few moments to scribble down a couple more notes for her article but it was long enough to make her the last person out of the building.

The heavy glass door automatically locked behind her, the metallic sound echoing ominously. Had she taken longer than she thought? There wasn't a goddamn soul left on the street. Even the hockey arena next door was deserted, although a senior men's play-off game earlier had made parking difficult to find. Now, her truck—a sturdy, old red Bronco that handled the snow much better than her poor little SUV had—was the only vehicle in sight.

The freezing rain made the three-block trek to the truck seem even longer. Not only did the cold wind drive stinging pellets of ice into her face, but her usual businesslike stride had to be shortened to tiny careful steps. Her knee-high leather boots were strictly a fashion accessory—her bedroom slippers would have given her more traction on the ice. If she slipped and broke her ankle out here, would anyone even find her before morning?

The truck glittered strangely as she approached and her heart sank. Thick sheets of ice coated every surface, sealing the doors. Nearly frozen herself, she pounded on the lock with the side of her fist until the ice broke away and she could get her key in. "Come on, dammit, come on!"

Of course, the key refused to turn, while the cold both numbed and hurt her gloveless fingers. She tried the passenger door lock without success, then walked gingerly around to the rear cargo door. No luck there either. She'd have to call a tow—

Except that her cell phone was on the front seat of her truck.

Certain that things couldn't get any worse, she tested each door again. Maybe one of the locks would loosen if she kept trying. If not, she'd probably have to walk all the way home, and wasn't that a cheery prospect?

Suddenly a furtive movement teased at her peripheral vision. Zoey straightened slowly and studied her surroundings. There wasn't much to see. The streetlights were very far apart, just glowing pools of pale gold that punctuated the darkness rather than alleviating it. Few downtown businesses bothered to leave lights on overnight. The whispery hiss of the freezing rain was all she could hear.

A normal person would simply chalk it up to imagination, but she'd been forced to toss *normal* out the window at an early age. Her mother, aunts, and grandmother were all powerful psychics—and the gene had been passed down to Zoey. Or at least a watered-down version of it. The talent was reliable enough when it worked, but it seemed to come and go as it pleased. *Like right now.* Zoey tried hard to focus yet sensed absolutely nothing. It was her own fault perhaps for trying to rid herself of the inconvenient ability.

No extrasensory power was needed, however, to see something large and black glide silently from one shadow to another near the building she'd just left. *What the hell was that?* There was nowhere to go for help. The only two bars in town would still be open, but they were several blocks away, as was the detachment headquarters for the Royal Canadian Mounted Police. There was a run-down trailer park a block and a half from the far side of the arena, but

Zoey knew there were no streetlights anywhere along that route.

A dog? Maybe it's just a big dog, she thought. *A really big dog or a runaway cow. After all, this was a rural community. And a northern rural community at that, so maybe it's just a local moose, ha, ha. . . .* She struggled to keep her fear at bay and redoubled her efforts on the door locks, all the while straining to listen over the sound of her own harsh breathing.

The rear door lock was just beginning to show promise when a low, rumbling growl caused her to drop her keys. She spun to see a monstrous shape emerge from the shadows, stiff-legged and head lowered. *A wolf?* It was bigger than any damn wolf had a right to be. *Jesus.* Some primal instinct warned her not to run and not to scream, that the animal would be on her instantly if she did so.

She backed away slowly, trying not to slip, trying to put the truck between herself and the creature. Its eyes glowed green like something out of a horror flick, but this was no movie. Snarling black lips pulled back to expose gleaming ivory teeth. The grizzled gray fur around its neck was bristling. Zoey was minutely aware that the hair on the back of her own neck was standing on end. Her breath came in short shuddering gasps as she blindly felt for the truck behind her with her hands, sliding her feet carefully without lifting them from the pavement.

She made it around the corner of the Bronco. As soon as she was out of the wolf's line of sight, she turned and half skated, half ran for the front of the truck as fast as the glassy pavement would allow. *Don't fall, don't fall!* It was a litany in her brain as she scrambled up the slippery front bumper onto the icy hood. With no hope of outrunning the creature and no safe place in sight, the roof of the truck seemed like her best bet—if she could make it. *Don't fall, don't fall!* Flailing for a handhold, she seized an ice-crusted windshield wiper, only to have the metal frame snap off in her hand. She screamed as she slid back a few inches.

The wolf sprang at once. It scrabbled and clawed, unable to find a purchase on the ice-coated metal. Foam from its snapping jaws sprayed over her as the beast roared its frustration. Finally it slipped back to the ground and began to pace around the truck.

Zoey managed to shimmy up the hood until she was able to put her back against the windshield, and pulled her knees up to her chin. She risked a glance at the roof behind her—she had to get higher. Before she could move, however, the wolf attacked again, scrambling its way up the front bumper. Vicious jaws slashed at her. Without thought, Zoey kicked out at the wolf, knocking one leg out from under it. It slid backward but not before it clamped its teeth on her calf. The enormous weight of the creature dragged at her and she felt herself starting to slide. . . .

One hand still clutched the broken windshield wiper and she used it, whipping the creature's face and muzzle with the frozen blade until she landed a slice across one ungodly glowing eye. The rage-filled snarl became a strangled yelp; the wolf released her leg and slipped from the hood. This time Zoey didn't look, just turned and launched herself upward for the roof rack. She came down hard, adrenaline keeping her from feeling the impact of the bruising metal rails. She was conscious only of the desperate need to claw and grasp and cling and pull until she was safely on the very top of the vehicle.

Except she *wasn't* safe. Not by a long shot. *Crap.* She could plainly see that she wasn't high enough. *Crap, crap,*

crap. The enraged wolf leapt upward in spite of the fact that its feet could find little traction on the ice-coated pavement. What it couldn't gain in momentum, the wolf made up for in effort, hurling itself repeatedly against the Bronco. Its snapping jaws came so close that Zoey could see the bleeding welts across its face, see that one of its hellish eyes was now clouded and half-closed. She slashed at it again, catching its tender nose so it howled in frustration and pain as it dropped to the ground. Snarling, it paced back and forth like a caged lion, watching her. Waiting.

The wind picked up and the freezing rain intensified. Huddled on her knees in the exact center of the icy roof, Zoey's adrenaline began to ebb. She was cold and exhausted, and parts of her were numb. But she wasn't helpless; she wouldn't allow herself to think that way. The thin windshield wiper was badly bent with pieces of it missing, but she'd damn well punch the wolf in the nose with her bare fist if she had to. If she still could. . . .

The wolf sprang again.

And continues with CHANGELING DREAM . . .

In times of stress Jillian Descharme has always found calm in her dream of a great white wolf with haunting blue eyes. But she is startled when the visions return and this time seem so real. Late at night he comes to her, speaks to her, touches her. It's almost as if he's alive . . .

Thirty years ago James Macleod lost his wife and unborn child to a killer bent on destroying the Changelings. Though he longed for death, his animal instinct fought for survival and James has been a wolf ever since. Yet now a woman has reawakened the man in him, taming wild instincts but arousing still wilder needs. With his ancient enemy hunting the legendary white wolf, James must fight for new life, new hope, new love.

W *hat kind of woman runs after a wolf?*
James was no closer to answering that question than he had been many hours before when he had paused in the clinic loft, two bounds away from the open window, and listened to the human calling after the white wolf. He had been startled to find the woman up and about so close to dawn, but more surprised by her reaction when she spotted him. She should have been terrified, should have been screaming. Instead she had stopped still, remaining quiet until he melted back into the darkness—then had plunged forward in a vain attempt to follow him. She acted as if she knew the wolf, but how could that be? There was something else too; something in her voice had almost compelled him to—what? Answer her? Reveal himself? He didn't know. The woman had gone from room to room then, switching on every light, searching.

He wasn't surprised when she didn't check the loft. After all, it was fifteen feet above the ground floor and accessible only by a vertical ladder. A wolf couldn't climb it, and she had no way of knowing that what she pursued was not a wolf and that the ladder was no impediment to him at all. The stack of bales outside, from which he had initially leapt, was more than thirty feet from the loading door of the loft. Only a very large tiger might cross such a span. Or a Changeling.

James felt a strange disappointment tugging at his senses, almost a regret that the woman had not found him. *Who are you? Why do I know you?* Within his lupine body, James chuffed out a breath in frustration. *And why do I care?* The angle of the fading light told him it was time to hunt, that deer would be on the move. Weary of human thoughts and human concerns, he relaxed into his wolf nature and disappeared beneath it.

"What a tourist I am!" Jillian berated herself for not bringing a cell phone, for not paying more attention to the time, for traveling in the bush alone, for not packing at least a chocolate bar. Two chocolate bars. Maybe three. The energy bars she'd brought tasted like wet cardboard. She made a long mental list of the things she was going to do to be more prepared for the next hike, because as difficult as the trail was, she simply had to go back to that rocky plateau, had to see if the wolves would return. Was it part of their territory or were they just passing through?

The sun was long gone. Stars were pinning a deep indigo sky, and a full moon was floating just above the horizon. It had climbed enough to glimmer through the trees and lay a broad swath of light over the surface of the river when Jillian finally found the marked hiking trail. Compared to the goat path she'd been traveling, the graveled corridor was like a wide paved highway, level and free of overhanging brush and fallen logs. It promised easier, faster travel in spite of the darkness. She was still two and a half, maybe three, miles from the truck she had borrowed from the clinic, but at least now she had a direct route.

The flashback broadsided her without warning.

It might have been the crunch of gravel beneath her feet, the rustle of leaves in the trees, or the scent of the river, but whatever the trigger, she was suddenly on another trail by another river. Phantom images, sounds, even smells burst vividly upon her senses. Jillian stumbled forward and fell to her knees, skinning them both right through her jeans. She rolled and sat, but clasped her hands to her head rather than to her wounds. "Don't close your eyes, don't close your eyes. You're not there, it's not real, it's over. Jesus, it's over, it's over and you're okay. You're okay." She spoke slowly, deliberately, coaching herself until the shaking stopped. "It's a different place and a different time. I'm not back there, I'm here. I'm here and I'm okay." *I'm okay, I'm okay.*

But she wasn't, not yet. She rocked back and forth in the gravel. "My name is Jillian Descharme and I'm a licensed veterinarian and I'm okay. I'm thirty-two years old and I'm in Dunvegan, Alberta, and I'm okay. Nothing is threatening me, nothing is wrong, I'm okay." She drew a long shaky breath and rubbed her runny nose with her sleeve like a child. "I'm okay. Jeez! Jeez goddamn Louise!" She was cold, freezing cold, her clothes soaked with sweat and her skin clammy, but the fear had her by the throat and she couldn't move. She had to think of something fast, something to help her break away from this terror, break out of this inertia or she'd be here all night. And then it came. The image of the white wolf—the memory, the dream, flowed into her, warmed her like brandy. Jillian clung to that mental picture like a life preserver in rough seas, let the wolf's unspoken words fill her mind and calm it. *Not alone. Here with you.*

She rose at last on trembling legs and cursed as her knees made their condition known. The sharp stinging cleared the last of the flashback from her head, however, and banished the nausea from her stomach. She stood for several moments, hugging herself, rubbing her hands over her upper arms. She sucked in great lungfuls of the cool moist air until she felt steady again, and took a few tentative steps along the dark path—but had to resist the impulse to run. If she ran, she might never stop.

"Think of the white wolf, think of the white wolf." Calm, she had to be calm. Take big breaths. "Walk like a normal person. It's okay to walk fast because I'm busy, got things to do, places to go, people to see, but I don't have to run. I can walk because nothing's wrong, I'm okay." She was in control, she would stay in control. As she walked, however, she couldn't stop her senses from being on hyper-alert. Jillian's eyes flicked rapidly from side to side, searching the darkness, her ears straining to hear any rustle of leaf or snap of twig. She noticed the tiny brown bats that dipped and whirled in the air above her. She noted the calls of night birds, of loons settling and owls hunting. A mouse hurried in front of her, crossing and recrossing the path. A few moments later, a weasel followed it, in a slinky rolling motion. Jillian was keenly aware of everything—the blood pounding in her ears, the sound of her footsteps in the gravel, the liquid sounds of the nearby river—but not the tree root bulging up through the path.

She yelled in surprise, then in pain as her knees hit the gravel again. She rolled to a sitting position, cursing the sharp stinging and her own clumsiness—hadn't she *just* successfully negotiated a rugged game trail down a steep hillside for heaven's sake? She couldn't see much even with the moon's light, but a quick examination showed both knees were bleeding, her jeans in shreds. She cursed even more as she picked out a few obvious shards of gravel, but cleaning and bandaging were just going to have to wait until she reached the truck. At least it wasn't anything worse. Annoying, damn painful and embarrassing, but not a broken ankle or snakebite. Her eyes strayed to the underbrush in spite of herself—there weren't any poisonous snakes this far north, were there? "Good grief!" Jillian yanked her mind firmly away from *that* train of thought and was pondering whether it was possible to stand without bending her knees when she heard the howl.

She sat bolt upright as if an electric current had suddenly passed through her, every hair on end, every sense alert. The call came again, closer. Deep, primal, long and low. Drawn out and out and out, an ancient song, mournful yet somehow sweet. When it fell silent, Jillian felt as if time itself had stopped. And she found herself straining to hear the song again, fascinated, even as her brain told her to run and instinct told her to freeze.

The moon was higher now. The pale light filtered down through the trees and laid a dappled carpet of silver on the stony path. There was no wind, no breeze. Jillian held her breath, listening, watching, but all was still. Her heart was pounding hard with both excitement and fear. Normally she would have loved to get a glimpse of a wolf in the wild, but the idea was a lot less attractive when she was alone in the dark. There were few recorded incidents of wolves attacking or killing humans, but all the data in the world wasn't very reassuring when she was sitting there bleeding. Immediately she wished she hadn't thought of that. It was just a little blood, but she struggled to get the image of a wounded fish in a shark tank out of her head.

A movement at the edge of the path beyond seized her attention. A pale shape emerged from the shadows, seemed to coalesce in the moonlight and grow larger until it was a vivid white creature of impossible size. Jillian's heart stuck in her throat as the great wolf slowly turned its massive head and stared directly at her.

Oh, Jesus. She had studied wolves more than any other wildlife, but only from books and captive specimens. Wolves don't attack humans, she reminded herself. Wolves don't attack humans—but there had been cases in Alaska. She gritted her teeth and sat perfectly still, afraid to breathe as the wolf began to slowly move in her direction. The creature approached within ten feet, then abruptly sat on its haunches and stared at her.

It was enormous. She swallowed hard, realizing if the wolf attacked there would be nothing she could do. Nothing. She wouldn't even manage a scream before it was on her. Not one bit of her martial arts training would help, especially when she was sitting on the ground. Nevertheless she scanned the ground with her peripheral vision for anything she might use as a weapon. Her fingers inched toward a rock, closed around it as the wolf rose, took a slow step toward her, into a pool of moonlight. Instantly its snowy fur gleamed and its eyes were . . . its eyes were . . .

Blue.

Jillian felt as if the air had been knocked from her body. The rock rolled out of her palm. Trembling, shaking, she reached a tentative hand toward the animal. "You. It's you," she choked out. "Oh, my God, it's you, isn't it? You're real."

The wolf closed the gap between them and licked her outstretched fingers. *Omigod, omigod.* She couldn't move at first, both enthralled and terrified—until the animal nudged its head under her hand like a dog asking to be petted. Jillian moved her fingers lightly across the broad skull, scratching hesitantly at first. Then fear fell away, and she worked both hands behind the sensitive ears, into the glossy ruff.

The wolf stood panting mildly, the immense jaws slack and the great pink tongue lolling out in apparent pleasure. Jillian had no illusions about the animal's power—it might behave like a big dog but those jaws could easily crack the leg bones of a moose, those teeth could tear out the throat of a bull elk in full flight. And as surely as she knew those facts, she knew the wolf would not hurt her. It wasn't sensible, it wasn't logical, but the certainty was core-deep. Instinct? Intuition? Insanity? She didn't know and didn't care. The wolf held steady as Jillian wrapped her arms around its great neck and buried her face in its thick white fur. "I thought I dreamed you. You came to me. You came when no one would come, but they all told me I dreamed you because no one saw you but me. And I looked and looked for you, but I couldn't find you."

Here now. Found you.